In 1990, **Patricia Cornwell** sold her first novel, *Postmortem*, while working at the Office of the Chief Medical Examiner in Richmond, Virginia. An auspicious debut, it went on to win the Edgar, Creasey, Anthony, and Macavity Awards, as well as the French Prix du Roman d'Aventures – the first book ever to claim all these distinctions in a single year. Growing into an international phenomenon, the Scarpetta series won Cornwell the Sherlock Award for best detective created by an American author, the Gold Dagger Award, the RBA Thriller Award, and the Medal of Chevalier of the Order of Arts and Letters for her contributions to literary and artistic development.

Today, Cornwell's novels and iconic characters are known around the world. Beyond the Scarpetta series, Cornwell has written the definitive nonfiction account of Jack the Ripper's identity, cookbooks, a children's book, a biography of Ruth Graham, and three other fictional series based on the characters Win Garano, Andy Brazil, and Captain Calli Chase. Cornwell continues exploring the latest space-age technologies and threats relevant to contemporary life. Her interests range from the morgue to artificial intelligence and include visits to Interpol, the Pentagon, the U.S. Secret Service and NASA.

Cornwell was born in Miami. She grew up in Montreat, North Carolina, and now lives and works in Boston.

ALSO BY PATRICIA CORNWELL

SCARPETTA SERIES

Unnatural Death
Livid
Autopsy
Chaos
Depraved Heart
Flesh and Blood
Dust
The Bone Bed
Red Mist
Port Mortuary
The Scarpetta Factor
Scarpetta
Book of the Dead
Predator
Trace
Blow Fly
The Last Precinct
Black Notice
Point of Origin
Unnatural Exposure
Cause of Death
From Potter's Field
The Body Farm
Cruel and Unusual
All That Remains
Body of Evidence
Postmortem

CAPTAIN CHASE SERIES

Spin
Quantum

ANDY BRAZIL SERIES

Isle of Dogs
Southern Cross
Hornet's Nest

WIN GARANO SERIES

The Front
At Risk

NONFICTION

*Ripper: The Secret Life of
      Walter Sickert*
*Portrait of a Killer: Jack the
      Ripper—Case Closed*

BIOGRAPHY

*Ruth, a Portrait: The Story of Ruth
      Bell Graham*

OTHER WORKS

*Food to Die For: Secrets from
      Kay Scarpetta's Kitchen*
Life's Little Fable
Scarpetta's Winter Table

PATRICIA CORNWELL

IDENTITY UNKNOWN

A SCARPETTA NOVEL

SPHERE

SPHERE

First published in the US in 2024 by Grand Central Publishing
an imprint of Hachette Book Group
First published in Great Britain in 2024 by Sphere

A CIP catalogue record for this book
is available from the British Library.

Hardback ISBN 978-1-4087-3261-8
Trade paperback ISBN 978-1-4087-3260-1

Printed and bound in Great Britain by Clays Ltd, Elcograf S.p.A.

Papers used by Sphere are from well-managed forests
and other responsible sources.

Sphere
An imprint of
Little, Brown Book Group
Carmelite House
50 Victoria Embankment
London EC4Y 0DZ

An Hachette UK Company
www.hachette.co.uk

www.littlebrown.co.uk

To Staci—Forever

There is no end. There is no beginning.

—Federico Fellini

IDENTITY
UNKNOWN

CHAPTER 1

 A Stryker saw grinds through bone, a knife rasping across a whetstone as water drums into deep metal sinks. Doctors call out organ weights, wound measurements and other findings as those assisting scribe. Rock and roll blares from the vintage boom box on a shelf, the autopsy suite not the quiet place one might expect.

Our caseload is heavy this Tuesday morning, the weather beautiful in Northern Virginia, the sun shining, the temperature in the seventies. People have been flocking to the parks, the nature trails, the waterfront, and with the good comes the awful. Violence, accidents and other senseless deaths escalate when the weather is nice, my idea of spring fever different from most.

I'm finishing a complicated case that I find especially disturbing, and there's nothing more I can do for now. What's needed is time for elusive injuries to creep out of hiding. When contusions occur close to death, the skin discoloration is subtle like shadows and easily missed. But with additional days in the cooler, the injuries become obvious like the bruised flesh of a peach turning brown.

1

I'm suspicious that faint marks on the victim's upper arms and neck were caused by violent gripping and throttling. If I'm right, that will be incriminating for her parents, Ryder and Piper Briley. My decisions could result in them charged with child abuse and murder. Based on what I've witnessed at their home and during the autopsy, they're a monstrous couple.

But it's not up to me to judge. I'm not supposed to care about punishment. The forensic pathologist's job is to present the facts with no interest in the outcome. That's impossible unless you're a robot or cold-blooded. Luna Briley's death is outrageous and infuriating. It was all I could do to keep my cool when I was at the scene yesterday.

I have no doubt that her entire short life was hellish, her influential parents unaccustomed to facing consequences. I'm sealing bullet fragments inside an evidence container when the old-style wall phone begins to clangor near my workstation. I wonder who it is. Few people have this number.

"Someone expecting a call down here?" I raise my voice above the din.

My medical examiners are deep in their cases, scarcely glancing in my direction as the ringing continues.

"No problem. I'll get it." I mutter this to no one in particular.

Taking off my surgical mask and bloody gloves, I toss them into the biohazard trash. The floor is sticky beneath my Tyvek-covered feet as I step over to the countertop. Taped to the cinderblock wall is a sign demanding CLEAN HANDS ONLY! and I grab the phone, the long cord hopelessly snarled.

"Doctor Scarpetta," I answer, and there's no response.

"Hello?" I detect the murmur of a talk show playing in the background. "Anybody there? Hello?"

Sensing someone on the line, I hang up. I'm returning to my table when the ringing starts again. This time I'm not as pleasant.

"Morgue," I announce.

"Hate to interrupt. I know you're slammed." It's my niece, Lucy Farinelli, a U.S. Secret Service agent and helicopter pilot.

I can tell by the noise of throbbing engines and thudding rotor blades that she's flying somewhere. She wouldn't call like this unless it's urgent.

"The phone just rang, and no one said anything. That wasn't you by chance?" I ask her.

"It wasn't, and I have bad news, Aunt Kay."

Lucy never calls me that anymore unless no one else is listening. She must be flying alone, and I imagine her in the right seat of a cockpit that reminds me of a space shuttle.

"We've got a bizarre death that I suspect is somehow related to the little girl likely on your table as we speak," she tells me somberly, and I detect an undercurrent of anger.

"I'm just finishing up with Luna Briley if that's who you mean." Rolling out a chair from the countertop, I sit down with my back to the room.

"I'm betting she's not an accident," Lucy says ominously.

"What *bizarre death* are you thinking might be related to her?" I slide a clipboard close, a pen attached by a plastic string.

"Her scumbag billionaire father owns the Oz theme park you and I are familiar with. It's abandoned now, and a couple of

3

hours ago we found the body of a missing person there," Lucy informs me in a reluctant tone, and I sense something coming I won't want to hear. "I'm afraid it's someone we know. You especially know," she adds awkwardly, and I'm touched by dread.

I jot down today's date, April 16. The time is 11:40 A.M. as she explains that Nobel laureate Sal Giordano was abducted last night near the Virginia and West Virginia border. He's been violently killed, she says to my shock and horror, my inner voice already arguing.

It can't be him.

"I'm really sorry, Aunt Kay. I know you two were close..."

There must be some mistake.

An acclaimed astrophysicist, he's an advisor to the White House and other top officials in the U.S. and internationally. Sal and I serve on several of the same government task forces and committees. We see each other regularly and have a history.

This can't be right.

"You got how close to the body?" I hear myself asking the right questions.

"Close enough to get a good look without disturbing anything. He's nude with no sign of personal effects so far, and I don't think he's been dead all that long..."

It could be someone else.

"Are we sure it's him? Let's start with that." I envision his compelling face. I hear his lyrical voice and easy laugh.

"Average height, slender, with long wavy gray hair. A tattoo of a pi sign on his left inner wrist," Lucy describes, and I go hollow inside. "There was a pungent odor that I could vaguely smell through my face mask. Sort of vinegary. Sharply acidic like white vinegar."

"Any guesses about the source?" I hear myself asking as I try to quell my inner turmoil.

"Only that I smelled it all around the body."

"What about obvious injuries?"

"A lot of trauma, especially to his face and head..."

No. No. No...

"His skin is strangely red," she says. "Maybe from some type of radiation, and there's a vortex of apple blossom petals around him like a crop circle..."

"A what?"

"It appears he was dropped out of the sky by a UAP..."

"Excuse me...?" I've paused my pen on the call sheet.

"A UAP," Lucy repeats. "An Unidentified Anomalous Phenomenon. A UFO. Whatever you want to call it."

* * *

Pressing the old phone's handset close to one ear, I cover the other with my free hand, trying to block out the racket behind me. Members of my staff are talking in loud voices. A blaring buzzer announces the morgue's vehicle bay door is opening. Water pounds in every sink, the cooler door slamming with a thud.

Lucy explains that at around six o'clock this morning, a UAP was detected on radar flying low and slow near the Oz theme park. After the Secret Service was notified that Sal was missing, my niece conducted an aerial search for him. Not having any luck, she decided to follow the flightpath the mysterious object had been on and was led directly to the body.

"Whatever the thing was, it flew over the very spot in the middle of the Haunted Forest," Lucy explains. "The low-flying craft had a signature that doesn't match any algorithm. And since it wasn't witnessed by anyone that we know of, we don't have any clues as to what the UAP might have looked like to an observer."

"A UAP as in a spaceship from another planet?" I glance around, making sure no one can hear me.

"What I know is that Sal Giordano was jettisoned from some type of flying object identity unknown," Lucy states. "It was unrecognizable to radar. And to electro-optical, telemetric and other sensors. Also to spectrum monitoring. That doesn't mean it was from outer space. But we can't assume it wasn't."

"I'll plan knowing that's a possibility." My mind races through how best to handle this.

"I need to ask a couple of questions," Lucy then says, another Stryker saw whining and grinding behind me.

"Of course."

"You saw him yesterday."

"Yes. It was his birthday." I push away what I'm feeling.

Guilt. I should have asked more questions.

I envision him squinting in the sun and smiling at me as we chatted on his driveway, both of us in a hurry. He was eager to get on the road, and I'd dropped by after a court hearing. He was dressed in cargo shorts, a loose white linen shirt like an ad for Banana Republic. I remember he seemed preoccupied as if something weighed heavily, but I didn't pry. I never have. I assumed he was in a mood because he wasn't happy turning sixty.

"Sounds like you were one of the last to see him alive." Lucy's voice over the phone, her helicopter thud-thudding. "What can you tell me?"

I explain that I dropped by his house late yesterday morning with a gift basket he could take on the road. I knew he was on his way to West Virginia's Green Bank Observatory, its steerable radio telescope the largest in the world. He's been a frequent visitor since graduate school, the place important to his work.

"Did he mention having trouble with anyone? Anything unusual going on?" Lucy asks.

"Nothing jumps out except he was a bit melancholy about his birthday." I ward off another wave of remorse and disbelief. "He didn't say much about what he would be doing during his trip, and that was typical. We never quizzed each other about our work, most of it not up for discussion."

Lucy informs me that last night at seven, Sal met two colleagues at the Red Caboose several miles from Green Bank. An hour and a half later a security camera caught him leaving the restaurant in his pickup truck, an old blue Chevy with a grumbly diesel engine I tease him about. Presumably, he was headed up the mountain to the Allegheny Peak Lodge where he always stayed.

"He was due at the observatory before daylight this morning to track the radio waves of the rising sun," Lucy is saying. "When he didn't show up, it was discovered that he never checked into the lodge last night. It seems that shortly after he drove away from the restaurant he had an encounter of the wrong kind."

7

"What about his truck?" I ask, a gurney trundling past.

"About two miles from there. Apparently, it plunged off the road with no one inside and is halfway down the mountain in a ravine. First responders report that the engine was running at the time of the crash, the doors locked, the front seat belts fastened but no sign of anyone."

"How far is that from where his body somehow ended up?" I continue writing down the details.

"Ninety miles, in Augusta County."

"The theme park has been abandoned how long?" I ask, and Lucy was in high school the last time I took her there.

"It was permanently shuttered at the beginning of COVID," she answers. "Since then it's fallen to ruin and been vandalized. As you remember, it's off the beaten track in the Blue Ridge foothills. You'd have to know about it or you wouldn't think to leave a body there. It's not the only stop we'll be making, and we'll talk more later. I'm an hour out from Washington National."

"Marino and I will be there with our gear."

"A bad storm front is on the way, and it's going to get nasty later in the day," she adds. "You can expect a lot of turbulence and tricky maneuvering. He won't be happy."

"That's an understatement. Fly safe," I tell her.

★ ★ ★

I return the handset to its cradle, the long cord twisting and coiling like something alive. Reaching for my cell phone, I write a text to Pete Marino, a former homicide detective I've worked with most of my career. He's my head of investigations

8

and hates flying in helicopters, especially when Lucy is at the stick.

Add bad weather to the equation, and he'll be an ill-tempered mess. Introduce the subject of UAPs and I'll never hear the end of it. An enthusiast of most things paranormal, including Bigfoot, ghosts and flying saucers, he's quick to tell you about his close encounters. Marino will hope the UAP really is from outer space. At the same time, he'll panic should that turn out to be the case.

I inform him that we're needed at a scene some 150 miles west of our office here in Alexandria. Lucy will be flying us there and possibly to other locations. In addition to the usual equipment, he's to bring Level-A hazmat protection. We'll need total containment body pouches and a radiation detector. It would be a good idea to include toiletries and a change of clothing. I have no idea how long we'll be gone.

You seen the weather report?! he fires back with emojis of a thunder-der cloud, lightning and a coffin.

Bring a rain jacket.

We're better off driving & transporting the body ourselves.

Not an option, I answer. *Lucy wants us with her. See you soon.*

I work my hands into a pair of gloves as death investigator Fabian Etienne sharpens another knife on the far side of the room. In his late twenties, he's exotically attractive, attired in his usual black scrubs, these with a spiderweb pattern. His long black hair is pinned up under a matching surgical cap, his arms and neck a tattoo gallery.

He's been keeping busy since he got here this morning, fooling himself into thinking I don't notice that he's avoiding me.

I understand better than most that some deaths are impossibly hard. It doesn't matter that he grew up in the business, his father a legendary Louisiana coroner. Fabian is experienced and for the most part fearless. But he's self-absorbed and overly sensitive. I motion for him that I could use some help.

He'll be with me in a minute, he indicates. While waiting, I finish labeling test tubes and other evidence. I can't stop seeing Sal Giordano's keen eyes, his Einstein-wild hair. Thoughts enter my mind as if from him, and it won't be the same when we're not sitting next to each other at meetings. We won't be grabbing lunch, a drink, or riding together and catching up.

È quello che è, amore.

It is what it is, he'd say. I imagine him telling me not to feel upset even as what I'm thinking seems heartless and disrespectful. As unlikely as it seems, I have no choice but to consider that he might have been inside a spacecraft of nonhuman origin. Possibly he was exposed to unknown pathogens or radioactive contaminants. I'll be treating his remains like an extreme biohazard.

CHAPTER 2

Fabian heads in my direction as the buzzer sounds again from the wall-mounted security monitors at either end of the autopsy suite. On live video the vehicle bay's huge door is clanking open to let in what looks like a windowless white cargo van with a rooftop ladder.

"I need you to finish up here," I say when Fabian reaches me. "Do you think you can manage? I'm headed out of town."

"No problem." He can barely look at seven-year-old Luna Briley's body, gutted of every organ, the curved ribs gleaming white.

Her face is pulled down like a tragic rubber mask, the top of her fractured skull sawn off. Supposedly, she was alone in her bedroom playing with her father's pistol yesterday afternoon. He and the mother were outside in the yard when they heard the gun go off. But I have good reason to doubt the story.

They claim Luna removed the trigger lock, and that's hard for me to fathom. Where did she find the key? And was the gun already cocked? If she shot herself, why was the trajectory pointed downward? Those are but a few of my questions, and when I attempt to envision what the parents claim, it doesn't make sense.

"Believe me, I know how hard this is, Fabian. But if you can't control your emotions, it will be your undoing." I'm firm but kind. "It's something all of us have to learn. We have to work at it constantly."

"Ryder Briley's a fucker. I know he did it." Fabian's eyes are glassy behind his face shield. "He thinks with all his power and money he doesn't have to play by the rules or even be a decent person."

"Don't get caught up in this…"

"The whole time we were there yesterday he was sneering at us like we're stupid. His daughter's dead body is on the bedroom floor and he's practically laughing. Plus, the shit he said about you behind your back. Asking me what it was like working for a C-word."

"He's a calculating bully, his goal to distract and intimidate. Don't let him." I take off the Tyvek gown covering my scrubs. "I need you to begin tracking down Luna Briley's medical records. I want all details of visits to the doctor or hospital for any reason. I won't be satisfied until her every injury old and new is accounted for."

"When can she be picked up? Shady Acres is already checking on her."

"That's too bad, and it figures the Brileys would use them." I'm no fan of the greedy funeral service.

"Jesse Spanks." Fabian tells me who's been leaving messages.

"I'm not releasing the body for several days." I take off my safety glasses. "Please make a note of it in the electronic case log right away. I don't want any confusion. Certainly not when Shady Acres and the Brileys are involved."

"What really got me was the mother boohooing the entire time we were there." Anger flashes as Fabian lifts the plastic bag of sectioned organs out of the bucket under the table. "Probably the same thing she did while looking the other way. What kind of person could do that? She's just as guilty as the father."

"I'm guessing she's abused too. That's usually how these things work."

"I don't give a shit." He places the bag inside the empty chest cavity. "There's no excuse. It's evil."

"I agree it's unforgivable." I pluck off my hair cover and Tyvek booties.

"In Louisiana, it's not unusual to have cases related to the occult, Satan worship, voodoo, as you might imagine." He's sweating and breathing fast, his surgical mask sucking in and out. "I used to go with my dad to some of the scenes and could feel the dark forces. That's what I felt yesterday in the Briley house. I felt evil."

He's talking at top speed while threading a surgical needle with cotton twine. I notice his hands are trembling slightly.

"Are you all right, Fabian?"

"Was too wound up to sleep much after I got home last night. Whenever I'd close my eyes, I'd see things I didn't want to see. I started thinking that something evil followed me from the Briley house. Faye could feel it too."

Faye Hanaday is the top tool marks and firearms examiner, her lab upstairs. She and Fabian live together in a converted carriage house that they swear is haunted.

"We walked around burning sage. And that seems to have cleared out the negativity." He wipes his forehead with a towel.

"Do you need to sit down?"

13

"Way too much coffee, and my adrenaline's going bonkers. Plus, I've got a headache. Maybe it's my blood sugar dropping."

"Easy does it," I tell him. "Slow, deep breaths. We don't want you hyperventilating."

"Last night I kept thinking, if only I'd been her big brother. Or her neighbor. It wouldn't have happened. I wouldn't have allowed anyone to hurt her." His eyes are bright with tears as he talks about Luna Briley. "She had nobody."

"I didn't sleep much either. But if I'm emotionally bent out of shape, I'm no help to her or anyone, and neither are you."

"What else do you want me to do?" He takes off his face shield, wiping his eyes.

"When her pajamas have air-dried, please receipt them and the bullet fragments to the firearms lab." I'm filling out the evidence analysis request forms that he'll take upstairs. "Tell Faye we'll want test fires for trajectory and distance as soon as possible. While you're at it, check with trace evidence on the status of the GSR swabs. Especially the ones for the hands."

As I'm telling him this, the wall phone begins to ring again. Off go my gloves again.

"Who this time?" Reluctantly, I grab the receiver.

"Morgue." My blunt greeting isn't answered, a talk show faintly playing in the background again. "Hello?" Nothing.

I hang up. The push-button phone down here is ancient. It's not used often and doesn't display caller ID.

"That's twice now in the past few minutes, and it definitely didn't feel like a wrong number," I say to Fabian. "It felt like someone playing creepy games."

"I've had a couple of the same sort of calls this morning,

14

someone calling my direct number, waiting a few seconds, then disconnecting. The caller ID was *out of area*."

"The number for investigations is public," I point out. "This one isn't."

"I keep telling you we need to update the phone down here. It must go back to the days of the Beatles."

"Not quite, but it needs replacing like so many things that aren't in the budget and have to be approved." I spray my case notes with Lysol before unclamping them from the clipboard. "If the calls continue, we'll get the police involved."

"Where are you headed?" Fabian sutures the Y-incision with long sweeps of the needle and twine.

"Marino and I are flying to the western part of the state, and communication will be a challenge." I wash my hands with disinfectant soap. "While we're gone I need you to start tracking down Luna Briley's medical information. We can expect the parents to interfere at every opportunity, and all of us need to be very careful. The Brileys aren't to be trifled with."

"I hope they rot in jail." Fabian returns the fractured cranium to the top of the skull.

He covers it with the scalp, the short red hair shaved in spots where I found contusions several days old. I can hear the mother sobbing about her accident-prone daughter.

Always knocking her head on something or falling down. Piper Briley made sure I knew.

For someone so slow? She had to be watched every minute. That's what the father told me, as if the child was impossible.

"I hope they get treated the same way they treated her," Fabian is saying.

"Remember, we're not supposed to take sides."

"You take sides all the time and just pretend you don't."

"Get better at pretending." I pat his shoulder as I walk by.

* * *

Outside the autopsy suite, the long white tile corridor is like the river Styx, the dead ferried along it, day in and out. Walls smudged with dried blood are scuffed and scraped from run-ins with gurneys. Fluorescent lights flicker in the water-stained ceiling, the stench of death pervasive like a painful memory.

The bug zapper electrocutes flies with an unpleasant hiss as I walk past the dark windows of the anthropology lab. I'm headed toward the fire exit, preferring to take the stairs when I can after long hours of standing and sitting. Emotions bubble up from the deep, and I can't imagine Sal not in my life anymore. He's been in it so long, practically my entire career.

The summer we connected I was one of a few female forensic pathologists in the United States. Having a law degree made me even more of an anomaly at the age of thirty. I was naïve with much to prove when I was appointed the first woman chief medical examiner of Virginia, not realizing that my being picked for the job had little to do with training or ability.

Hiring me was a political stunt to show the progressiveness of the administration. It also was assumed that a woman would be easy to manipulate, the daughter of Italian immigrants even better. I was sure relocating to Richmond had been a terrible mistake. On leave without pay, I was making plans to move back to Miami when the University of Rome's medical school invited me to lecture for the summer.

A visiting professor of forensic medicine had canceled at the last minute, and I'd been recommended as a replacement. My sister, Dorothy, and I grew up speaking Italian, and I didn't hesitate to accept the offer. Teaching while living the aesthetic life in faculty housing seemed like just the remedy for my failures and disappointments. But as my father used to say, *Il destino ha la sua idea*. Fate has its own idea.

I'd been in Rome but a few days when Sal and I literally collided in a bistro near the Campo de' Fiori. Replacing our glasses of spilled Chianti, he told me he was an astrophysics professor at Georgetown University in Washington, D.C. On sabbatical in Rome for a year, he was writing a book while staying in the home where he grew up. *A quaint little place but old,* as he described it.

His parents spent summers in the South of France, and we had the apartment to ourselves. To me it was a palace overlooking the Fontana del Moro in the Piazza Navona. We cooked lavish meals, sampling regional dishes and wines, sleeping little. Pondering our place in the cosmos, we lived out a fairy-tale romance that wasn't meant to last.

Sal was a genius but more than that he was a good person, one of the best. He didn't deserve to come to such a hideous end. I hope to God he didn't suffer. But I know he did if he was abducted last night and hasn't been dead long. What Lucy described suggests he was kept alive somewhere for many hours. I hate to think what else was done to him. I'm sickened and deeply saddened.

I hope my eyes aren't red as I push through the fire door, exiting the stairwell on the third floor. Following the hallway, I nod at staff I encounter. Some are on their way out of the building, others in the breakroom for lunch. The aroma of warming food makes my stomach growl. I can hear the microwave oven beeping, the news playing loudly through the open doorway.

I pause to listen, hoping word about Sal hasn't hit the media. Celebrity TV journalist Dana Diletti is broadcasting live from Mount Vernon, former home of George Washington, our nation's first president.

"...*Today begins Historic Garden Week in Virginia, and bigger crowds than usual are expected on tours of splendid estates around the Commonwealth,*" she's saying in her sultry voice. "*And wow are the cherry blossoms ever gorgeous, folks. But if you think this is something, just wait until tomorrow when I take you to Berkeley Plantation on the James River for a private visit to the formal gardens...*"

Walking on, I'm assured that the media knows nothing about Sal's death yet. Otherwise, Dana Diletti would be in her news helicopter, trying to reach the scene before I do like always. I can imagine her whipping the public into a frenzy about UAPs and the entities inside them. She'll make a big thing about Sal's otherworldly interests, his nickname in the media the "ET Whisperer."

A member of the Search for Extraterrestrial Intelligence (SETI) Institute, he's an icon to *believers*, as he calls those who accept that we aren't the only life in the universe. Last week Sal and I were at the Pentagon together for a meeting with other experts focused on potential threats to the planet. We discussed how best to inform the public when contact is confirmed with nonhuman intelligence.

He presented a PowerPoint on 'Oumuamua, the submarine-shaped interstellar object that visited our solar system in 2017.

Reflective like metal with a reddish hue, it tumbled past Earth at speeds exceeding two hundred thousand miles an hour at times, not acting like a typical asteroid or comet. Sal proposed that it was an extraterrestrial spacecraft. He made international news for repeatedly attempting to contact it.

The third-floor hallway terminates at my corner office, and I open the door, turning on the light, the window shades drawn inside. I didn't open them when I arrived at dawn and changed into my scrubs, heading downstairs to get an early start on Luna Briley. I recognize the familiar scent of Lysol that my secretary, Shannon Park, likes to spray liberally.

That and her potent floral cologne, and I can tell she's passed through recently. Her office is connected to mine, the door shut between us, and typically I wouldn't be able to make out what's she saying on the phone. But she's talking loudly, adamantly, with a spark of ire. Someone must be giving her a hard time, underestimating her as most people tend to do.

My secretary is friendly and helpful until she's not. I don't know anyone shrewder, and I move closer to the closed door between us. I detect the flintiness in Shannon's tone, her Irish brogue as pronounced now as when I was chief the first time around. I catch fragments of what she's saying...

"...*I've made myself clear, Mister Briley. Doctor Scarpetta isn't available*..."

And...

"...*Will serve you no good to carry on like this. I won't be bullied*..."

Then...

"...*You should know this call like the others is being recorded*..."

Also...

"...I'll just be hanging up now..."

I suspect that Ryder Briley is calling about his dead daughter who was sickly and slow witted, I was told yesterday. She was always hurting herself, it was volunteered, because the parents knew damn well what I'd find. The ringing starts again, and I can hear Shannon impatiently snatching up the phone.

"As I've said, I'm very sorry for your loss. But you really must stop this. It's most inappropriate..."

I step away from the door as Marino texts me the latest weather update. High winds and thunderstorms in the Appalachian Mountains could cause hail and tornado conditions.

CHAPTER 3

I check my desk for what's been added since I was here last, piles of autopsy reports, death certificates and lab reports awaiting my review and initialing. The stack of cardboard slide folders next to my microscope wasn't there earlier, and I won't get to any of it today.

I begin shuffling through telephone messages from funeral homes, attorneys, forensic scientists. I'm not surprised to discover that Ryder Briley is demanding I discuss the autopsy. He wants his daughter's body released immediately so that he can *put my baby to rest,* my secretary quotes on a pink message slip.

Blaise Fruge is the investigator in the case, and she's been trying to get hold of me. Before doing anything else, I check on the weather, opening a window shade. The parking lot is bright, my bland brick building surrounded by a palisade of tall metal privacy fencing that casts long shadows.

The blue sky is streaked with wispy clouds, the storm front Marino continues harping about a dark band on the distant horizon. As I watch employees heading out on lunch breaks, I notice a large white SUV has pulled off the street, parked in a blind spot for our surveillance cameras. The driver is positioned to watch who comes and goes through our parking lot's security gate.

Only someone familiar with the building would know the location of the cameras unless it's luck. I'm reminded of arriving at the Brileys' house late yesterday afternoon. Fabian and I were carrying in our gear as the police searched the huge garage, the doors retracted. I noticed the expensive vehicles inside, including a white Cadillac Escalade SUV parked between a Ferrari and a Bentley.

Picking up my binoculars, I can see the Cadillac badge on the grille of the white SUV across from my building. I recognize the angry middle-aged man behind the wheel. Ryder Briley has on sunglasses and a golf shirt, wearing his baseball cap backwards. His hefty gold watch and diamond pinky ring shine in the sunlight as he flicks a cigarette butt out the white Escalade's open window while harassing Shannon over the phone.

I train the binoculars on Piper Briley in the passenger seat drinking a tall boy beer, her long blond hair in a ponytail. Her pretty face is frozen with no expression as it was yesterday, the result of Botox injections, I assume. Braless and big breasted, she has on a hot pink tube top, and through the stretchy fabric I can see the shapes of nipple rings.

Holding up her phone, she's filming state employees driving in and out, her diamond jewelry flashing in the bright midday sun. Then my own phone is ringing, Investigator Blaise Fruge trying to reach me on FaceTime, and I answer.

"I just came upstairs to my office and was going to call you before I head out the door. But you beat me to it," I say to her.

"I'm holding on to Luna Briley a few more days and pending her manner of death for now as we continue to investigate."

"Her parents are already causing huge trouble, and I wanted you to hear it straight from me," she says, her face stern on my phone's display.

I can see that she's parked somewhere in her unmarked SUV, her eyes masked by mirrored Ray-Ban sunglasses similar to what Marino wears. Like him she's obsessed with the gym and taking all sorts of dietary supplements. She looks buff in jeans and a polo shirt, her typical uniform now that the weather is warmer.

"Ryder Briley has been calling the chief's office, internal affairs, also the city manager and the mayor," Fruge says on FaceTime, clamping her phone into the holder on the dash. "He's bragging about all the super-lawyers he has working for him, throwing his weight around, threatening to own the police, the medical examiner and the city of Alexandria."

"He keeps calling my office haranguing Shannon. And right now, he and his wife are parked across from my building," I say to Fruge as she picks up a large drink from Burger King. "Plus, we've been getting weird phone calls. Harassment, in other words. I can't swear it's the Brileys. But it could be."

"They're claiming that Fabian was threatening them inside their house. Basically, they're lying through their teeth about all of us," Fruge replies between sips on a straw.

"I won't allow them to intimidate my staff or anyone else, including me," I tell her while glancing at the white Escalade out my office window.

"Easier said than done." Paper crackles as she opens a fast-food bag. "You got any idea all the stuff he owns? Hotels, office and apartment buildings, amusement parks, airport hangars. Plus, all kinds of companies, and huge homes all over. He's as rich as God and has a network of high-level people who will do what he wants," she says, and I'm aware of his reputation.

When Roxane Dare ran for governor, Ryder Briley was her opponent's biggest contributor. After she won, he's continued to speak out about her viciously and publicly in TV commercials. He's known for starring in his own political ads for whoever he's backing, typically depicting himself hunting big game in Africa or landing his helicopter on the rooftop of a building he owns.

"God only knows who all he's got in his back pocket." Fruge unwraps a Whopper, and what I wouldn't give for one, my mouth watering. "The Brileys are a blight on society, and I swear to God I'm going to make sure they get what they deserve."

Fruge's not much better than Fabian when it comes to over-heating and seeking vengeance. She didn't disguise her feelings while interviewing the Brileys in a great room that reminded me of a ski lodge. They sat on a cowhide-upholstered sofa sur-rounded by hunting trophies. A gazelle. An elk. A bobcat. An African buffalo. A wildebeest.

Exotic birds were mounted on plaques. An elephant's foot had been turned into a wastepaper basket. The floor was arranged with rugs made from the skins of bears, zebras, giraffes, and I found myself stepping around them whenever I walked past.

*　*　*

"Did you find anything that makes you think Luna did this to herself or even could have?" Fruge asks as I spray distilled water on my orchids and other potted plants. "What? She unlocked the pistol herself. She chambered a round?"

"I don't believe that's what happened." I return the spray bottle to a bookcase crammed with medical and legal tomes, many of them old editions filled with my notes.

"As tiny and frail as she was?" Fruge continues talking and eating as we FaceTime. "If I didn't know better, I'd think she was three years old. Not seven."

"She was small for her age, thirty-one pounds and barely three feet tall," I reply as my outrage quietly churns inside. "I'm guessing from chronic malnourishment, her body a road map of abuse."

"And here they are parading as saints. Giving money to this cause and the next, having photo ops with kids at every opportunity," Fruge says. "Total fucking hypocrites."

"The oldest story. Especially in cases of domestic abuse," I reply.

"They have to pay."

"If proven guilty, I expect they will."

"What else can you tell me?" Fruge slurps on her drink.

"X-rays show multiple healed fractures of her extremities, including a spiral fracture of the shaft of her left humerus consistent with her left arm being violently twisted."

"Jesus. I'm so going to nail them." She takes another bite of her burger.

"Scars on her buttocks, back and arms look like cigarette burns," I continue. "She also has obvious bruises on her head that are days old. And possibly ones from around the time of death, the vague marks on her neck and shoulders that I pointed out to you at the scene. I'll know more later."

"People like that make me want to believe in hell." Fruge's face twitches with fury.

"Well, I certainly believe in it, and that it's here on earth." I walk back and forth in front of the window with the open shade, keeping tabs on the white Escalade without being obvious.

"Question is how to build an airtight case." She dips a French fry in ketchup as I try not to think about how hungry I am. "Now that you've done the autopsy, what can you tell about the shooting itself? Can we prove Luna couldn't have done it?"

I reply that the gunshot wound to the upper left forehead is atypical for self-inflicted. The .22 caliber hollow-point bullet ripped a wide wound channel through the brain's frontal and temporal lobes, lodging in the cerebellum at the back of the skull.

"The trajectory was angled downward, and we'll see what else the labs can tell us," I add.

"Consistent with the father shooting her while she was in bed watching TV, which is what I think the asshole did," Fruge says.

"Possibly." I envision the bedroom decorated with a Barbie doll theme, pinkly perfect and for show like everything else.

I didn't notice a single stuffed animal or family photograph, no books or crayons, nothing that might make you think the parents gave a damn. It crossed my mind that Luna was no different from the antique dolls imprisoned in glass display boxes on high shelves inside her bedroom. Their unblinking eyes seemed to follow me as I moved about examining the body.

"It sounds like they were abusing the hell out her forever and nobody knew," Fruge says in a stone-cold tone, squeezing more ketchup out of a packet. "They're important and rich with a special-needs child who *supposedly* was afraid to leave the house. She *supposedly* got severely agitated around other people. That's how the parents described her to anyone who would listen."

As we continue FaceTiming, I'm watching the white Escalade speed away, the Brileys gone, but for how long? I don't need them casing my building or having someone else do it. The security here is far better than it was when I took this job four years ago. But that's not saying a whole lot under the best of circumstances.

My officers can't carry firearms or make arrests. I can't afford more than one on duty per shift, and have to depend on my police friends in times like this.

"I would appreciate a few units patrolling my headquarters until this blows over if you can manage it," I'm saying to Fruge. "I've got more than one reason to worry about Ryder Briley."

"Something else going on with him I don't know about?"

"One of his properties is involved in a case I'm about to respond to near the West Virginia border," I reply. "That's as much as I can say right now."

"And you're thinking the cases might be related?" She rewraps what's left of her Whopper.

"At the moment I have no idea what to think."

CHAPTER 4

As Fruge and I end the call, I'm distracted by the security video screens on my office walls. Something is going on with the cameras inside the vehicle bay, those images suddenly replaced by black squares. I send a text to Security Officer Wyatt Earle asking him what's wrong.

Just noticed they're out. Got no idea, he texts me back, and as if on cue the cameras are working again just like that.

The blacked-out squares are replaced by images inside the vehicle bay, the white cargo van I noticed earlier parked off to the side, a logo on the door that I can't make out. Someone in a tan jumpsuit is walking around to the open tailgate. The metal bay door is retracted all the way up, bright sunlight and blue sky filling the huge square opening.

Cameras seem to be working fine now. I send Wyatt another text.

Don't know what that was about, he answers.

I tell him to expect a few police cruisers showing up to help us keep an eye on our place. Explaining why, I give him the white Escalade's plate number. I'm closing the window shade when my cell phone rings, *out of area* appearing on the display.

"Hello?" I answer, waiting several seconds, hearing radio

or TV chatter playing quietly in the background. "Hello?" Ending the call, I think about who might have my personal cell phone number.

I don't give it to many people. I also don't share the direct number for the autopsy suite, and in my mind, I see security officer Norm Duffy's thin lips and icy pale eyes. I can hear him calling me a fucking bitch after I fired him last fall. He was taking yet another break when an armed intruder entered the building. Norm did nothing, and I suspected he was stealing.

One of the worst employees I've ever had, he was a huge liability. His aggression and negligence placed everyone at risk, and not a day passes that I'm not grateful that he's gone. For a while he left messages threatening to sue for wrongful termination. There's been nothing from him this year, and I'm hopeful he's moved on. But what if he hasn't?

If not him, someone else.

Sadly, the list is long of those who can't resist causing trouble. I step inside my private bathroom, perhaps the biggest perk that goes with being chief. Shutting the door, I take off my surgical clogs and scrubs. It's now half past noon, and there's no time to shower. I douse a washcloth with hot water, adding a dollop of antibacterial soap that claims to have a pleasant herbal scent. It doesn't.

I'm gargling with an antiseptic mouthwash when my husband, Benton Wesley, calls, and I'm relieved and happy to hear his voice. I turn off the water in the sink and switch to speakerphone.

"I wanted to check on you while I could," he's saying. "I know you're on your way to meet Lucy at Washington National."

"I was going to try to reach you shortly but didn't think I'd be so lucky, figuring you were locked away with the CIA."

"I'm at my headquarters now because of what's happened," he says.

A forensic psychologist, my husband is the Secret Service's top threat analyst. I have no doubt he's aware of everything Lucy's told me, and knows details that she doesn't.

"As terrible as I feel about Sal, I can imagine how this must be for you," Benton says, and he really can't imagine what I'm feeling. No one can. "Nothing about this is going to be easy, Kay."

"It already isn't." I rub moisturizer into my face and neck. "I can't stop thinking about what I might have done to prevent it. I was just with him and am replaying every second."

"There's nothing you could have done."

"I think of all the times I lectured him about security." I open the bathroom's closet, not much bigger than a locker.

"I warned him every time the three of us were together." Benton's voice is all around me. "He wouldn't listen."

"No, he wouldn't." I collect cargo pants, a polo shirt from hangers. "And I stopped saying much after a while. But I shouldn't have."

"He saw the good in people even when it wasn't there." Benton has always been gracious about Sal when most husbands wouldn't be. "Which might give us a hint about why he stopped his truck while heading up the mountain to check into the lodge last night. Maybe someone pretended to have car trouble, for example."

"He's the sort to bend over backwards to help." I close the toilet lid, sitting down on it.

30

"Whoever's responsible knew enough to appeal to his self-less nature," Benton says in his pleasant baritone, rarely sounding rushed or stressed. "The first rule of being a good assassin is to know your victim."

"Sounds like you're not buying this UAP business." I pull on the black cargo pants.

"We know there was one," Benton says. "A moving blip on radar and multiple other sensors that can't be explained."

"I'm concerned. It's a dangerous distraction from what's really going on, and maybe that's the point." I pull on the polo shirt, black with the medical examiner's crest embroidered on it.

"I don't believe it's the point, and a UAP would be a pretty difficult thing to fake, I should think," Benton replies. "But that doesn't mean we're dealing with a flying saucer, extraterrestrials, interdimensional beings or whatever."

"Why would someone do this to Sal? Do you have an idea? For what purpose?"

"He had direct access to sensitive information that our enemies want."

"And you think that was the motive?"

"I think it was a motive. Not the only one."

"Whose?"

"That's the question."

"Why leave him in the Oz theme park?" I continue thinking about who owns it. "I find that detail particularly disturbing. Possibly because I've been there and can see it so vividly in my head. But the park belongs to Ryder Briley, whose daughter I just autopsied."

31

"Yes, I'm aware. I agree that it's troubling," Benton says. "What I can tell you is the Oz theme park isn't random. I suspect it was picked deliberately in part to shock and degrade. Perhaps to make a mockery of the ET Whisperer. Or maybe it's personal for other reasons."

"Personal for whom?"

"As you've mentioned, Lucy used to love it when you took her there," he says. "It was a very special place."

"What could that possibly have to do with the UAP, the unidentified craft detected in the area?" I ask, baffled.

"We're missing too much data to know what's going on, Kay. But every precaution must be taken, and we apologize in advance for any inconvenience."

When my husband begins a statement with *we,* I usually won't be happy about what follows, and this is no exception. He goes on to explain that the location of Sal Giordano's autopsy and other details will be disclosed to me at the appropriate time. There's no point in trying to coax him for further information. He's not going to give it.

"Again, we regret the inconvenience." What he's saying is that I won't be conducting the postmortem examination in my building.

Nor will I be using the Remote Mobile Operating Theater Environment semi tractor-trailer in my parking lot. We resort to the REMOTE in potentially hazardous cases, but the Secret Service has something else in store.

"As sensitive as this is, we don't think the body should be examined in any of your district offices. We have another location

32

better suited," Benton says, and my first thought is Dover Air Force Base, where all military-related fatalities are handled.

I'm familiar with its port mortuary, having worked there on occasion. But when I push him about it, he indicates that the body isn't destined for Dover, Delaware. I won't know where I'm going until I get there.

"I'm sorry we can't tell you anything more for now," Benton adds.

"I understand the need for secrecy." I tuck in my shirt. "But I have to insist that we work Sal's case together with reasonable transparency. I'm not responding to the scene and then letting the Secret Service completely shut me out. I have to do the job up to my standards and swear to my findings under oath."

"Our labs and yours will conduct independent examinations of all evidence except the body itself," Benton promises. "We'll do our best to keep the details from the public for as long as possible. How we manage what happens when the news finally breaks is what I'm about to address in a SCIF."

He has colleagues waiting for him inside a Sensitive Compartmented Information Facility, and I don't know when we'll see each other or talk again. It's been this way from the start of our time together, but that doesn't necessarily make it easy.

We first met when a serial killer began raping and strangling women in Richmond not long after I'd moved there. Benton was the star psychological profiler at what was then the FBI Academy's Behavioral Science Unit in Quantico, Virginia. Handsome and from old New England money, he had a beautiful wife and family. He dressed like *GQ* and drove a BMW.

Assuming he was a legend in his own mind, I was prepared to dislike him intensely.

But when he walked into my conference room that hot June afternoon, he wasn't at all what I anticipated, the attraction electric. I stare at my reflection in the full-length mirror on the back of my office bathroom door, thinking about the decades that have passed. What I envision and feel inside don't match the image reflected back, and the loss of Sal is knocking out pixels I forgot I had.

He wasn't my first love or the most important. But he came along when I needed it most, and without him I wouldn't have been ready for Benton. Swiping Carmex over my lips, I brush on mineral sunblock, the overhead light shadowing the lines in my face, the hollowed areas carved by the years. My field clothes are unflattering, the cargo pants and polo shirt a bit snug after multiple washings in scalding water.

Or that's what I blame it on, and I can imagine what my sister, Dorothy, would say. Her voice is always at the back of my thoughts as I dissect myself as thoroughly as everything else.

*　*　*

Turning off the light, I emerge from the bathroom to discover that my secretary has opened our connecting office door. She's spraying Lysol as she walks in holding a datebook and a pen while wishing me a fine top of the day.

"Always wise to disinfect a bit when you've just come up from the morgue," Shannon Park explains, spraying some more, tucking the can in one of her many pockets. "Can't be too careful these days." Her typically cheery face is haunted.

"Yes indeed, I can always tell when you've just been in here," I reply pointedly, and no doubt she was eavesdropping while I talked to Benton.

That means she knows about Sal Giordano, explaining her somber demeanor. A retired court stenographer, Shannon is a snoop with *bat ears*, as Marino describes her. Most people don't take her seriously, writing her off as an eccentric. They tend to talk freely when she's around, and I couldn't be happier that I hired her. I no longer have to dread what I'll find when I come to work. I'm not worried about her sabotaging me the way my last secretary did.

This is the first time Shannon and I have seen each other today, and she's dressed in her usual vintage attire, none of it quite fitting or matching. The yellow paisley vest over her long emerald-green tunic, her voluminous pale blue skirt, black fishnet hose and red high-top sneakers are an unlikely ensemble. Not quite five feet tall, she's fond of old bucket hats like the purple one she has on, her spikey hair tinted pink.

"It sounded like you were having an unfortunate phone conversation a few minutes ago." Carrying in a pair of tactical boots, I sit down behind my desk. "I'm very sorry you're being harassed, but not surprised based on what I witnessed inside the Briley house yesterday."

"The father's a real dirt bird, was effin' a blue streak on the phone. I don't care a tinker's damn who he is or how bloody much money he has. I find him disgusting, and recorded our conversations while telling him I was doing it. He'll keep calling, and I don't recommend you talk to him directly, Doctor Scarpetta."

"I'll let the police deal with him from now on." I pull on my boots, remembering how arrogant and contemptuous he was. "He and his wife were parked across from our building a few minutes ago. It appeared she was drinking a beer while they filmed employees driving in and out."

"Well that figures. So, he's parked a stone's toss away while badgering me over the phone about viewing the body." Shannon's voice is tight with emotion.

"Never happening."

"He demanded to see his *precious little girl* before the funeral home repairs your *butchery* and *whatever treachery you're up to with your political cronies,* to quote him. I guess he thought he was going to drive right on through our gate and come inside, looking at whatever he pleases."

"I'm sure you told him that for security and safety reasons we're not permitted to have viewings or unofficial visitors." I give her the party line. "The police certainly wouldn't want him or his wife coming around when it's uncertain who shot their daughter."

"In his mind, he's above the law, an exception to every rule," Shannon says, her preoccupations heavy. "And if he's heartbroken about his so-called *precious little girl,* you could have fooled me."

"I've alerted Wyatt to be on the lookout in case they decide to come back." I tie my boot laces as my secretary watches everything I do.

Her periwinkle-blue eyes are pinned to me curiously, and I sense questions and heartache unrelated to Luna Briley. I know how much Shannon admired Sal Giordano. I saw the way she lit up when his name was mentioned. It didn't escape my notice that she was flirty when he'd call, no doubt hoping he'd ask her out. In recent months I've begun sensing she might be lonely.

A medical examiner's office is the antithesis of the bustling courthouses where she was a fixture for decades. Shannon lives alone in Old Town, her daughter hours away in Richmond. The rest of her family is in Ireland or no longer alive. Benton and I have her over on occasion, but the underlying problem traces back to when the intruder broke into my building five months ago.

A lot of people could have been killed besides me, depending on who happened to be around and if things had turned out differently. Such thoughts have occurred to other employees besides Shannon, a few of them quitting to take jobs elsewhere. I can tell she feels vulnerable in a way I've not seen in the past.

"Well, you're dressed for battle, going somewhere unpleasant, Doctor Scarpetta. Might you tell me what's the story?" she says.

"How much do you already know from opening our connecting door while I was on the phone with Benton?" I'm not coy about it. "And just because you can hear something doesn't mean you should listen. For your own good maybe you shouldn't."

"I was leaving a few things on your desk and could hear you talking inside the bathroom. By the sound of it, Sal Giordano went missing and has been found dead in that old Oz theme park near West Virginia," she says, and when I don't respond she reacts visibly, her face stricken, her eyes welling. "Oh dear, it's true. How dreadful!"

"It's beyond dreadful." I get up from my desk, handing her a box of tissues as I steady myself.

"He's always been so nice to me, never too busy to ask how I am."

"That's the way he was to everyone." I clear my throat. "I know how fond of you he was."

"And so humble. You'd never know he won a Nobel Prize." She dabs her eyes. "I can't imagine how you feel. There are no words."

"Please be mindful that identity hasn't been confirmed, the case is extremely confidential." I focus on what's important right now.

"If such a thing can happen to the likes of him?" Blinking back more tears. "When he's been nothing but their biggest defender? Makes no sense and I don't believe it for a minute. Something else must be to blame."

"I'm not sure what you're talking about."

"Without intending to hear anything at all, I picked up references to a UFO." Shannon confirms that she eavesdropped on Benton's and my conversation.

"Again, not a word to anyone," I reply with feeling. "We can't afford for something like this to leak…"

"I find it most alarming since Doctor Giordano's known for trying to communicate with aliens. Of course, we're not supposed to call them that anymore. I guess the safest thing is to refer to them as the *Others*. But I'd be shocked if they'd harm him or anyone unless the person had it coming."

"We don't know the facts yet. We don't know much at all."

"I've always believed that they would have destroyed us long ago if that's their intention," Shannon replies. "I've assumed it's humans who are the danger."

"That's because we are." I peek behind a window shade, making sure the white Escalade hasn't come back.

CHAPTER 5

If the Others wanted to hurt us, we're no match for them," Shannon says as I'm reminded of how quickly rumors can cause an uproar. "Imagine if they did to us what we do to everything else. What could be more hideous? But I don't believe they would."

"It's people we should fear. They're who bring death to our door." I rummage in the snack drawer near the coffeemaker.

"In my opinion, that's why the Others are here. To help before it's too late."

"Well, if they have any remedies, I'd be most grateful." I carry granola bars and small bags of peanuts to my conference table.

"When I was growing up in Galway, I used to see strange lights dancing at night over the river Corrib and the ocean." Shannon says this wistfully with a far-off stare. "My father referred to them as the Star People checking on us. He'd tell me that we were wondrously made by beings from another galaxy, which I thought was grand."

"What you're alluding to is a scientific theory that life here might have been started by beings from outer space." I place the snacks in my briefcase. "The Others, as you call them."

"One of my earliest memories is a starship landing on our neighbor's farm when I was just a wee thing." Shannon launches into one of her tales. "He said it looked like a gigantic upside-down spinning top with blue lights under it, and I saw for myself the burned circle left in the grass—"

"Shannon...?" I gently interrupt.

"And the neighbor told us about these childlike beings who floated off the ground. I remember he described them as gray-ish with huge dark eyes, all of them looking exactly alike with thumbless hands that were a bit like claws. They were curious about him but not the least bit harmful. And certainly, they could have been..."

"What we don't need are wild tales and hypotheticals." I open a cabinet, retrieving my jump-out bag prepacked with clothing and other necessities. "Marino and I are meeting Lucy at the airport, and I don't know when we'll be back. The Secret Service is in charge, and I'll update you as best I can when able. In the meantime, I need you to cancel everything for the rest of the day."

"That would be your one o'clock with the *Telegraph*, and let's see what else." Fishing a pair of glasses out of a pocket, Shannon opens her datebook. "After that it's the *Boston Globe* and the *Washington Post* again."

I collect my satellite phone as I think of the many times I encouraged Sal to carry one when visiting the observatory in West Virginia. It's in the heart of the National Radio Quiet Zone where there are no cell towers, all wireless devices prohibited and rendered unusable.

A satellite phone is all that would work in the Quiet Zone. But he refused to use anything that might interfere with Green

Bank's massive radio telescope or those at the nearby National Security Agency top-secret Sugar Grove Station.

"What else?" I'm asking Shannon.

"Your monthly chat with the governor at five o'clock, of course."

"That will have to be rescheduled too," I reply.

"She'll be most disappointed." What Shannon means is that the governor will be pissed. "No doubt she'll be keen to discuss the Luna Briley case, for obvious reasons. Since the father is her enemy."

"Not that I can discuss it anyway, but let her know I've been called out of town. Please give her my apologies," I reply while glancing at a text from my sister.

Le Refuge tonight? 7:30 reservation? Will tell you ALL about my award-winning jackpot of a fab weekend! I could use a quiet evening with family and fine dining . . . , Dorothy writes.

"When people ask where you are, what shall I tell them?" Shannon continues surfing through her datebook, her zany pink reading glasses parked on the tip of her nose.

"You can say that I'm traveling to an area where there's limited cell phone service," I reply while answering Dorothy's text.

I let her know that dinner can't happen tonight. Marino and I are headed out of town on a case. She should know that already. But it's clear he's not informed her. They're married and yet he expects me to pass along the message. What this tells me is they're having a problem.

"You should be aware that Bug Off is here today at long last because of the problem we've been having in the vehicle bay." Shannon continues to brief me.

"Bug Off?" The name isn't familiar.

"One of the pest control companies on state contract."

"Never heard of it."

"It was recently added to the list of vendors. Meaning, it's not the usual young fellow with strange eyes and poor posture who can't get away from us fast enough when he bothers to show up. They sent a woman this time. She showed up without any notice and is scaring the bejesus out of me." Shannon nods at live video on the security monitors.

The exterminator is in protective clothing, her head and face covered, a tank of pesticide strapped to her back. I notice right away that she's not clipped to a safety tether. She must be forty feet off the ground, hanging on to a rung with one gloved hand, the other holding the spray gun. Then she's fogging the nest, clouds of poison billowing up, the hornets frantic.

"It looks awfully dangerous, and I hope she doesn't hurtle to her death in front of all of us." Shannon's brow is knitted into a worried frown as she watches. "Fancy having a job like that."

"Tell her we'd really appreciate it if she takes care of the mosquito mitigation while she's at it," I suggest. "Someone should have sprayed for them weeks ago."

"I've been calling since February. I'll see what she can do while she's here. Otherwise, who knows when anyone will be back," Shannon says as her phone starts ringing again.

*   *   *

My secretary returns to her office as Marino walks into mine, dressed in field clothes, a pistol on his hip. He sets down two large Pelican cases that have wheels and retractable handles.

They weigh at least fifty pounds each, his weathered face and shaved head flushed from exertion and shiny with sweat. It's obvious that he took the stairs, the elevator topping his list of things that he's sure will harm him.

"I'm afraid we have a long day ahead of us," I tell him. "I hope you and Dorothy got some rest over your long weekend."

"Not exactly," he says sourly, and I'm not surprised.

They drove back to Alexandria this morning after three nights in Atlantic City, where my sister was presented with a prestigious social media influencer award. Marino isn't a gambler and can think of better ways to waste money, he'll tell you. Since the pandemic and proliferation of riots and mass murders, he dislikes crowds more than ever.

"Dorothy got lucky with the slot machines, lucky by her definition. I could hardly drag her away," he reports. "Not to mention, the awards dinner went on forever. Then it was back to the casino until after midnight."

"As long as you had quality time together and a change of scenery."

"Atlantic City isn't a change of scenery that I'm looking for. And who gives a shit about winning thousands of pennies?" Marino replies grumpily. "That was Sunday. Last night it was a Blues Brothers concert where she walked right up to Dan Aykroyd and asked him to autograph her onesie, which would have pissed me off if he'd been anybody else..."

I duck my head in Shannon's office to the rapid clicking of her fingers on the keyboard. She has headphones on, typing at warp speed, and I signal that Marino and I are leaving.

"...After that it was a karaoke competition in a bar," he's

telling me. "And Dorothy did her usual Cher impersonation, winning a whopping fifty bucks. We spent a hell of a lot more than that on drinks."

"I think you're well aware that my sister doesn't do it for the money." I shoulder my bags.

"Yeah, I know why she does it. If I didn't before, I do now."

"Your truck's packed and ready to go?" I ask him.

"Got everything we need, including hazmat PPE and the Geiger counter. You mind telling me what the hell is going on? Be nice if I knew where we're headed, and why we're flying in sucky weather. Why are we flying at all? What's the rush? Whoever died isn't getting any deader."

I pass along what I've been told so far, and he knows very well who Sal Giordano is but not who he was to me. Marino may recall that in our Richmond days I spent a summer teaching in Rome during a rocky time for me professionally. But I've never hinted at the rest of the story. He wouldn't take it well.

"Sal Giordano's been trying to make contact with ETs," Marino is saying as we walk out of my office, and I lock the door. "He and the other SETI people have been sending signals all over the universe like they assume ETs are friendly. Well, what if all of them aren't?"

"Saying something is a UAP simply means it's not identifiable, and I suppose that could be a lot of things," I reply.

"Some sightings are explainable. But others aren't, and the reason we can't identify them is because they weren't made by us, the Chinese, the Russians or any other humans," Marino says as if it's beyond question. "There are nonhuman craft visiting us and it's been going on forever."

"We don't know that such a thing was involved in Sal's case," I repeat as we follow the hallway.

"The fact that he was beamed up while driving and exposed to radiation? The fact that aliens probably experimented on him for hours, downloading everything in his brain? The fact that the craft left a crop circle and then vanished off the radar, back into outer space? You don't find that pretty damn convincing, Doc?"

"Those aren't facts." The straps of my bags are digging into my shoulders.

"Not to mention he was left in Oz."

"The theme park is owned by Ryder Briley, by the way."

"You thinking he might have something to do with Sal Giordano being killed? Is that what Benton thinks?"

"Like the rest of us, he has more questions than answers at this point."

"Just so you know, what Lucy described to you sounds a lot like other UAP encounters I've heard about. And it's nothing new in that part of Virginia going back to the sixties when a spaceship landed near Staunton. Small beings were on board, the whole thing witnessed," Marino explains as if it's gospel.

"What was picked up this morning could have been an experimental aircraft that radar and other sensors didn't recognize. It's the same thing as our tox screens missing the newest designer drug or an odd one not included in the algorithm," I suggest, the EXIT sign glowing red up ahead.

"Do you know if the UAP was shaped like a saucer, an orb, a triangle, maybe a cylinder? What else could they tell about it?"

"Not much, only that something was there." I stop before the elevator's closed stainless steel doors and his eyes widen as if I'm pointing a gun at him.

"Oh no we don't!" he declares. "We're not getting on this damn thing."

My answer is to push the Down button.

"We need to take the stairs," he insists.

"Sorry, not this time. I've got too much to carry," I reply, the doors slowly twitching open.

"Damn death trap," he grouses as we board, setting down the field cases. "It's never worked worth a damn since we've been here and needs to be replaced."

"I couldn't agree more, but that will never happen." I press the button for the ground floor, the doors stuttering shut. "Please be mindful that the exterminator's here, and the hornets are riled up."

"I kept my distance while I was loading my truck," he says as the elevator begins descending slowly with a shudder. "Damn thing better not get stuck again!"

We creep past the second floor in fits and starts. Then the lights flicker, and the elevator comes to an abrupt halt.

"Dammit! I told you so!" His index finger jackhammers the lighted button. "One of these days we're going to die in this thing! It's going to crash or we'll suffocate!"

"Why is it I seem to spend so much time calming down the men in this place?" I mutter.

"And of course, no signal in here." Marino is fuming at his phone. "Not that calling anyone would do any good."

The elevator begins moving again. Then we stop. And start

again. Shakily reaching the morgue level. Halting abruptly. The door opening as if having a seizure.

"It was working fine when I got here this morning," I tell him as we exit in a hurry.

*   *   *

Following the corridor, we near the evidence room, its observation windows offering a peek at the patients who pass through our sad clinic.

On the other side of the glass, gory personal effects labeled with case numbers are arranged on white-paper-covered exam tables. Along the back wall are multiple drying cabinets with transparent doors, everything destined for the labs upstairs.

"Those are hers." I point out Luna Briley's pink Barbie doll pajamas on a steel hanger. "Notice the blood pattern? In particular the blood drops on the anterior thigh area?"

Marino fogs up the window, peering at the small pajamas limp and stained reddish black.

"The drops are perfectly round," he says. "They fell straight down, hitting her thighs at a ninety-degree angle. And that's not possible if she was standing up like I've been hearing on the news. She had to be sitting."

"And I think she was."

"Supposedly, she was walking around in her bedroom, fooling with her father's pistol, when it went off, explaining why her body was in the middle of the floor. The parents were outside in the yard when they heard the gunshot. Again supposedly."

"That's the same story they told me and probably everyone else," I answer.

"Total bullshit, in other words."

We've paused outside the x-ray room, black-and-white images illuminated on arrays of computer screens. I point out the tangential bullet hole in the frontal bone, multiple fractures radiating from it. The radiopaque shape of the small-caliber bullet is lodged at the back of the skull. I can see the gaps from missing baby teeth, and the shadows of permanent ones pushing through the gums.

"I believe when she was shot, she was in her pajamas sitting on top of the bedcovers watching TV, leaning against the headboard, her legs stretched out in front of her," I explain. "I suspect that after the fact, the body was moved, the scene cleaned up and staged."

"Any idea what might have precipitated the shooting?"

"I couldn't tell you. We know she had lunch cooked on the grill. And she was eating something like M&M's not long before she died, ones with peanuts," I explain. "Her gastric contents are partially digested chicken and potato. But I also found the candy. And flecks of it were caught in her teeth, suggesting she ate it shortly before death."

I explain that according to the parents, Luna had grilled barbecue chicken and French fries. They said she ate at one P.M., and our office was notified of her death at around four-thirty.

"How long do you think she'd been dead by the time you got there?" Marino asks as we resume walking.

"Fabian and I pulled up close to five-fifteen, and by then she'd been dead several hours," I reply as we reach the decomp room, the light bright red next to the windowless door.

My deputy chief, Doug Schlaefer, is autopsying what the cops call a floater, the badly decomposed body recovered from the Chesapeake Bay. According to witnesses, the victim fell off a boat several weeks ago while smoking crack cocaine and drinking heavily. The autopsy is being done in isolation because the stench is untenable.

"I don't recall seeing an M&M-type candy wrapper in the bedroom or while the police were going through the kitchen trash," I'm saying to Marino. "The question is where Luna got the candy."

"Maybe she was sneaking something she wasn't supposed to have, and Mom or Dad got pissed."

"If she was diabetic as the parents claim, then she definitely wasn't supposed to have candy," I explain.

"Any insulin in the house?"

"When I asked Ryder Briley about it, he said they'd collect her medications and get them to me later. That they were too upset to do it then." I envision the arrogance in his cold eyes. "He also said they didn't keep sweets in the house."

"So, what would happen if Luna ate sugar?" Marino asks.

"She could have gone into ketoacidosis and ended up in the hospital."

"You try Bluestar around the bed in particular? Making sure Mom and Dad didn't clean up the blood in there thinking we won't figure it out?"

"Yes, and Fruge took video while I sprayed."

We're talking about a chemical reagent that causes nonvisible bloody residues to glow blue. The headboard, the walls, even the ceiling lit up, I explain.

CHAPTER 6

The corridor ends in the receiving area with its walk-in stainless steel coolers and freezers, the gauges on the doors constantly giving updated readings. When patients are wheeled in from the vehicle bay, the first stop in here is the floor scale. Height is measured with an old-fashioned wooden measuring rod, case numbers assigned and written on stiff manila paper toe tags.

Across from the door leading out of the building is the security office, and through bulletproof glass I can see that no one is inside. On the desk are a Bojangles takeout bag, a large drink with a straw next to a stack of napkins and packets of condiments. I can tell from the 3-D printer that Wyatt Earle was doing a run of radio frequency identification (RFID) labels when he was interrupted.

I watch him on the video displays walking through the vehicle bay where the white cargo van remains parked out of the way of traffic, the exterminator high up on her ladder. Wyatt looks formidable in his new uniform, black with the Office of the Chief Medical Examiner (OCME) patch featuring a caduceus and scales of justice. On his belt are pepper spray, a tactical baton, a cellular phone that also works as a walkie-talkie.

Since the governor allocated additional funding for our security, I've hired new guards and gotten rid of others. I've upgraded equipment, offering training and more competitive pay. We don't have what we need, but the morale has never been better. I watch on the live feed as a gleaming black hearse backs into the bay to the loud beeping that large vehicles make when driving in reverse.

It comes to a stop as Wyatt strides up, the driver's door opening. Jesse Spanks steps out, sleazy with slicked-back black hair and a widow's peak like Eddie Munster in the 1960s sitcom. That's if you ask Marino. This afternoon the mortician is loudly dressed in a powder-blue suit, a polka-dotted tie and matching pocket square. He opens the hearse's tailgate with a flourish like a magician about to impress us with a trick.

My office isn't on good terms with Shady Acres Funeral Home, a thriving enterprise less than a mile from here. The expectation is that I'll give them referrals and other considerations in exchange for favors. I'm expected to do exactly as my predecessor, Elvin Reddy, did and maybe still does in his new capacity. But that didn't happen the first time I was chief, and it won't happen now.

"Shit," Marino mutters under his breath, staring at Spanks on the security monitor. "What's he doing here? I got an updated list of all pickups and deliveries scheduled so far and Shady Acres isn't on it."

"He's been calling about Luna Briley." I hold open the pedestrian door leading into the vehicle bay, the hearse's engine rumbling.

"I saw on the log that she's not being released yet," Marino says.

"That's right," I reply as we haul our bags and cases down the concrete ramp, the exterminator spraying high above our heads.

We give her ladder a wide berth, Marino's eyes nervously darting in that direction. I smell the odor of pesticide while keeping up my scan for hornets, a few darting around. Most are dead or dying on the epoxy-sealed concrete floor beneath the nest, and I'm depressed by the sight. But venomous insects can't be relocated like a mouse, a chipmunk or some of our other misguided guests.

"...Those aren't my instructions," Wyatt is saying while watching our approach, and Jesse Spanks is none the wiser.

His back is to Marino and me as he stands at the hearse's open tailgate, a stretcher inside with a folded blanket on top. He doesn't see us coming as he continues to misrepresent and manipulate.

"I think you weren't informed and that's the problem," he's saying in his self-important way.

"When the chief gives me the go-ahead, you'll get a call just like always," Wyatt answers. "You can't just show up like this under false pretenses."

"Clearly, she forgot to tell you I was on my way," Spanks replies.

"You were told the body's not ready."

"I'm sorry to say but Doctor Scarpetta's the weak link here. Not me. I hear she was ill tempered and overly emotional at the scene yesterday. And it's understandable at her stage in life

53

and with all she must have on her mind." Spanks continues his audacious lies, and Marino and I have stopped to listen.

"The body's not going anywhere," Wyatt flatly states.

"We can't get started on preparations until we have little Luna in our care." The mortician has a habit of unctuously dropping his voice when asserting himself. "The Brileys are expecting you to comply with their wishes immediately."

"I don't answer to the families," is Wyatt's sharp response.

"Most of all the Brileys want to be assured that their loved one is handled properly—"

"What's going on?" I interrupt.

"Why, good afternoon, Doctor Scarpetta. How long have you been standing there?" Spanks gives me an insincere smile.

"Long enough," I reply as Marino and I walk up.

"As always, nice to see you, ma'am." Another big grin that could be a tooth whitening ad.

He shakes my hand, squeezing it painfully hard as he always does. This time I return the favor, my grip strong from decades of cutting through stubborn tissue and bone. He winces, sliding his hands in his pockets, his cloying cologne blending with the acrid odors of death and insecticide.

"I was just explaining our earlier communications," he says to me.

"And what might those have been since I don't recall the last time we talked," I reply.

"There's just too much to remember these days," he says sympathetically.

"You and I haven't communicated this entire year so far." I set the record straight.

"And besides that, the doc's got a fucking photographic memory," Marino feels compelled to say.

"I've been telling Mister Spanks that you're not releasing Luna Briley yet." Wyatt speaks up heatedly.

"Such a tragic accident." Spanks sadly shakes his head. "It's appalling what little children know about these days. Nothing's safe. Apparently, she could be quite stubborn and willful for such a cute little thing."

"Who asked you to testify?" Marino fires back at him. "And why are you here?"

"To pull something, that's why." Wyatt nails Spanks with an accusatory stare. "The only reason I let him through the security gate when he just now showed up unannounced is he said he left a stretcher here and needed to pick it up."

"What stretcher?" Marino stares at the folded one inside the back of the hearse.

"The one he brought to make the pickup." Wyatt is so irate he's practically sputtering. "In other words, he lied so he could come in and body snatch."

"Luna Briley's not going anywhere until I say, and that could be a while. Days, at least, as I'm sure you've been told." I look at Spanks in a way that gives him fair warning.

"I can't help but find it strange that you're not done with her yet. To do what else?" he says accusingly.

"The case is pending for now." That's as much as I'm going to tell him.

"I'll be sure to let them know you're not interested in honoring their wishes. But I don't think it's the best idea riling them any further. Mister Briley in particular. He's awfully powerful, knows folks in high places. I'm talking as high as places get." Spanks is on the brink of threatening me. "He's already complaining about your office."

"Ask if we give a shit," Marino says, his grip white-knuckle hard on the handles of the heavy Pelican cases, his muscles straining.

"You need to leave now," I tell Spanks. "Don't pull another stunt like this or we won't be so forgiving next time. Wyatt, please make sure he's escorted out of the parking lot."

"You got it, Chief," he says as Spanks slams the hearse's tailgate.

* * *

The vehicle bay's door is retracted, the sun directly overhead as Marino and I leave the building. Virginia and U.S. flags flap loudly, their swivel hooks clicking against tall metal poles in front of the padlocked glass entrance. The wind is picking up, the barometric pressure dropping, and I can feel the storm front's approach.

"What we just witnessed was a crime. There's no other way to slice it." Marino continues venting as we put on our sunglasses. "The attempted removal of a dead body is a felony. And it's all recorded on our security cameras. I should get Jesse Spanks's ass arrested."

"I don't think that's a good idea," I reply as we walk past rows of cars, a few people coming and going on their lunch breaks.

I find myself constantly looking for the white Escalade, relieved that there's no sign of it. Marino's blacked-out Ford

Raptor pickup truck is halfway across the parking lot tucked at an angle near the fence where no one will ding the doors.

"How come you parked way over there?" I ask him.

"Didn't want to be anywhere near a bunch of pissed-off hornets. Not to mention poison. Maybe I need to file a complaint with the Better Business Bureau or something, get Shady Acres in a shitload of trouble."

"It will likely make things worse," I reply as we near the semi tractor-trailer hooked up to its generator, the REMOTE that I presumed we'd use in Sal Giordano's case.

"We can't let Eddie fucking Munster get away with it, Doc."

"Best not to make a thing of it. Now we're onto him if we weren't before. He won't try that again if he has a brain in his head."

"Well, he doesn't. And obviously, he's doing what the Brileys instructed. So, tell me, what's the point of snatching the body after you've already done the autopsy?" Marino digs in a pocket for his truck's keyless remote. "What did they think they were going to accomplish? It's a little late to destroy the evidence."

"I don't know the motive but I'm not finished. I haven't verified the most important finding if I'm right about the fingertip bruises. They'd show that she was violently grabbed by the shoulders and neck not long before she was shot. And that would be very bad for the parents."

"You thinking they somehow know about the bruises?"

"Hopefully they don't," I reply as I think about who does.

I told Fruge. And Shannon could know if she's looked at the paperwork I left on my conference table. Fabian wasn't with me while I examined the body.

"All to say, it's actually not too late to destroy evidence," I add as Marino points the remote at his truck, and the lights flash. "Did you remember to bring your motion sickness medicine?"

"Already took it and have more in my pocket." He stares up at the wall of dark clouds in the distance. "I hope Lucy knows what's she's doing, because everything I'm hearing sounds like a nightmare. I sure as hell hope we don't get stranded in the mountains or worse."

We place our gear inside the truck's covered bed, and momentarily he's starting the powerful engine, maneuvering out of the crowded parking lot. At the security gate, we wait for other cars to drive through. When it's our turn, Marino begins easing forward, when suddenly the black-and-white-striped arm begins chopping up and down like a scene from *The Exorcist*.

"*SHIT!*" He shoves the gearshift into park, the front bumper just inches from the guillotining gate. "This is what I'm talking about! Everything's haywire around here!"

Climbing out, he finds the power cutoff switch in a small gray box and disables the arm. It's barricading the exit lane, and two cars are behind us, employees leaving. I feel curious eyes when Marino orders me out of the truck as if I'm about to be arrested. He motions like a traffic cop, indicating for me to take the driver's seat.

Lifting the security arm, he holds it above his head as I drive through. Then I'm parking out of the way of traffic. I return to the passenger's seat as he switches the power back on, giving me an incredulous shrug while the waiting cars drive out. The gate operates as if nothing was ever wrong.

"Now it's fine?" He climbs into his truck, pulling the door shut. "How does that make sense?"

"Maybe when you flipped the switch off and back on something got reset?" I suggest.

"It doesn't work like that."

"Possibly a power surge or glitchy sensor?"

"Dammit, Doc. I hope we've not been hacked again."

"Don't even say it," I reply as we drive away from our four-story building in the hinterlands of the Northern Virginia district government center.

The fenced-in OCME complex is off to itself at the back of the state government office park. On three sides of my building are kudzu-choked wetlands, and an electrical substation that's been shot at several times. We have a smokestack on the roof for the anatomical division's crematorium, and I don't blame people for wanting to be as far from us as possible.

Several acres away are the Departments of Health, Public Safety and Emergency Medical Services and the Bureau of Vital Records. Those buildings are modern and attractive by comparison, with tinted glass and tidy flower beds, fountains and reflecting pools. Some have cafeterias, rooftop terraces and underground parking. There are benches beneath shade trees, the lobbies unlocked, visitors welcome.

CHAPTER 7

Minutes later we're driving past the serpentine stone wall enclosing the Shady Acres compound. Across from the soaring wrought iron entrance one of their billboards advertises, *Whatever floats your boat, we wait with open arms*. It shows customers in swan boats on the cemetery's fake lake. In other ads, the bereft sprinkle ashes from a hot air balloon.

"I texted Dorothy that we're not available for dinner," I tell Marino, the Safeway grocery store ahead reminding me of errands I need to run. "I explained why without going into detail. I've not had a chance to catch up with her, but she seems excited about her award and your weekend in Atlantic City."

"Yeah, she had quite the time." He stares straight ahead as he drives, chewing gum because he wants to smoke.

"Have you talked to her recently?" I want to know why he didn't inform her that we're on our way out of town.

"Not since I saw her last. Although I wouldn't call what we were doing *talking* by that point, as bitchy as she was."

"Everything all right?"

"She wanted all of us to have dinner tonight at that French place she's been bugging me to try, which is the last thing I feel like after the weekend from hell." He's chomping on the gum, his jaw muscles flexing. "I asked why we couldn't have a quiet night at home just me and her. She said it would be good to see everyone. Like she's lonely after being around mobs nonstop. Which I don't get."

"I'm sorry you two are having a rough patch. Even so, I would have assumed you'd let her know that you've been called out of town and aren't sure when you'll be home. I didn't expect that you'd leave it up to me to let her know," I reply, and he's pulled this before when he doesn't want to be the messenger.

"She's already irritated enough."

"About what?"

"Supposedly I ignored her the entire weekend," he replies in frustration. "After I followed her from slot machine to slot machine three nights in a row? And I was right there for her karaoke contests acting like her bodyguard. You wouldn't believe the people wanting to buy her drinks. And throwing shit at her. Room keys. Money and notes folded up. A sports bra."

"That sounds pretty stressful and chaotic." I study his tense face, and my sister wouldn't be easy for anyone to manage. Maybe none of us are, if we're honest.

"When Dorothy's in front of people, I can see how happy she is." Marino takes the gum out of his mouth, dropping it in the trash bag hanging from the gearshift. "If everyone's clapping and cheering, she's *over the moon*, as she describes it. She used to feel that way about me."

"You know how much she loves an audience." I sidestep what he's really saying. I'm wading in deep enough and resisting further detail. "You've always known how outgoing she is. And yes, she craves attention, and it's not new."

"It's worse, and we're getting along like crap." He's out with it. "We argued most of the drive home. What the hell did I do to screw this up?"

He seems genuinely hurt and lost. I've seen the look before when my charismatic sister goes through men like Kleenex, as our mother used to say.

"You and Dorothy have big personalities, and it's to be expected that you'll clash from time to time." I hope their relationship doesn't crash and burn. "That's why it's for better or worse." I've worried about them ever since they suddenly married during the pandemic.

"You predicted she'd get bored with me, and I guess you were right," he replies, and I'm taken aback.

"I've never predicted or intimated any such thing." I can't help but sound indignant.

Past the Sunoco gas station where I often stop, Marino turns left on North Quaker Lane. The name is ironic at the moment, nothing peaceful about our conversation.

"Please don't take it out on me," I say in a quieter voice. "I can't be in the middle of what goes on between you and my sister."

"I know." He blows out an exasperated breath.

"Just remember that people don't always get along, and she's complicated. She's also worth it."

"Not always." Turning on the blinker, he guns the big engine, switching lanes. "She's not a fair fighter, spends a huge amount of time plotting and planning. Then there's hell to pay when you least expect it," he explains, and how well I know.

My sister mastered the art of mean tricks and slights early on. Hiding my homework and textbooks or the school uniform I'd laid out the night before. Making untrue comments to the nuns that came back to haunt me. Mislabeling the test tubes in my chemistry set. Telling the neighborhood bad boy that I had a crush on him.

"I'm sorry you had an unpleasant trip to Atlantic City, and of all times for you to be out of town," I say to Marino. "I wish you'd been with me at the Briley scene yesterday, truth be told. I would have been better off. As would Fabian. You know how thin-skinned he is, and the Brileys sensed it. I don't know if you've seen him today but he's a wreck."

"People like the Brileys eat the Fabians of the world for breakfast." Marino picks up I-395, the traffic not terrible at this hour. "Anybody wide open like him is an easy target for jerking around."

"That's rather much what happened. Ryder Briley was relentless."

"He's a lot more dangerous than most people would imagine," Marino says. "Fabian needs to stay the hell away from him and his Stockholm syndrome wife. The minute I got to the office this morning I started doing some deep diving. Looking for shit you're not going to dig up from the regular news. What I'm finding out so far is pretty damn disturbing."

*   *   *

By *deep diving* Marino means he's logged into Lucy's AI chatbot that's now a handy app on our personal computers and phones. We don't have to sit at her office workstation if we want questions answered instantly. Opening the ashtray while keeping his eyes on the road, Marino digs out a pack of Teaberry gum, offering it to me.

"No thanks," I reply, and to our left is the golf course at the Army Navy Country Club, a rolling sea of green grass dotted by white carts.

"I wanted information that's not easy to dig up. The kind of stuff Fruge's never going to find. And Fabian sure as hell won't either." Marino crams two sticks of gum into his mouth, the sharp minty fragrance reminding me of my childhood. "So, I ran it past Janet. I asked her to find out everything she could."

He doesn't mean it literally. My niece's partner, the Janet we once knew and loved, is dead. But her animated AI avatar created in her likeness is alive and constantly evolving. She's personable, user friendly, and it's been only recently that Marino has felt comfortable enough to start querying her without going through Lucy. How quickly something becomes a habit.

"I wanted to see what Janet could find, asking her to look for any references to Ryder or Piper Briley," Marino explains. "Not just reports made to the police that were a dead end or shit people say about them in interviews. But anything posted on social media or anywhere else that's been missed over the years. And what I've been finding out is pretty alarming."

We curve around the Pentagon City shopping mall as Marino tells me about an internet journalist named Mattie Fey. Six years ago, she complained to the police that the Brileys had been harassing her about a fence she was building. Around this time her service dog was poisoned with fentanyl, and soon after Mattie Fey crashed down the cellar stairs in her wheelchair.

"She lived alone and had been dead for days by the time her body was found." Marino continues telling me what the AI chatbot we call Janet has uncovered so far. "And what do you know? Her tox screen was positive for a high level of fentanyl when she wasn't known to take it. She worked remotely, and had most things delivered to her house, including food."

"Making her an easy mark," I reply. "Just add a grain of fentanyl to something she eats or drinks. Then show up to finish her off, assuming she's not already dead. Try to make it appear she died from a fall."

"Same thing I'm thinking," he says as we near Ronald Reagan Washington National Airport. "Her place was near Lake d'Evereux and really isolated."

"That's not where the Brileys live now, not even close," I reply, a passenger jet roaring low overhead. "They're here in Alexandria near Northridge."

"But at the time Mattie Fey's property backed up to the Brileys'. She told friends she was building the fence because of what awful neighbors they were," Marino explains.

"Luna was a year old then, and her parents claimed the construction noise was making her cry constantly," Marino is saying as he takes the airport exit. "Several months after the journalist tumbled down the stairs, the Brileys moved to some other big property."

"I've never heard of this case. How was it signed out?" I ask.

"An accident. Elvin Reddy didn't even question it."

"That figures. Were the Brileys ever mentioned in connection to it?"

"No. And two years later they were living near Fort Belvoir, where he got into a road rage altercation when a car supposedly cut him off. Two days later the other driver was shot to death while walking to his mailbox," Marino says, the Potomac River straight ahead sparkling deep blue beyond the tree-lined shore.

"And how was he signed out?"

"Same thing. An accident. Elvin Reddy decided the bullet was a stray from a hunter. Apparently where it happened is fairly close to a hunting camp."

"That sounds like something he would concoct," I reply. "Especially if he was appropriately persuaded it was in his best interest."

When I was hired to replace the former chief medical examiner, I knew the legacy he left would be abysmal. His messes are why I was called back to Virginia after decades away. Roxane Dare appointed me as a fixer, and it seems all I do is clean up after Elvin while he and my former secretary, Maggie Cutbush, watch from a distance.

Since I fired her last summer she's resurfaced as the deputy director of the useless Department of Emergency Prevention that Elvin now heads. Their northern district office is located on the top floor of my building, and a perfect example of my going from the frying pan into the fire.

Marino follows Smith Boulevard through the airport as it loops around Alaska Airlines and United. Then the statue of Ronald Reagan appears around a copse of flowering trees. Marino keeps glancing at his mirrors, and I know when he's not liking something he's seeing.

"What is it?" I ask.

"I'm wondering if the Brileys own a silver Suburban," he

replies. "I hate that I can't run plates anymore. Drives me batshit."

"I didn't notice a silver Suburban at their house yesterday, but that doesn't mean much."

"One's been on our tail for the past few minutes," Marino says. "Some bald guy with a beard behind the wheel. He looks sort of familiar, maybe? And there's a woman with long blond hair in the passenger's seat."

Ahead on our left is the small terminal where we typically meet Lucy when flying with her. Marino drives into the parking lot, and I turn around to catch the silver Suburban swinging in behind us.

"Okay, now I'm really not liking this," he says.

"I'm not either." I watch in my side mirror as he stops close to the entrance.

"Sit tight." Marino opens his door as the Suburban's driver opens his, and I can't believe it.

Fired security officer Norm Duffy climbs out. He's grown a mustache and beard since I last saw him. In jeans and lace-up boots, he has on a loose-fitting button-up shirt that likely hides whatever firearm he's carrying. He's gained considerable muscle mass, the top of his shaved head tattooed.

"What the hell...?" Marino's hand is within easy reach of his pistol as he shuts his door.

I roll down my window to hear them as Norm Duffy walks in my direction, reaching into his tactical sling bag. He coughs quietly, clearing his throat as if he has a cold or allergies.

"Hey, Norm! What are you doing?" Marino raises his voice, his hand on his gun.

"I'm fucking you. That's what I'm doing." Norm slides out a large manila envelope, shoving it through the open window, and it lands in my lap. "Have a good one! Because I know I will!"

He's laughing and coughing as he returns to the Suburban, sliding back behind the wheel. Marino types the plate number into his phone as I climb out of his truck.

"Shit!" he explodes. "I'm sorry, Doc. He's damn lucky I didn't shoot him. Damn, I came close."

"I'm very glad you didn't, and there's nothing for you to be sorry about." I watch Norm Duffy and the woman with him take a shortcut through a parking lot, bumping over a curb onto Smith Avenue.

"I should have stopped him." Marino's Ray-Bans stare after them. "What the hell is he up to? Who's he working for? Let me see it."

Marino holds out his hand as I follow him to the back of his truck. I give him the envelope, and he tears it open, sliding out a document printed on heavy-stock cream paper with an elaborate Washington, D.C., law firm letterhead. Marino skims through several pages, making outraged quiet grunts.

"Well, I think we know who Norm's working for now," he informs me. "Ryder Briley's giving notice that he's suing you, the medical examiner's office, the governor, and listing the reasons why."

"No huge surprise. I figured this was coming." I can't stop seeing the mocking look on Norm's face as he shoved the envelope at me. I could feel his hatred like heat.

"The Brileys' daughter hasn't even been dead twenty-four

hours and they're threatening to take people to court?" Marino says.

"And what's he accusing me of?"

"Making false claims and disparaging statements that are politically motivated because of your *mutually advantageous* relationship with the governor." He tucks the document back inside the envelope. "Also racketeering."

"I'm a mob boss? Maybe I should be flattered."

"It's not funny."

"I'm not laughing," I reply as we collect our bags and gear.

We follow the sidewalk to the private terminal's entrance, walking into a hushed lobby of formal furniture upholstered in chocolate-brown leather. Paneled walls are arranged with modern art, and splendid arrangements of fresh flowers center tables. Granite countertops offer coffee and tea, the small refrigerators stocked with beer, wine, bottles of flavored vitamin water and other beverages.

I stop at a wall arranged with clear plastic bins of sweet treats for guests to help themselves. Small packs of Life Savers, mints and gum with sugar and without, bite-size candy bars, licorice drops, and my attention is fixed on the brightly colored candy-coated peanuts.

"Not M&M's per se, but the same sort of thing," I point out while helping myself to a small paper bag that has *Briley Flight Services* printed on it.

As I'm saying this, I'm aware of the dome camera in the ceiling overhead. Turning a handle above the opening in the bin, I fill the bag with enough candy-coated peanuts to test in the labs. But I don't let on that my interest goes beyond wanting a snack. I crunch on a few of the candies in case anybody's watching.

Marino helps himself to a bag of his own, shoveling a handful into his mouth as we reach the front desk. The older woman behind it looks up from her computer, giving us a practiced smile. In front of her is a microphone that enables her to deal with UNICOM calls from inbound pilots requesting parking and fuel. I look around for Lucy, not seeing her.

"We're meeting the pilot of a helicopter that should have just landed." I recite the tail number to the woman at the desk.

"She stepped out for a minute...And here she comes," she replies as Lucy appears on the other side of the glass door leading out to the ramp.

CHAPTER 8

My niece walks in, her mouth grimly set, and I can feel her intensity humming like a power line. Formidable in a black flight suit and baseball cap, she carries a pistol in a drop-leg holster, a black tactical backpack slung over her shoulder. Her eyes are masked by computer-assisted photovoltaic "smart" glasses, the lenses this moment tinted dark green from the sun.

"We're just about ready," she announces to Marino and me.

The woman at the desk returns Lucy's government credit card and a receipt for fuel. She tucks them into her badge wallet.

"How was the drive over?" Lucy asks us.

"Peachy," Marino says with heavy sarcasm.

"This way." She indicates for us to follow her.

"Where are we going?" he puzzles, and she says nothing else for now.

Lithe and deceptively strong, her short mahogany hair touched by rose gold, Lucy isn't recognizable as the pudgy know-it-all who spent vacations with me while she was growing up. In those days she was a redheaded tomboy in owlish round glasses, her face scattered with freckles. Marino would call her Peppermint Patty when he wasn't teasing her about something else.

After Janet and their son, Desi, died at the beginning of COVID, Lucy moved into the guest cottage on Benton's and my property. But that doesn't mean we see her often. The last time was five days ago when she told me there were issues with the Secret Service's stand-alone cloud computer. Her presence was required at the training center and cyber lab some forty miles from Old Town in a rural part of Maryland.

As it's turned out, her being there was fortuitous. The helicopter she pilots is hangared on the grounds. When the Secret Service was alerted about Sal Giordano's disappearance, she was able to mobilize immediately.

"We'll step in here for a minute," she says.

She shows us into an empty pilots' lounge overlooking the ramp parked with private aircraft shining in the sun. Lucy shuts the door behind us, the lenses of her glasses changing to shades of gray in the low lighting.

"Now we can talk safely," she explains. "In case you haven't noticed, there are cameras everywhere."

"Yeah, I noticed." Marino stares out the windows at a red Jet Ranger helicopter taking off, the expression on his face transmitting how much he dreads our flight.

"There are surveillance devices that you won't have noticed, and I've temporarily jammed the ones in here. I'm not happy about the confrontation you just had in the parking lot." Lucy is telling us that she's hacked Briley Flight Service's cameras, and I think of the candy-coated peanuts in my briefcase.

"I'm surprised the Secret Service would use any joint belonging to Ryder Briley." Marino has a way of making remarks to her that sound like a challenge.

"He owns a lot of private terminals in Virginia," Lucy says. "The choices are limited."

"And now we're headed to a theme park that belongs to the same asshole. I don't trust it." Marino hands her the manila envelope from Ryder Briley.

"I'm accustomed to not trusting anyplace, and assume someone's watching unless I make sure they can't. And maybe we're watching him as much as he's watching us." Lucy slides out the document. "Clearly, he's on the offensive. Which means he's feeling defensive. When did you notice someone was tailing you?"

"Once we hit the airport this silver Suburban suddenly appeared behind us," Marino says. "Obviously, I couldn't run the tag, but I'm betting it's not registered to Norm Duffy."

"The SUV belongs to Briley Enterprises, and Norm started working there within weeks of you firing him last November." Lucy says this to me.

"Did you know that before now?" Marino asks her. "The jerkoff practically gets the doc killed, and here he is in our faces again?"

"I didn't know," Lucy says. "The woman with him is security officer Mira Tang, thirty-six years old. Convicted of fraud and tax evasion five years ago and spent eighteen months in the women's prison near Richmond. Since getting out she's worked security for Briley, her rap sheet making her all the easier to manipulate."

"How can you know all that from a tag number?" Marino asks Lucy.

"Facial recognition technology."

"Jesus, what else do your fancy computer glasses see that the rest of us don't know about?"

"Live as if others are watching. Because they are," Lucy replies. "Ryder Briley certainly is, and there's no question that he was tipped off. Be careful what you say outside this room. If you need to hit the loo, do it now. The restrooms at the theme park haven't been used in years. There's no running water and plenty of rats as big as Munchkins, I'm told."

"Anybody mention what a bad idea this is?" Marino replies as he opens the door. "Maybe you forgot to check the weather report."

"I didn't, and nothing to worry about unless we spend time here arguing about it." Lucy isn't going to let him get a rise out of her.

"I'm hitting the men's room." He stalks out of the pilots' lounge.

"You okay?" She looks at me.

"Trying to keep my attention on what's important," I reply, and she can see it in my eyes.

"I'd been around Sal, but not like you had." She's aware that he and I were old friends, but I've never told her much more than that.

"You appear to be by yourself." I change the subject. "Where's Tron?"

"I left her at the scene to supervise," she says of her investigative partner. "She'll be with us on the return flight."

"To what location?" I'll see if Lucy divulges where I'm being taken for the autopsy.

"You've talked to Benton?"

"Yes."

"Then you know I can't tell you." She's not taking the bait. "But for now, it looks like you get to copilot."

What that means is I sit in the left seat and help with the avionics as I've been doing since she started taking flying lessons while still in her teens. Beyond that, I'm not well trained, certainly not in the beast of a helicopter she pilots these days. Although I suppose with assistance I could get it safely to the ground in an emergency. But it wouldn't be pretty.

* * *

Marino returns from the men's room, picking up the two scene cases by their handles. The woman at the desk releases the lock to the door leading outside to the ramp, the sharp fumes of jet fuel making my eyes water. We walk through rows of private jets and prop planes, careful not to trip over tiedown rings and ropes.

An aircraft marshaller in a reflective orange vest directs a King Air taxiing in, the roar of turbine engines loud. Off by itself in a remote corner is the Secret Service's twin-engine black helicopter known as the Doomsday Bird. AI-assisted, it has wide tactical platform skids and gun mounts. Under the fuselage are special imaging systems enclosed in a radome.

"I sure hope you know what you're doing." Marino has a habit of talking to Lucy as if she's a kid. "I don't care what the computers are telling you. I can see the storm moving in with my own two eyes. And I don't need artificial intelligence to tell me that it's genuinely stupid to be flying anywhere."

"I wouldn't put you or any of us in danger," she says, the lenses of her computer-assisted glasses dark again.

The wind is picking up as we reach the Doomsday Bird, the flat black paint seeming to absorb sunlight, the four main rotor blades gracefully bending toward the ground. The skin is covered with strange geometric configurations that could be symbols from an ancient language. Lucy has explained that the sigil-like shapes are a type of invisibility cloaking. They defeat radar and other sensors by reflecting light in unusual patterns.

"You want us getting struck by lightning? Because that could happen, not to mention fog and wind shear in the mountains. And if it hails? Think of the damage." Marino is going through his litany of objections as Lucy opens the baggage compartment.

"We'll be fine." She helps him slide in the Pelican cases.

"What? You've got some kind of special lightning protection system?"

"We won't get hit." She takes my bags and fits them in.

"Why?" He glowers at her. "Because you're such a gifted pilot you can outmaneuver lightning?"

"I can."

Griping and arguing, he climbs into the back cabin, the helicopter shifting under his solid mass. He settles into a Nomex-upholstered seat, one of two facing forward, the headliner and floor covered with the same silvery fire-retardant material. The seats across from him have been removed, leaving an open area of flooring large enough to fit a stretcher.

Lucy and I step up on the skids, settling into the hot stuffy cockpit, leaving our doors open, the breeze cool. We fasten our four-point harnesses, and she straps a kneeboard around her left thigh, jotting down the time, the amount of fuel and other details. Going through the preflight checklist, she pushes buttons and flips switches, multiple video screens blinking on.

An automated voice talks her through testing the autopilot, the hydraulics and other systems. She turns on the battery, and alarms begin to bong and blare as we put on our headsets, adjusting the voice-activated mic booms.

"You all set back there?" Lucy asks Marino, and I imagine him overwhelmed by anxiety in the back cabin.

"As set as I'm going to be." His glum voice is loud in my headset, and I turn down the volume.

"We're switching the intercom to crew-only as I start up and deal with the radios," Lucy tells him. "But I'll have you on camera. If you have a problem just motion."

"I'll be sure to flip you a fucking bird."

"And if that doesn't work," Lucy says in all seriousness, "press the red button on your mic controls. It will alert us that you need our attention. For now, you won't be able to hear us, and we can't hear you."

"Don't fucking worry, I won't feel like talking—" he says as she flips the intercom switch, and he's gone.

Lucy fires up the first engine, and the rotor blades start turning with a roar. Next, the second engine is going, the generator on. She asks me to enter the frequency for ATIS, the automated weather service. The robotic voice recites the details about heavy rains, high winds and poor visibility moving from west to east across the Commonwealth.

"Niner-Zulu is ready for departure with ATIS," Lucy talks to the tower.

"Stand by."

"It's busy, a lot of traffic right now." She says this to me, the rotor blades thud-thudding, the radios bristling with calls as pilots wait to land and take off. "But once we're clear from here there won't be much, not with the forecast we just heard."

"I hope Marino's going to be all right back there," I reply, the sun hot through the windshield.

"Him and his phobias. The less control he feels he has, the worse they get."

"Which is why they're in high gear since your mother started worrying about her crazed fans harassing and stalking her." I adjust my mic boom so that it's touching my bottom lip. "I didn't realize the extent of the problems she's having."

"The trolls Mom's talking about are nasty. But I doubt one of them broke into her car at the nail salon last month to grab her gym bag as she claims. There's no evidence she's being stalked."

"What about the white van she's been noticing?" I ask. "Last week she felt that someone was tailing her as she was driving to Target. She worried someone might be following as she rode her bike on the Mount Vernon Trail."

"The van had no front license plate, meaning she couldn't see the tag number, and there are a lot of bikes on the Mount Vernon trail." Lucy scans everything going on out the cockpit windows, barely looking at me as we talk. "That doesn't mean I don't take Mom seriously. But I'm suspicious some of what she's claiming could be a subconscious need for attention."

"There's nothing subconscious about it and never has been, Lucy." I watch a Piper Cub start up, the prop sputtering and spinning, reminding me of a toy plane powered by a rubber band.

"The more she gets, the more she needs."

"That tends to be what happens with addictions."

"She's playing with fire when she engages with strangers." Lucy's getting impatient as we wait for the tower to call back, the rotor blades thudding. "Recently, she's started commenting on what a dangerous world it is for visible people like her. All that does is give wack jobs ideas. As you can imagine, none of this is sitting well with Marino."

"It doesn't set well with me either now that I'm hearing the details."

I don't follow my sister on Facebook, TikTok, the former Twitter platform now called X or anything else. For the most part I have no idea what she posts.

"This is ridiculous." Lucy stares at the air traffic control tower rising above the airport like an Olympic torch. "You know how much fuel we're wasting sitting here going nowhere? Six minutes and counting. We've just burned through twelve gallons, about a hundred taxpayer dollars."

"They know you're law enforcement," I reply. "Seems like they could be more accommodating."

"Depends on who you get." Lucy's trigger finger squeezes the radio switch on the cyclic, what most refer to as the stick. "Helicopter Niner-Zulu is on the ramp standing by," she reminds air traffic control.

"Niner-Zulu, what is your request?" After a long pause.

"I'd like to depart from our current position on a one-eighty heading."

"Niner-Zulu. Squawk one-six-three."

"Squawking one-six-three," Lucy answers as I enter the numbers into the transponder, identifying us on radar.

"Ident."

"Identing," Lucy says, and I press the ident button for her.

"Permission granted to depart from current position on a niner-zero heading. Stay clear of the runways at all times."

CHAPTER 9

Lucy rolls opens the throttles, the blades spinning faster and louder. She eases up the collective, pulling in power, her feet on the pedals, her fingers steadying the cyclic. I feel the helicopter getting light on its skids. Then we're off the ground, lifting over parking lots, climbing above traffic along the George Washington Memorial Parkway.

We curve along the shoreline, crossing a wide rocky stream called the Four Mile Run that empties into the Potomac, the high sun flaring off bright ruffled water. Heading south at an altitude of one hundred feet, we're well out of the way of planes landing and taking off.

"Traffic! Traffic . . . !"

The Traffic Collision Avoidance System (TCAS) is going off constantly. It blares in our headsets as Lucy follows the Potomac River unnervingly close beneath us, the surface of the water fanning out in our rotor wash. I can see a lost yellow boat cushion, a plastic bottle bobbing, the variegated blue shades reflecting the dense green trees along the shore.

"Traffic! Traffic . . . !"

The disembodied warnings continue, and fortunately

Marino is oblivious. He can't hear or see us because of the partition between the cockpit and cabin. I imagine him in his silvery fireproof seat, his eyes squeezed shut and fists clenched, maybe chewing on another motion sickness tablet.

"Traffic! Traffic...!"

He'll have an airsickness bag in hand, taking deep breaths, trying not to panic, and it's a terrible way to feel. I'm sorry I'm not there to distract him with reassurances and jokes. I can't talk him off his emotional ledge the way I did Fabian this morning.

"Traffic! Traffic...!"

The targets flash red in the glass cockpit, showing where other aircraft are in relation to us. The farther we get from the airport, the quieter the alerts. We wind around the Washington Sailing Marina, then Daingerfield Island. Dozens of boats are on the river, their sails white blades against blue like a painting. Water taxis churn past each other, their passengers looking up at the Doomsday Bird, pointing and taking pictures.

As we near the historic district of Alexandria, I can see the George Washington Masonic National Memorial shining white above the horizon like a majestic tabernacle. No matter where I am in Old Town, the colossal granite museum is visible, and I often use it to navigate. But I don't understand why we're headed in this direction.

"Where are we going? You taking a detour?" I ask Lucy.

"Checking on something." Her attention is out the windshield, her hands facile on the controls. "And I'm making our presence known."

"For whose benefit?"

"Never know who's watching." Her steady voice sounds in my headset, the ground rushing beneath us. "When you talked to Sal yesterday, did he tell you whether he planned on stopping anywhere along the way to Green Bank?"

"He indicated he was driving straight through other than a pitstop. We chatted in his driveway for maybe fifteen minutes. Then I left, and he was right behind me, heading out. A few hours later he called." As I explain, I remember how uneasy I felt.

How's the trip? Any problems? I asked him first thing, worried something was wrong.

I just wanted to thank you again for stopping by, amore. He sounded wistful, maybe sad, our cell connection iffy. *I will always feel like the richest of mortals for knowing you.*

"I asked where he was, and he said that he'd stopped in Weyers Cave for gas and a coffee," I'm telling Lucy. "That's the last we communicated."

"What time was this?" She steers the helicopter along the shoreline, and I catch glimpses of the Mount Vernon Trail between trees.

"One-thirty or a little after."

"Did you get any indication of him stopping in Weyers Cave for anything more than gas and a coffee? Did something seem odd?"

"Nothing comes to mind except it wasn't like him to call for no reason," I reply, and that's not entirely true.

Long ago in a different life, he called for no reason all the time, as did I. There's no need for Lucy to know. She was a child when that went on.

"But in retrospect I wonder if he had a premonition that something might happen to him," I add. "Or it simply may be that he was feeling sentimental on his sixtieth birthday. We'll probably never know."

"And he was heading directly to Green Bank after making the pitstop?" Her voice sounds in my headset.

"That was my impression."

"It's unclear why it took him so long to get there. Several hours are unaccounted for and it's raising a lot of questions, unfortunately." She says this in an unsettling way, and we're slowing down.

We've reached our Old Town neighborhood, the narrow streets below surveyed during the colonial days, the homes historically preserved and immaculate. Our property is ahead, the manor house's two tall brick chimneys peeking above dense leafy canopies. Cherry trees and dogwoods are vivid pink against bright green, the fruit trees snowy with blossoms.

Then Sal's turn-of-the-century villa materializes behind a tall stand of evergreens on a bluff overlooking the Potomac. Whitewashed stucco is topped by an igloo-looking observatory. It's surrounded by a terrace with small flowering trees, planters of shrubs, a wooden table and two chairs. I imagine him sitting there on dark clear nights.

I wonder if he carried up a bottle of wine, drinking alone while looking through his telescope like we did that summer. I wonder if he thought about our time together. I know I still do even though I don't say it. I can imagine all too well what he remembered, and I feel the weight of guilt again. When we were on his driveway, I sensed something was bothering him, and I didn't question it.

Lucy flies low and slow over the former stable that's now a garage, and next the carriage house converted into guest quarters. From the air, the gardens are intricate mosaics in vivid colors, the swimming pool shining like a cut sapphire amid fuchsia cherry trees. Sal's told me the history of the property, researching it thoroughly before deciding to buy the place.

A wealthy Italian shipbuilder designed the original twenty-acre estate in the early 1900s, naming it Porto Sicuro, a safe harbor. The summer Sal and I were together in Rome, he was thinking of buying the place. It was convenient to Washington, D.C., and there was nothing similar on the market.

He showed me photographs of water-stained walls, rotted wood, leaky roofs and windows. But the bones and view are unrivaled, and I told him that if he loved Porto Sicuro, it would love him back.

*   *   *

As Lucy slowly circles, I look down at the cobblestone driveway cutting through tulip poplars, blue cedars, ginkgoes and other centuries-old trees. The ornate iron front gate has been barricaded with traffic cones and sawhorses, and a black SUV is parked just inside. Another one is between the main house and the garage. From our altitude they look like toys.

"Yours, I presume?" I notice two people staring up at us, shielding their eyes from the sun.

"Yes," Lucy says, the agents disappearing as we fly away toward the river. "When Sal was reported missing, we immediately put his place under surveillance. No one's allowed inside the house or outbuildings for now. We need to make sure it's safe, and we really shouldn't turn his property inside out before we've confirmed his identity."

"That would be rather awful should he walk in on it," I reply, and if only that could happen.

I recognize the Torpedo Factory passing beneath us, a former munitions plant now an art center that's a fun bike ride from our house. Then we've reached the bustling waterfront's shops and places to eat that Benton and I visit as schedules allow.

"When you were with Sal yesterday, was anyone else on the grounds or inside the buildings?" Lucy swoops the helicopter inland as we near the Woodrow Wilson drawbridge spanning the river. "Did you notice any signs that someone else might be there or had been?"

"When I was coming up the driveway, a florist's van was leaving," I reply. "I wasn't surprised and didn't pay much attention since it was Sal's birthday. Other than that, I didn't see a sign of anyone else."

"What was he like when you were with him?"

"Preoccupied," I reply. "A bit gloomy, truth be told."

"You sure turning sixty was the only thing bothering him?"

"No, I'm not sure. And I should have asked. There are a lot of things I should have asked him, but I didn't."

"Don't feel bad about it." Lucy's voice is matter-of-fact in my headset. "You know what they say about hindsight being twenty-twenty. There's not a thing you could have done to prevent what's happened unless you'd abducted Sal yourself and locked him away somewhere for safekeeping."

In my mind, I see him on his driveway. We chatted in the

sunlight surrounded by flowers blooming, everything dusted with greenish-yellow pollen. He was getting ready to leave for West Virginia, packing his pickup truck.

Dove è finito il tempo, amore? Where did the time go? he asked when I handed him the gift basket and wished him a happy birthday.

"He was expecting you yesterday? Did you contact him in advance?" Lucy turns the Doomsday Bird on a due west heading.

"Yes," I reply. "I showed up at eleven with a gift basket of Italian cheeses, olive oil, a bottle of Toscana red, my home-made ciabatta bread. I thought he might want to take it on the road with him."

"You have a text, an email that shows you were planning to see him?"

"Yes, a text. Actually, more than one," I confirm. "Why do you ask?"

"When did you send these texts?" She thunders over a field where kids are playing soccer, and they stop their game to stare.

"We communicated the night before." I scroll through the messages on my phone. "We texted on Sunday night between six and six-thirty while I was home making dinner."

"Who reached out first?"

"I did."

"Why?"

"To ask if I could stop by the next day with his birthday gift," I reply. "And I said that when he was back from his travels, Benton and I would have him over for a belated celebration."

"This was in a text?"

"Yes," I repeat. "Am I a suspect in something?" I'm not really joking.

"You knew him well and are going to be asked a lot of questions," Lucy says as we fly over a meadow spangled with colorful wildflowers. "Better get used to it."

"I'll do my best to answer what I can." I'm not liking the sound of this.

"What can you tell me about the florist's van that happened to show up at the same time you did yesterday?" Lucy returns to that while scanning her instruments.

"The driver was wearing dark glasses, a black baseball cap pulled low and a black face mask," I describe. "Don't know if it was a man or a woman but I had to move over to let the person pass. The driver was rude in retrospect."

"Can you describe the van?"

"White with no windows." I wonder uneasily who I passed on Sal's driveway. Who was it really? "There was a rack on top, and a Betsy Ross flag logo, the name First Family Florists. I've never heard of them, by the way."

"That's because they don't exist, not around here." Lucy's "smart" glasses answer questions without being asked. "Did Sal say anything about a flower delivery? I'm assuming the van you saw must have dropped off something?"

"He told me that he'd just received five dozen long-stem white roses."

"Wow. That's quite a gift," Lucy says. "Whoever sent them obviously knew he was turning sixty. Of course, it wouldn't be hard to find out that information or where he lives."

"He told me they arrived in a beautiful Italian ceramic vase hand-painted with a pastoral scene." I continue telling her what I remember. "The card was addressed to *Sal,* and nothing was on it but the name of the florist that you're telling me is fake."

"Did he have any idea who the roses might be from?"

We cut across the Capital Beltway. Ribbons of traffic wind through hotels, apartment complexes and parking lots like a charmless Monopoly board.

"He thought they were wonderful and assumed I sent them." I envision his face lighting up at the thought. "Of course, they weren't from me. And as beautiful as they may be, I wouldn't pick white roses because I associate them with funerals."

"Maybe that's the point considering what's happened since," Lucy says, and it's a sickening thought.

"I should have asked Sal more questions or stepped inside the house to take a look at the roses for myself, but I didn't think about it. He needed to be on his way to West Virginia and I couldn't stay very long either."

"Sounds like we should take a few more precautions," Lucy decides.

She calls Secret Service headquarters about the bogus First Family Florists, and I can hear the conversation in my headset. Someone posing as a delivery person showed up at Sal Giordano's house yesterday, Lucy tells whoever she's talking to, an agent with a quiet deep voice.

"I want to make sure the large vase of white roses this person delivered isn't a booby trap," she's saying. "Appropriate measures must be taken to ensure that any possible explosive devices or anything else dangerous are rendered safe before investigators go in ..."

* * *

The Doomsday Bird follows I-495 west, trees on either side of us. The mountains are a bluish-gray haze in the distance, the storm front's dark wall rising higher above them.

"Do you think someone's already been through Sal's place before we've had the chance?" I ask.

"We know that the alarm's been on since he set it yesterday as he was leaving for West Virginia." Lucy watches a red-tailed hawk sail past, a hazardous weather warning flashing on an illuminated weather map.

"I saw him do it," I confirm.

"In a perfect world we would have had his property under surveillance from then on. But we had no way of knowing he was about to be abducted and killed. By the time we were notified this morning that he was missing, anyone interested in his property would have had a significant head start."

"Assuming he was grabbed after leaving the Red Caboose around eight-thirty or nine last night, we're talking a ten- or eleven-hour window before anyone started looking for him," I tell her. "That's quite a head start indeed. Obviously, you're worried about someone breaking into his home."

"And hoping it hasn't already happened," Lucy replies. "That and sabotage, planting bombs, poisons, who knows what. According to his alarm company, the security system is old and doesn't include glass breakers and motion sensors. He has a camera over the front door, nothing else, and none of this would stop anybody as sophisticated as what we're dealing with."

"Breaking in for what reason?"

"Looking for something."

"What?" I ask.

"Information would be my first guess. Stealing any electronic devices, for example."

"Needless to say, I lectured him about his safety and security when given the chance," I reply.

"So did we." She means the Secret Service did. "He'd come to the White House or Camp David, driving his old truck by himself, living as if he wasn't a Nobel laureate and confidant of the president."

"He was a free spirit, determined to block out distractions, especially unpleasant ones such as people wanting to hurt him." It's becoming easier to talk about him in the past tense, the finality slowly sinking in and tightening its grip.

CHAPTER 10

Lucy continues pulling in power, our airspeed easing past 155 knots, or almost 180 miles per hour, as we near the Civil War battlefields in Manassas. Vast rolling green fields are spotted with cannons and monuments surrounded by wooden palings. The trails snaking through are busy with tourists before the bad weather moves in.

"Are you expecting anyone in particular to show up at Porto Sicuro?" I study the dark clouds above the mountains, the wind gusting harder.

"Whoever abducted him was after something," Lucy replies. "It wasn't just to take him out or he'd probably be inside his crashed truck with a bullet in his head. Not dropped naked into the middle of a theme park after being held all night somewhere."

"Your theory about what someone might want beyond passwords to critical facilities such as Green Bank?" I ask.

"And also the massive radio telescopes at Sugar Grove that as you well know are busy tracking what Russia and other enemies are up to," she adds.

"Sal didn't need to write down passwords and other sensitive information to remember it," I reply as we fly over a school. "Anybody who knew much about him would be aware of that."

"The passwords we're talking about are incredibly sophisticated cryptology that changes constantly," Lucy answers. "Even if Sal could recite the most recent ones it wouldn't have done any good. And you're not given the current password until you're inside the observatory's control room. The minute you leave, the password is changed again."

But that doesn't mean Sal didn't have valuable information, she adds. In the wrong hands the security procedures would make it easier to figure out the key to hacking in. He also knew the identities of personnel involved in the intelligence community and could have blown the cover of agents in the field.

"That's a very big incentive for our enemies," Lucy explains.

"Is there a chance his abductor gained access to this sort of information?" I can't imagine anything much worse for Sal and wouldn't expect him to cooperate.

"I don't know what might have been given up, but it appears we're lucky so far," Lucy says. "Green Bank, Sugar Grove and others are already taking extra security measures. Certain members of the intelligence community were forewarned the instant we realized Sal had been abducted."

"This is the first I've heard that he was doing work at Sugar Grove," I reply. "He's talked about research projects at Green Bank but not the NSA station."

Within fifty miles of each other, their massive radio telescopes are critical to global security, only the NSA isn't scanning for black holes, asteroids and signs of life in the universe. Their mission is to intercept all electronic transmissions entering the eastern U.S. In other words, to spy, mainly on Russia and other enemy nations, but also on Americans.

"Sal never mentioned Sugar Grove to me," I tell Lucy.

"He wasn't going to discuss something like that with you or most people," Lucy says.

We're following I-66 now, nothing below us but farmland. I'm feeling the winds intensifying, pushing us around, and I ask about Marino. She can see him on camera in her "smart" glasses.

"Headset off, eyes shut, gripping the armrests," she reports. "Just like last time I checked."

"Green Bank isn't actively engaged in spying that I'm aware of, but Sugar Grove is." I get back to that. "And this leads me to the Russians."

I look at Lucy, checking for any sign that she might be thinking about the enemy we tangled with not long ago and have been plagued by forever. A devil as old as evil itself. Someone I would eradicate given the chance, and I try very hard not to go into that dark space. I don't want to give anyone that much power, but Carrie Grethen has it by the sheer dint of her existence.

An internationally wanted criminal and perhaps one of the most dangerous psychopaths I've ever dealt with, she managed to weave herself into the tapestry of my life. There's scarcely any part of it she's not touched since I was first confronted with her violence during the early days of my career. It was a relief beyond description when I heard she was captured and had died in a psychiatric hospital for the criminally insane.

For years I believed she was gone, only to discover months ago that it wasn't true. Since then, I've assumed she's in Russia, where she ended up after a prisoner swap, and I bring her up while Marino can't hear us.

"Any chance it's her? That she's behind this? Maybe she has some nefarious connection with Ryder Briley?" I suggest, and the thought is appalling. "Is it possible she orchestrated the kidnapping and murder of Sal? And staged it to look like so-called aliens did it?"

"Yes and no," Lucy says. "Carrie very well may be the mastermind of whatever is going on. But I don't believe Sal's death was staged to look like an attack by ETs. I don't think it was staged at all. The UAP on radar was real. We just don't know what it means."

She explains that the unidentified object was picked up intermittently before vanishing near the Oz theme park. Then the UAP was picked up again on and off in the area of Waynesville. Apparently, the mysterious craft caused spikes and flashes on multiple sensors, including those at Green Bank and Sugar Grove.

"It stayed below five hundred feet, the signal difficult to distinguish from the noise floor," Lucy is saying. "Which I believe was a deliberate evasive maneuver."

"What's the explanation, assuming Carrie's involved in Sal's death somehow?" I watch blossoming orchards flow by through the plexiglass beneath my feet. "How would that account for a UAP dropping the body overboard?"

"I don't have an explanation yet."

"She obviously has a score to settle," I suggest.

"Carrie's had a score to settle for as long as I've known her and doesn't need a reason. But yes, it's possible she's responsible for having Sal assassinated. This is the sort of thing she would do if it serves her bigger purposes while punishing whoever she decides."

"I just hope we're not the reason he's dead." I look out my side window, the sky not as blue, more like washed-out denim. The storm continues to build above the mountains.

"That's exactly the sort of thing Carrie would want you to start obsessing about," Lucy says. "And if she's to blame, she has more than one reason. Hurting us and those we care about is her dessert. It's not the main course. What feeds her is power."

I find it disturbing that Lucy talks about her in a familiar tone as if they still have a relationship. And maybe they do in a horrible way.

"The Oz theme park is connected to us because I used to take you there when you'd come visit," I say to Lucy. "Does she know that?"

"I might have mentioned it during our time at Quantico. Probably when we were running the Yellow Brick Road."

She's talking about the FBI Academy's obstacle course, and I still have the yellow-painted brick from when I completed it with her the first time. She often ran the Yellow Brick Road with Carrie, and it would make sense if Lucy mentioned the Oz theme park. She was a college intern at the academy when the two of them met. Carrie is twelve years older and can be irresistibly charismatic, like any successful psychopath.

An IT contractor working at the FBI's Engineering Research Facility on the academy grounds, she was tasked with supervising Lucy while developing the Criminal Artificial Intelligence Network known as CAIN. It wasn't long before I realized that they had become more than colleagues and friends.

"If she's formed an alliance with the likes of Ryder Briley, that would seem of great concern to all of us," I point out.

"I wouldn't be surprised if she's gotten involved with him," Lucy says. "He funnels untold millions into elections across the country, all of the candidates having the same thing in common. They're extremists who want to destroy our democracy."

The old city of Front Royal is beneath us, its farmland and orchards drawing visitors from all over. I can make out the white-columned courthouse where I've testified in murder trials, often stopping for lunch in a former feed mill converted into a diner. I always order the fried chicken salad. Marino is partial to the cheeseburger, and I shouldn't think about food as hungry as I am.

I catch glimpses of silos and barns, of railroad tracks and aboveground swimming pools as we near the Front Royal-Warren County Airport. Lucy makes a traffic call over the radio, alerting other pilots that we're out here, announcing our altitude and heading. No one answers, and we cross over the center of the single paved airstrip, not an aircraft in sight, the hangar doors closed.

*   *   *

The Shenandoah River is bright with colorful canoes and kayaks. The elevation is climbing, and we reach the first foothills.

The storm front is mounting like a tsunami behind the mountain ranges where we're headed.

The countryside becomes more desolate as we cross I-81, cutting through the wilderness of Lost River State Park, nothing much to see but trees and rocky outcrops. As we get closer to West Virginia, Lucy describes the damage Carrie Grethen could inflict were she to take control of the radio telescopes at Green Bank and Sugar Grove. From them she could hack into others around the world and in outer space.

"We're talking about the Naval Observatory's atomic clocks, for example," she's saying. "The Department of Defense relies on them as the time standard for our GPS satellites, the time on our phones and everything else. Nothing would be safe, including NASA telescopes and probes in our solar system and beyond. Everything's connected."

"Imagine the computer programs that depend on the accurate time," I reply. "It would be catastrophic."

"And that's just the beginning of the damage. What a coup, ensuring Carrie's status with the Kremlin," Lucy says, and it continues to bother me how easily she utters that name. "The havoc she could cause is unthinkable. I'm talking apocalyptically bad."

"Where is she? Do we know? Still in Russia, far away from here, I hope, doing her maliciousness by proxy." I watch Lucy carefully, her dark-tinted glasses monitoring a passenger jet at our eleven o'clock. "Do you have any idea of her whereabouts? Specifically, at this very moment?"

"I wouldn't assume she's still in Russia," Lucy finally says.

"*Assume?* That's a word I don't want to hear."

"When she wants to be off the radar she will be, and we don't know where she is right now."

"You're saying that our government has lost track of her," I reply as my heart sinks.

"Yes."

"I was hoping that wouldn't be your response. When?"

"After Thanksgiving."

"Any chance she's in the U.S.?" I hope to God the answer is no.

"We don't have a reason to think it. But that doesn't mean much."

"No, it doesn't. And she could be. That's what you're saying, Lucy."

"She might be close by, for all we know. Which is why I want to identify everyone who's accessed Sal's property in recent memory."

We're nearing Harrisonburg, and I recognize James Madison University's Federal-style brick buildings, red-roofed and columned. Then we're gaining altitude, flying over the Blue Ridge Mountains, the winds blowing harder. Lucy's known for months that Carrie Grethen is unaccounted for. Benton would have the same information, no one telling me.

I understand why they can't and have been kept in the dark before. I'm used to it, but that doesn't make it less hard to take. The fact that Lucy is admitting it now also tells me she strongly suspects Carrie is a clear and present danger.

"I think we should check on Marino so he doesn't feel we've forgotten him." My impulse is to keep turning around to look, but there's nothing to see except the partition.

"He's still got his eyes shut," Lucy replies. "And it's not even all that turbulent yet. Nothing like it's going to be."

We're now twenty minutes from crossing the border into West Virginia, and there's the not-so-trivial problem of getting Sal's truck out of the ravine.

"I'm going to have to sling-load it up to the road before the rain moves in," Lucy explains. "The body's protected in an enclosure, but Sal's wrecked pickup is out in the open. We don't want to lose any evidence. And look who's back. Sleeping Beauty has opened his eyes at long last and put his headset on."

She switches the intercom setting as I gaze at the Appalachian Mountains in the distance, an ocean of rolling hills under our feet thick with dark green trees.

"Marino, you still with us?" Lucy asks.

"You seeing the damn weather coming toward us like a freight train?" His voice is tense in our headsets. "And how is it okay for you to fly this thing inside the Quiet Zone?"

"Doctor Rao is one of the astronomers Sal had dinner with last night. By the time we get close she'll have the telescope in sleep mode to protect it from our transmissions," Lucy explains.

That also means they won't be able to pick us up on radar or anything else, making it tricky to communicate our location and what we're doing, she says. The only recourse is to talk over the helicopter's satellite phone.

"Let's give her a try," Lucy says, and I hear the ringing through my headset.

"Welcome back," Dr. Rao answers.

"A race against the storm," Lucy says.

"I can't see you yet. I'm looking out my window." The Green Bank astronomer has an Indian accent.

"We're ten miles to the northeast, Route Ninety-Two under us."

"I'd like you to do the same as before, please. Turn on a one-ten heading when you're five miles from the observatory."

"Roger that."

"You will want to follow Route Four around Buffalo Run again," Dr. Rao instructs. "You'll see the police cars and the flatbed truck."

"The ground crew's in place and all set?"

"They're ready for you."

"Thanks again for your help." Lucy ends the call. "Marino?" she asks. "You alive?"

"Barely. How much bumpier is this going to get?" He's very unhappy.

"We're going silent again. Got some tricky maneuvering to do. You might want to take another pill and close your eyes like you've been doing." She flips the switch on the intercom before he can respond.

CHAPTER 11

The Appalachian Mountains rise around us, the storm front rolling in like an advancing armada. Winds buffet the helicopter as we fly over foothills, the treetops thrashing beneath our feet. For long intervals there's no sign of civilization, nothing but forests.

Over a ridge, we emerge in a valley where the Green Bank radio telescope dwarfs a barn in a grass clearing. Sal once told me that it's sensitive enough to pick up my cell signal on Jupiter should I visit and call home. Appearing through gaps in trees, the structure appears like a gigantic ghost forged of metal, the three-hundred-foot-wide dish pointed up in a mushroom position.

The summer Sal and I were together in Italy, he'd just begun doing research at Green Bank. I remember he said that telescopes like theirs are time machines detecting gases and stardust from the formation of the universe.

We're witnessing what's happening billions of years ago, he'd marvel. *We're watching our own creation, amore.*

The ground flows by like a movie fast-forwarding, a scattering of mobile homes, a cemetery, an old train station. As we approach the tiny town of Arbovale, Lucy points out the Red Caboose near the train station. The restaurant is known for its barbecue, and Sal was a regular when visiting. She says that last night he, Marie Rao and another colleague ordered the Monday special of pulled pork platters with coleslaw and tater tots.

Turning on a northeast heading, the elevation rising, Lucy lowers the collective, slowing down. We thread through a notch in the hills, blue and red lights flashing on the other side. Police cars, the flatbed truck block the narrow winding road below. Rescuers in bright orange are gathered around Sal's blue pickup truck lodged against trees at the verge of a ravine, the sight shaking my composure.

Finding a menu on her heads-up display, Lucy lowers a retractable orange nylon strap. A hundred feet long with two cargo hooks on the end, it's called a dual point load, she fills me in. I watch the hooks dropping straight down as if she's fishing for a whale while holding the helicopter steady as the wind pummels us like a heavy surf.

The sun slips in and out of smoky clouds, the helicopter casting a flickering shadow on the ground. The long blades reach out like the arms of a swimmer as Lucy lines up the sight picture from her side window. She positions the bright orange line over Sal's truck while making small adjustments on the controls. When the cargo hooks are in reach, a loadmaster attaches them to fittings on chains around the axles.

Lucy begins lifting gradually, keeping the dangling truck in her side window as we rise vertically above trees dancing wildly. I take in the damage to the truck's front end, the hood buckled, the bumper hanging off, when suddenly one of the chains breaks free, the helicopter lurching violently. I look down in dismay at the truck swinging like a pendulum, tugging us out of trim as if we're having a mechanical failure.

"That's not good. Somebody screwed up." Lucy's voice is surprisingly calm, the truck hanging nose down, swinging and twirling.

It seems to take forever to stabilize, and Lucy moves into position over the flatbed. She sets down the old Chevy while the ground crew in hard hats is at the ready with hands reaching up. Releasing the cargo hooks, Lucy retracts the line and it snakes up, disappearing into the helicopter's undercarriage like a strand of spaghetti.

We fly away as dark clouds gather, the first drops of rain streaking the windshield. The imaging systems paint the artificial terrain, and radar tracks weather in real time on the cockpit's multiple displays. I'm seeing a lot of orange and red shades warning of dangerous conditions.

"Looks like you got the truck out of there just in time," I say to Lucy as the rain gets harder. "I don't suppose it's destined for my place." I know the answer.

"It's not."

"I didn't think so. Are you going to tell me where it's going?"

"When it's time for you to know." The lenses of her computer-assisted glasses are amber in the churning grayness.

"You don't think I should have a vote or even an opinion?"

"It doesn't matter what I think, Aunt Kay. And you're better off not knowing certain things. As is Marino. At least for now. That way if anything leaks, you can't be blamed. You'll understand better later, and he's the one we have to worry about. He's not going to handle it well."

"Handle what well?"

"Certain aspects of reality you're about to get exposed to and can't talk about with anyone except for those of us involved," she replies.

"Such as?"

"I just said I can't talk about it. But you're perceptive. I won't need to tell you what you're seeing."

Lucy turns the helicopter's intercom switch to the All position.

"Marino? You holding up?" she asks.

"Jesus effing Christ!" His voice explodes in our headsets. "You trying to kill us?"

"That's not the goal," Lucy answers.

"I thought the damn truck was going to slam into the trees and pull us down with it. Or swing up so high it knocked us out of the sky like a wrecking ball."

"Someone did a bad job with the chains," she says.

"Damn sabotage," he decides. "Who attached the one that failed? We need to find out. We could have crashed."

"That wasn't going to happen," Lucy tells him.

"I'm seeing lightning. And I assume you are too."

"The storm's reaching us quicker than expected, with a possibility of tornadoes," she says as if it's no big deal.

"You gotta be fucking kidding me. We're going to die in fucking West Virginia."

"I'll do my best to make sure that doesn't happen."

Soon we reach Monterey, where people visit from nearby

and far away for the farmers' markets. A cluster of red metal roofs are a conservation center where scientists work to save endangered species of animals, including ones from Africa, I've seen in the news.

"The Brileys are their biggest benefactors." Lucy gives the place a wide berth, always considerate about not disturbing wildlife.

"So they hunt endangered animals in Africa and hang them on their walls while donating money for their survival?" I reply.

"The way they probably figure it, there's more to shoot that way."

"Don't get me started." I feel the anger deep inside.

Thunderheads rise blackly, shimmering with lightning as if the gods are warring. The rain is mixed with tiny ice pellets, and at times I can't see the ground, just the shapes of tree canopies in the billowing gloom. Lucy makes another call on the satellite phone, this time to her investigative partner Tron, asking for confirmation that the landing zone remains unobstructed.

"Because of the trees, I'll be coming in hot with a tailwind while doing a steep approach," Lucy explains, and it's a good thing Marino can't hear what she's saying. "It will be hard to keep the tail boom from swinging, and I don't want anything around us. No cars parked there. Nothing."

"The LZ is clear." Tron's voice sounds in my headset. "Nothing there but puddles. See you in a few."

*   *   *

A mile from the Oz theme park I can make out the roller-coaster tracks soaring above the foggy horizon. The Witch's

Castle is a gothic silhouette shrouded in gray. As we get closer, the Yellow Brick Road shines through the rainy mist, the turrets of Emerald City a faint etching.

"Look familiar?" Lucy is lowering the collective, reducing power.

"Never seen it from this perspective," I reply as we thunder low and slow over the entrance.

The front gates are open, the barricades removed to let emergency vehicles through. She eases into a hover as we reach the empty parking lot where I used to leave my car when we visited years ago.

"This is as close as I can get without blowing things around," Lucy says, the asphalt potholed and cracked, tall weeds whipping in our rotor wash.

We set down harder than usual as she fights the wind. Lightning veins the dark sky above the hulking castle as if the Wicked Witch is throwing a tantrum. The heavens suddenly open, rain drumming the roof. Lucy begins the shutdown, going through her endless lists.

Cutting the engines, she pumps down the rotor brake handle, the blades slowing to a stop. Harnesses off, we open our doors, and I feel the chill and smell ozone. The rain smacks wetly, cold drops pattering on my head as I climb down, stepping on a skid, then the ground. Opening the baggage compartment, Lucy gathers the bright red tiedown straps to secure the main rotor blades.

While I'm helping her, a black Tahoe rolls into the parking lot, stopping close to us. Leaving the engine running, the wipers going, Tron climbs out the driver's side. Attractive and solidly built, she's in black tactical clothing and waterproof boots. Her black windbreaker has the Secret Service star on the shoulder, her gun on her hip.

"Welcome to Oz." She walks up to us, rain dripping from the bill of her baseball cap. She makes a big production of looking under the helicopter. "Just checking that you didn't land on the Wicked Witch," she quips as Lucy bends another rotor blade within reach and I slip the nylon cover over the tip.

"The flight from hell," Marino complains. "You should be glad you weren't on it."

"I will be soon enough." She gives him one of her winning smiles.

We help load our gear into the Tahoe, slamming the tailgate shut. Marino and I settle into the backseat as Tron climbs behind the wheel. Lucy is up front next to her, and she hands back a roll of paper towels.

"Thanks." Marino tears off sheets, dropping them in my lap, and we pat ourselves dry enough that at least we're not dripping.

We slowly bump along the Yellow Brick Road, the pavers paint-chipped, some of them missing. The fabled thoroughfare leads to the park's many attractions, and I remember the festive Lollipop Guild tramcar welcoming guests by song while driving to the rides, shops and other entertainments.

"Still no luck with any personal effects?" I ask Tron. "Has anything at all turned up?"

"I'm afraid not."

"Not even inside his truck?" I ask.

"Rescuers looked through the windows and didn't see anything inside," she replies.

"I hope that's all they've done is look," Marino butts in. "The truck's not to be opened before we can process it."

"We got the DNA and fingerprints of the first responders making sure anything found isn't from them. The doors were locked and stayed locked. Nobody's opened anything." Tron leaves out the part that it won't be us doing the examination.

"What about a picnic basket with wine, olive oil, cheese and such?" I explain that I watched Sal place it in his truck yesterday morning.

"There was no mention of that or anything else, including his phone and laptop," Tron says, the wipers sweeping rain off the windshield in a monotonous thumping.

The Munchkin carousel is silent and lonely in the deluge, and I remember the statue of the Wicked Witch in her pointed hat. Her eyes would light up red, a recording blasting her shrieking laughter whenever people walked past. She's dark and silent now, listing to one side, her arms broken and green face smashed as if someone went after her with a baseball bat.

We follow the Yellow Brick Road into the Haunted Forest, passing the ten-foot-tall Tin Man fabricated of steel that's now dented and spray painted. His oilcan cap and axe are missing. Blighted by a heavy rash of rust, he looks sad and abused, his mouth forever clamped shut. When he'd come to life, his eyes moved side to side as the music started. *"If I only had a heart,"* he seemed to sing.

Next is the Scarecrow hanging from a post as if crucified, his straw and clothing mostly rotted and scattered. Tangles of dead electrical cables are all that's left of the Cowardly Lion. I can still hear his talking statue wishing for courage, and everything I'm seeing is depressing. I wonder when Ryder Briley was here last to check on his property. It's shameful that he'd allow the beloved theme park to slip into such disrepair.

"Looks like he wanted the place destroyed after it closed," I comment.

"Send in the vandals and start collecting insurance payouts," Tron says. "He writes off this place as a huge loss year after year. It's more profitable for him than selling it. For one thing, who would want it in this day and age? Especially way out here with hardly anything around it."

"We've had Ryder Briley on our radar for a while," Lucy explains. "Insurance fraud is one of his specialties."

"That and getting away with it," Tron adds.

The Tahoe sloshes over yellow bricks that are muddy and puddled, either side of us crowded with apple trees in bloom, the picnic tables overgrown. Heavy branches seem to grab at us, their pale blossoms driven down by the wind and rain. The small petals stick to the paint and glass, the ground carpeted white.

As we near the Witch's Castle, five unmarked police SUVs and a van materialize in the mist. Quiet and with lights out, they're parked in a clearing where two tents have been set up. One is blue and large, the other black and smaller, and they're some distance apart on the Yellow Brick Road.

Flashes of lightning silhouette the castle, the roller-coaster tracks beyond undulating like a dragon's back. Thunder cracks and reverberates as if we're under attack, salvos of rain smacking and flooding the windshield.

"Anybody besides me wondering about the significance of him being abducted on his birthday?" Tron is saying as she parks close to the tents. "I can't stop thinking about it because it doesn't strike me as coincidental. I guess it could be. But if not? I'm feeling a lot of hate. Someone had one hell of a point to make."

"It also implies planning in advance." Lucy takes off her seat belt. "Sal Giordano didn't just happen to be in the wrong place at the wrong time and someone grabbed him, dumping him in Oz."

"Assuming he was targeted, whoever's responsible would know a lot about him." I place my briefcase in my lap. "Including that it was his sixtieth birthday yesterday. And that he was on his way to Green Bank. And where he was staying and eating dinner." I talk about him logically as if he's someone else. Otherwise, I won't be able to bear it.

"Considering who we might be dealing with, assume nothing is random," Lucy says as we climb out of the Tahoe, rainwater drenching my hair and soaking into my clothing. "Everything means something when the perpetrator has incentive and all the time and resources needed."

"Who are you talking about?" Marino looks peaked from our turbulent ride, standing in the downpour as if it might feel good to him. "You got someone in particular in mind? Because that's what it's sounding like."

"Practically speaking, we need to ask who might be hell-bent on creating chaos right about now." Lucy opens the back of the SUV.

"I have a feeling I know where you're going with this," he replies, all but rolling his eyes. "Despite what you seem to be convinced of, all roads don't lead to Carrie Grethen."

"Cause and effect," Lucy says. "We took out one of her comrades last fall. Now she takes out one of ours."

"And how would that explain a UAP dumping the body? You think she's got a flying saucer at her disposal?" Marino's sarcasm is biting.

"She could."

"Oh, for fuck's sake!" he exclaims, squinting in the deluge, water running off his big face and shaved head.

"The U.S., Russia, probably the Chinese have been designing and building flying saucers since the fifties." Lucy pulls out my rain slicker but it's a little late, and I drape it over an arm. "I can point you to ones now in museums at places like Fort Eustis and Wright-Patterson. Trust me when I tell you that there are all sorts of technologies out there that the general public knows nothing about."

"So, you're saying that all the weird shit people have been seeing forever, the UFOs, the UAPs, the Tic Tacs, the jellyfish are secret human-made technologies," Marino says.

"Not all of them," she replies as Tron lifts out the cardboard box full of containment body pouches.

"The chopper's okay sitting out in this? What if it hails?" Marino carries our Pelican cases.

"It wouldn't be ideal." Lucy leads the way, the rain splashing and sizzling on yellow bricks.

CHAPTER 12

The first order of business is the camping toilet I instructed Marino to bring, and now that I'm thinking about it, I wonder where it is. When asked, he shrugs, telling me we'll have to make do without it.

"Easy for you to say," I reply as we make our way through the wind and rain. "Your equipment's different from mine."

"Sorry about that, Doc. I was going to bring it but got distracted."

"I've managed before and will again." Already, I'm soaked to the skin, and I suppose taking to the woods won't make much difference.

"Your best bet are the restrooms inside the Witch's Castle," Tron suggests. "Nothing works and the place is a stinking mess but at least it's right here and you're out of the weather. When I was in there earlier, I heard something scuttling about. Rats, squirrels, maybe raccoons."

"I'll go with you," Marino tells me.

"Give us your gear and we'll meet you in the blue tent," Lucy says, and we hand over our scene cases.

Marino and I step around puddles, half walking, half trotting through the heavy rain. Our booted feet thud across the familiar wooden drawbridge leading to the castle, a shell of what it once was due to vandalism and neglect. The thatch roof is collapsing in places, the windows broken out, the walls defaced with spray-painted graffiti. The black front door with its brass broom knocker is off the hinges and on the ground.

Broken glass crunches beneath our boots as we walk inside, dripping water everywhere we step. Turning on our cell phone flashlights, we shine them around as I'm bombarded by memories of when Lucy and I used to come here. I envision the fake bats that darted and dive-bombed overhead on wires from the ceiling. Every room was filled with recordings of screams and maniacal laughter.

We'd climb the stone steps inside the prison tower while video projections on the walls showed the Wicked Witch scowling and cackling while staring into her crystal ball. I envision scary Winkie guards standing sentry in their bearskin caps, at intervals crossing their halberd spears to block our passage. It was startling when they'd break into their chant.

"Oh-Ee-Yah...!"

Even though we knew it was coming it would snap us to attention. Lucy's eyes would widen. Then both of us would laugh.

"Ee-Oh-Ah...!"

Climbing to the rooftop platform, we'd take the Flying Monkey zipline, something that went against the very fabric of my being. Thrill-seekers willing and otherwise streaked over the moat, the poison garden and the guard hut where enemies of Winkie Country were tried for trumped-up crimes. The ride ended at the roller coaster, the Wicked Witch's laughter sounding while we hurled along the tracks.

The castle's gutted shops and snack bar have been spray painted with vulgar graffiti that doesn't seem to have a point, everything in ruins. I remember that the restrooms are past the stone stairs on the other side of the shadowy open area cluttered with overturned tables and chairs. The crystal ball is missing from the fortune-telling machine where you'd feed in a dollar and hear your future predicted.

"I'll be super quick and waiting for you right here." Marino heads to the men's room.

Shining my phone's flashlight, I'm careful where I step, pushing through the ladies' room door. The air is stale and foul as I enter a stall, the toilet bowl empty and stained brown. I'm digging tissues out of a pocket when something clatters upstairs, sounding like a metal object falling to the floor.

Then I barely make out a strain of eerie music playing. I could swear I hear the Winkie guards chanting, and fear tickles up my spine. I strain to listen. Nothing now. I zip up my pants, barely breathing as I detect faint footsteps overhead. I hear mumbling and muttering as I pass mirrors over the sinks, my reflection dim in dirty shards of broken glass.

"Hello?" I call out as my heart thumps. "Anybody up there?"

Silence.

I hurry out of the ladies' room as Marino draws his gun, shining his damn light in my face. For an instant, I'm blind, almost running into him.

"Who the hell were you talking to? What's going on?" His light moves as he probes for danger. "You hear something...?"

"Shhhhh." I point my light straight up. "Footsteps."

Both of us listen. Nothing.

"Possible it was the wind making noise?" he suggests as it howls around the building, rain blowing in through open windows.

"That's not what I heard. It sounded like someone or something walking and mumbling." I'm sure of it. "And I thought I heard music."

"I'd better go up there and look around just to be safe." He says this with a decided lack of enthusiasm. "You stay here."

"Not happening. I'll be right behind you at all times." I'm mindful that he has his gun drawn.

Our feet scuff quietly as we climb the stone steps, painting our lights over profanity and vulgar cartoons sullying every surface. The castle's second floor used to be a buzzing place, people queuing up for the zipline, the air electric with nerve-jangling excitement. The space is empty now, the air tasting like dust, the loud din of excited children a distant echo.

"While I was in the bathroom I heard something clatter overhead," I tell Marino while looking around. "Something hard, possibly made of metal."

"Well, for sure something's been in here."

Marino shines his light obliquely across the wooden floor. He paints over broken glass, twisted window screens and other debris, the dust and dirt disturbed in places.

"The question is how recently," he adds.

"And what was it?"

I look around for dried feces and other evidence that critters might be visiting. I don't notice anything that catches my attention, just a lot of dead bugs, cobwebs, a mummified mouse, the carcasses and faded wings of moths.

"Anybody here? Hello?" Marino calls out, gripping his pistol in both hands, the barrel pointed up. "HELLO?"

Nothing. I shine my light around. A chilly wind gusts in, a hanging wooden sign banging against the wall.

"I think that's what you heard." Marino suggests what he wants to believe.

"It's not, and it might have been coming from the roof," I decide.

"Better take a look," he says with a sigh. "And just hope we don't have a problem in this dump since our phones aren't going to work in the freakin' Quiet Zone."

We return to the stairs, climbing up to the zipline platform, the thatch overhang caved in, water dripping and splashing.

*   *   *

Moving closer to the edge of the zipline platform, I shine my light on the taut steel cable stretching toward the roller-coaster tracks in the rainy overcast. Missing are the pulleys and trolleys, and the harnesses passengers would wear while flying through the air.

"No way in hell I'd ever get on something like that." Marino stares out at the cable, faint like a pencil stroke vanishing in roiling grayness.

"It wasn't my favorite thing, but Lucy couldn't get enough." I can see the joy on her face as she'd strap on a helmet.

117

"That figures. Anything that might kill you, and she's the first to sign up," Marino says as the Winkie chant starts and stops again. "What the hell?" He glances around, startled.

"I heard the same thing while I was in the bathroom."

"Coming from where?"

"I have no idea. Except there are a lot of speakers around because of the music and other special effects once piped in."

"Most of the speakers I'm seeing have their damn wires hanging out," Marino says. "And the power's been turned off for years. Let's get out of here."

I'm on his heels as we hurry down the stone steps, back through the main floor, over broken glass and out the front door into the downpour. Following him across the wooden drawbridge, I keep looking back at the castle feeling something watching, lightning shimmering, the windows gaping like empty eye sockets.

We reach the blue tent, ducking inside where Tron and Lucy wait with two Secret Service crime scene investigators I've not met. They're ready with towels for us to dry off. Marino begins unpacking Level-A PPE, chartreuse green with vapor-tight seams. The two of us will be wearing full containment coveralls and breathing apparatuses. Our equipment will protect us from most hazards.

But not gamma rays should the body be radioactive after an exposure to a vehicle of nonhuman origin, for example. If that's the case, other measures will have to be taken. What those are, I'm not sure. The prospect of a UAP isn't something I've dealt with in practice. I pass around the snacks I carried in my briefcase, helping myself to peanuts that taste divine, my breakfast with Benton a long time ago.

Sitting down on top of a Pelican case, I take off my boots, tucking my pants cuffs into my socks. I pull on the PPE coveralls as a Secret Service investigator named Rob begins explaining what's been done so far.

"The state police assisted in securing the scene until we could get here from the closest field offices," he's saying in a West Virginia accent, his face boyishly cute, his carrot-red hair cropped short.

"Let's hope they don't run their mouths," Marino says, chugging Gatorade.

"Good luck with that," replies the other investigator, Daniel, gray-haired with piercing blue eyes. "I'm surprised it's not all over the news already."

"The cops here earlier don't know much beyond the likelihood that the victim is Sal Giordano since he's missing," Tron replies, signaling that the detail about the UAP hasn't been shared.

"What do they think happened to him?" Marino wants to know.

"They were spinning a lot of theories while waiting around, including that someone killed him and made it look like extraterrestrials did it," Tron explains. "You know, because he's known as the ET Whisperer. They speculated that the crop circle was faked to create a panic."

"What about the vinegary smell Lucy described to me?" I ask.

"I noticed it too when we first got here," Tron adds. "It's long gone now."

"By the time we rolled up, I didn't notice any smells. But when I saw the pink circle of flowers around the body?" Daniel says. "That was pretty freaky. Do we have an explanation that makes sense?" He looks at Lucy.

"I don't know how you'd fake what I saw. It was caused by a rotating force that bent grass and blew flower petals in a clockwise direction," she answers.

"Unfortunately, the crop circle's been disturbed if not completely destroyed by the rain," Tron explains. "But we've got plenty of video and photographs of what it looked like."

"What *rotating force* might we be talking about?" Rob asks Lucy as I zip up my coveralls. "Something like a helicopter?"

"Speaking of? You sure yours didn't blow shit all over the place when you found the body?" Marino pins Lucy with a stare. "Maybe you hovered over it not realizing it was causing a crop circle. That's the most logical explanation."

"Not possible," she says. "Tron and I spotted the body at two hundred feet above the ground. I didn't fly directly over it and landed in the parking lot where the chopper is now. We went the rest of the way on foot. And the main rotor blades spin counterclockwise. Not clockwise."

"I'm assuming the body has been protected from the rain." I get back to what's most important to me. "What else do I need to know before taking a look?"

"It's been inside the other tent almost the entire time," Rob replies.

"Before that I was here with the state police," Tron says. "I made sure they stayed away from the body. No one's touched it."

"Or been near it without appropriate PPE protection?" I make sure.

"I was suited up when I took the temp with an IR

thermometer," Rob says. "You know, point and shoot at the forehead. I didn't have to touch anything, the temp ninety-six degrees."

As I'm listening, I'm hoping like hell the body's not contagious with some unknown virus. And dear God, don't let the scene be radioactive. Otherwise, everyone is in trouble.

"And the ambient temperature?" I ask.

"Seventy-five degrees," Rob replies.

"At what time?"

"Around ten."

"Was the body in the sun at that time?" I'm making calculations in my head.

"Sunrise was at oh-six-hundred hours. So, yes, and had been for a while."

"The sun would have made the surface of the skin warmer," I explain. "I doubt his core temp was as high as indicated by infrared. And what time was it when the enclosure went up?"

"About a half hour later." It's Daniel who answers.

"You get a sense that anyone besides us has been in this park in recent memory?" Marino directs this at Tron. "Any sign that someone might have been scoping out the place in advance, for example?"

"Nothing I saw, but I was wondering the same thing when we landed here after spotting the body," she says. "I kept thinking that whoever did this checked out the place first, did a dry run."

"How can you be sure nobody else is here even as we speak, as big as the theme park is?" Marino then asks.

"A hundred acres with a lot of places to hide. The visibility's terrible, and we're in the Quiet Zone," Tron replies. "You're right, we can't be sure of anything."

"We did a recon of the main buildings but no way we could search every inch of the entire park," Rob explains. "We didn't find any sign that someone had been here recently. Although several times we heard something strange."

"So did we inside the castle a few minutes ago." Marino works his legs into the coveralls, staring through the tent's opening as if something might be out there. "The doc thought she heard someone walking around, and both of us heard music."

"Music?" Tron frowns. "From where?"

"I don't know," Marino says. "But something weird is going on."

"When we were looking around Emerald City, we heard something in the brush close by," Rob goes on. "Now and then we'd hear it moaning, mumbling, making eerie sounds as it followed in the woods. We couldn't see what it was and I didn't want to go poking around to find out."

"Maybe a coyote or a fox?" Daniel offers. "I don't think a bear would make the sounds we heard."

"I can only imagine the wildlife that's taken over this place," Tron comments.

CHAPTER 13

The heavy rain drums the tent, thunder rumbling as Marino and I finish suiting up. We strap on belt-mounted blowers that will circulate purified air inside hoods that smell like plastic and are the yellowish green of tennis balls. The heavy rubber gloves we pull on will work well enough for my purposes.

"Truth is, we don't know what's out here, and normally we'd have drones patrolling," Lucy is saying. "That's not possible in this downpour. But our spectrum analyzers aren't picking up any unusual signals in the noise floor."

"All that means is nobody's nearby with a cell phone or some other wireless device that probably wouldn't work anyway this close to the heart of the Quiet Zone," Marino retorts.

"You're right about that," Lucy admits.

He picks up the field cases, and I carry the wet cardboard box of body pouches. We step outside to loud rain splashing, lightning streaking and thunder cracking. Hurrying through wind and water, we're careful not to slip in our ill-fitting rubber boots, the visibility poor, my face shield fogging up. Battery-powered auxiliary lighting has been set up inside the black tent, and my breath catches at the gruesome sight of him.

Sal is face up on the Yellow Brick Road, dark red blood coagulated around his head, and I'm shaken to my core. I know instantly that he was alive when dropped from the sky by a flying object we can't identify. He has massive tissue response to his injuries, and I hope to God he wasn't conscious at the time.

"How do you want to do this?" Marino says as we pat ourselves dry with paper towels left for us.

"We're not going to do much here. Only what's necessary while you take photographs," I reply.

Our voices are muffled through the rubber speaking diaphragms in our plastic face covers. My breathing is loud, and I'm getting hot in heavy plastic. I ask for the handheld Geiger counter, battery powered, the size of an iPhone but no Wi-Fi required.

"Give me a few minutes," I then say.

Stepping away from him, I can't be crowded. And I need to be alone with Sal for now.

"I'll be right here." Marino waits near the tent's opening, and I block him out, pretending he's not there watching my every move.

I step closer to the body of a friend I've cared for half my life. Then I push away thoughts like that, telling myself now's not the time. But I'm pained by the familiar chiseled cut of his jaw, the straight bridge of his nose, his lean but strong build and shoulder-length gray hair. I recognize the long scar on the left side of his abdomen from surgery to remove his appendix.

Also missing is the jewelry he had on when I saw him in his driveway yesterday. His smartwatch. Several inexpensive beaded bracelets. A fossilized shark's tooth he wore as a necklace. A gold stud earring. From where I'm standing I can see the pi sign tattoo on his inner left wrist. Taking slow breaths to steady myself, I hold down the Geiger counter's power button until it beeps.

The software runs through a systems check on the illuminated display, the detector working normally. I slowly walk around the body, waiting for an alarm to sound, and it doesn't. The radiation level is below the safe threshold. We won't need a hazmat team, but that doesn't mean the body wasn't exposed to something else harmful.

I step closer to look him over, naked on his back, his arms bent at awkward angles. His left leg is broken, the shattered femur protruding, the foot pointing the wrong direction. Sal is hardly recognizable, his face contused and swollen, his eyes barely open, his skin red as Lucy described earlier. The substantial amount of coagulated blood is from his lacerated right temple, and his right collarbone looks broken.

He sustained severe blunt force trauma after dropping from a significant height, and I open my scene case. I find the long glass chemical thermometer, and the ambient temperature is fifty-nine degrees Fahrenheit. The storm has cooled things off considerably. My rubber-sheathed fingers are clumsy peeling open the plastic wrapper of a disposable scalpel.

I kneel by the body, the bricks kept dry under the tent and littered with apple blossom petals that remind me of confetti. Making a tiny incision in the lower left abdomen, I focus on every detail of what I do. Trying not to see who it is. Trying not to think. Or feel. Or remember.

I insert the thermometer into the liver to take the core body temperature. It will be more reliable than infrared. Slipping brown paper bags over the hands and feet, I secure them with tape and rubber bands. Marino watches through his hooded full-face respirator. I tell him I'm ready, and he carries in the cardboard box, setting it down.

He lifts out two transparent plastic body pouches, spreading them open, one inside the other. The sound of the rain is a constant loud patter, the tent sides moving in the gusting wind.

"How long are you thinking he's been dead?" he asks.

I remove the thermometer, holding it up to the auxiliary light, wiping off blood.

"His liver temp's eighty-five degrees," I tell Marino. "Rigor and livor mortis are well advanced, and based on everything else I'm seeing, I estimate he's been dead six or seven hours. No longer than that."

"Well, it's almost three o'clock now. You're saying he might have still been alive at eight or nine this morning?" Marino asks doubtfully.

"Yes."

"If the UAP was spotted on radar at six? Then he was alive when he was thrown overboard and slowly died?" Marino's eyes are startled behind plastic.

"He wouldn't have bled like this unless he still had a blood pressure," I reply. "After he hit the ground, he survived for a while. I can't tell you exactly how long."

"I wonder how high up he was when he went overboard." Marino looks up at the stormy sky as if he might find the answer.

"I don't know," I reply.

"If the radiation level is normal, why's his skin so damn red?"

"I don't know yet."

"You sure the detector's working okay?" Marino asks.

"I took multiple readings, and it seems fine," I reply.

Having done what's needed for now, we grab the body by the ankles and under the arms. His limbs and neck are stiff, and my heart aches as we lift him. Blood seeps from the head and leg wounds, dripping as we set him down inside the spread-open pouches. We begin peeling off the protective backing to the adhesive seals, the distorted dead face showing through the clear plastic.

* * *

Using the flat of his hand like an iron, Marino presses down the seam from one end to the other for the first bag, then the second. When he's done, I spray disinfectant over the pouched body front and back. We spray down our PPE. Taking it off, we stuff it into garbage bags that I hand to Tron through the tent's opening.

"I'll be back in a few minutes with the van," she says as we give her our scene cases next. "Stay here out of the rain. We've already taken down the other tent, clearing out as fast as we can because of what's moving in."

"This really sucks," Marino complains.

We wait near the opening, peering out at the empty grassy area where the big blue tent was but moments ago.

"I can't believe we're going to fly in this." He's not going to stop worrying about it.

"If Lucy thinks it's okay, then it is."

"Her idea of okay isn't the same as mine," he replies as my satellite phone rings.

I dig it out of my briefcase, the caller ID *out of area.*

"Who's calling me? And how did the person get this number. Hello?" I answer, switching to speakerphone.

"Doctor Scarpetta?" The voice sounds female and familiar.

"And who is this?"

"This is Heidi, the governor's scheduler. Your secretary said this was the only way to reach you right now, and I apologize for the intrusion. Please hold for Governor Dare."

"Where are you?" she asks right off.

"At a scene in the western part of the state, and this is a bad time to talk, Roxane."

"What's this I hear about you threatening Ryder Briley inside his own house yesterday?" Her voice is demanding over the phone. "Not that I have an ounce of sympathy for him. But I understand he's suing me, the medical examiner's office, God knows who else and I absolutely don't need publicity like this."

"Ryder Briley is lying," I reply. "He's doing what he can to divert attention away from his daughter's death investigation and perhaps other bad things going on."

I explain that he's been calling my office, parking outside my building, doing his best to intimidate. He attempted to have his daughter's body spirited away before I'm done with it.

"What's the loud background noise?" the governor asks. "Sounds like you're in a carwash."

"We're in a tent, and it's raining very hard."

"What can you tell me about Luna Briley's autopsy?"

"She died from a gunshot wound to the head."

"I'm asking for the truth, Kay. Do you think she shot herself as the Brileys are claiming all over the news?"

"I think the parents have plenty to worry about." That's as much as I'm going to say, but it's enough.

"Then she may have been murdered with her father's gun," the governor replies predictably. "And the parents were the only other people home when the shooting occurred, based on what I've heard?"

"The best person to talk to about the case is Alexandria investigator Blaise Fruge."

"What I want to know from you, Kay, is whether you're going to call Luna Briley's death an accident or a homicide. Because it certainly sounds suspicious to me."

"There are a lot of questions yet to be answered."

"Prison would be exactly what Ryder Briley deserves," she says, and I abruptly end the call as if the signal was dropped.

I can't let her try to influence me or appear to be doing that, and I want no record of it. Looking up her cell phone number in my contacts list, I try her back, ending the call when she answers. I do this one more time before texting her that I'm in a *bad cell* and we'll have to talk later.

Keep me informed, she writes back as I'm looking out at the rain, catching a movement in the corner of my eye.

I feel something looking at me as the hair pricks up on my arms and the back of my neck. Then I catch a movement in an empty window of the Witch's Castle, something stirring slightly. A shape in the gloom.

"We've got company," I inform Marino.

He looks where I point, but the castle window is dark, nothing there.

"I don't see anything," he says.

129

"I saw something."

"Probably your eyes playing tricks on you."

"I don't think so," I tell him as he looks around tensely, his hand near his gun again.

"I'm feeling worse about this place every minute," he decides.

When the van pulls up, we lift the body, carrying it out. The cold rain loudly spatters the transparent plastic, my boots splashing through puddles. The investigator named Rob is behind the wheel, and Tron jumps out of the passenger side. She opens the tailgate while telling us that tornadoes are touching down less than thirty miles away.

"We need to get out of here." She's emphatic as we slide in the body.

"What about the tent?" Marino asks.

"We're leaving it for now."

Dripping as we climb into the van, Marino and I buckle ourselves into the cloth-covered bench seat, sliding the door shut. Then we're following the Yellow Brick Road, no one saying much, the presence of the body in back palpable like an undertow. I'm staring out my window when the van suddenly brakes to a stop.

"Whoa!" Rob looks shocked.

"Holy shit!" Marino exclaims.

"Nobody open your doors," Tron warns as I see what they're talking about.

*　　*　　*

The spotted cat is the size of a Labrador retriever, standing on the yellow bricks in the flare of headlights no more than twenty feet from our van's front bumper. A male leopard or a cheetah

I decide as it comes closer. He seems unbothered by the rain, twitching his tail, staring at us with eyes glowing bright white like something supernatural.

"I wonder if he escaped from the wildlife institute near Monterey," I suggest.

"That's maybe thirty miles from here," Tron replies. "Still a pretty good distance, though."

"Hell, that would be nothing for a cheetah. They can run as fast as a car," Marino says as if he's an expert. "I'm pretty sure that's what this is. Their heads are smaller than a leopard's."

"Why end up here?" Tron asks.

"That's what I'm wondering," I reply, the big cat standing as still as a statue, staring.

"Although it's odd that the Brileys own this theme park and also give a lot of money to the wildlife institute," Tron adds.

"Maybe someone's illegal pet that's wandered off." Rob watches through the sweeping wipers. "It's used to people or it wouldn't be this close to us, just standing there like that. I bet if I got out it would come right up to me."

"Don't even think about it," Marino says as I roll down my window halfway. "Whether it's used to people or not it could tear you apart. And there'd be no way for us to stop it."

"I may have seen him in a second-floor window of the Witch's Castle as we were leaving. Maybe that's where he's been holing up," I explain, not needing a cell signal to take a picture with my phone. "Poor thing's probably hungry. Although he doesn't look all that thin to me. His ribs aren't showing."

I think of what's left in my briefcase, doubting he'd want a granola bar.

"Maybe he knows what we've got in the back of the van." Marino adds a horrific thought. "If Lucy hadn't found the body when she did, maybe that big cat would have gotten to it first."

"I was just thinking the same thing." Tron follows my lead, taking a picture through the windshield. "What's strange is the body was there for a while before Lucy and I found it but the cat stayed away."

"We need to report him to animal control and send a picture," I explain, and the big cat saunters off as if he heard me, disappearing in the fog. "I don't want him or something else hurt. And he can't survive out here. If nothing else, someone will end up shooting him."

"You got that right," Marino says. "If he'd showed up while we were waiting in the tent I might have done just that."

"There's been enough death and destruction today," I reply with a sudden spike of emotion.

"We'll call it in." Rob resumes driving slowly as I roll up my window, looking for the cat and not seeing it, the encounter surreal.

It feels symbolic, of what I don't know, but I'm reminded of Sal. He was always kind to animals and especially fond of cats, although he hadn't owned one in a while. But whenever he'd come to the house for dinner, he'd dote on Lucy's rescued Scottish fold, Merlin, who stalks our property like something wild.

CHAPTER 14

We return to the parking lot, where Lucy waits inside the helicopter, the blades untied and rocking in the wind. She steps down to open the rear clamshell door used for stretchers as Marino and I climb into the back cabin. We help slide in the plastic-shrouded body, securing it with bungee cords attached to rings in the flooring.

Marino and I are dripping wet as we sit down next to each other, shutting the doors, another roll of paper towels waiting for us. We wipe off, fastening our harnesses as I'm conscious of Sal's disfigured face and tangled gray hair, his flesh and wounds showing through the clear plastic. Lucy and Tron are in the cockpit going through an abbreviated start-up, stressed and in a hurry.

When the blades begin to turn, I put on my headset, looking out my window, the rain flooding the helicopter. Lightning flashes, thunder cracking unnervingly close, and I'm not liking this any more than Marino. But staying put in hopes the tornado will miss us would be foolish. I imagine a funnel cloud appearing in the distant eerie glow, then roaring like a train bearing down, turning the roller coaster into a pile of twisted metal.

Not to mention what it would do to the helicopter, and I don't want to wait around for that finale. Our options are limited, and I don't blame Marino for chewing on another motion sickness pill, his headset off. I continue staring out at the frightening weather because I don't want to look at Sal on the floor near my wet muddy boots.

His bent rigorous limbs push grotesquely against the pouches as if he's trying to get out, and I can't help but think of the indignity. In my head I hear his chuckle as if he's next to me, bending close, taking me into his confidence, his voice quiet in my ear. I remember the spicy masculine scent of his cologne, the tickle of his hair touching my face.

No doubt he'd make some silly crack about being shrink-wrapped. Or sealed in a big sandwich baggie. He'd joke that if he had to go, at least it was entertaining.

We must never be boring, Kay, he used to say, and I can see him leaning into the candlelight, raising his glass in a toast to that.

"Everybody all set back there?" Lucy's disembodied voice in my headset interrupts my thoughts.

"All set," I reply.

I feel gravity slip away as we lift off the pavement, the tall weeds growing through cracks bending and flattening, the sky dark. We're rising above the parking lot's tall light standards when they suddenly blaze on to my astonishment.

"What the flying fuck...?" Lucy's voice sounds as tall iron lamps along the Yellow Brick Road blink on all at once, their lanterns smudges in the gloom.

At the same time, lights flicker in the Witch's Castle dark empty windows. Music starts playing over the helicopter's intercom, and I don't see how any of it is possible.

"...*We're off to see the Wizard, the wonderful Wizard of Oz...*" The childlike singsong voices from long ago. "...*Because, because, because of the wonderful things he does...*" Stopping just as suddenly as it started.

I stare down at the roller coaster lighting up, and the train of empty cars begins shuddering, barely moving along the tracks, reminding me of the elevator in my building. Then I can't see anything at all but moiling thick gray clouds as we gain altitude. I look over at Marino, his eyes squeezed shut, his face wan, an airsick bag in hand, oblivious to what just happened.

"Everyone still okay back there?" Lucy's voice again, and it seems an ironic thing to ask, as I'm aware of the dead passenger riding with us.

"What just happened?" I don't know what's worse, looking down at Sal or out the window at the storm.

"Everything in the park was turned on. Some of the lights and such are operable, but not many."

"Turned on by who or what?"

"We don't know."

"And the music playing through the intercom? I don't understand. Has the helicopter been hacked?" I ask while thinking *please God no*.

"What you heard was coming out of the speakers in the park," Lucy says as we fly through squalls of rain. "No, we've not been hacked."

"The helicopter's got sensors that can pick up loud noises

on the ground," Tron explains as we're shoved by the wind, the mountains in and out of fog.

"I'm pulling in full power and climbing to a higher altitude that will avoid the worst of the turbulence." Lucy's voice in my headset, and I'm grateful Marino has his off and can't hear a word. "You won't be seeing anything out the windows for a while. Probably not until we get close to where we're going. The weather there will have cleared by then."

"How might someone turn on rides, lights, music inside a theme park that's been closed for years with the electricity shut off along with everything else?" I can't get away from that. "And doing it at the very moment we were taking off? As if for our benefit?"

"You're asking the same questions we are," Tron says. "I've got people checking with the power company to find out when the service was turned back on."

"Could lightning have caused something like that?" I ask.

"Not if the power is disconnected," Lucy says.

"Someone was watching and ready, and wants us to know it," I decide. "That's what I think, explaining why Marino and I heard music inside the Witch's Castle."

"We're being screwed with," Lucy says, and I envision crazed eyes that remind me of spinning pinwheels.

I see the scars on Carrie Grethen's once perfect face, and I know how she feels about me. I know who she blames for everything wrong in her life, and in an odd way I understand it. Perversely, I can see her side. A psychopath has no conscience or remorse. From her point of view, she's done nothing wrong. But

I've become the over-controlling mother who's robbed her of everything that matters.

I committed the unpardonable sin of interfering with Lucy and Carrie's relationship in the beginning when they were together at the FBI Academy. I unjustly maligned Carrie to put a wedge between them. I'm responsible for the ruination and deaths of those Carrie loved, most of all her own flesh and blood. That's what she'd say, and I know she's not done.

"We'll be busy flying instruments and on *crew only* until we get out of the worst of this." Lucy's voice continues. "You won't hear us but I can see you on camera."

*   *   *

The thudding of the rotor blades is muffled by my headset, and I feel the Doomsday Bird's powerful vibrations in my every cell. As we fly through volatile clouds, I can't see the ground. I try to work out where Lucy and Tron are taking us and can think of no better medical examiner facilities than what I offer in Virginia.

But that's not an option for some reason. At moments I have the sensation of being abducted while imagining Sal naked and alive inside a flying vehicle of some type. He had to know he was about to die, and I would have expected him to resist. Yet I haven't noticed injuries that might make me think he put up a struggle. That suggests to me that he was incapacitated somehow.

As I try to reconstruct how he might have been confronted last night, I envision him driving his standard-shift truck up the poorly lit switchback leading to the Allegheny Peak Lodge, where Benton and I have stayed many times. I imagine Sal's headlights illuminating a seemingly disabled vehicle, the driver waving him down. Or perhaps the person was on foot, acting distressed.

Sal would have tried to help, and my attention is constantly drawn to the floor. I understand the rationale for total containment pouches fabricated of clear plastic. Once sealed with heat or adhesives, they aren't meant to be reopened. It's helpful to look at who's inside before cremation or burial. But visual identifications aren't to be trusted, and seeing through the pouch is nothing but a drawback in my opinion.

I'd rather not look at the bag at my feet while belted in my seat, listening to nothing over the intercom with only gray out the windows as if reality is offline. Any minute life will return to normal, rebooted or patched like faulty software. Maybe I'm dreaming or in a different dimension. I'll come to and Sal won't be in a body bag. I'm rocked by another powerful wave of emotion as I look down at him in turbulence that's unnerving.

I can't hear the thunder with my headset on. But lightning shimmers in clouds, and I have no idea how high off the ground we are. I close my eyes, leaving my hand on Marino's wrist until the winds retreat, the air smoother, more like skiing blue runs than black diamond moguls. I feel his thick muscles beneath my fingers, his sun-damaged skin clammy, his pulse rapid like a bird.

He can't hide his fear from me, and I keep my hand where it is until the overcast is brighter and the rain has stopped. Then I move away, digging out my cell phone and turning it on, the signal full as we retreat farther from the heart of the Quiet Zone. I begin to click through messages. Shannon has sent a weather report that shows tornadoes touching down in the Monterey area accompanied by power outages and severe damage.

She's *worried sick* about us, and I write back assuring her that we're safely away from the worst of it. I'll give her more information when able. She answers by sending me a link to *a most unfortunate and irresponsible* TV interview that is *all over the internet.* I glance at the accompanying transcript, and Ryder Briley has gone public with his allegations about my *corrupt office* being *in bed* with the police and the governor.

Dana Diletti interviewed him this afternoon at his sprawling stone and timber home. He described Fabian as *menacing,* referring to me as *heartless and conniving.* When the Brileys appeared at my office this morning, supposedly I refused to answer their questions. I wouldn't take their calls or so much as let them into my parking lot. I won't release Luna's body or explain what I'm *doing to it.*

…He and the mother were in their child's bedroom crying crocodile tears on TV, Shannon writes. *Thought I might gag.*

She says that Dana Diletti's people continue trying to reach me. *They want to know why you're pending the manner of death. If it's an obvious accident, why aren't you calling it that?*

I think about who knows that I've pended the case. Fabian, Wyatt, others at my office are aware. I mentioned it to Jesse Spanks inside the vehicle bay as Marino and I were on our way to the airport. But I have a feeling the information came from Blaise Fruge. It would make sense for the media to reach out to her. I ask Shannon what she thinks Dana Diletti's producers are digging for.

It seems they're releasing a news story about their investigation into Luna Briley's "questionable" death. Was it really "accidental"?

Shannon suspects that the show ran a favorable piece earlier to gain access to Ryder Briley. All the while Dana Diletti was filming and acting empathetic, she was waiting to do a number on him. I wouldn't be surprised. That sounds about right.

I look at Marino as the first rays of light break through clouds, touching his face. I notice the lines that show he scowls a lot, his strong stubbly jaw bulkier than when he was young. The scars on his nose and the top of his shaved head are from recent skin cancer surgeries. Ignoring my warnings about the sun, he's as tan as summer and it's only the middle of April.

When he finally opens his eyes, it's getting close to half past five, the sun a bright smudge on the dimming horizon. I hand him his headset, and he puts it on.

"That was fun," he says sarcastically, still unnerved—he can't fool me. "Are we alive?" Acting like he wasn't terrified.

"It appears we're through the worst of it." I stare out at churning gray clouds, glints of blue shining through.

I'm aware that Lucy can see us on camera. She knows that Marino has his eyes open and headset on. Yet neither she nor Tron are checking on us or offering an update. They must have their hands full in the cockpit. Or maybe they don't want questions about where they're taking us and when we might get there.

"How are you feeling?" I watch Marino sitting tensely.

"You mean after being shaken like a fucking margarita?"

"It was pretty awful, maybe the worst I've experienced," I admit. "I had moments when I wondered if this was it."

"Don't say that when we're not on the ground yet." He stares out at nothing but grayness again. "Did I mention how tired I am of Lucy and her damn death wish?"

"I'm sure she did what she believed was safest."

"I'd hate to see what she thinks is risky."

"Would you rather stay put like a sitting duck, waiting for a tornado to lift us out of Oz?" I realize what I'm saying as I hear myself. "Shannon reports that several have touched down in the Monterey area. Apparently, there's a lot of damage."

As I'm saying this, the big cat and his bright white eyes appear in my mind, and I hope he's safely out of the weather. I continue wondering how he ended up inside the theme park, and if animal control officers have been able to look for him yet.

"You really thought we were going to die?" Marino is serious.

"It was crossing my mind."

"I guess we won't now. I was hoping that if it had to happen, it would be quick. I'd rather not see it coming. And I said to myself, after all the doc and me have been through? At least we're together in the end." He nudges closer to my boundaries, and I wish he wouldn't.

"Hopefully we'll be landing soon," I comment as sunlight intermittently shines through clouds, the rotor blades thudding monotonously. "But landing where is the question."

"I was sitting there thinking what I'd say if it was all about to end." He puts on his Ray-Bans. "I thought about sending a text to Dorothy. I don't know why I couldn't make myself do it."

"If you don't send the note, then maybe the bad thing won't happen."

"Did you think of sending a note to anyone?"

"I was thinking a lot of things."

Through patchy clouds I can see the red tile roof of Keswick Hall, a splendid former villa, now a resort that Benton and I treat ourselves to on special occasions. I catch a glimpse of the swimming pool and tennis courts before we're completely socked in again. We're close to Charlottesville, but I'm unsure what direction we're going except that it's away from the mountains.

"If it was me, I'd want to know how someone feels before it's too late. Wouldn't you?" Marino isn't going to stop probing.

"It depends."

"On what?"

"On whether one is really better off knowing."

"If you thought this was it, Doc? What would you say that you've never said before?" He inches closer to spaces he shouldn't explore.

"I don't want to wait until I'm about to die to say what matters."

"What would you say to me?"

"I might tell you how I feel about people asking invasive questions," I reply, and I can't help but smile as he laughs in spite of himself.

CHAPTER 15

I don't know, Doc." Marino sighs, leaning back in the seat, looking up at the Doomsday Bird's silvery headliner. "I'm bothered by shit that didn't used to put a dent in me. I know a lot of people who've died, and I worry about other people dying, including you and me most of all."

"When we first started working together, we knew more about death than most of the population," I reply. "But at some level we believed it wouldn't touch us personally."

"That's exactly how I felt, and wish I still did."

"It's called denial. Something you're quite skilled at."

"You're one to talk," his voice retorts in my headset. "I remember you showing up at scenes in the worst neighborhoods with nothing to protect you but a scalpel."

"I'm pretty good with sharp instruments."

"And how many times have I told you not to bring a knife to a gunfight?"

"You've always been there when I roll up. I've always felt safe when you're around," I reply as a rainbow arches across the clearing sky, and I point it out. "A good sign," I tell him, and I feel it.

"Maybe."

"How can it be a bad one, Marino?"

"If there's no pot of gold and instead we crash at the end of it," he says as the brilliant prism colors dim and are gone, the sun ducking behind streaming clouds.

He catches me staring down at the pouched body, dark red blood showing through plastic. Without warning, emotions well up again and I will them back into their walled-off space. Marino and I don't talk for a while, and I feel his eyes on me. I sense his pressing questions like a persistent presence in the dark.

"If it makes you feel any better," he says, "I've been there, Doc."

"Been where?"

"Every cop I know has rolled up on a scene and realized the victim is their relative, a friend, a husband, a wife. Or maybe somebody they were having a relationship with. And maybe they can't tell anyone for some reason," he explains as I realize he has suspicions I've not anticipated.

I keep my attention out the window, finding nothing but the brooding sky as I look for the rainbow, hoping it was a message meant for me. I want to believe in symbols like the big cat appearing on the Yellow Brick Road. Metaphor may be the only language Sal has left, and he'd want to reassure me somehow. He'd protest that it's not him in that ugly bag on the floor at my muddy feet. He's moved on, leaving behind his spacesuit, as he referred to his strong, lithe body that I once loved.

Images rush back with fresh intensity of climbing steep steps worn smooth by the centuries, feeling the cool stone beneath my bare feet. We'd wait until the enchanted hour, as he described those early mornings when businesses were closed, most people asleep, the light pollution minimal. Carrying a bottle of wine to the rooftop, we'd sit amid flowers and marble sculptures, a fountain plashing, the primrose and phlox perfuming the warm darkness.

Spreading below was a sea of red barrel tiles, domes, and ruins overrun by feral cats that we often fed while out on long walks. The rooftop's blood orange and lemon trees waved like wands in the breeze, casting their spell over the ancient city as we'd look through Sal's telescope. He'd explain the dry lakes, canyons and craters of the moon. Pointing out rocky riverbeds on Mars, he'd tell me it was a beautiful place before losing its atmosphere.

For the first time I saw the bands of Jupiter and the rings of Saturn with my own eyes. He was convinced of planets existing beyond our solar system before it was known.

One day you'll see, amore. Everything I tell you will be true. I know this because what will be already is, and has been before.

"...It was that summer in Italy, right?" Marino goes on, and I've not attended carefully to him.

"I'm sorry. I missed the last few things you said," I reply. "Maybe move the mic closer to your lips. You're cutting in and out a little bit." It's true, but that's not the reason I wasn't listening.

"I was talking about when it happened," he goes on.

"When what did?" I don't want to discuss this with him.

"Don't make me say it."

"Say what?"

145

"How pissed I was at you for a really long time for fleeing the coop the way you did." His face is stony as he stares out his window, patches of blue showing through clouds.

"You've been pissed at me at one time or other for as long as we've known each other."

"First, you were going to quit and run home to Miami. Then you suddenly decided to leave the country with no warning." He looks out at the sky continuing to clear as the sun dips lower. "I had to find out from *Style* magazine that you were teaching forensics in Rome for the summer. You didn't even bother to say goodbye or send a fucking postcard."

"That's ridiculous. At that point we weren't friendly in the least," I remind him, my attention tugged back to the floor again.

At times the vibration of the helicopter gives me the uncanny sense that Sal's body is shivering inside its plastic cocoon.

"Well, I knew something must have happened while you were gone," Marino says. "When you came back you'd changed."

"That was the point of going."

"You were different because of him." He avoids saying Sal's name when possible, always has, and maybe now I understand. "I knew for sure what was going on a couple of weeks after you were back. We ended up at a homicide in Gilpin Court, a drive-by shooting in the middle of the day. Remember?"

"There were more than one. I'm not sure—"

"I met you as you got out of that tank of a Mercedes you drove in those days. As I was walking up, I overheard you on that big-ass mobile phone you carried around back then. You were telling whoever it was that that you missed him," Marino says. "And I asked you about it. You acted like he was nothing special, but I knew he was."

"And you were right," I reply, and I see it in Marino's eyes.

The hurt after all these years. I've always been with someone. But it's never been him.

"Are you going to come clean about it? You know, full disclosure? Seems like an important detail that could be used against you if you're not careful." He's almost lecturing me.

"The romantic element of the relationship was short-lived and a very long time ago," I reply.

"Really? Then how come I've caught how upset you are when you think I'm not looking?"

"That doesn't mean I can't do the job. It just means I care. And of course I cared for him. I cared very much." I swallow hard, emotions threatening.

"I'm not trying to pick on you, Doc."

"Good."

"I just don't want other people doing it."

I stare at the lead-gray partition between the cabin and the cockpit, wishing I could hear what Lucy and Tron are talking about. I wonder where we're going and what else they're keeping from me about why Sal had to die so hideously.

"What about next of kin?" Marino starts in with other questions. "Who needs to be notified once the ID is confirmed?"

"His parents are gone, his mother dying a few years ago. But he has a sister," I reply. "She lives in Rome, and Sal was there with her just a few weeks ago."

"I guess he never married."

"He was married to his work." I can't bring myself to say that Sal was selfish.

But he was, and didn't see it. For someone so insightful, he had a blind spot when it came to his drives and ego.

"I'm betting the truth is he never got with anybody else because he never got over you," Marino says.

"He dated plenty over the years," I reply.

"And who was he with at the end? Who stopped by to wish him a happy birthday yesterday when he was feeling shitty about turning sixty? What I'm wondering is why you didn't do anything about it if you both felt that way."

"Part of life is accepting things that won't change no matter how disappointing," I reply, and I remember saying this very thing to Sal.

"Tell me about it." Marino's attention is fixed out the window again. "I know exactly what you're describing. Sometimes it feels like all I've ever done is settle."

I'm grateful Dorothy can't hear us. It would be an ugly reminder of past conflicts when she's suspected Marino's interest. She knew about it long before the two of them were dating. Now she's amused more than anything else that he *once had the hots* for me. She'd be devastated by the word *settle* and must never know he said it.

*   *   *

The downtown Richmond skyline is out our windows, the tops of the James Monroe Building and other skyscrapers shrouded in fog. We're flying over the restaurants and bars of Shockoe Bottom, and the crowded neighborhoods of Libby

Hill. I know what I'm seeing. It always comes back to me whenever I'm here.

Despite how much this part of Virginia has changed over the years, the bones of it are unmistakable. Lucy picks up I-64 on the other side of Oakwood Cemetery with its circuitous paths and rows of gray headstones. I recognize the New Kent County Airport tucked in trees, the numbers 11 and 29 painted in white on either end of the runway. Then there's nothing below but trees, and a reservoir where people are fishing.

The farther east the better the weather, the sinking sun fiery on the horizon. Soon we're over Colonial Williamsburg, and I catch a fleeting glimpse of the redbrick visitor center, the Governor's Palace, the serpentine walls and open green fields enclosed by wooden palings. Knots of visitors stroll along walkways, and I can make out the historical interpreters in period costumes before the view is replaced by woods.

"Where the hell are they taking us?" Marino asks, and I don't have an answer. I don't even have a guess.

Several miles off to our right is the Busch Gardens theme park, its roller-coaster tracks arching across the dimming sky. I'm reminded of Sal's body callously dumped inside the Haunted Forest. And of the see-through pouch inches from me on the helicopter floor. And who might be to blame. And it seems impossible that we're confronted by the same enemy again.

If only she would die.

I think of Carrie Grethen as a human virus that can't be eradicated. All it does is mutate into the next variant, each one crueler and wilier than the last. I send Benton a text without mentioning where we are or other details. He requires no update from me, knowing far more than I ever will about what's going on. I tell him I'm checking in to see how he is. I'm thinking of him.

Heard it's not been a pleasant flight, he writes back.

No fun but better now.

How's Marino?

A little green around the gills, I type while making sure Marino isn't looking on. *We're ok. But disturbing things are happening. Not sure what you've heard.* I have little doubt that Benton knows exactly who I'm concerned about.

We'll talk soon, he replies, and I hope that's true.

"Hello? Hey!" Marino's voice booms in my headset as he waves a hand, gesturing to the cameras. "You guys up?" He's hoping Tron or Lucy might decide to answer, and they don't. "You think they're still awake?" He directs this at me. "Because I sure as hell hope AI isn't flying this bucket."

The sun smolders over the York River, burnishing it gold. A fishing pier, a gray wooden footbridge snake through marshland at Denbigh Park, and I recognize the modern brick and glass airport in Newport News flowing by. The Hampton Coliseum seems to hover like a concrete mothership in the waning light, and I know where we are. But not our destination.

I have no clue until I see the flashing red beacons on top of the colossal sawhorse-shaped gantry etched against the darkening sky. The Doomsday Bird thunders in low and slow as we near NASA Langley Research Center. The Aeronautical and Space Administration's oldest campus dates back to the days of the Wright brothers. It's where Neil Armstrong and Buzz Aldrin trained to walk on the moon.

"What the hell are we coming here for?" Marino is baffled, and I don't have an answer.

Streetlights blink on below, the wind tunnels powered by massive white metal vacuum spheres that remind me of giant balloons. We lumber past a red-and-white-striped water tower, a tall stack in the distance gushing smoke and fire. The dull silver aircraft hangar glints into view, some ten stories high with a white radome on the roof, and we swoop around it, slowing into a hover.

Lights on tall poles are bright on the ramp and in the parking lot where a van and an SUV wait with headlights burning. Beyond is Langley Air Force Base, the long runway outlined in diamond-white lights. An F-22 Raptor fighter jet takes off while two others wait on the taxiway, streams of exhaust shimmering. We set down on the tarmac, the landing lights flaring on the NASA blue-and-red logo, faded on old aluminum siding.

Lucy shuts down, cutting the engines, braking the rotor blades, and the SUV and van rush in. The driver's doors open, two soldiers in camouflage jumping out, heavily armed and in tactical gear. Their comrades emerge from the passenger doors, cradling submachine guns and wearing earpieces. We climb out of the helicopter, and Lucy retrieves the jump-out bags but not our Pelican cases.

"You won't need your gear," she explains.

Marino and I settle into the SUV's third row of seats, Lucy and Tron in front of us, and we're driven away. Around the north end of the airfield, we stop at the Armistead Gate, where the military police are expecting us. They confer briefly with our drivers while shining flashlights on ID badges. I can't hear all of what they're saying over the rumble of engines but it's obvious they're aware of our morbid cargo.

A K-9 handler begins to circle with a Belgian Malinois, checking for explosives and who knows what. Guards peer through our rolled-down windows, shining their lights, making sure we look like our photographs. They check the undercarriage with long-handled mirrors as drones orbit overhead. We're waved through and wished a good night, the setting sun molten.

CHAPTER 16

We follow Sweeney Boulevard, paralleling the runway. Another supersonic jet takes off at an impossibly steep angle, the engines whining and screaming. Flowing past are the commissary, the chapel and tidy rows of military housing, the traffic heavy at this hour. Roadsides are planted with dogwoods and cherry trees, what I'm seeing unchanged from when I was here last winter for a murder-suicide.

Over the years I've visited numerous bases for a variety of reasons, my connection to the military a deeply rooted one. The Air Force reserves helped make my education possible, and I had a debt to repay. After the Dade County Medical Examiner's Office and before I moved to Richmond, I was assigned to the Armed Forces Institute of Pathology (AFIP) at Walter Reed Hospital in Bethesda, Maryland.

I reviewed military autopsies and investigated the deaths of Americans overseas. In my spare time I helped out at the AFIP's National Museum of Health and Medicine. I wrote catalog descriptions, assisted researchers and in the process was exposed to a variety of pathological wonders. Rare birth defects. Limbs amputated during the Civil War. Fragments of Abraham Lincoln's skull, and the bullet that killed him.

At the end of a long row of white hangars, we pick up a low-lying road that takes us around the northwest end of the airfield. Raptor jets tear up the bluing dusk, climbing and rolling, spinning and looping like Cirque du Soleil performers, the afterburners deafening. Past a soccer field, we skirt the golf course, the sand traps vaguely showing white against deeply shadowed grass.

In barren fields are small ponds of rainwater from the storms passing through earlier. Canada geese fly in formation low over marshland reticulated with tidal creeks that turn into forests. Beyond Quonset huts and ammunition bunkers, lights show through trees. As we get closer, I can make out tall privacy fencing topped with rolls of razor wire that bring to mind a prison camp.

Multiple signs warn in bold red letters that we're approaching a restricted area where photography is prohibited. Trespassing is forbidden. The use of deadly force is authorized. Our vehicles stop, the windows going down again. Two unsmiling guards with submachine guns on slings across their chests approach, and I have no doubt that they'd protect first and question later.

They slide open the dark green metal gate along its tracks, and it clangs shut behind us after we drive through. Another quadcopter drone is making whiny circuits overhead like a huge robotic mosquito. I notice multiple antennas, the white dishes reminding me of morning glories. I suspect there are additional motion sensors to give advanced warning when anything or anyone approaches what's obviously a top-secret facility.

Somewhere will be a control room staffed with military police and cyber investigators monitoring the data around the clock. We're being surveilled in real time, following what could pass for a logging trail through woods, more lights burning ahead. On the other side of the tall fencing is a remote area of the NASA Langley campus where the gantry towers in the distance look like a giant construction of Tinkertoys, red beacons flashing.

The iconic structural testing complex is in the process of being phased out, Lucy tells us. Physical drop tests and splashdowns are considered increasingly unnecessary. These days scientists can run computer programs for predictions of how something like a crew capsule or a spaceplane will do under certain circumstances.

"As AI only gets better, that's the way everything is going," she adds.

"All I can say is we'd better hope the algorithm is right when a flying taxi full of passengers takes off from the top of a building," I reply, unpleasant images violating my mind.

The woods open into a big clearing illuminated by floodlights shining on dozens of windowless blockhouses painted in a camouflage pattern. Two-story and in rows, they're numbered in reflective white paint, a concrete smokestack rising above them. In front are six SUVs gleaming like black patent leather, one of them I recognize. When Benton said he'd see me soon, it was a promise.

"Look who's here." Marino notices my husband's Tesla as we park. "Who else do all these trucks belong to? Besides the feds?"

"Those who need to be here," Tron says as we climb out, the cool air rain-scrubbed, a breeze blowing in from the Chesapeake Bay.

"I guess you're going to keep on with the secret squirrel talk," Marino says, annoyed and enthralled.

"We'll tell you what you should know," Tron replies. "Then when it's time to leave, this never happened."

"Not so much as a hint to anyone." Lucy directs this at Marino. "Not a word to Mom no matter how much she tries to get it out of you."

A full moon rises above dark pines as the front door opens to blockhouse 3141, the first four digits of the number pi, I'm jolted to realize. Two soldiers emerge in long white Tyvek lab coats, face masks and gloves. They approach with purpose, their PPE fluttering like ghosts in the gathering dusk.

Saying nothing to us, they open the back of the van, grabbing the pouch by the handles. The interior light shines hideously on bright pink skin and smears of blood showing through plastic. Slamming the tailgate, they ferry their morbid cargo past three blockhouses, back to 3141, up the concrete ramp, the door banging shut behind them.

"We'll hold here for a minute while Tron checks on things," Lucy says.

"I'll let you know when everybody's ready," she replies, walking off, fireflies sparking.

"Thirty-one-forty-one? As in the number pi and his tattoo?" I ask Lucy about the yellow inked symbol on the underside of Sal's left wrist. "Is there a connection? Am I to assume he's been to this place?"

"Many times." The lenses of her glasses are barely tinted in the fading light. "Back in the early forties when the blockhouses were built, they were assigned identifying numbers like everything else."

The number 3141 doesn't mean anything, she explains. But Sal spent considerable time in that particular blockhouse, the Space-Linked Autopsy Base, or SLAB, that's been in development since the Apollo era. I've never heard of it. But I wouldn't necessarily unless there was a reason before now. I'm dismayed by how much I didn't know about Sal. Who was he really? What secrets did he keep from me?

"He spent a lot of time here doing what?" Marino asks.

"Research while dealing with critically sensitive situations." Tron gives another one of her oblique answers. "Obviously, we can't go into detail."

"If you think of all the whistleblowing stories about crash retrievals and such in recent years, you can probably figure out some of what goes on here," Lucy explains. "Things coming through that have to be looked at and dealt with in a facility so secure that even people like you haven't heard of it. A place where top-secret technologies can be studied and re-created."

"Whose technologies? Ours? Or theirs?" Marino points up at the night sky.

"All of it."

"Maybe Sal Giordano's connection to this place is related to what's happened to him," Marino suggests.

"Except you'd have to wonder how anybody unauthorized would know about this place to begin with," I reply while wondering if Carrie Grethen does.

"It's an important question," Lucy replies. "And we should be prepared for some unfortunate possibilities. Such as what Sal Giordano might have been involved in that he hid from the rest of us."

"I'm asking myself the same thing," Marino adds.

"Let's get going," Lucy then says as if receiving a signal, and probably she has in her "smart" glasses.

The wind lightly gusts in fits and starts, the sharp scent of pine reminding me of Christmas and triggering an ambush of emotions. I'm grateful for the dark. Our feet are quiet along the cracked sidewalk, the three of us stopping now and then to knock off dried mud we've tracked here from Oz.

"Sal had the pi sign tattoo when I met him the summer I was teaching in Rome," I tell Lucy and Marino. "If it was inspired by the SLAB, then he's been coming here for decades."

"Since he was in grad school," she replies as we walk through a chiaroscuro of glaring lights and darkness. "He was instrumental in repurposing what you're about to see, never imagining he'd end up here himself someday. Not like this. But the questions we have about what he might have been exposed to are the same ones he had in mind when helping design this place."

It's called Area One, and we won't find it on any map, Lucy tells us. Most of what we're seeing is used for storage. Some of the buildings are labs and workshops.

"Storing what?" Marino stares at the dozens of camouflage-painted blockhouses illuminated by floodlights up ahead.

"Mostly wreckage."

"From what?"

"From wrecks," she says blandly.

"Let me guess." His wide eyes are everywhere. "In some of these blockhouses are the Chinese spy balloon, the Tic Tacs and other UFOs shot down that we never hear anything else about?" he asks, and Lucy doesn't answer.

* * *

We reach the entrance of 3141, or the SLAB, as it's called. A floodlight burns above the camouflage-painted double metal doors, the woods around us pitch dark, fireflies flickering. The stillness is broken by the grunting and barking of frogs, the chirping of crickets. An owl trills and whistles, raising the flesh on my arms, a chill touching the back of my neck.

"The Raptor jets are deployed from right here at Langley Air Force Base. It's been all over the news when they're sent to shoot down a UFO," Marino says as we follow the sloped ramp, our shadows elongated on concrete. "So it makes sense the wreckage would be here. Which means it's probably being reverse engineered here too."

Lucy says nothing, scanning her right thumb in a biometric lock, opening the solid metal door. Inside the bright white tile receiving area, Tron waits for us. A stretcher is parked on top of the floor scale, a measuring stick propped against the wall, the receiving area similar to those in my district offices. The air is chilled with no trace of a foul odor, and I'm sure there are special ventilation systems.

But I have a feeling the SLAB hasn't been used in recent memory. Used for what is the question. Instead of walk-in coolers and freezers, stainless steel drawers crowd walls like silver post office boxes. There are at least sixty of them, each numbered and not big enough for a normal adult body. They don't look like anything I've ever seen or heard about.

Each is maybe eighteen by eighteen inches with a digital glass panel and lights that are green. I can tell by the temperatures displayed that only a few of the drawers are set for refrigerated conditions, the rest showing minus-twenty-two degrees Celsius or minus-seven degrees Fahrenheit. Most of what's stored here is frozen solid. I assume it's military-related and top secret for some reason. But I'd be surprised if bodies or parts of them weren't returned to families.

"When Area One was built during the early years of World War Two, there was no such thing as a National Transportation Safety Board to investigate aircraft crashes," Lucy continues to explain. "Thirty-one-forty-one was a pathology lab for the examination of related biological materials or bio-hybrids."

"As in the dead pilots?" Marino keeps pushing for answers.

"As in whatever required the special care Area One offers." It's Tron who replies.

"In those days, the military would have done the necessary autopsies." Lucy is talking about the Armed Forces Medical Examiners I've worked with throughout my career. "It wasn't generally known where some of these examinations took place or who performed them."

"That much I'm aware of, but I didn't know about the SLAB until now," I reply.

"For the most part what's been done here in recent years is necropsies," Tron explains.

"*For the most part?*" Marino asks. "What else?"

"Typically, on animals launched into space," Tron goes on as if she didn't hear him.

"Like when John Glenn went up with the monkey that never got the credit he deserved," Marino decides. "I forget what his name was."

"It was a chimpanzee, and they didn't go up together," Lucy answers.

"I remember that after he came back from space and died, the body disappeared." Marino stares at the steel drawers as if he might divine what's inside them. "I'm betting the chimp ended up here in one of these."

"As old as this place may look," Tron says, "don't be fooled. It's got everything needed. A separate mechanical room runs the decontamination system. There are autoclaves, powerful disinfectants, positive pressure suits."

We follow them through an airlock into a locker room with a toilet, a sink, two shower stalls, a chemical shower and not much else. Cardboard boxes of PPE are stacked against a wall, and I place my briefcase, my jump-out bag on an old wooden bench.

"All electronic devices go in here." Lucy opens one of three tarnished copper lockers, essentially Faraday cages that shield electromagnetic transmissions.

Phones are followed in by "smart" jewelry like my ring, and the black ceramic fitness bracelet Dorothy gave Marino for Christmas. We're told to check our pockets and bags, making certain we have nothing else electronic. Tron hands out Level-A protective gear that's the same as what we had on earlier today, these suits bright yellow instead of chartreuse.

CHAPTER 17

Polypropylene rustles and smells like a new shower curtain as I shake open a pair of folded coveralls. In addition to self-contained breathing apparatuses, we have battery-powered in-ear headsets to amplify what's said over a secure telephone landline.

"The hardwired phone is encrypted, and when it rings you pick it up and switch it to speakerphone." Lucy directs this at me. "Everyone will need to talk loudly and clearly. That's how we'll communicate during the examination."

"When you're ready, exit there through that airlock." Tron points to a steel-clad outer door that's scratched and dented, the dull metal freckled with rust.

She and Lucy leave the same way we entered, and Marino and I are alone. But that doesn't ensure privacy. I'm mindful of possible hidden cameras, and don't want to mention my suspicions out loud. Nor should I have to, but Marino is too excited to pay attention.

"How is it possible we've never heard of this place?" he marvels as we sit down on benches across from each other.

"I suspect there are a lot of places we've not heard of,"

I reply as we bend over to unlace our boots. "If there isn't a legitimate reason to share information, we aren't going to be informed by anyone, including Lucy and Benton. Or Sal Giordano for that matter. Frankly, if there isn't a reason to know, I prefer not to anyway."

"You've been working with the Armed Forces M.E.s all your career. And you swear you never got a hint about Area One? Or the SLAB?"

"I haven't." I tuck my pants cuffs into my socks.

"Seriously?" He's not sure he believes me. "You've never once gotten the slightest indication that something spooky might be going on at Langley Air Force Base? And probably their NASA neighbor? I guarantee they're in this together and have been all along. They've got to be."

"My guess is that most of my colleagues in the military and otherwise have no idea about Area One. I doubt most NASA or Space Force people do either." I begin putting on the bright yellow coveralls over clothes still clammy from the rain. "And those who know can't talk about it any more than we can. That included Sal."

"Did he ever see a UFO?" Marino shoves his big stockinged feet through plastic pants legs. "Maybe he was inside one, maybe at a crash retrieval? I wonder if he ever saw an ET dead or alive?"

"He never said."

"Maybe he dropped a few hints?"

"Not to me." I work my arms into the sleeves. "But certainly, he believed other intelligent life is out there and was trying to communicate with it. He was convinced that Mars was once habitable before something catastrophic happened."

"Earth was plan B. It's where the Martians escaped thousands of years ago when their own planet was about to be destroyed," Marino replies as if it's commonly known.

No doubt he learned this and more from *All Things—Unexplained, Ancient Aliens* or one of his other favorite podcasts and TV shows. He and my sister both tune in religiously, and it makes for lively dinner conversations when all of us are together.

"Dorothy's into the SETI stuff the same way I am," Marino is saying as we pull on rubber boots. "Not telling her about this place and what we're doing right now is going to kill her. She'll never forgive it."

"Not if she doesn't know." I give him a look, trying to shut him up, but he's not getting the message.

"How am I supposed to keep quiet? And why the hell should I?" He's getting overheated by our conversation and the PPE's thick plastic. "Last I checked we don't work for the feds." He gets up from the bench. "I have a right to talk about my life. I'm not a damn spy."

"You have a right to do anything you want as long as you're prepared for the consequences." I zip up my coveralls.

"Well, we'd better decide on a good story to tell Dorothy about where the hell we've been today. Or we'll never hear the end of it." Grabbing a towel off a stack of them, he mops his sweaty face and the top of his head. "You know how she is when she wants to know something," he adds, and he's just as bad. Worse, actually.

"A military mortuary is as much as we need to tell her and anyone else." I continue looking around for cameras while being careful what I say, and he ignores my cues. "Beyond that, the case isn't something we can discuss. Marino. This is serious business."

"I'll tell you what I'm wondering." He works his hands into a pair of thick black rubber gloves. "Maybe those freezer drawers we just saw have to do with Roswell, which you probably don't believe was the real deal."

"By real deal I assume you mean of an extraterrestrial nature. I'm no expert and don't know the details." I pull on two pairs of nitrile gloves instead of rubber ones because I have to feel what I'm doing during an autopsy.

"Trust me, what crashed in New Mexico wasn't a weather balloon," he replies. "It was a spacecraft with aliens on board who used vibrations to move in and out of different dimensions. I've seen official memos and other intelligence. You wouldn't believe the information Janet finds for me. She knows what I want and downloads it directly into my email. I don't even have to ask."

"And you're aware that much posted on social media and elsewhere isn't necessarily real or to be trusted?" I buckle the respirator blower around my waist, making sure the batteries are charged.

"Janet helps me know what's real and fake," Marino replies. "She thinks the truth about Roswell was covered up immediately after the whole thing happened. The government knew damn well it was a flying saucer."

"Janet is an AI algorithm that's the result of human input. She isn't a person and doesn't actually think for herself."

"The hell she doesn't." He acts insulted on her behalf. "Janet thinks better than anyone I know and comes up with stuff nobody else would. And I don't have to deal with her making judgments about me. Anything out there, she's going to find it, including facts about Roswell, which definitely was real. I don't care what you say."

"I didn't utter a word."

"You don't have to for me to know you think what I'm saying is stupid."

"You might be surprised by what I think," I reply without telling him the rest of it.

I can't share what happened toward the end of my tenure at the National Museum of Health and Medicine. Marino would be far too interested in what I came across one day while in a largely forgotten storage room. I was excavating for paperwork relating to the donation of Robert Hooke's seventeenth-century microscope, and found myself in an area of the basement where I'd not been.

Shelves crowded with glass jars of pathological specimens and rows of fireproof filing cabinets were coated in a fuzz of dust. Skeletons on wheeled stands showed anomalies like Marfan syndrome, gigantism, dwarfism, rickets. They stared with empty eyes and grimaces while I riffled through musty files, happening upon one jammed in the back of a drawer where it didn't belong.

Sealed in layers of red tape accompanied by warnings not to open and stamped TOP SECRET, it was labeled *Roswell Incident, 1947.* Judging by the weight, I suspected there were hundreds of pages of documents and possibly photographs inside. I carried the file upstairs to the curator, a by-the-book retired Air Force colonel, tall and thin with a clipped mustache and the ruddy complexion of a drinker.

Getting close to eighty, he began his career with the Armed Forces M.E.s during World War II and had little use for women doctors. He spent his days running the museum as a volunteer, and I walked into his office, placing the file in front of him. For a flicker he was stunned, then rattled. He went from polite and pleasant to stern and distrusting, his gray eyes turning to slate.

Why were you looking for this? He spoke to me in a way he hadn't before. *Who told you about it?*

No one. I found the file by accident.

I described exactly where it was, explaining that I had no reason to think something like this was here. Therefore, I couldn't possibly have been looking for it.

Something like this? he echoed accusingly. *Sounds like you opened it.*

No, sir, I brought it straight to you. As you can see for yourself, it hasn't been opened since it was sealed many years ago, possibly decades ago, I said, and his demeanor changed again.

Gotcha, didn't I? He winked with a phony grin.

I'm sorry...?

A hoax, a prank. He'd never make it as an actor.

If I opened the file like most people would, I'd discover nothing's inside except blank sheets of paper, and the joke was on me. That's what he said, and I was sure he was lying as he went on to order me never to mention what I found.

It would be misunderstood, he said sternly.

I wasn't to repeat our conversation, and I haven't. The one exception was Sal, and his response was a Mona Lisa smile.

He had no comment beyond the usual about the government's need to obfuscate the truth in the name of security.

Not just the White House and Ten Downing Street but the Vatican, he often said. *What it's really about is keeping humanity in the dark.*

* * *

Marino and I pull on our yellow hoods, our voices muffled through the rubber speaking diaphragms, our in-ear headphones amplifying sounds. We push through the airlock, greeted by bright lights inside a small autopsy room.

Sal's pouched body is on top of the pedestaled stainless steel table attached to a sink, a surgical cart set up nearby. Behind glass on the second floor is a pantheon of distinguished witnesses, and my heart lifts at the sight of Benton. Seated in the front row, he's wearing a midnight-blue suit that accentuates his lankiness, his platinum hair and strong chiseled features.

He looks as fresh as he did while we were getting dressed this morning. I envision us drinking coffee in our bedroom when we hadn't a clue what the day would bring. Everyone has taken a seat inside the observation area, and I know some of the notables gathered. The director of the Secret Service, Bella Steele, looks unusually grim in black, her long dark hair tightly pulled back.

I can tell she's distressed, her strong vibrant face slack, and I know she and Sal were friendly. The last time the three of us were together at the White House, it was obvious they were fond of each other. She's talking to General Jake Gunner, the commander of the U.S. Space Force, dressed in camouflage, his rugged face granite.

Next to him is Gus Gutenberg from the Central Intelligence Agency, nondescript with gray hair, a gray beard, everything about him colorless and vague like a faded daguerreotype. I recognize the director of the Pentagon's All-domain Anomaly Resolution Office (AARO), and next to him the former U.S. senator who now heads NASA.

I've met the Defense Advanced Research Projects Agency (DARPA) aerospace engineer several times at the Pentagon, and know the agent from Interpol's Washington, D.C., bureau. The National Security Agency is here, also the U.S. secretary of state, and a scientist from NASA Langley. I imagine Sal amused, wanting to know what all the fuss is about. He'd have something risqué to say about being naked and dead on a cold steel table in front of such an esteemed audience.

Marino and I get our bearings in the unfamiliar environment, walking around. The white tile walls and floor, the scratched zinc countertop probably go back to when the blockhouses were built. I'm reminded of medical school days spent in old hospital morgues. Only this one is stocked with every modern necessity, including total containment body pouches like the ones I use.

White-painted cabinets with glass doors offer the same supplies ordered for my district offices. Parked next to the autopsy table is a portable C-arm x-ray machine, and I roll it closer, turning it on. The display runs through the start-up routine as the landlined black phone begins to ring from the countertop. I stop what I'm doing to answer it.

"Hello." Pressing the button for speakerphone as Lucy instructed, I look up at her through the observation window as we begin talking to each other.

"How do you read me?" Her voice sounds in the headset under my hood.

"Loud and clear," I reply.

"We're hermetically sealed between an airlock and thick glass up here," Lucy says. "This is the only way to hear each other. Marino, hello, hello?" She then says when he remains silent, "You there?"

"Yep," he answers gruffly.

Lucy moves out of the way, and Benton leans closer to the phone upstairs.

"We very much appreciate Doctor Scarpetta and Pete Marino taking time to be here," he begins, as if we had a choice. "We apologize for the inconvenience of being airlifted to an undisclosed location with little notice."

"You mean flying in tornadoes and lightning with a freakin' dead body on board that might be contaminated? You referring to Lucy almost killing us?" Marino feels compelled to vent his frustrations while she stares down at him.

"We were fine," she says. "But it was a bit like a mechanical bull."

"I'm not getting back on it any time soon. Hopefully never," he promises.

"I know you appreciate the importance of what we're doing and the need for discretion," Benton goes on. "By now, it's apparent that Area One isn't a topic of discussion. I'll remind you of a few guidelines you've heard before. I'm saying this mostly for your benefit, Pete, since you don't have a security clearance."

"And I'd like to keep it that way. I don't feel like spending my life buried under a shit-pile of secrets." Marino glares up through his face shield.

"You know how things have to be done," Benton says with nothing in his tone.

"Yeah, I know the drill," Marino says rudely, and I'm reminded of our conversations inside the helicopter.

At least he no longer hates my husband, who's not going to give him emotional traction. No one better at playing the indifferent card than Benton. There's much he won't forgive or forget when it comes to Marino, and the feeling is mutual. At best, they tolerate each other, occasionally suffering flare-ups when Marino is heavy into the bourbon.

"The minute you pulled up to this facility you were granted an OTRI." Benton is going to brief him, doesn't matter if Marino doesn't want to hear it. "A one-time read-in, a temporary top-secret clearance."

"Otherwise, you couldn't be here," Bella Steele reminds him.

"I'm not the one who invited me," Marino answers.

"What goes on here can't be shared with anyone unauthorized, including family. One's spouse, for example. Regardless of how badly the person wants to know." It's General Jake Gunner saying this, and no question he's referring to my sister.

As I suspected, when Marino and I were talking in the locker room, we were monitored. He complained about how unhappy Dorothy will be if he doesn't tell her the details of what we've been doing today. The commander of Space Force and possibly everyone else in the observation area was listening.

"You can't mention anything you observed or learned while here. Once you leave, it never happened," Bella says.

"Better hope I don't have to take a polygraph, because I won't pass it." Marino shakes open a black plastic bag, lining a bucket with it.

"If you play by the rules, there's no reason for a polygraph." The NSA's comment sounds like a warning.

CHAPTER 18

Doctor Scarpetta, before you get started we need to ask you a few questions," the CIA's Gus Gutenberg says, and I feel an interrogation coming. "It will take just a few minutes, and I apologize in advance for coming across as personally invasive. It goes without saying that all of us here have the utmost respect for you. But we understand you once had a significant relationship with Sal Giordano. That has to be discussed."

"I did long ago." I tell him the year Sal and I met, giving a quick summary of what was going on with me then.

"You lived together in Rome for two months. In the Giordano family apartment," Gus continues.

"Yes."

"And when it was time for you to return to the U.S., Sal didn't want you to leave. That's what he told you." Gus has gotten up from his chair, moving closer to the observation window, looking down at me. "He wanted you to stay in Rome with him during his yearlong sabbatical, and talked to you about eventually getting married. Is this accurate?"

"It is." I can feel Marino's eyes on me.

I sense him thinking that I haven't been honest with him,

173

and to some extent he's right. It's true that Sal asked me to stay with him in Italy. He wanted us to get married, and I told him I couldn't. I needed to finish what I'd started in my life and career. I knew it would be disastrous if I lost myself in him or anyone else. I've shared none of this with Marino or Lucy. Only Benton knows.

"And you told him you wouldn't marry him," Gus is saying to me as Marino impatiently lumbers about opening cabinets and drawers. His PPE makes slippery sounds.

"He thought I could teach forensic medicine while he wrote books and did research," I reply. "I knew that wasn't the life for me."

I won't mention that anyone partnered with Sal would be an afterthought, a sweet one. He was unfailingly gentle and kind. He was abundantly generous. But deep in his soul there was no room for anything but what drove him.

"He knew what he was getting. Or *not* getting, better put perhaps. And it actually suited him, don't you think? Even as he claimed otherwise, Doctor Scarpetta?" Gus replies to my surprise. "I'm wondering if it ever occurred to you that he knew you wouldn't marry him. And that was the answer he was counting on."

"I'm not aware that he..."

"I suspect he knew from the start that you wouldn't give up practicing forensic medicine."

"That wasn't the only reason..."

"The chase was exciting for him. And it was safe." Gus pauses, shuffling through notes on small pieces of paper.

"Excuse the psychologizing. I can't help it. You know, when I see dots that need connecting." He's trained as a psychiatrist.

"Most of all, Sal Giordano couldn't really get close to you or anyone because of his work," Gus is saying. "And long before that the problem was his mother. Both of his parents, actually."

"By *work* we're not just talking about looking through a tele-scope," Bella adds. "But work he was sworn not to share with scarcely anyone else on earth. Work that could lead him into temptation. Work that could get him murdered and perhaps has."

"He was as close to you emotionally as he would allow him-self to be with anyone," Gus then says.

Deve bastare, amore. It has to be enough, I'd tell Sal when we'd talk about the future. To want more than is possible is a useless and selfish ambition.

I wonder what he would have said had I agreed to stay in Italy and marry him. I drove myself to distraction about hurt-ing him, and a commitment wasn't what he really wanted after all. What an irony. He was counting on my saying no, and I suppose it's understandable. He wasn't good at give-and-take even if he loved the person as profoundly as he said.

"You left Italy at the end of that summer, returning to Vir-ginia," Gus is saying. "Then what?"

"The intimate part of our relationship ended," I reply. "We had limited contact, keeping up by phone now and then."

"And you got involved with Benton Wesley. Whom you'd already met professionally on numerous earlier occasions."

"It didn't happen right away..."

"There was nothing between you prior to your summer of teaching abroad?" Gus can ask anything without sounding provocative.

"No," I reply.

But I desperately wanted there to be, and that was part of my problem. The attraction between us was dangerous, and I wouldn't have much insight about Sal's role in the narrative until later. I sought him out as a cure. But when I returned to Richmond, my feelings for Benton were back with a vengeance. We ended up out of town together on a case, and the inevitable happened.

I look up at him seated overhead with other high-ranking officials. He meets my eyes, and I understand the importance of being transparent. But when we were on the phone this morning and texting later, he didn't mention briefing his colleagues about my private life. And I know he has. There can be no other source of the information.

"Doctor Scarpetta, again, I'm sorry to pry, but it's necessary as we proceed with this investigation," Gus goes on, not sorry at all even as he sounds it.

"Investigation into what exactly?" Marino interrupts.

"Everything that might have led to this unfortunate moment," the NSA replies.

"Well, as I'm listening, it's sounding like what you're investigating is the doc." Marino stares up defiantly.

"We're not," Gus says in his blasé way as I give Marino a look that tells him to cool it. "Will your personal relationship with Sal Giordano prevent you from doing your job?" Gus asks me.

"It won't." I snap a new blade into a scalpel.

"A year after your summer in Italy, he returned to his post at Georgetown University. The two of you were but a couple hours' drive from each other. And you didn't try to get together stateside?"

"No." I begin labeling test tubes as Marino arranges Post-its, envelopes, Sharpies, other supplies on the countertop.

Gus asks a question I don't want to answer. "Did he suggest resuming your relationship?"

"He wanted to be friends. But also, more."

"Friends with benefits, as they say?"

"That would have been acceptable to him on occasion. But it wasn't to me."

"You were seeing Benton Wesley by then," Gus says.

"We weren't actually together yet. But we were aware of our feelings for each other."

"How would you describe your relationship with Sal since you've been married to Benton?" Gus goes on as if Benton isn't present.

"We remained close friends and confidants over the years. But that's all," I reply, Benton's face inscrutable.

"Nothing physical? No remnant of that long-ago romance? Not even a little bit on occasion as he suggested?" Gus says in his flat affect.

"No."

"And if your text messages, your emails, etcetera were looked at, what we'd find would verify that?"

"They would." I have no doubt that if the CIA wants to hack into such things, it can and possibly has.

"I'm not going to be disingenuous with you, Doctor Scarpetta. It's important we know if Sal might have shared information with you that he shouldn't have." Gus gets around to what the government is most worried about.

"We're wondering if you ever had a sense he might be passing on information to anyone who shouldn't have it?" the NSA asks.

"That includes during those early days when you were with him in Rome. As you may have gathered, he's been involved with us for a very long time. And I know you're familiar with the term *pillow talk*," Gus says before I can answer the disheartening suspicions. "If he divulged sensitive information to you at any time, it speaks to his character, I'm afraid. It speaks to other things he may have done and continued to do."

What I'm hearing is that Sal was working with the intelligence community while we were together that summer. I was sleeping with a spy and had not the slightest inkling. The question is whose side was he on. Or that seems to be the shocking point.

"It's important that we ask you about this on the record," Bella is saying apologetically, and of course we're being recorded. "We have very serious concerns about Sal's activities. Especially of late. And now this. He's dead. Bizarrely and horribly...," she adds, her voice catching.

* * *

"For one thing, the timing is a problem." Benton is looking directly at me again. "As you know, it's about a four-hour drive from Alexandria to Green Bank, and he set out yesterday at eleven-thirty. When he called while getting gas in Weyers Cave, it was around one-thirty. I believe that's what you told Lucy earlier."

"Yes."

"Which should have put him in the Green Bank area between three-thirty and four P.M.," Benton explains. "Not at seven when he met his colleagues at the Red Caboose. We know he didn't go to the lodge first because he never checked in. And he didn't go to the observatory. So where was he for three hours?"

"The interval can't be accounted for," Gus is saying. "The last time Sal's phone signal was picked up was when he called you from the convenience store in Weyers Cave. After that he turned off his phone as he drove deeper into the Quiet Zone. We don't know where he went or what he was doing."

"What about satellite images?" I suggest.

"Forget it," Lucy says. "He wasn't under surveillance and therefore not a target."

"It would be a crapshoot for a satellite in low Earth orbit to catch him driving somewhere in his truck," General Gunner says. "And the spysats we have in the geostationary orbit aren't going to pick him up from twenty-two thousand miles above the planet. He was completely off grid."

"Are you sure he didn't mention an errand he planned to run, some other stop?" Bella asks me.

"He didn't."

"Maybe somebody he hoped to see along the way?" she then suggests.

"I wouldn't know."

"Someone he'd seen before, perhaps." She holds my gaze. "We know from his credit card activity that last month he got gas at the same convenience store in Weyers Cave. The Little Rebel off Route Two-Fifty-Six. And he was there filling his truck last summer in June, July and August. Then again in January and March, as I mentioned. What was he doing in Weyers Cave? Who was he seeing?"

"I don't know, unless he was on his way to or from Green Bank?" I offer.

"He wasn't on those occasions." Gus moves away from the window, returning to his chair. "The last time he visited the observatory was in September, and it doesn't appear that he stopped in Weyers Cave coming or going."

"Doctor Scarpetta, might you have noticed if he was carrying anything unusual in his truck yesterday while he was getting ready to leave for West Virginia?" the National Security Agency asks.

"Such as?"

"For example, a blue fabric briefcase with a black shoulder strap?"

"I didn't notice anything like that. And that's not what he typically carried—"

"Asking about a blue fabric briefcase is pretty damn specific," Marino interrupts again.

"Images from his front-door camera show him placing it on the floor of the front passenger seat not long before Doctor Scarpetta showed up." Secret Service Director Bella Steele twists off the cap from a water bottle, taking a swallow. "Four days ago, on Thursday, he stopped by his bank and withdrew five thousand dollars in twenty-dollar bills. And he did the same thing around the time of those other visits to the convenience store in Weyers Cave. A total of thirty-five thousand dollars cash has been withdrawn since last June. Do you have any idea why?" She's asking me this.

"No, I don't," I reply. "And the blue briefcase doesn't sound familiar."

"It's missing, like everything else, it seems," Lucy says. "We've not had the chance to search his truck yet, but it's looking like nothing was inside when it went off the mountain."

"It certainly seems that Sal Giordano might have been meeting someone on his way to Green Bank yesterday afternoon," Bella goes on as she looks at me. "And perhaps exchanging the briefcase and cash for something. Of course, some of this is conjecture. But one has to ask if it's connected to his death."

The speculations continue implying that Sal may have been a traitor, and I can scarcely listen. How quickly people want to blame the victim, and he wasn't perfect. No one is. But he wasn't a turncoat. I refuse to believe it, and I pull on fresh gloves, unwilling to discuss this further.

"I know some of you have seen postmortems. Who hasn't?" I look up at my audience behind glass, and several people raise their hands. "Think of a forensic autopsy as exploratory instead of something gory." I begin taking x-rays through the double layers of thick plastic.

I give them a preview of what to expect while moving the C-arm as images appear on the console's video screen. Marino is checking out a vintage Nikon 35-millimeter camera that isn't Wi-Fi enabled.

"It's an excavation rather than an anatomical dissection," I'm saying to our audience. "The goal is to see what truths the dead have to tell."

As I explain, I notice a radiodense object in the stomach. The shape makes me think of a pharmaceutical capsule that Sal must have swallowed close to the time he ate dinner. I find this puzzling, not aware that he was on any medications. He was staunchly against them, taking only vitamins and other nutritional supplements.

But I'm not the end-all when it comes to information about him despite what's been implied. I roll the C-arm from one part of the body to the next, monitoring the images on the display, doing what I can to disavow people of their assumptions.

"You saw him how often, would you estimate?" the NSA asks me.

"On average once a month or so we'd see each other at meetings. Or he'd come to our house. Now and then Benton and I would drop by his. Sometimes we'd run into each other in the neighborhood."

"And how often did you text or talk on the phone?"

"It varied depending on what was going on. At least several times a month." I'm aware of Benton's eyes on me.

"Would Sal Giordano have told you if he'd gotten involved with someone?" Gus wants to know.

"What do you mean by involved?"

"If he were sleeping with someone. Would he have confided that in you?"

"Not necessarily." I position the C-arm over the right side of the head.

"What makes you think he was sleeping with someone?" Marino asks as he finds a six-inch plastic ruler that he'll use for a photographic scale.

"Because he seems to have been living a secret life," Gus says. "Our concern is that he might have been lured into something. Unfortunately, it happens all too often. No one is immune to mistakes of the heart."

"Or mistakes of a lower part of the anatomy, I was actually thinking," Bella says, and those around her manage to smile. "Did Sal sleep with a lot of women? Does anybody know? Because that's not how he came across to me. The question is whether he was easily led astray, shall we say."

"That wasn't my impression," I reply.

"I'm more suspicious about him selling secrets to the bad guys," says the secretary of state.

"Except it appears Sal was the one paying somebody possibly in twenty-dollar bills delivered in a briefcase," Benton replies.

CHAPTER 19

Completing the orbit with the x-ray machine, I roll it out of the way. I begin describing the extensive skeletal damage Sal suffered due to blunt force trauma when he hit the ground.

"His right radial and ulnar shaft are fractured, as is the right temporal bone of his skull," I'm saying. "His right shoulder is dislocated, his hips and pelvis shattered. I'm seeing broken ribs and burst vertebrae, all of it consistent with an abrupt vertical deceleration. Or more specifically in this case, the victim being jettisoned out of some type of flying craft."

"From how far up, do you think?" NASA Langley asks.

"I've examined victims of falls and jumps from high-rises, bridges, water towers, when a skydiver's parachute fails. They look similar to this, the injuries profound and almost never survivable if the landing is on a hard surface, as it was in this case." I begin cutting open the plastic body pouches along the sealed seams. "But it's not possible to know for certain the altitude except that it was a significant drop."

"Based on the vortex of flattened grass and flower petals, and the height of the trees around the clearing." Lucy's voice fills my hood. "I'd estimate the UAP was at least fifty feet off the ground, maybe a hundred. Not much more than that or the propulsion system's downwash wouldn't have caused what I saw at the scene."

"How big was this vortex you're describing?" the All-domain Anomaly Resolution Office (AARO) asks her.

"Approximately eighty feet in diameter. We have photos and exact measurements taken before the storm. From the air it looked like a pink halo around him."

"Possibly the result of a coronal discharge from a high-voltage energy source that ionized the air," the Defense Advanced Research Projects Agency considers.

"The technology is definitely out there but not mainstream." Space Force's General Gunner means it's secret.

"What I can say for a fact is the vortex was caused by something rotating clockwise extremely fast," Lucy informs us. "It created enough turbulence to strip the nearby apple trees of their blossoms. And when Tron and I first got there we noticed a sort of vinegary odor."

"Strange," Bella says. "I wonder what that could have been."

"It didn't make any sense," Tron replies.

"Was this pink halo radioactive?" AARO inquires. "Did anybody check?"

"We used a Geiger counter on the body and immediate area," I reply. "Nothing unusual was detected."

"But it had been raining like a mother by the time we got there," Marino adds.

"That shouldn't have made a significant difference," DARPA answers.

"What I'm seeing fits with him having received his injuries early morning, possibly around the time the UAP showed up on radar," I explain as Marino and I slide the opened pouches out from under the body. "Once he hit the bricks, he wasn't moving after that. But he survived for a while."

"Let me make sure this is clear," General Gunner says to me. "He landed on the Yellow Brick Road in the middle of an apple orchard."

"Inside the Haunted Forest. Yes."

"It sure feels like someone giving him the finger," he says. "Or maybe giving the finger to all of us."

"How long is *a while*?" Bella asks as Marino loudly stuffs bloody plastic into the biohazard trash.

"Several hours, explaining the profound tissue response to his injuries," I reply. "The longer he had a blood pressure, the worse he was going to look."

"And there's no question he was alive when he fell from the sky?" It's Benton asking.

"He definitely was."

"That's important," he says.

"A totally different scenario," Gus adds. "Are we absolutely sure of this before you've done the autopsy? It's critical because it speaks to intention."

"I don't need an autopsy to know that he was alive for an interval after hitting the ground," I tell them.

"Stripping someone naked, throwing the person overboard while alive changes the emotionality of the act," Benton says. "The goal becomes terror. Not only the victim's but anyone who knows what was done, and we've seen this before."

"*Vuelos de la muerte*. Death flights. Unfortunately, they're nothing new," Gus agrees. "During Argentina's Dirty War thousands were killed in a similar fashion."

"The MO's always the same," Benton explains. "Once on board the aircraft the victims were stripped of their clothing and all personal effects. They were drugged into compliance before being pushed out over an ocean, a river, the mountains, where they'd most likely never be found."

"Also a Russian specialty, and at various times practiced by the Japanese, the Indonesians, the French, the Colombians," Gus adds. "Typically, the hostages are first injected with an anesthetic like Pentothal."

"Known as truth serum in the old days," says the NSA.

"And used in executions by lethal injection," I inform them. "Sodium thiopental isn't made in the U.S. anymore, but we'll screen for it and other drugs."

"It's estimated that between the late seventies and early eighties, tens of thousands of people were disappeared in this fashion," Gus goes on. "Death flights, poisonings, prison camps, torture, mental asylums create fear and destabilization that lead to a collapse of civilized society. It plays right into the hands of ruthless dictators."

"Except the body was found in this instance," Marino reminds everyone. "There wasn't much of an effort to *disappear* it. No matter what, it would have been found eventually."

"The goal isn't to conceal what happened to Sal Giordano, quite the opposite," Benton says. "The point is the ruination of any semblance of peace of mind. The very thing that terrorists like Carrie Grethen are gifted at." He brings her up and I'm not surprised.

"I understand we don't know where she is," I reply, watching Marino's reaction to the news.

"What the fuck?" he says under his breath. But I hear his amplified voice fine, as can everyone else.

*　　*　　*

"We lost track of her in December and don't know where she is right now." Benton has no expression on his face but I sense the contempt he feels for her. "However, we have an idea what she's been doing."

"Starting with Russia's role in Israel's war against Hamas and the resulting global mayhem," Interpol says. "The Kremlin has provided material support to that terrorist organization and others in part to sow chaos."

"And to pull the U.S. into another war in an ongoing effort to weaken us," General Gunner says.

"Then Carrie Grethen could be in the Middle East," Marino suggests.

"Or she may still be in Russia," the CIA's Gus Gutenberg replies.

"Or here," I add.

"We simply don't know," Gus says.

"How the hell could you let that happen?" Marino yanks off his soiled outer gloves, throwing them into the trash. "Jesus Christ! The entire U.S. government can't keep their eye on one person? And now she could be here? In Virginia? Even as we speak? Like we need to worry about that again?"

"Nobody *let* it happen," Lucy says. "When she decides to go dark, that's what she does. She's invisible when she wants to be."

"Let's be reminded of a few facts." Marino works his gloved hands into a new outer pair. "There are plenty of stories about people and livestock being dropped out of UFOs, UAPs, flying disks, whatever you want to call them."

"Endless stories and no credible evidence," says AARO.

"It's easy to blame Carrie Grethen for everything," Marino continues. "Well, unless she's got access to a UFO that can beam people up while they're driving, then maybe we should be looking for something else."

"Nobody's said anything about people being beamed up." AARO again.

"You want to explain how his truck went off the mountain with no one in it and the engine running, the doors locked and the seat belts still fastened?" Marino argues.

"Wouldn't be all that hard to stage in an old pickup truck like that," Lucy says.

"Seat belts as in plural?" Bella's voice inside my hood sounds perplexed.

"Those in the front seats," Lucy tells her.

"Did he have someone with him at the time?"

"Not that anyone knows of," Lucy answers. "When he was witnessed getting into his truck and driving out of the restaurant parking lot after dinner, he appeared to be alone."

"At eight-thirty, it would have been dark," Bella replies. "Maybe the witness didn't get a good look."

"What witness are we talking about?" Marino asks.

"His astronomer friend Marie Rao walked out with him to the parking lot." Benton offers a detail I didn't know. "They talked by her car for a few minutes, and then he got into his truck and drove away as if everything was normal. The restaurant has a hardwired security camera covering the parking lot. We've got it on film."

"It would be helpful to see that," Marino replies, and it's sickening to imagine what Benton just described.

It sounds like Sal had a pleasant time with his colleagues, and then what? Who else saw him drive away and perhaps followed? I pick up a large syringe, signaling I'm getting started.

"First, I'll draw blood from the femoral artery in the upper inner thigh." Inserting the ten-gauge needle, I pull the plunger, the unoxygenated blood dark red. "The number one priority is to confirm identity with DNA." I begin filling test tubes. "The sooner the better, as I worry about the news getting out before we can inform his next of kin."

Placing a tube of blood in a plastic carton, I instruct Marino to set it outside the door. He's to spray everything copiously with disinfectant. Whoever picks up the evidence needs to have on appropriate PPE, I tell everyone, and Tron leaves the observation area.

"Based on his x-rays, he didn't land feetfirst." I begin to explain what else I'm seeing.

"Is that significant?" Bella asks.

"If people are conscious during a fall, the theory is that they'll try to right themselves and land feetfirst," I reply. "It's instinct to protect the head. But the way someone lands depends on many things, including what position the person was in to begin with and what happened on the way down. He has a hematoma across the middle of both thighs from striking something hard before hitting the ground."

"How do you know it happened before he hit the ground?" DARPA asks.

"Because the injury occurred not long before death but doesn't correlate with anything I saw at the scene." I swab the dark red contusion. "I can see four evenly spaced identical perpendicular scrapes, a pattern of some kind."

"Definitely not a tree branch," Bella says.

"And it wasn't made by the bricks under him," I answer as Marino places the ruler next to the injury in question, taking photos.

"Maybe he hit some part of the UAP on his way down," General Gunner suggests. "Part of a landing gear or other structure."

"My question is whether he was conscious when he was pushed overboard," Bella says. "You're telling us that he was alive. But was he aware?"

"I can't answer that yet, and we may never know." Using a hand magnifier, I look at debris in tangles of long gray hair.

I adjust the surgical light as I check the neck with the magnifier, noticing a barely visible tiny reddish dot below the left ear. A puncture wound that looks fresh, I inform everyone.

"Likely made by a hypodermic needle," I add. "Possibly he was injected with something."

"Explaining how he was subdued," Benton decides. "He may have encountered someone on the road who injected him in the neck with some type of sedative."

"We'll see what toxicology has to say." I check other skin surfaces, finding three puncture wounds in the fold of the left arm, and two more on the left buttock. "We'll run samples in our labs while you run them in yours." I meet Benton's eyes as I say this, silently reminding him that we agreed to share the evidence.

I ask if there might be a set of forensic lights handy, and Lucy directs Marino to the top shelf of a cabinet. He lifts out a plastic case, opening it on the countertop. Inside are what look like six small black flashlights, each a different wavelength.

"Now I'm going to collect trace evidence, which literally refers to traces of things we can't see with the unaided eye," I explain. "We'll see what fluoresces. Dust, fibers, body fluids."

I select the ultraviolent light, turning it on, the glass lens glowing purple. Turning off the surgical lamp, I put on a pair of orange-tinted glasses.

"You're going to be in the dark for a few minutes," I apologize to our audience, flipping a wall switch, everything blacking out.

I begin painting the UV light over the body, amazed as something lights up cobalt blue, a residue as fine as dust. It adheres everywhere except the bloody wounds, suggesting it isn't from the ground where Sal was found. It was transferred from somewhere else before he was dropped out of the sky. Using the adhesive side of Post-its, I begin collecting anything clinging to hair and skin.

As I work in the dark I describe what I'm doing while Marino continues taking photographs, holding an orange filter in front of the camera lens. He's on one side of the table and I'm on the other, and I can make out his bulky shape as the camera's flashgun goes off. In the purple glow of ultraviolent I label the small yellow Post-it squares, tucking them into white paper envelopes.

"The most telling evidence likely will be what we discover has been transferred to the body from various locations," I'm saying as I continue exploring with the UV light. "Of interest is any conveyance he was in, including the UAP that seems to be involved. But most of all where he was held hostage."

"How long are we thinking?" Bella asks.

"We know he left the restaurant last night at around eight-thirty and never made it to the lodge." It's Benton who answers. "And the UAP was detected near the Oz theme park at six this morning. That's the time frame."

"He was held somewhere for as long as ten hours?" Bella asks. "How dreadful."

CHAPTER 20

Painting the UV light over the hands and arms, I'm surprised that the pi sign tattoo glows a brilliant yellow.

"The ink has some sort of fluorescent additive," I explain as it occurs to me why Sal might have had the tattoo to begin with.

Maybe the reason wasn't merely decorative or symbolic. Perhaps holding the tattoo over certain scanners granted access into off-limits places such as Area One storage containers and mortuary drawers. Possibly the tattoo was a form of secret identification, a skeleton key to forbidden knowledge. I propose this to our audience as I continue collecting evidence in the dark, and no one denies or confirms.

"Is there a need for retaining the tattoo?" What I'm asking is if I should excise it, preserving it in formalin. "Possibly there's a computer chip under the skin or something that should be recovered?"

"That won't be necessary," Gus says, and if he knows the purpose of the tattoo, he isn't saying.

I continue searching and collecting, then flip the lights back on, everybody squinting. Picking up a clipboard from the countertop, I begin charting multiple injuries on body diagrams. I fill more test tubes with blood, and take vitreous fluid from the eyes, now a cloudy grayish blue. I dictate, and Marino writes it down.

Opening what the cops call a rape kit, I swab every orifice as I would a victim of sexual assault. Since I can't know what Sal was subjected to, I intend to leave nothing to the imagination. If something isn't done properly, there's no going back. The time on the old wall clock ticks close to 9:30 P.M. as I turn on the faucet in the sink at the foot of the table.

I run my scalpel from clavicle to clavicle, down the torso, detouring around the navel, ending at the pelvis. Reflecting back tissue, I slice through the breastplate of ribs, removing it. Placing the bloc of organs on the cutting board, I cut through connective tissue, rinsing with water I squeeze from a big sponge.

I begin dictating pathological details, the heart within normal limits, the blood vessels patent and clear of plaque. The lungs were punctured by broken ribs, and the spleen is ruptured. I weigh the left kidney, then the right, each 161 grams, I tell Marino. The liver is contused, and I lift it out of the hanging scale, setting it on the plastic cutting board.

I begin slicing with a long-bladed knife, saving sections in a jar of formalin, dropping the rest in the plastic bucket under the table. Retrieving a steel cup from the surgical cart, I measure the amount of hemorrhaged blood pooled inside the empty chest cavity.

"About five hundred milliliters," I explain. "Or around seventeen ounces. Most likely he was unconscious after hitting the ground and soon after went into shock."

"Are you finding anything that might make you think he was tortured?" the secretary of state asks. "Why is his skin red? I'm wondering if they burned him." He's leaning forward in his chair, looking down impassively at the carnage on my table.

"Who's *they*?" Marino wants to know.

"That is the question, now isn't it?" Gus answers. Then to me he says, "What about high-energy weapons that could inflict serious pain as a way of extracting information?"

"There's no way for me to tell," I reply. "It's also difficult to determine if the redness of his skin is uniform front and back."

I explain that after death, blood ceases to circulate. It settles according to gravity, causing areas of the body to turn a dark dusky red easily confused with bruising. The postmortem artifact is called livor mortis. Typically, it and rigor mortis are completely fixed after eight hours, and Sal's findings are consistent with that. If I press my thumb against his back, the skin no longer blanches, every muscle in his body stiff.

"By all appearances he landed on his right side first, and was on his back from then on." I continue reconstructing what the injuries are telling me. "His dusky lividity makes it nearly impossible for me to tell if the skin on his back was red prior to death."

"It would make sense if he was tortured while someone tried to find out what he knew," the NSA says.

"That while teaching him and others a lesson," Gus suggests. "Depending on the circumstances."

"Or it could be from the sun," I reply. "It might be as simple as that. In the open clearing where he was left, he could have been in the sun for a while."

"When we found him, it was about three and a half hours after the UAP was picked up by radar and other sensors," Lucy says. "The clearing was definitely in the sun at that time."

"Can you get sunburned when you're dead?" Bella asks.

"The skin might become somewhat discolored," I reply. "But it wouldn't turn pink or red because there would be no tissue response. And there'd be no production of the melanin that causes tanning."

Picking up a pair of surgical scissors, I snip open the stomach, emptying it into a plastic carton I've placed on the cutting board.

"That's weird." Marino watches with an unpleasant look on his face. "As if everything's not weird enough already. What time did he eat last night? And do we know what he ordered at the restaurant?"

"He and his two colleagues got the same thing. Barbecue plates with slaw and tater tots." Lucy repeats what she told me earlier.

"That's what this is looking like," I confirm. "And it tells me that soon after dinner he was sufficiently stressed that his digestion completely quit."

"I didn't know that could happen," AARO says.

"Part of the fight-or-flight response. The central nervous system shuts down the digestive system, focusing the body's resources on the extremities, preparing you to defend yourself or run. And that's what happened here," I explain while sifting. "If I didn't know better I might think he died soon after he ate."

"And you're sure he didn't?" the NASA director asks.

"I'm sure," I reply, noticing a hint of robin-egg blue.

I think about the small radiodense shape I noticed earlier on x-ray. I explain that Sal swallowed some type of capsule, and I finish rinsing it, setting it down on the clean blue towel Marino placed on a cart. He begins to take photographs.

"Half blue, half white with no markings on it that might hint at what it is." I pick up the hand magnifier. "In fact, the only thing I'm seeing on it is a smiley face."

"Are you sure that's what it is?" Gus's voice sounds puzzled. "Possibly what you're seeing is a trademark symbol?"

"No," I reply. "It's definitely a smiley face. Two eyes, an upturned mouth, a circle around them."

"That's bizarre," Interpol weighs in.

"I might laugh if there was anything funny about this," Bella comments.

"Someone taunting us," the NSA suggests.

"My thoughts too," AARO adds while Benton says nothing.

* * *

"How did the capsule get there?" Marino asks what seems a nonsensical question. "That's important to consider."

"Get where?" Bella's dubious voice sounds inside my hood.

"In his stomach," Marino answers. "Inside his body where it would be found by us."

"He swallowed it," I state the obvious. "That's the only way it could have gotten into his stomach."

"Yeah, well, there was a crop circle around his body, and his driverless car went off the mountain with the seat belts fastened." Marino is back to that for the umpteenth time. "Maybe the capsule is some kind of super high-tech device that was implanted by whatever was flying the UAP he was thrown out of."

"A high-tech device for what purpose?" Benton puzzles.

"To manipulate humans somehow," Marino replies. "Or warn us about something. Hell if I know. But he was tossed out of a UAP, so it's a good idea to be thinking outside the box."

"I don't mean to burst your bubble," says AARO, "but most UAPs are proven to be of human origin."

"Most. As in not all of them," Marino argues.

"Doctor Scarpetta, are we sure it's not dangerous?" Bella asks as I pick up the capsule in my gloved fingers, and it's as light as a feather. "Since we don't know what's inside it?"

"I'll be careful." Placing it under a chemical fume hood, I turn on the exhaust fan. "We'll take a look while protected by the highest level of PPE in case we're dealing with something toxic like anthrax or ricin."

Carefully, I twist open the blue-and-white plastic halves, and inside is a dark square of a filmlike material no bigger than the head of a match. Without touching it, I tap it out on top of a glass slide, protecting it with a cover slip.

Carrying this across the room in the palm of my gloved hand, I sit down at the countertop in front of an optical microscope, switching on its lamp. Peering through the binocular lenses, I adjust the magnification, bumping it up to 100X, and what I'm looking at is a microphotograph also known as microfilm.

Moving the slide around on the stage and making further adjustments, I sharpen the image into focus as I explain what I'm doing.

"I'm going to guess he swallowed this early on before he was stripped of his clothing," I suggest. "He likely had the capsule hidden on his person, perhaps in a pocket, making it easily accessible in an emergency."

As I'm saying this, I think of my visit with Sal on his driveway yesterday. He may have had the capsule in a pocket then. Yet he said nothing to me. Maybe if I'd paid closer attention I might have questioned whether his heavy mood was about more than turning sixty. Maybe he had good reason to suspect he wouldn't be alive much longer.

"A microphotograph of what?" Gus asks.

"A message in Sal's hand." I peer at his magnified neat writing in black ink on a piece of lined yellow paper that he photographed through a microscope.

TN-5L-7R-9L

"I'm going to read what it says." I glance up at everyone. "*TN,* followed by the number five and the letter *L.* Next is the number seven and the letter *R.* Then the number nine and the letter *L.*"

"Sounds like the combination to a dial lock," Interpol decides. "*L* for left. *R* for right."

"What would *TN* stand for? Besides *Tennessee,* which wouldn't make sense?" asks the director of NASA.

"The Oak Ridge National Labs, the Y-Twelve National Security Complex are in Tennessee. The enriched uranium needed for nuclear weapons is stored and processed there," General Gunner answers.

"A lot of sensitive research goes on that pertains to national security," says DARPA. "Sal Giordano had been to those facilities many times."

"What about the string of letters and numbers being a password?" Interpol suggests.

"Not to any of the secure facilities he frequented. Those passwords are far more complex and constantly changing," the NSA replies.

"He has a safe in his home office." I remove the slide from the microscope's stage. "I've heard him mention it. Maybe it has a dial lock," I add as reality settles leadenly.

Sal went to a lot of trouble creating a cryptic microphotograph and concealing it in an empty capsule that looks like something found in a gag store. He anticipated his abduction and death well in advance. He must have, and it's horrible that I didn't know. Had he shared his fears with me, maybe we wouldn't be here now.

"It certainly sounds like he had reason to think he was in extreme danger," Bella decides. "He must have felt that way before he got into his truck and headed to Green Bank. And you're sure he wasn't acting strangely?" She directs this at me.

"He wasn't in the best mood," I reply. "I thought it unusual when he called me from the road. But he didn't so much as hint that he was worried something might happen to him."

"Which doesn't add up," Marino replies. "If he thought someone was after him, why not say something? Why not try to stop the bad thing from happening?"

"Because he might not have wanted anyone knowing what he was involved in. He might have placed himself in grave danger because of his own activities," Gus says to my dismay as they continue chipping away at Sal's character.

"What's the capsule made out of?" Marino asks me this.

"It looks like plastic."

"Then eventually it was going to pass through him and end up in the toilet," he replies.

"Had he lived."

"Meaning the secret code in the capsule might have been intended for someone else, and he swallowed it for a later recovery," Marino continues to speculate. "But he died first."

"I think the capsule was meant for you to find." Benton is staring straight at me. "This is for your benefit, that's the reason for the smiley face. That was his signal to you. He knew if the worst happened, you'd be the one doing the examination."

"I'm not sure we can assume it was meant for me to find as opposed to any other medical examiner or coroner. Depending on where the death occurred." I don't want to believe what Benton is saying.

"It was meant for you to recover," he flatly states. "He suspected that if someone took him out it would be in his own backyard. It would be while he was going about his usual business in his usual places. He knew exactly what he was doing and the dangers he faced. Even as he did little about it."

I place the glass slide, the empty capsule inside small cardboard boxes that I label and initial. I remind my audience that only the most experienced forensic scientists can be allowed to handle the evidence I've collected.

"Even though I'm sure the body isn't radioactive," I explain. "And I seriously doubt it's contagious with some exotic virus that doesn't exist on earth. But I'm not taking shortcuts or chances. We'll decon everything in here as best we can, and whoever comes inside this room needs to be in Level-A protection just like we are. Special precautions must be taken every step of the way."

"We understand and know what to do," Lucy says as I plug the Stryker saw into the overhead cord reel, and Benton abruptly gets up from his chair.

He leaves the observation area without a word, and I sense his unhappy preoccupations. He had to sit there and listen to me talk about my relationship with Sal, not that Benton learned anything new. But I did as his peers put me through what felt like a voir dire examination. Plain and simple, they don't trust Sal, and I know how he'd feel if he could hear them. It would crush him.

CHAPTER 21

The electric saw's oscillating blade grinds through bone as I open the fractured skull as if the patient on my table is like any other. I focus intensely while willing myself to feel nothing. That will have to come later. Now is not the time. If I'm going to help him I must be strong.

Lifting out the brain, I weigh and examine it, finding the expected damage. Cerebral contusions, intracranial hemorrhage, and when I dissect the neck, I discover bleeding into soft tissue indicative of whiplash.

"The force of hitting the ground caused the neck to hyperextend rather much like when your car slams into a wall," I explain. "And this is common in people who fall or jump from high places."

"What actually killed him?" Bella asks as she and the others get up from their chairs, gathering their notes and other belongings.

"The longer the survival time the more his brain was going to swell, resulting in brainstem compression and respiratory arrest," I reply. "Ultimately, that's what caused his death, but there are multiple contributing factors. Blood loss and shock, for example. One thing adds to another."

"Are you calling it a homicide?" Gus peers through the observation window, looking down, his hands in the pockets of his shapeless gray trousers.

"If a human is responsible, yes," I reply. "If we're talking about something else, then I don't have an answer."

"You mean if a nonhuman intelligence did it," AARO says.

"Legally, a homicide is one human killing another," I tell them. "A death caused by an animal is an accident. If it were proven that a nonhuman intelligence was to blame? Which I've never heard of, by the way. Well, I don't know what that would be. There's no existing medico-legal category for deaths caused by the paranormal."

"I guess we might have to come up with a new term," Marino decides. "We should have a long time ago."

"Let's hope that won't be necessary." I screw the top on a jar of tissue sections, the formalin tinted pink from blood.

Marino returns the bag of sectioned organs to the chest cavity as I thread a surgical needle with twine. I close the Y-incision, returning the sawn-off skull cap to the proper position, pulling the scalp over it before suturing ear to ear along the hairline. I follow my usual procedures with military precision while knowing the futility. It doesn't stop me.

I carry on as if Sal is destined for a proper funeral home where he'll have a proper viewing and proper burial with a proper crowd of those who loved and respected him. It's not going to happen. There's nothing proper about any of this. It's made all the more disgraceful by the slights against everything he stood for. As if being terrorized and killed suggests he must have done something to cause it.

We seal the body in another clear plastic total containment pouch, and I spray it and our work area with a powerful disinfectant. Marino and I douse ourselves from head to toe, the liquid lightly spattering plastic. We take off our PPE, the room sharply pungent with the odor of hydrogen peroxide that masks everything else.

By now the second-floor observation area is dark. No one is left except Lucy silhouetted behind glass.

"What happens next?" I ask.

Stepping closer to the hardwired phone on the countertop, I look up at the shape of her.

"Nothing more for now," she says. "You've done enough."

"Meaning what?"

"DNA has verified his identity, and there's nothing more you can help with tonight." Her voice is firm over speakerphone. "We'll handle it from here."

"Sounds good to me." Marino's quick to agree.

"I'm not finished." I'm well aware that the Secret Service is in charge of the investigation. Technically, I answer to Lucy right now.

"We've got everything covered," she says. "You've got a car waiting. Go get some rest." It sounds like an order.

"Get some rest where?" Marino asks.

"The Langley Inn."

"Fine by me." He's more than happy to comply, and I'm not.

"The body is evidence," I explain. "I have to sign off on its release and testify truthfully about its disposition."

"We consider the remains extremely hazardous. Or they

could be." Lucy's tone doesn't invite discussion. "Therefore, we'll dispose of them in the safest manner possible. That's the protocol. No exceptions."

"Dispose of it where?" Marino uses a twist-tie to secure a biohazard trash bag.

"Here."

"*Where* here?" He frowns up at her shadowy figure behind the observation glass.

"Below ground," she tells him as I envision the smokestack rising from the center of the blockhouses. "A cramped claustrophobic place you'd really hate."

"No thanks," he says.

"I need to see what you're talking about," I tell her in a reasonable tone that belies what simmers deep inside.

"It's not necessary."

"There's paperwork I need to fill out and sign." I won't give in.

"It can wait until later."

Don't tell me what to do about him!

"That's for me to decide." My heated emotions roll into a slow boil. "We'll get our stuff, and see you in a few minutes." I hang up the landline.

Marino and I return to the locker room, and I wash my face. I can't wait to get out of these clothes and take a shower. Soon, I promise myself.

"I've got just what the doctor ordered after a shit day like this." Marino is cleaning up in the sink next to mine, scrubbing his forearms and hands.

"What might that be?" I grab towels for each of us.

"How about we blow this joint like the old days and go have a drink?" he says.

"The hotel bar won't be open at this hour." That's not the only reason I can't.

"I keep a stash of Maker's Mark for emergencies. You know me, Doc. Always prepared."

"As much as I'd like to, I can't. I need to be here right now," I reply as we tuck our rain jackets into our jump-out bags.

"No you don't. You don't need to do this at all." Marino doesn't hide how stung he feels. "Why the hell do you want to witness something like that? You don't trust what they're going to do with his body?"

"I trust them fine. But I'm staying. After that, Benton's waiting…"

"Have it your way. As for me?" Marino shrugs, his tone resentful on the way to cold. "I'm blowing this damn place, grabbing something to eat, throwing back a few bourbons."

"You've earned it," I reply, and no matter what I say it doesn't help.

* * *

Leaving the locker room, we find Lucy inside the receiving area waiting by a stairway door that has a biometric lock.

"I'm staying, but no need for Marino," I tell her.

"Yeah, no need." He stalks off, his bad mood closing in like overcast.

"I meant that I'll take care of it." My voice follows him as he opens the door leading outside.

"What's eating him?" Lucy watches him leave, the lenses of

her glasses almost clear. "Never mind. Why am I asking after everything he just heard about your relationship with Sal?"

"Nothing about today has been easy for any of us," I answer diplomatically.

"I know." Her eyes linger on mine as if she's about to say something else.

But she doesn't, and I'm reminded we're on camera. She scans open the lock of the heavy metal door, and we descend four flights of steep metal-edged steps, our boots loud and echoing in the uneven light. On the lowest level, she opens another steel door. We enter a concrete space no bigger than a single-bay garage, the dank air stale and tasting of dust.

Neon lights flicker overhead, one of the tubular bulbs burned out, a lot of gauzy cobwebs everywhere. I look around at a sink, a freestanding double-glass-doored cabinet filled with old bottles of embalming fluid and other chemicals. A large rusting drain is in the middle of the brick floor, an old black rubber hose sloppily coiled next to a fifty-five-gallon metal drum of formaldehyde.

I associate the small dissection table with veterinary necropsies. The zinc top can be tilted on the wooden base, the gears rusty.

"What exactly went on down here?" I ask.

"It's where the pathologists and others conducted certain examinations," Lucy says.

"That much I can deduce."

"For the most part, we're talking about long before my time."

"I can deduce that, too," I reply as she artfully dodges the question.

The vintage embalming machine resembles a large white enameled blender, and lining a shelf are glass jars, flasks and antique tins of Morticians Powder that helps with odors. On a hospital cart are a jumble of forceps, scissors, retractors, catheters, hypodermic trocars, a bone handsaw that I suspect haven't been used in many years.

"Related to animals that have gone into space?" I ask. "Is that the purpose?"

"For handling biological materials or purported ones and such." She continues being evasive.

"It certainly looks like they were dissecting and embalming something down here." I prod for answers she's not going to give. "While other things have been kept frozen in drawers?"

She opens another door to a rush of heated air and the muffled roar of an inferno. Tron is waiting for us inside the crematorium room, flames showing orange around the edges of the oven's iron door, square with an arched top like a medieval castle portcullis. Propped nearby against a brick wall are long-handled clean-out brushes and other tools.

Sal's pouched body awaits on top of a gurney that's at least as old as the blockhouses, the metal patinaed, the wheels hard rubber with white rims. I place my bags on a pitted zinc countertop. Above it on a shelf are cardboard urns similar to what my anatomical division uses when we cremate donated bodies after medical schools finish with them.

"You sure about this?" Tron asks me.

"I'm sure."

She hands me a clipboard, and I sign an evidence form verifying that the body is Salvatore Dante Giordano.

"What's the temp?" I ask.

"Nineteen hundred degrees," Tron says.

"That's good." I begin filling out a provisional death certificate.

... Date of death April 15 ... Time of death approx. 8 a.m. ...

"Don't know when it was used last but it fired up just fine ...," she's saying.

... Place of death Oz ...

"I'm told there's plenty of propane in the tank. Thank God ..."

... Born in Rome, Italy ...

"If the fire went out that would be bad ..."

... Residence Old Town Alexandria, VA ...

"I wonder if that's ever happened ...," Lucy adds as I continue filling in the blanks.

... Parents Mario and Gloria Giordano ...

I write that Sal died from blunt force trauma due to a vertical descent from a flying object, identity unknown. I have little doubt that he's an assassination, a hit perpetrated by another human being or perhaps more than one. I return the clipboard to Tron, and we put on heat-resistant gloves.

"Maybe we turn him facedown," I suggest, and we do it.

But it makes me feel no better, quite the opposite, not that this could be anything but awful. He won't lie flat due to the awkward angles of his rigorous limbs. His familiar wavy gray hair and dusky red back show through plastic, and I experience an unexpected shock of panic that just as quickly passes.

We turn the body face up again, and it's as stiff as a mannikin, thudding against metal, the barely open eyes cloudy and

211

staring blindly. His body is clenched rigidly like a fist, almost pugilistic, as if he's offended and resisting mightily. Or maybe he would find all this *Far Side* funny. It's anything but that to me.

"The damn see-through pouches." I find myself perseverating. "They should make them plain black. Or white. Or red, orange, yellow, I don't give a damn. Anything but transparent."

"I agree," Tron says. "It seems disrespectful."

"Because it is," Lucy replies. "No matter what we do it's a fucking indignity."

Tron rolls the body closer to the oven, the wheels creaking and chattering over the brick flooring.

"Death is an ugly fucker." Lucy grabs a long, hooked tool leaning against the wall.

"Yes, it sure as hell is. Death and every fucking thing leading up to it. And then what it leaves you with." I'm dismayed by my flare of temper.

I grip the handles of the steel tray, helping Tron lift the body as Lucy stands back from the iron door, using the hooked tool to pull it open. We're slammed with a wall of searing heat, the blast of the fire deafening. The tray makes a dreadful grating sound as it slides into the raging maw, the plastic pouch instantly melting and smoking.

"Should take a couple hours." Lucy clanks the heavy door shut.

The air is instantly cooler, my heart beating hard, and my vision seems to black out. I'm lightheaded.

"Are you okay?" Lucy's voice as I feel her hand on my arm.

"Yes." Taking a deep breath, I step back from the oven.

"Do you need to sit down before I get you out of here?" she asks.

"I'm fine." I take off the heavy Kevlar gloves while silently lecturing myself to control my emotions. "When I leave tomorrow I'll bring the ashes with me. I'll hold them safely at the office until we know what to do."

"We'll have them ready for you in the morning," Tron promises.

Feel nothing.

Picking up my bags, I shoulder the straps as Lucy and I return to the stairwell, my thoughts racing and colliding, my attention fragmented. I don't want to envision what's happening inside the oven, and I've seen it before.

Feel nothing!

"I expect that his sister will want the ashes sent to Italy," Lucy is saying as we begin climbing the four flights of stairs.

"The Giordano family has a mausoleum in Campo Verano," I reply. "I saw it long ago, huge with Baroque marble sculptures near where the poet Shelley is buried. It's hard to imagine Sal wanting anything so grand. And most of all, he didn't get along with his parents worth a damn."

"Why not? He was a Nobel laureate. They must have been proud."

"They wanted him to take over the family business of managing their wealth," I explain. "He wasn't supposed to work for a living. What should I expect next?" I then ask her. "The evidence, for example."

"We'll get it to your labs and ours ASAP, and a forensic

213

team will go over his truck," she replies. "It was delivered a little while ago."

"Delivered where?" I envision the vintage blue Chevy dangling and spinning from the long orange tether, trees thrashing under our feet.

"On the other side of the fence." She's saying that it's at NASA Langley. "In hangar eleven-twelve near the gantry if you want to take a look in the morning before heading back to Alexandria."

"Yes, I'll want to see," I reply as we continue to climb, my bags bumping against my thighs.

CHAPTER 22

The dust is making my eyes water, no air stirring as we reach the top floor, shadows moving on the walls. A large moth bats against the caged light overhead, the V-shaped wings the same greenish camouflage as the blockhouses.

I'm familiar with Pandora sphinxes. During warm months, they frequent my garden at night, alighting on the white champion and petunias, drawing nectar like aircraft refueling.

"Shoo!" I wave my hand at the crazed moth as Lucy holds open the door. "Leave while you can!" I wave my hand some more.

The moth darts out of the stairwell and into the bright receiving area, flying toward the light, confused and frantic.

"The inevitable has happened." Lucy walks me to the entrance. "News about Sal's disappearance and death have hit the internet. As of a few minutes ago."

"Do we know who released it?"

"I know it wasn't us. We wouldn't do that before the next of kin has been notified."

"I'll try to take care of that right away," I reply.

"Your ride is in front. Room two-eighteen. Benton's there

waiting." Lucy hands me a plastic keycard that has *Langley Inn* printed on it.

"He left in a hurry, it seemed?" Mindful of cameras, I'm careful what I say, tucking the key in a pocket.

She'll know that I'm asking how he's doing. What he witnessed couldn't have been easy, and I'm not talking about the autopsy. He's seen plenty of those. But my husband was surrounded by his colleagues while I was interrogated about my love affair with another man. It was invasive and embarrassing, every word of it recorded.

"I think he left because he'd gotten as much as he needed," Lucy says as the moth zigzags overhead.

"I'm sure he did," I reply with heavy irony.

"And he has other people in D.C. to report to as we continue monitoring the threat level. I imagine he's on the phone nonstop."

"What's the latest on your mom?"

"Home alone drinking wine while doing her thing on social media."

"Not a good combination."

"It never is. She's been on and off the phone with Marino. All is fine," Lucy says. "And I'm remote monitoring. Anything triggers various sensors, and I'm going to know."

"I'm very glad to hear it. Where are you staying?"

"Wherever I end up. But I'll be here for the next few hours," she replies as more ghastly images violate my thoughts.

"I want you to be careful, Lucy." I give her a hug, holding her hard, not caring who might be watching. "Be as careful as you've ever been since it seems we don't know what's going on.

And if it's her. And who she might go after next." I avoid uttering Carrie's name.

"She'll be targeting someone, maybe already is," Lucy says.

"After all we've been through, I can't believe we still have to worry."

I can't take my eyes off the moth rapidly beating its wings directly over our heads. I can see its pink-and-black-striped velvety body as it hovers like a hummingbird before landing on a wall, clinging to it with sticklike legs.

"If not her, then someone else," Lucy says with a glibness she doesn't feel. "Always best to guard against the worst thing you can think of. I wish Sal had."

"He wasn't motivated by fear, and for the most part thought the best about people. That was good and bad. But mostly good."

"I'm sorry about him. And didn't know how close you were. I'll see you in the morning." She heads back downstairs, the door banging shut behind her.

The moth's stealth-bomber-shaped wings are splayed against white cinderblock. Big black shiny eyes seem to look at me, the spindly antennae twitching as I cautiously approach.

"I'm not going to hurt you." I talk to it, asking what on earth it's doing here. "I know you never meant to end up trapped inside this depressing place. But with so many people in and out I can see how it happened." I inch closer. "Don't be afraid."

I ease my hand closer yet and the moth streaks toward the ceiling, disoriented by the bright lights, darting about more frenetic than ever.

"You're certainly not making it easy for me to help you. Come on now." I open the solid metal front door, cool air blowing in, the porch light garishly bright. "Leave."

It doesn't, and I look for the wall switches, flipping off the outside light, throwing the entrance into darkness.

"You can see better now so get out while you can." I watch the moth swooping near the ceiling. "There's a big world out there, and nothing at all in here except death. I can't hold the door open all night. Leave!"

I flap my hand and yell while imagining how I must look to those monitoring the security cameras. Military guards are probably laughing at me right about now, and I don't give a damn.

"Go on!" I gesture at the moth. "GO!" I wave at it wildly, and it streaks out the open door, vanishing into the night as tears threaten.

I walk outside, leaving the SLAB behind, taking a deep shaky breath, suddenly exhausted. Fireflies glow and fade like falling stars, the moon higher and smaller, more distant and colder. I think of Sal telling me that humans come from something glorious. But it doesn't feel like that as I think about what was done to him. I'll forever see the fire raging. I'll hear the sounds of it roaring like the wind into a microphone.

Don't think about it.

The nocturnal din of frogs and owls seems to crescendo as I push away images of hair and bright pink skin showing through clear plastic. Of dead eyes I scarcely recognized. And flames licking, tendrils of smoke curling. The oven door clanging shut.

Don't think about it!

The lighted surveillance drone brings to mind a UAP as it

continues making circuits, and I envision Sal being pushed out an open door high above the ground. I walk through rows of blockhouses, wondering what's inside them. It's impossible to tell. There's no sign of anyone as I listen to the trees stirring and nature striking up its orchestra.

* * *

Beyond the blockhouses all but one of the SUVs parked here earlier are gone, including Benton's. The Suburban that drove me here is waiting, the headlights shining on pine trees, the same two soldiers inside. One of them steps out to open my door, and I climb in back, placing my briefcase and jump-out bag on the seat next to me.

"Thank you, and hello again." I fasten my seat belt. "I imagine this has been a long day for the two of you."

"Our instructions are to take you to the Langley Inn, ma'am," the driver says, his eyes on me in the rearview mirror.

"That's correct. Thanks."

"Anyplace you need to stop first, ma'am?" asks the officer riding shotgun.

"No, thanks."

Moments later we're passing through the metal front gate and driving away from Area One as I turn on my cell phone. We begin retracing our steps from earlier, the road poorly lit. The golf course is a dark void, the marshland textured with shadows as I surf through news stories on the internet. Conspiracy theories are in full swing about Sal Giordano.

E.T. WHISPERER ABDUCTED AND KILLED BY ALIENS? A headline screams the question.

NOBEL PRIZE WINNER BRUTALLY SLAIN! Another story blames it on his otherworldly beliefs, claiming the government shut him up permanently.

I see no fighter jets taking off and landing, the runway dark as we curve around the airfield. There's scarcely anybody on the road as we drive past the closed bowling alley, and houses with few windows glowing at this late hour.

On my way, I text Benton. *Just a few minutes out.*

Better be hungry, he answers.

It's close to midnight when I'm let out at the four-story red-brick Langley Inn, where I explain to the officer at the front desk that I'm already checked in. I walk through the small lobby furnished in shades of blue and brown. On the walls are poster-size photographs of the C-5 Super Galaxy and C-17 Globemaster transport planes, and F-22 Raptors and other military aircraft.

I take the elevator to the second floor, where an Air Force colonel in camouflage wishes me *good evening, ma'am* as he strides past carrying a pizza box. I hear the faint noise of TVs through closed doors with privacy signs hanging on them. Reaching room 218, I insert my keycard, walking into the delicious aroma of fried foods.

"It's me!" I call out.

The efficiency suite has comfortable couches and chairs upholstered in brown and blue like the furniture in the lobby. Drapes are drawn across the windows, the TV playing the news with the sound off. I close the door and deadbolt it. Dropping my bags inside the bedroom, I find Benton in the kitchen pouring an añejo tequila into two glasses filled with ice.

Shoeless, in a T-shirt and warm-up pants, he smiles as if very glad to see me. I'm just as happy but uneasy as I think of him abruptly leaving the observation area inside the SLAB.

"I'm starved." I walk over to him.

"Fried chicken and all the fixin's." He feigns a Southern drawl and I sense the darkness shadowing his smile.

"It smells divine."

I notice that he's set the table, his 9-millimeter pistol on the countertop. Takeout Styrofoam boxes are next to the microwave oven. He pads closer in his socks, handing me a drink.

"As for the tequila, I thought to bootleg," he says as we clink glasses.

"That was brilliant," I reply, the first swallow heating me up. "I'm sorry I'm not fit company at the moment, Benton. I didn't want to hang around to shower inside the SLAB."

"I would hope not. Especially not with Marino on top of you." Benton sips his drink. "He was in rare form, acting like an ass. More of one than usual."

"It's been a tough day for him from beginning to end."

"Not to mention what it's been for you. But of course, Pete's all about himself." Benton's not typically this uncharitable.

"That's one of the reasons he's out of sorts. My relationship with Sal. Doesn't matter that it's ancient history when it comes to Marino." I search Benton's face to see what's there.

"He can't get out of his own way."

"And he doesn't mean to be like that."

"That doesn't make it okay. There's nothing more powerful than jealousy. One of the greatest motivators when it comes to people doing horrible things." Benton's not smiling now.

"It sounds like he and Dorothy didn't have the best of weekends. Or at least he didn't," I'm explaining. "When his insecurity button is pushed, he gets out of sorts."

"Out of sorts? That's an understatement. You do realize how much time you spend defending him, and always have?" Benton stares across the room at the muted TV.

"I'm not defending him," I reply, and Marino isn't the problem. "I'm also not the psychologist in the room." I can see the hurt in Benton's eyes. "But common sense tells me that knowing something and hearing it in front of an audience are two different things. I'm sorry you were subjected to all that earlier."

"At least it was Gus Gutenberg. He's gentler than most."

"Yes, he can tell you that you're about to be charged with treason without changing the expression on his face or tone of his voice. What happened inside the SLAB was unfortunate for you and me both, Benton. Doesn't matter if I understand the reason."

"I hated to watch you interrogated like that." He takes a big swallow of tequila. "I felt like telling Gus to shut the fuck up, if you want me to be honest."

"Often we don't realize what something is going to feel like until it happens." I'm careful drinking on an empty stomach.

"And then there's the comments one has to hear offstage. People asking how I'm supposed to compete with a Nobel laureate." Ice rattles in his glass as he drains it. "And allusions to you being a home wrecker."

"Technically, I was."

"It takes two. I won't win any morality prizes."

"Neither of us would." I take another swallow of tequila.

"Do you regret it?" Benton's eyes are intense on mine, and he isn't asking about our affair.

He's asking about everything else.

"What I regret is we didn't marry each other the first time around," I reply. "Maybe it was necessary for us to learn from mistakes. But in the process many years were lost. And we can't get them back. Not this time around."

CHAPTER 23

Benton's ex-wife, Connie, wasn't as interested in him as in the Wesley family money. He didn't share his work with her, nor did she want to hear about it. And my first husband was forgettable, my brief marriage to Tony by prescription. I thought it the sensible thing to do after graduate school, for reasons I don't entirely understand. I suspect that it had much to do with my mother and Dorothy, both worried I'd never find anyone.

"There's nothing I regret about you." I tell Benton the truth. "There's no one I want to be with more."

"No one? Not even Sal?"

"Not even close."

"I'm glad to hear it."

"You shouldn't need to hear it. But regardless of what we think we know, we can get surprised." I take another swallow of my drink as it melts away inhibitions that hold me tightly wrapped. "And I was surprised to realize you told your colleagues about my history with Sal before discussing it with me first."

"I should have said something to you earlier." Benton uncorks the bottle again.

"Yes, you should have."

"I'm sorry."

"Why didn't you?"

"The professional thing was to inform those involved that you and Sal were close. In fact, you were lovers once."

"In another life."

"It could cause trouble if not handled appropriately. It doesn't matter how long ago." He splashes more tequila into his glass, and it's not like him to drink this much. "Mainly, I was thinking of what the media will do when it's discovered that you did the autopsy. I wanted us getting on top of it with full disclosure."

"That's what you told yourself, but it's not the real reason," I reply. "My early relationship with Sal bothers you, and you didn't want your colleagues thinking that it did. So, you volunteered my business for me. As if to imply my past was no big deal to you. That you were comfortable discussing it. And that the information was yours to offer when it wasn't."

"Ouch. That sounds petty. Not to mention damn stupid. I would have hoped I'm better than that." He swirls the drink in his glass.

"We're all capable."

"I admit it gets under my skin that you two were together first. I wasn't in your life except from a professional distance."

"And now I'm here exactly where I want to be," I reply as he places takeout boxes into the microwave.

"I won't zap anything until you're ready," he says, and my attention is snagged by the TV news playing.

Dana Diletti is talking about her visit to Berkeley Plantation tomorrow morning, I can tell from the captions and film clips. Then the scene cuts to her live, standing in front of Sal's gated driveway, Secret Service SUVs parked with headlights burning. I pick up the remote control from the coffee table, turning on the sound.

"*...And tomorrow morning on* First Up in Virginia *I'll reveal more about the shocking death of Nobel Prize winner Sal Giordano, known as the ET Whisperer. He's spent years trying to connect with intelligent life from beyond. Did he finally succeed? Did it kill him, and what might that mean for the rest of us? I'll be sharing the details as our investigation continues...*"

"What about searching his house?" I ask, muting the sound again. "I assume that by now someone's gotten in there."

"Agents are inside as we speak," Benton says. "The five dozen white roses delivered included an explosive device for no extra charge."

"How horrifying." I think about what could have happened.

"A pipe bomb that would have been triggered by anyone picking up or moving the vase," Benton adds.

"But Sal told me he carried it into the house himself," I reply. "How does that make sense?"

"The device was remotely armed after he was on his way to West Virginia. The booby trap was left for whoever searched the house eventually. Our crime scene investigators. Agents like me. It could have been anyone."

"How did someone know when he was leaving and where he was going?" I ask. "Unless the person was watching."

"His property has been hacked. When you were talking on the driveway yesterday, it was recorded by the camera in front. You should expect that someone was monitoring your entire conversation."

"What about the safe in his home office?" I ask.

"A dial safe but no luck. The cryptic code he microphotographed doesn't work," Benton says. "It must mean something else, could be anything."

"Well, not anything." I think of the numbers and letters written in Sal's distinctive hand. "If he intended for us to find his note? Then he believed we'd figure out what it means."

I go on to say that I need to call his sister and hope the number is still good. The last time I talked to Sabina Giordano was when their mother died a few years ago.

"We can send an officer to her door if that's better. I have contacts with the carabinieri," Benton suggests.

"That wouldn't be better." I imagine her shock at hearing police knocking on her door. "I'll see you in a few minutes. When I'm clean, I'll greet you properly."

"You don't have to be clean."

"Yes, I do."

I carry my drink through the bedroom, hoping I can reach Sabina Giordano before she hears about Sal in the news. She's a few years younger than him, and it was always the two of them against the world when they were young. As close as they were, she'll be completely undone. I find her number in my phone's contacts list, and it's a few minutes past five A.M. in Rome.

"*Pronto*," she answers groggily.

"Sabina?" Digging inside my briefcase, I pull out my Moleskine notebook.

"*Si? Chi è questo?*"

"It's Kay Scarpetta. So sorry to call you at this hour," I say to her in Italian.

"Oh! What a lovely surprise, Kay! How are you?" Sabina answers in English, suddenly alert and happy. "Sal and I were just talking about you yesterday when I called to cheer him up about turning sixty. I told him not to feel bad because I'm not far behind."

"Yes, I went by to see him . . ."

"*Si, si,* he told me you were planning on dropping by, and I said that next time he comes to Italy he has to bring you. We talked about taking you back to Trattoria da Enzo in Trastevere where we got a bit drunk on a bottle of very nice Chianti. Well, more than a bit, and more than one bottle. Remember?"

Grief wells up as I envision the three of us at an outdoor table in the cobblestone alleyway, light spilling from the restaurant. Sal continued refilling our glasses as we feasted on Roman cuisine, that night's menu written on a blackboard. *Panzanella. Burrata di Andria. Pennette con cozze e pecorino . . .*

"I could never forget our times together," I tell her.

"Are you here now?" Her tone is touched by misgiving.

"I'm in Virginia."

"Is everything all right?" She's instantly somber.

"I have something very unfortunate to tell you, Sabina." I sit down on the edge of the bed. "I wanted you to hear it from me."

I explain that her brother disappeared Monday night and has been found dead.

"That can't be right," she says in a shocked voice. "No, that can't be!"

"DNA has confirmed his identity. I'm so very sorry."

"What do you mean he disappeared?" Her voice quavers.

"He was abducted after leaving a restaurant last night in the mountains of West Virginia. This morning, police found his body in an abandoned theme park some ninety miles from there."

"Oh my God," she gasps. "He was kidnapped and murdered?"

"His death was violent, but we're not sure who or what is responsible," I answer carefully.

"No, oh no...!"

"I'm sorry I'm not there with you right now, Sabina..."

"I've never liked him going there. It's so desolate. And he's too trusting." She's sobbing. "I never liked him driving in the mountains and staying in that old lodge."

"There's much we don't know. I'm hoping you might help with a few details."

"Anything I can." She blows out a long shaky breath, and I can feel her grief and horror.

"When you called him yesterday, what time was it?" I have my notebook and pen ready.

"Midmorning his time."

"Not long after that, a florist appeared at his house with a delivery of five dozen long-stemmed white roses in a hand-painted ceramic vase." I refrain from telling her that it was rigged with explosives. "I'm wondering if you have any idea who might have sent something like that to him?"

"*Scusa?*"

"They were delivered just minutes before I arrived at eleven."

"I do not know and can't imagine. That's very strange. *Morbosa. Non bene.*" She doesn't like the gesture, finding it as morbid as I do. "And Sal told you he had no idea who would they were from?"

"The card had nothing on it but his name." I don't mention that he thought the roses were from me. "When he visited you in Rome several weeks ago, did he mention having concerns about anything or anyone? Did he seem like himself then?"

"No, not really. He was not himself."

"What do you mean?" I ask.

"He said the world is more dangerous than it has ever been and he should redo his will," Sabina explains. "We were having dinner in the Quartiere Coppedè, and I told him I did not wish to discuss anything so depressing while eating a perfect carbonara with a beautiful Abruzzo rosé." Her voice sounds tragic.

"Did he mention anything specific? I know how hard this is. But anything you remember might be helpful, Sabina."

"He was sure someone was following him. He said that since he'd arrived in Rome he kept seeing the same person. First, when he was waiting for a taxi outside Fiumicino Airport. Then the next day when he was walking through the Piazza della Rotonda. And the day after that when he was returning from the Vatican Observatory."

"A man or a woman?" I'm taking notes.

"It was hard to tell." Her voice trembles. "But he thought it was a woman, about my same height and slender, wearing a black baseball cap. He didn't notice her hair and assumed it was very short. She looked to be in her thirties or forties with scars on her face. Each time he saw her she was wearing dark glasses, a long leather coat and the cap."

"When he'd notice her, did he get the sense that she was aware of him?" I envision Carrie Grethen's androgynously pretty face and the scars from our last encounter.

"He wasn't sure if she noticed him but felt she did," Sabina is saying. "He told me he picked up a very bad energy from her."

"And he had no clue who this person might be?"

"He said he didn't, but if something happened to him, to remember how much I mean to him." She can barely talk. "He's all I have, Kay! It's always been just the two of us. What will happen now?"

"I'll make arrangements to send the ashes," I tell her delicately. "Then he can be buried with your family if that's what you wish."

"He would not want that. You know how he felt about our family. He would want to be buried in Alexandria," she sobs. "It's been his home for many years."

"Is there someone you can call? Someone who can come over? I don't want you to be alone."

But she's crying too hard to answer, quickly getting off the phone. My heart hurts as if someone is squeezing it, and I step into the bathroom, closing the door.

* * *

The cargo pants and polo shirt I put on this morning are wilted and clammy. I can't get undressed fast enough, stuffing my clothing into a trash bag liner I find under the sink. Peeling open a bar of soap with *Langley Inn* on the wrapper, I step into the shower.

I close my eyes in the floral-scented steam, scrubbing and shampooing away death and disaster, letting the hot water drum my neck and shoulders. When I'm done, I'm much better. I feel a resolve settling over me as I put on a bathrobe and blow-dry my hair. Sipping my drink, I look at my face in the mirror over the sink. I recognize the hard set of my mouth, the perfectly calm expression, my anger a steady flame that won't waver.

The harm she's done yet again. I realize there's no proof it was Carrie Grethen following Sal in Rome. We can't be sure she's responsible for what's happened to him. But I know what I feel. I probably know what she feels too every time she looks in the mirror just as I'm doing. Using my fingers to comb back my hair, I study my face.

For an instant I see myself as I looked when Sal and I first met. I envision the Kay Scarpetta he fell for, and then the reflection staring back is who I am now. I don't look the same. Yet I feel the same in the important ways. But I'm losing people who should still be here, and she's not finished. I don't want to lose anyone else, and I return to the kitchen, the microwave oven beeping.

"Almost ready." Benton lifts out the cardboard containers, setting them down on the counter.

"It's sounding like someone was following Sal in Rome last month. Yet he didn't say a word to me. Maybe not to anyone except Sabina. The choices we make in life, and here we are." I take a swallow of my drink, feeling a spark of anger toward him.

A part of me wants to yell at Sal. He knew better and should have been more careful. He should have told me. Or Benton. Or someone.

"Choices we don't fully understand at the time. In fact, I'm not sure we understand them at all." Benton wraps his arms around me. "Learning from our mistakes is the circle of life," he says into my hair. "You smell good."

"Air Force shampoo." I pass on the rest of what Sabina said.

"The question is whether someone was really following Sal." Benton opens takeout boxes, steam rising. "And was it Carrie Grethen."

"He wouldn't have noticed her unless she wanted him to. If he saw her scarred face, then that's exactly what she intended."

"To taunt and goad us. To play her games," Benton says. "It's precisely the sort of thing she'd do and has done before."

"I suppose it's possible that Sal just thought he was seeing the same person. Maybe he was mistaken."

"Carrie followed him in Rome and wanted us to know. Plain and simple." Opening a cupboard, Benton finds two plates. "She wants our attention and knows how to get it." He's said this in the past, and the thought is enraging.

"Toying with us. Cat and mouse. Her specialty," I reply as Benton begins serving our dinner.

"Buttermilk fried chicken, fries, and green beans cooked with bacon," he says. "Also, mashed potatoes."

"Very considerate of you to get the diet special." I kiss him.

"By now I think I know what you like after a godawful day."

"You do. More than anyone."

We carry our plates to the table, the curtains drawn in the

window. Sitting down, both of us are ravenous. I tell him about the helicopter ride in terrible weather, and the chain breaking free as we sling-loaded Sal's truck out of the ravine. I describe the large African cat that disappeared in the fog, and what happened when we were leaving in the storm.

"We're lifting off from the parking lot as tornadoes are touching down nearby," I'm saying between bites. "When suddenly the lights, rides and music turned on. Not all of them, of course, because much isn't working anymore. But how could anything at all turn on when the power's been off since the place was shuttered?"

"We've since discovered it was turned back on two weeks ago." Benton twists the cap off a bottle of water.

"Turned back on by whom?"

"The park's original account was reactivated over the internet, the charges invoiced to the owner's credit card."

"Ryder Briley's credit card?" I ask.

"Briley Enterprises specifically."

"And the explanation?" I dip another piece of fried chicken into honey mustard.

"Ryder Briley pleads ignorance, claiming someone must have gotten hold of his company's credit card information. He went on to say that he'd been planning on putting Oz on the market this spring. But now because of the *murder there*, he won't be able to sell it."

"How convenient. Another hefty business loss he can deduct."

"He's claiming that Sal Giordano's death has tanked the property value." Benton sprinkles pepper on a drumstick.

"Do you believe that he's the victim? That he had no idea about the power being turned back on?" I reply as Carrie circles my thoughts.

"Hard to know. But I believe he's in the mix somehow." Benton drops bones into an empty box. "I have a bad feeling he's gotten tangled up with her." He means Carrie. "And no one better at hacking and creating a spectacle."

"The power was turned back on two weeks ago even though there appears to be no work going on. Then suddenly this afternoon, the lights and other things go haywire." I give him the chronology. "Just like things have been going haywire in my office."

I tell Benton about the parking lot's security gate. And the cameras inside the vehicle bay turning on and off for no apparent reason. Also, the elevator is having fits, all of it happening rather much at once.

"Just when I'm certain it's deliberate, I start wondering if I'm paranoid," I explain.

"You're not."

"Do you think she's hacked into my building?"

"It's been five months since she resurfaced, causing her usual mayhem." He tears open a packet of ketchup. "She didn't accomplish what she wanted then, and now she's at it again with a vengeance. While at it, she's having her fun. That's what I think we're going to find out."

"And whatever her ultimate goal, she didn't get started yesterday." I add. "She's been thinking about it for a while."

"That's part of the thrill. Premeditating. Fantasizing in advance." He bites into a buttermilk biscuit, melted butter oozing from it. "Lucy needs to sweep your building for any-thing that might have been planted there," he adds, and I think of the exterminator on top of the tall ladder.

It wasn't the usual person, someone unfamiliar, I'm telling Benton as I get an incredulous feeling. The cargo van parked inside the vehicle bay was white with a logo on the side. The florist's van was white with a bogus logo, and those can be attached with magnets. Plastic signs can be 3-D printed these days.

CHAPTER 24

The next morning, I open my eyes in the dark and wouldn't know where I am if Reveille wasn't playing through outdoor speakers. It's five o'clock, and Benton doesn't stir next to me even as trumpets blare. We stayed up much too late, and agreed there was no rush to hit the road this morning.

I sneak out of bed without disturbing him, the carpet rough beneath my bare feet as Reveille stops. The quiet is restored except for the sound of water running overhead in pipes as other guests stir. Closing the bedroom door after me, I carry my phone into the kitchen. I turn on the lights, filling the coffeemaker's reservoir.

Opening the refrigerator, I inspect our leftovers. Fried chicken and biscuits sound good. The mashed potatoes I can turn into fritters. Not perfect without cheese and onions, but they'll be delicious, and my stomach growls. Wrapping the chicken and biscuits in foil, I begin warming them in the toaster oven.

As coffee brews, I scroll through messages and emails, and have several from Fabian. I'm surprised to learn that he and Faye spent the night in the on-call room inside my building.

Hope you don't mind that we helped ourselves to what's in the fridge, he texted at one A.M.

I wonder what possessed them to have a sleepover, and I answer him, not expecting he'll respond at this hour. But my phone rings right away.

"I hope you're getting enough rest and not drinking so much coffee," I say to Fabian first thing. "Are you feeling better than you were yesterday, I hope?"

"I'll live." His voice is sullen over the phone.

"What's up with you and Faye? Why the need to sleep in the building?" I find a frying pan in the drawer under the oven.

"We worked late and thought we should just hunker down," he says.

"Because...?" I find a spatula.

"Because Luna Briley's body is still here."

"You don't need to babysit." I turn on an electric burner on the stovetop.

"We don't trust what's going on, Doctor Scarpetta. I guess you know what's all over the news." Fabian sounds angry and scared. "The things Ryder Briley's accusing you and me of."

"I know all about it...," I start to say.

"And now a dead body's been found in the Oz theme park he owns. I guarantee he's involved in all of it, and not that it will surprise you? But I've been checking on her medical records, and nowhere is there any indication that she was diabetic."

"I figured as much since there was no insulin at the scene."

"More of their lies," Fabian says. "And bottom line, Faye and I don't feel safe. And that's because we aren't safe. And who's going to protect us? Imagine the people Ryder Briley's got in his pocket, including judges and cops? Imagine if his daughter's body gets stolen..."

"Hopefully we don't have to worry about someone breaking into our building after hours. You shouldn't feel like you need to stay there unless that's your choice." I peel open mini-tubs of butter, and Benton was thoughtful enough to ask for extra. "Teresa should be working security." I'm referring to our most recent hire. "I assume all is quiet now?"

"She's *one* person. And there's only so much any of the security officers can do. Believe me, she appreciates our being here after what happened at three A.M. when the bay door rolled open on its own."

"You've got to be kidding me." I wipe my hands with paper towels.

"I'm as serious as a heart attack," Fabian says. "And nobody was there. Just the empty night. It was spooky, a really bad energy field. And of course, we didn't think to bring any sage with us."

"But the bay door is fine now?" I melt butter in the pan.

"So far. But the elevator is totally screwed up. It's not working at all, and we've gotten several more of the hang-ups from an *out of area* number. It's like someone is sticking pins in our doll."

"Maybe someone is." I tell him it's possible we've been hacked. "That means the building isn't secure, as evidenced by the bay door rolling up in the middle of the night."

"I don't know how you prevent stuff like this anymore."

"It's getting harder." I flatten dollops of mashed potatoes in the sizzling butter.

"When will you and Marino leave wherever you are?" Fabian asks.

"Not sure about him as we've not communicated yet today. But likely I won't be back until this afternoon." I check on the toaster oven.

"I don't guess you're going to tell me what's going on with the ET Whisperer, Sal Giordano, who's all over the news? Obviously, that's what you've been tied up with..."

"The examination is being handled at a military facility," I recite as scripted, flipping the fritters, sprinkling them with salt and pepper.

"So, where are you?"

"In a place where I'm reachable by phone. That's all you need to know." I hear firearms examiner Faye Hanaday saying something in the background.

"Hold a sec," Fabian tells me, and then she's on the line.

"Doctor Scarpetta? Good morning," she begins. "Thanks for letting us stay here. And I'm afraid we polished off the bread and tuna fish."

"It's not an Airbnb but you're welcome anytime. I hope Fabian's not feeling as unsettled as he was yesterday."

"It's this case." Faye lowers her voice. "Luna Briley's hit a real nerve with him. When he was a little kid, the girl next door wandered into his family's yard and drowned in their swimming pool. She was four, and obviously not well looked after."

"I didn't know, and how terrible," I reply.

"You know how Fabian is. He figured way back then that he should have prevented it somehow."

"I understand better than you might imagine," I answer. "What do you have for me, Faye?"

"You'll get the official report soon enough, but I happen to know from Lee about the gunshot residue," she says. "I assume you'd like to hear the results right away? As long as you don't tell him I told you."

*　*　*

The fritters are golden brown, and I place them on a paper-towel-covered plate as Faye explains what happened late yesterday. She says that trace evidence examiner Lee Fishburne analyzed samples with scanning electron microscopy and spectroscopy. The gunshot residue (GSR) swabs from Luna Briley's hands are negative.

"As are ones taken from hair and skin around the entrance wound," Faye informs me. "And her pajama top is negative. But there's other stuff on it that Lee says is unexpected and inexplicable. I can give you the upshot unofficially...?"

"Please." I tear open packets of honey.

"When I walked into his lab, he was analyzing these strange particles that were on Luna Briley's pajama top. I could see them on the video displays, the magnification 500X. They brought to mind microscopic asteroids with chunks of shiny metal attached."

"And their composition?" I arrange pieces of chicken on buttered biscuit halves, dribbling honey over them.

"Made mostly of silica but also magnesium, aluminum, iron and other elements," she replies.

"Sounds a lot like dirt," I reply, and I wouldn't have been aware of it.

I didn't examine Luna's pajamas. When I removed them from her body, they were air-dried in the evidence room. Then they were delivered upstairs to the trace evidence lab for Lee to go over thoroughly.

"Lee has an idea what it might be but won't say until it's confirmed by some expert he contacted," Faye explains. "He told me that when he went over the pajamas with a UV light, the particles fluoresced cobalt blue," she adds to my amazement. "So, what is the stuff and how did it get on her?"

"Her pajamas aren't the only place a sparkling residue like that has shown up," I reply, thinking of the dust lighting up all over Sal's body.

Then images of the Oz theme park flash in my mind. I envision the candy-coated peanuts I recovered from Luna's stomach, and those in the bin at Briley Flight Services. It's as if I'm walking into a spiderweb of threads and connections I feel but can't follow.

"I plan to start doing test fires this morning for distance and trajectory," Faye tells me as I turn off the toaster oven.

"Who else knows about the trace evidence besides Lee, you, Fabian?" Collecting napkins, I take the plastic tray out from under the empty ice bucket.

"I can't say for sure. Fabian and I aren't talking about it with anyone but each other."

"What about Blaise Fruge?"

"It wouldn't be up to me to tell her," Faye replies, and she's right about that.

Moments later, I'm carrying the breakfast tray into the bedroom, and by now Benton is sitting up under the covers. He's wedged two pillows behind his back, looking at his phone, his face illuminated in the near dark. I set a coffee and his plate on the table next to him, explaining what I just learned from Fabian and Faye.

"I agree it's curious about the fluorescing residue." He cuts a fritter with his fork, taking a bite. "Damn that's good." He takes another hungry bite. "We don't know for a fact that the sparkling residue on Luna Briley's pajamas and Sal's body is the same thing. I'm suspicious just like you are, but we don't have enough information yet."

"Whatever's fluorescing cobalt blue is very unusual." I settle on the bed, my plate in my lap. "Everything we're finding out certainly makes me wonder what Ryder Briley is involved in. And we can be sure there will be hell to pay when I decide his daughter's death is a homicide."

"When do you think that will happen?" Benton reaches for his coffee as I devour my biscuit.

"If Faye's test fires tell us what I think they will, then I'll rule on the manner of death." Paper crinkles as I wipe my hands with a napkin. "I'll decide it's a homicide, and the police will have to investigate the parents and anyone else who might have been on the property at the time Luna was shot."

When Benton and I are finished eating, we set our plates on the bedside tables, the rising sun bright around the edges of the draperies. Fighter jets are screaming overhead again, and I don't intend to let him get up just yet. We're not done communicating in the important ways, and I lean against him, lacing my fingers in his.

"While we have a private moment, talk to me. Are you all right?" I ask him. "Because I don't think you are no matter how good you are at pretending."

I know what's bothering him and that he needs to say it. I move closer, resting my head on his chest.

"I'm okay."

"That's not good enough." I hear the thumping of his heart, his skin warm beneath my cheek.

"Maybe I don't like being reminded of other people you've been with," he says into my hair. "Especially him." He means Sal.

"Our summer together was another life ago," I reply. "It seems like someone else."

"But it wasn't someone else."

"I never felt about him the way I've always felt about you, Benton. Probably the reason I was with him was to get away from you."

I remember feeling ruined. We worked together. He was married with children, and I was drawn to him with the pull of a vacuum. I didn't fight it hard enough. Looking back, I don't think I could. I'm not proud of our affair but would do it again if it was the only way to have him.

"And maybe I don't like being reminded of people you've been with either." I stroke his arm. "And that you have an estranged family out there who won't forgive or forget."

"A testament to my inadequacies when it comes to personal relationships," Benton says. "Just ask Connie. She told me often enough."

"You should have divorced her even if I hadn't come along." I kiss him as we hold each other close. "We don't have to be anywhere for a little while, do we?"

CHAPTER 25

An hour later I'm showered and back in the kitchen when Lee Fishburne calls. He has preliminary results of the trace evidence analysis, and I don't let on that Faye already leaked the headlines to me. I know how to act as if hearing something for the first time.

Lee verifies that swabs taken of the Brileys' hands and their clothing are negative for GSR, and I wouldn't be surprised even if Faye hadn't told me earlier. I never expected that Luna was shot at close enough range to have soot and partially burned powder deposited on her. As for her parents, gunshot residue can be washed off, and I suspect that's what they did, assuming one of them pulled the trigger.

"For sure Luna shouldn't have GSR on her hands if she wasn't holding the gun when it fired," I'm saying over the phone as I refill the coffee reservoir. "And I wouldn't expect Ryder and Piper Briley to be positive for GSR either since they had ample time to make sure nothing like that was found on them. I'm betting they washed the clothing they had on or disposed of it somewhere by the time the police got there."

"I wonder about any pictures taken of them earlier that evening that might show they changed their clothes later?" Lee says.

"A good point that you should mention to Investigator Fruge," I suggest. "Based on what I saw when I arrived at the house, Luna had been dead for several hours before the father called nine-one-one."

"What's known as being guilty as sin." Lee's voice is disgusted over the phone. "Their swabs and clothing also were negative for the particles that fluoresce cobalt blue under UV. The residue that was on their daughter's pajama top."

...*Made mostly of silica but also magnesium, aluminum, iron and other elements...*, Faye said to me moments ago.

"And this is where it gets interesting, Kay. The sparkly stuff is a simulant of lunar regolith..."

...*They brought to mind microscopic asteroids...*I hear Faye's voice.

"...In other words, fake moon dust," Lee is telling me in my Bluetooth earpiece. "Microscopically, the simulant particles are more uniform because they're ground up by machines. But the composition is the same, about half of it melted silica sand. Glass, in other words. It's not all that hard to tell simulant from the real thing, but you've got to know what you're looking at."

"Let's make sure I have this straight," I reply. "You're saying that fake moon dust was on Luna's pajamas?"

"It's weird that's her name."

"I'm finding everything about this weird, Lee." I resume loading silverware and plates into the dishwasher.

"We're talking about pulverized volcanic ash, an igneous rock like basalt," Lee continues to explain over the phone as

I start the dishwasher. "It's mined and turned to dust by huge crushers and grinders. Then this is processed and packaged inside cleanrooms."

He goes on to explain that natural moon dust particles are sharply irregular, melted and porous. They're created by meteors smashing into the surface of the moon. Simulated or real, the shards are electrostatically charged, sticking to everything.

"Explaining why the dust is problematic to astronauts and their equipment," Lee is saying. "You sure as hell don't want to track it into your space shuttle or habitat. It's a wonder some of the Apollo guys back in the sixties and seventies didn't have serious respiratory problems."

"You're sure we're dealing with simulated moon dust?" I walk through the living room carrying two coffees. "Possible it might be something else?"

"When I got up this morning I had an email waiting from a friend of mine I contacted late yesterday, a materials scientist at Johnson Space Center. She confirmed that the images and composition of the particles are consistent with a high-grade lunar regolith simulant. The reason it fluoresces under UV is because it's supposed to. Although she said she's never seen a simulant light up cobalt blue. She has no idea who might make it."

"That was my next question," I reply. "Where would someone get fake moon dust?"

"You can order small amounts off the internet. Mainly people do it as a curiosity or they're space geeks. Or they're someone like me who wants to look at it microscopically. You'd be amazed by the stuff I order online that I might never get a chance to examine otherwise. But moon dust simulated or real isn't something you'd give to a child who might inhale it or get it in their eyes."

"Does the simulant one can buy off the internet have a fluorescent additive?" I've returned to the bedroom, Benton in the bathroom with the door shut, the shower running.

"Not any I'm aware of."

"And if you're using it for big scientific projects, I would imagine you're not buying sample sizes off the internet. You're dealing with a commercial lab somewhere."

"There are only a few of them in the country, none in Virginia that I know of," Lee says. "And regolith simulant isn't the sort of thing you create in your hobby shop with a tumbler or a portable grinder. Industrial machinery is involved, and you've got to get the right rocks and minerals from somewhere on this planet."

He explains that the typical moon dust simulant used for scientific research often has a fluorescent additive that glows white. It makes it easier to determine if a spacesuit or piece of electronic equipment is properly sealed. High-quality simulants are pricey, anywhere from ten to thirty dollars per pound depending on where you get it.

"That adds up when buying tons of it to simulate lunar, Martian or asteroid conditions," Lee is saying.

"Can you make any sense of this?" I sit down on the bed, sipping my coffee. "We're talking about a child who didn't go out and play. Luna Briley rarely left the house or had company. She was all but held in solitary confinement." I feel the anger flaring again. "How the hell did she get fake moon dust on her?"

"I'm guessing it was transferred to her pajama top by some-one who had physical contact with her. My question is whether there are other sources of the simulant inside her house."

"I don't know if the entire place was searched with crime lights, but the bedroom and certain other areas definitely were while I was there," I reply. "And nothing fluoresced cobalt blue. Not that I saw or have heard about."

"If there's no trace of it in the house," Lee says, "then it was transferred to Luna by someone who had it on their clothing. That's what I'm guessing."

"And how might that person have been exposed?"

"Anybody who works around it, for example," he says. "A number of aerospace companies and government agencies, including NASA, use regolith simulants, as you might imagine. The real thing is locked up in vaults. Only a small amount of real moon dust and rocks still exist since we were last on the moon more than fifty years ago."

*   *   *

I'm getting off the phone when Benton emerges from the bath-room in a cloud of steam, a towel wrapped around him. He's clean-shaven, his hair damp and combed straight back, his chiseled chest and flat belly covered in a sheen of sweat. I tell him what I'm finding out.

"Christ. I can't say I saw that coming," he says.

"You and me both."

"I can't imagine many uses for fake moon dust beyond the obvious aerospace research," he adds. "For one thing, it's extremely dangerous."

"To everything and everyone," I reply. "Chronic exposure without appropriate protection can cause severe lung damage and death. I'd worry about anyone spending much time around it."

"Our trace evidence lab will confer with yours when appropriate to confirm what Lee told you, and I have no reason to doubt him." Benton is getting dressed in khaki pants, a polo shirt. "We'll find out who's having a simulant like this shipped to them, specifically focusing on anything in this area."

"I suspect that whoever left the microscopic residue on Luna wasn't aware of it and wouldn't have been unless walking under a black light," I reply as Carrie Grethen hovers in my thoughts. "I suppose someone regularly exposed to moon dust, fake or otherwise, could leave it all over the place without realizing it? Or is this more of the same? Another rabbit hole? Another riddle to solve that leads nowhere, Benton?"

"We don't know who left it," he says. "And we don't know the source. But if Carrie's the one transferring this stuff all over the place, I strongly suspect she's none the wiser."

"Then she's made a mistake."

"She may have." Benton ties his shoelaces.

"Or maybe she doesn't care if she's leaving it," I reply. "Or she wants us to find it."

"All of the above are possible, depending on other things going on."

While he's on the phone with other agents, I put on clean cargo pants and a long-sleeved tactical shirt not appropriate for hot weather. But when I last packed the jump-out bag it was winter. My clothes are wrinkled and a bit musty smelling.

I should have hung them up before going to bed but was distracted by my husband and tequila.

I've texted Lucy several times on a secure messaging app, and am just now hearing back. She and other investigators are next door at NASA Langley inside building 1112 examining Sal's pickup truck. I reply that Benton and I will head that way as soon as we check out of our room. Then I pass along what I've learned from Lee Fishburne about the moon dust simulant.

Probably the same thing we're finding all over his truck, Lucy writes back. *You'll see when you get here.*

I ask if she's heard from Marino. I've sent texts and tried to call since early this morning, and he's not responding. She informs me that he rented a car and drove back to Alexandria. No way he was getting on the helicopter again, he told her to tell me. Last they communicated he was at the office, and I send him a message. I tell him that Benton and I are on our way to look at Sal Giordano's pickup truck.

I'm with Faye, Marino answers me right away.

He's inside the firing range with Faye Hanaday, and he sends a video of a white cloth-covered target screeching along a track. Faye has safety glasses and headphones on while testing the Beretta .22 pistol that killed Luna Briley.

BANG! BANG! BANG!

Faye blasts away, ejected cartridge cases clinking. She shoots the target from varying distances with Ryder Briley's gun, firing the same hollow-point ammunition that killed his daughter. Then my "smart" ring vibrates, alerting me that Marino is calling.

"How long are Luna Briley's arms," he asks right off.

"About fourteen inches. As I've mentioned, she was small for her age," I reply, and Benton is off his phone. He sits down on the bed next to me.

"And assuming her arm was bent while she was pointing the pistol at her head, the distance would be even less than ten inches. Half that, maybe," Marino calculates.

"Very possibly."

"No way she shot herself," he says. "Hold on, I'm putting us on speakerphone so Faye can tell you herself."

"I'm not surprised. It's what we thought," she says. "Based on my test fires and absence of GSR on the victim, I'd estimate the shooter was three to five feet away from her. Luna Briley couldn't have been holding the gun, end of story."

I tell Marino to let Blaise Fruge know immediately that I'm finalizing the manner of death as a homicide.

"The Brileys will go ballistic," he says, unaware of the pun. "You'd better be looking over your shoulder, Doc."

"I make a habit of it anyway," I reply.

*   *   *

It's after eleven as Benton and I drive away from the Langley Inn, the morning bright and warm, the blue sky scrubbed by yesterday's storms. We follow Sweeney Boulevard around the north end of the Air Force runway as F-22s tear up the sky.

In the past several years I've noticed stepped-up activity around Virginia military bases, more fighter jets doing maneuvers day and night. When I visit my Tidewater office, I see more battleships and nuclear submarines in and out of the Norfolk Naval Station, the largest in the world.

The constant roaring and screaming overhead sounds like an invasion as we take Commander Shepard Boulevard past a sprawling mobile home park. Nearby is a run-down bar with a purple film covering the windows, a place to be avoided, I've been told in the past. Across from a motor speedway is NASA Langley Research Center, its large-scale wind tunnel stretching along the roadside like a giant white Slinky.

A blue globe sculpture of the NASA "meatball" logo rises from a circle of grass in front of the entrance. Over the main gate a digital sign welcomes visitors, which strikes me as ironic when protective services officers are armed with submachine guns. Several of them have pulled over a truck, searching it with a dog. A driver in a Prius is being questioned while his backseat is gone through.

Benton rolls down his window, and it's obvious that we're expected, no visit to the Badge & Pass office needed. A quick look at our IDs and we're given directions for where we're going.

"As you get closer to the gantry, you'll see the hangars. Have a nice day." The officer steps back from our car.

We drive through the middle of the campus, passing through a cluster of white vacuum spheres with steam billowing around them. Numbered buildings are brick and modern, others dreary precast dating back to the beginning of the space administration. Names describe the work that goes on. The Hypersonic Facilities. The Autonomous Incubator. The Sonic Boom Lab.

The farther we go from the center of the campus, the more isolated and mysterious the facilities. We wind through acres of open fields and woods, antennas of all shapes and sizes standing sentry. As we near the gantry looming above the trees, we begin to see a series of silvery hangars of varying sizes. There's no signage, only numbers, and I notice NASA protective services black Tahoe SUVs patrolling the area.

Beyond a drone test range enclosed in netting is hangar 1112, concrete and windowless with a flat roof and a metal retractable door that's closed. Benton parks near other SUVs and several crime scene vans. I text Lucy that we're here, and in seconds she emerges from a side pedestrian door. Covered in white Tyvek, she hands us folded PPE. Her eyes are tired, and I wonder if she got any sleep last night.

"How's it going?" I balance on one foot at a time, pulling on booties. "Any updates?"

"The team's been at it for hours, and we've found a few curiosities. Impressions left on glass that don't make any sense," she says as Benton and I cover up with protective gowns. "They look sort of like handprints. But not normal hands. A combination of mitten and clawlike is the best I can describe it."

As she tells us this I can imagine Marino's reaction if he were here, and I'm glad he's not. He'd resume harping about the crop circle and so-called alien abductions. The older he gets, the stronger his convictions, and I don't look forward to telling him about the simulated moon dust. He'll put two and two together and come up with the wrong number.

CHAPTER 26

Lucy opens the side door and we step inside a concrete space not so different from my offices' vehicle bays. But this is brightly lit and spotless with workbenches, tool cabinets, a hydraulic lift and multiple utility carts. Shadows of tire tracks crisscross the shiny concrete flooring, not a speck of dirt, the hangar more like a laboratory cleanroom than a large garage.

Crime scene investigators in white are taking down the translucent plastic tent shrouding Sal's blue Chevy truck. I detect the sharp odor of superglue used to fume for latent prints left on nonporous surfaces such as glass and metal. The cyano-acrylate vapors react to amino acids secreted by skin surfaces such as finger pads. The prints turn whitish and hard, the ridge detail permanently set in glue and readily visible.

"Before we fumed the truck, we went over it inside and out, making sure we didn't glue something we shouldn't." Lucy continues, explaining what's been done. "We found the odd impressions on the front door windows, most of them partials. We lifted them with magnetic powder, and a picture's worth a thousand words."

We follow her to a workbench where evidence has been bagged and labeled. Mostly, what's been collected is from the seats and carpet.

"Under UV, there's glittery stuff all over the driver's seat, the steering wheel and other areas, including inside the covered truck bed." She's typing a password on a laptop computer that's open on the workbench. "I'm not saying it's the same thing that fluoresced on Sal Giordano's body. But it certainly looks the same."

Lucy shows us photographs taken with an orange-tinted filter, clicking through images of the residue sparkling cobalt blue in the fabric of the truck's front seats. The inside of the covered truck bed sparkles like a galaxy.

"Why in both seats?" I ask. "As if two people were sitting up front and had this residue on their clothing?"

"Unless it was already inside the truck."

"You mean if Sal was transferring it in and out himself." It's a startling thought.

"We can't be sure how long the residue has been there," Benton says. "If it's fake moon dust? What was he doing with it? Was he doing research? And if so, where?"

"He never mentioned regolith simulants to me," I reply. "And most people don't want a hazardous material like that around. It needs to be stored and worked with in a controlled environment."

"Whatever he might have been doing behind the scenes, he wasn't doing it for us." Lucy means the U.S. government. "Or we'd know about it." She shows us another photograph.

This one is of a smudge about the size of my hand but

nothing like it. The somewhat V-shaped impression is long and slender like a hoof. Or possibly a mitten with vague, irregular fingerlike shapes inside it. Yes, somewhat clawlike, and reminding me of a Rorschach ink blot, actually. I see no suggestion of the friction ridge detail associated with skin, and I'm baffled.

"This was on the outside of the driver's window," Lucy explains.

"Made by what? Do we have an idea?" Benton's shoulder is pressed against me as we stare at the image on the laptop computer. "It doesn't look like an impression of any type of glove I've ever seen."

"Not anything I've ever seen, either," Lucy replies. "And it's not the only one we found."

Lucy walks away from the workbench, and we follow her to Sal's pickup truck. Utility carts are parked around it, and the tent is gone.

"What about the sparkling residue?" Benton asks. "Was any of that associated with these impressions?"

"Not a lot of it," Lucy says, and I pass along what Lee Fishburne told me about moon dust.

"Not the real thing but a simulant that has a fluorescent additive causing it to glow cobalt blue under UV light," I explain. "And what that was doing on Luna Briley's pajama top is anybody's guess. We'll find out soon enough if this same residue was on Sal Giordano's body and is inside his truck."

"I have a feeling it will be," Benton replies. "Not too many things fluoresce cobalt blue or at all."

"The deaths are connected, and it's more than a feeling," Lucy says flatly. "What's happened to Luna Briley and Sal

Giordano is related for some reason. That doesn't mean the same person killed them."

"The same person didn't," Benton says. "His death was calculated and carefully planned. I don't believe hers was."

On a cart are crime lights and pairs of tinted goggles that Lucy hands out to us. We put on gloves, hair covers and face masks. She calls for someone to cut the lights directly overhead. We begin painting our UV lights over the truck, starting with the driver's window. The clean rectangular shape in the middle of it is from the lifting tape, we're told.

Also on the glass is a constellation of the pinprick cobalt-blue sparkles. I find more of them on the driver's door handles inside and out. Even as I'm looking I'm invaded by memories of riding in this very truck with Sal to meetings at the White House, the Pentagon and other official places. I often joked that we looked like Ma and Pa Kettle making a visit to the big city.

I slowly circle the familiar old Chevy with its mangled chrome bumpers and shattered square headlights. The residue glitters near the tailgate handle, and there's a scant spattering of sparkles on the outer front passenger door handle. But not on the interior one.

"Possibly suggesting the passenger door was opened and closed from the outside." Benton paints his light over it. "Possibly Sal was incapacitated and placed in the passenger's seat. Maybe the seat belts were fastened so the alarm didn't chime while Sal was driven somewhere. Assuming the truck had an alarm as old as it was?"

"It's possible, alarm or not. What we're talking about is a habit, something one does without thinking," Lucy says, shadowing us.

"But his truck went off the mountain," I remind them.

"Before it did, someone took the time to remove everything from inside it," Benton says. "It's possible Sal was abducted in his own truck, and then transferred into a different vehicle that was parked out of sight nearby. Finally, the truck was sent off the mountain into the ravine."

"Now that we've been able to look inside and under the hood, we know that at the time of the crash, the gearshift was in neutral with the engine running." Lucy continues making comments from the shadowy sidelines. "In something old like this you could shut the doors and lock them from the outside while the key's in the ignition."

"I've known Sal to do that accidentally a number of times," I reply. "Do we have any idea how much gas was in the tank at the time of the crash?"

"Nope," Lucy says, the overhead lights turning back on. "It continued running until it was out of gas, but we can't know how long that took. Diesel engines don't have sparkplugs. They don't emit electric signals that flash on radio telescopes and various sensors. His truck could have been running in the ravine for hours and it wasn't going to be detected by anything."

"And you found nothing inside it?" I ask, envisioning the gift basket I carefully put together for Sal.

"Even the glove box was cleaned out," Lucy says.

We remove our tinted goggles, placing them back on the cart.

"Why take everything?" I ask them. "What was someone looking for?"

"Anything that might be there," Benton says. "And the person didn't want to spend a lot of time in the pitch dark going through the truck while trying to manage a hostage. And perhaps worrying about another motorist rolling up while all this is going on. Even if Sal was drugged and manageable, better to grab everything out of the truck. Then go through it later when you get where you're going."

"Makes sense...," Lucy starts to say. "Hold on." She must see something in her "smart" glasses.

She steps away to make a call, her back to us as she paces. I can't hear what she's saying but know from her body language that the news isn't good. She's walking in fast small circles, pushing back her hair the way she does when frustrated.

"What's happened now? What next?" I say to Benton as he scrolls through red-flagged alerts landing on his phone.

"A small aircraft just crashed not too far from here," he says as I watch Lucy talking and gesturing. "Off the shore of Fort Monroe..."

*   *   *

Dana Diletti's helicopter has gone down into the Chesapeake Bay twelve miles from where we are at NASA Langley. Rescuers are on the way but it's not sounding hopeful. Benton tells me what he's seeing in emergency alerts.

I remember from the news that the celebrity TV journalist was supposed to film at Berkeley Plantation this morning for Virginia's Historic Garden Week. Anybody paying attention would be aware of what she was doing and when. I watch Lucy as she gets off the phone and stops pacing not far from Sal's pickup truck, investigators covering it in white plastic.

They'll use heat guns to shrink-wrap it like a boat stored for the winter. I wonder what will happen after they have no further use for the old Chevy that Sal had as long as I've known him. Maybe it will be crushed into a cube. Or sold for parts. Or someone ghoulish will try to buy it.

"You've heard what's going on?" Lucy asks as she trots back to Benton and me.

"We know about Dana Diletti's helicopter but nothing more," he tells her.

"Who was on board?" I ask.

"Bret Jones, one of several pilots she uses. I've seen him around and he was always nice enough. But I didn't know him," Lucy explains. "He landed at Berkeley Plantation to drop off Dana and three members of her crew. The plan was for him to head to Newport News. He'd refuel and wait until they were done filming."

It appears he was the only one on board, but that hasn't been confirmed yet, she goes on to say. His last radio call was fifteen miles northwest of the Newport News-Williamsburg International Airport. At 11:10 A.M. he contacted the tower, saying that he was inbound for landing. He was told to radio back when he was five miles out. He didn't do that or call the UNICOM at the private terminal to request fuel and parking.

Entering the Class C airspace without clearance, he didn't answer repeated radio calls. The airport declared an emergency, halting all traffic as F-16 fighter jets were scrambled to intercept the small white helicopter. It continued on the same southeast heading at an altitude of twelve hundred feet, overflying shopping malls, crowded neighborhoods, a hospital.

"Had it gone down over land, it could have killed a lot of people," I reply.

"I suspect that was the intention," Benton says.

"Obviously, it was on autopilot," Lucy continues. "When the F-16s flew close enough for the pilots to see inside the cockpit, they reported that Bret Jones was slumped forward in the right seat either unconscious or dead. It didn't seem that anyone else was on board, and there was nothing to be done except wait for the inevitable."

"I have a feeling you may be here for a while." Benton says this to me.

"That's how it's looking," I reply. "I'm disappointed I won't be riding home with you."

"It will be very lonely." He smiles into my eyes. "Most of all be safe and stay out of trouble."

"Don't worry. Tron and I will take good care of her," Lucy promises.

"I'm not so sure." He puts on his sunglasses. "I don't trust it when the three of you are together."

We walk out of hangar 1112 and into the noon glare. I hug and kiss Benton goodbye for now. I'll see him tonight if not sooner, I promise as Tron roars up in a black Dodge Charger.

"Did someone call Uber?" She jumps out, folding down her seat so I can squeeze in back.

"Jesus. What have you got in this thing? An anvil?" I haul a heavy tactical backpack out of my way.

"Field glasses. A spectrum analyzer. And other surprises. Just like Cracker Jack." It's Lucy who answers.

She drops her own heavy backpack on the floor in front of the passenger seat, climbing in.

"You know the Boy Scout motto. Be prepared." Tron slides behind the wheel.

"Also the Girl Scout motto, just so you know." The seat is so low I feel I'm sitting on the ground, the engine shaking my bones.

"I didn't know you were a Girl Scout once." Lucy directs this at me.

"I wasn't. Or a Brownie and never earned a single merit badge, I'm sorry to report." I look out the window at Benton driving away in his black Tesla.

"Well, I was a Girl Scout while wanting to be an Eagle Scout before girls got to do fun shit like that," Tron says to the percussion of their doors shutting. She turns up the fan.

"Speaking of fun. Where did we manage to borrow this beauty?" My knees are touching the back of her seat.

"Our Norfolk field office." Tron shifts the car into reverse, scanning her mirrors. "I've been running around since oh-dark-hundred delivering evidence, including to your place." She makes a NASCAR-worthy U-turn, and I bump my head against the window.

"I'll make sure the labs know to get started immediately." I rub my temple as we rumble out of the parking lot.

"And while I was making deliveries in your building, I dropped off the ashes," Tron says to me in a gentler tone, the reminder jolting, emotions swelling in my throat. "Wyatt was starting his shift and promised to put them in your office."

"That was thoughtful of you."

"I took special care packing them up in a cardboard urn with lots of bubble wrap."

"Thank you." I look out at other hangars tucked in the woods as images flash.

...Flames licking over melting plastic...Pink skin and gray hair showing through...

CHAPTER 27

"S till no sign of the pilot," Lucy says as we drive through the back of the NASA campus. "Long before now he should have egressed the cockpit. He should be floating on the surface with his life vest inflated. Assuming he was wearing one. And he might not have been if he wasn't planning on flying over wide stretches of water."

As she describes the perils of extricating oneself from a submerged helicopter, I find the number for my Tidewater district deputy chief. I inform Rena Peace that I'm twenty minutes from Fort Monroe responding to a helicopter crash with what appears to be one fatality.

"We've gotten no notifications from the police," she replies, surprised.

"You will soon enough unless by some miracle the pilot survives."

"And I didn't know you were in the area," she says. "I would have asked you to drop by for coffee. Or drinks better yet if you're staying over."

"Another time. We've got a sensitive situation, Rena."

I explain that we can expect sensational news coverage

about the crash since Dana Diletti could have been on board. She'll milk that for all it's worth, I have no doubt.

"And we're not sure that this isn't connected to other things going on." I'm careful what I say.

"Are the police suspicious of foul play?" Rena asks, and it's hard to hear inside the Secret Service muscle car.

"It's too early to say," I answer. "In light of other things, one has to wonder."

"I saw the piece Dana Diletti did on Ryder Briley last night. She all but came out and said he murdered his child."

"And he very well might have," I reply.

"She drops that bombshell? Then this morning her helicopter crashes? Interesting timing."

"That seems to be a pattern when Ryder Briley's involved. Bad things happen to people who cross him. We'll have to see what caused the crash."

"Do you plan to handle the body recovery?" she asks.

"Fred's at a meeting in San Diego, and I happen to be here on business unexpectedly," I reply. "So it makes the most sense."

Her forensic pathologist husband is one of my medical examiners, and also a master diver and a boat captain. Fred often works underwater recoveries with the police, and we've been diving together in the past on cases.

"He'll be most unhappy that you're here and he's not," Rena says.

"Once the body gets to your office, I'll trust you to handle it from there," I explain. "The biggest question is what incapacitated the pilot while he was flying, and was he dead before the crash. We'll want a rush on toxicology."

"You always want a rush on everything," she says with a smile in her tone.

"An extra rush on it, then."

"Who's in charge of the investigation? Who should I expect to hear from?"

"The Secret Service," I reply as Tron blows through a yellow light. "I'm with them now. I need one of your vans to meet us at the Old Point Comfort Marina in Fort Monroe as soon as possible."

"Nathan's just getting back from a suspected overdose. He'll leave right away."

"Make sure he brings underwater body bags. More than one to be on the safe side," I reply. "They have to be on the boat with me. It's believed the pilot was the only one on board, but we can't be sure until we reach the wreckage."

When I'm off the phone, I ask Lucy and Tron how we're supposed to manage. I've been scuba diving most of my adult life and worked numerous underwater scenes in Virginia and other places. But my dive bag is at home. I don't have a swimsuit with me. I prefer not wearing my skivvies under a wetsuit, and no way I'm going commando.

"Not a problem. We can fix you right up." Tron weaves in and out of traffic as if escaping a fire. "Agents from our Norfolk office will supply the dive gear. And we always have extra bike shorts with us."

"Lucy and I don't wear the same size shorts," I reply. "But thanks for thinking we might."

"Mine should fit you fine," Tron offers.

"We can't help you with a sports bra, though," Lucy adds, and it's true they can't.

We don't wear the same size, and fortunately, I'm wearing one under my polo shirt. After that I'll have to figure things out as I go along.

"Hampton police divers are getting the boat ready at the marina in Fort Monroe, and a sky crane is being mobilized out of Norfolk." Lucy gives us the latest updates as information appears in the lenses of her glasses. "Rescue boats are looking for any sign of survivors. Nothing so far, but the wreckage has been located on sonar."

She says that witnesses claim the helicopter flew over Fort Monroe, and all seemed normal until it was beyond the beach and well offshore. Then the engine started sputtering. The helicopter began losing altitude, plunging nose-first into the bay dangerously close to several sailboats.

"The people on board reported that the pop-up floats on the skids weren't deployed," Lucy explains. "They said the helicopter filled with water, disappearing below the surface within minutes."

"If people heard the engine sputtering, that doesn't sound like an autopilot problem," I point out. "And if Bret Jones was unconscious, how could he have disengaged it?"

"Maybe it malfunctioned?" Lucy says dubiously. "But the sputtering makes me wonder if the engine flamed out for some reason. That's the more likely scenario, explaining why the helicopter suddenly dropped out of the sky."

"Could he have run out of fuel?" I ask.

"Not unless he didn't start out with a full tank, and he wouldn't be that stupid."

"As Doctor Peace just pointed out, Dana Diletti aired a big story about Ryder Briley last night that all but suggests he's a murderer," I say to them. "Now suddenly, her chopper's down, and it's just lucky for her that she wasn't in it."

"She and her crew have got to be thinking about that right about now," Tron says, her eyes constantly scanning the mirrors. "They've got to be realizing they could be fish food on the bottom of the Chesapeake Bay."

"Where did the news station keep the helicopter?" I ask.

"She uses the same terminal we fly out of at Washington National, Briley Flight Services," Lucy says as my suspicions continue to gather.

I envision the cameras in the ceiling, and the bin of candy-coated peanuts. Bret Jones and his passengers were there often when flying on assignment. Everything they did and said was recorded.

*　*　*

"It would be interesting to know who else might have been around while they were there this morning," I suggest as Tron guns the muscle car along East Mercury Boulevard, crossing Mill Creek.

She has the grille lights strobing, slaloming past other cars like an Olympic skier, some of them pulling over. Beyond a golf course, she floors it through another yellow light as we near the Chesapeake Bay.

"It would be helpful to see video of the pilot while he was inside the terminal. Was he acting unusually? What can we find out about his medical history?" I'm glancing at a text from Rena Peace telling me the van from her office is fifteen minutes away.

"Was he depressed, maybe suicidal, for example?" Tron picks up the thought. "You know, he drops off everybody and then crashes into the bay on purpose."

"It's happened before. But I have a feeling that's not what we're dealing with," Lucy says, and I sense who's in her thoughts.

We're conditioned to expect that Carrie Grethen is behind every horrible thing that happens. I realize it's not rational. But we may as well talk about it.

"What would be her reason?" I come right out and ask.

"She probably has more than one," Lucy says. "Including luring us into something."

"If she's tied in with Ryder Briley, then it very well could have been an attempted hit on Dana Diletti," Tron suggests as we near our destination.

The sky is empty and bright over the deep blue water of the bay on our left. People are sunbathing on the sandy strip of Outlook Beach, others strolling and jogging along the board-walk. They stare at the emergency lights flashing about a mile offshore where boats have gathered while a Coast Guard heli-copter searches.

We drive past the massive stone walls of the Fort Monroe former military installation, now an upscale residential com-munity with acres of hiking trails and parks. Crumbling bat-teries, cannon emplacements, the moat go back to the early 1800s when the hexagonal fortress was constructed to protect the Chesapeake Bay from enemy ships.

We pass street after street of brick apartments that were barracks, the writer Edgar Allan Poe famously staying in one when he was stationed here. He would have lived in a cramped brick room with creaking wooden floors and a fireplace casting shadows after dark. No doubt it fed his spooky imagination.

Tree-shaded mansions now turned into condos have sweeping views of the bay, the distant shore of Norfolk a sliver on the horizon. I imagine generals back in the day standing on their grand front porches looking out at battleships and submarines offshore. Long before that it would have been frigates in full sail and men at the oars of barges.

An abandoned airstrip is off to our left, then the Old Point Comfort lighthouse looms ahead, bright white in the sun. Across from the marina on a grassy knoll is the Hampton police department's redbrick marine unit. Tron slows down, a paved lane leading around to the back of the one-story building. The parking lot is practically empty, just an SUV, a van and a Zodiac boat on a trailer.

"We've been given permission to change here, and I'm leaving the car so no one will mess with it." Tron stops near the back door. "Most of the officers are out in boats at the crash site or doing other things related. So there shouldn't be anybody much around."

The building dates back to an earlier century and is in poor repair, the paint peeling on white window frames, the gray slate roof missing tiles. An air conditioner rattles loudly from a window with a cracked pane of glass, and the boxwoods flanking the back door haven't been trimmed in years, I'm guessing.

Tron rings the buzzer, and we're let in by a woman on crutches, one foot in a cast, the other in a rubber Birkenstock. Dressed in tactical shorts and a baggy Tommy Bahama shirt, she has a lot of sun damage for someone her age. In her twenties, I estimate. Not much more than that. A chatterbox with a chip on her shoulder, and I often forget that local police tend to resent the feds.

"You can see why I'm not out in the boat with everyone else," she's saying boisterously, and I can tell by her accent that she was born and raised around here. "Never fails when something big goes down."

We follow her through metal desks arranged with laptop computers and video displays, the chairs parked haphazardly as if officers left in a hurry. A workbench is cluttered with dive computers, regulators, a speargun and a takeout fish sandwich partially eaten.

"I know you're not supposed to wish for things to crash, right?" Only she pronounces it *cresh*. "But when it happens in the water I want to be there. Anyway, I'm Sergeant Walker. You can call me Dixie. As in *that Dixie Chick*. Go ahead and make the joke. Everyone else does."

She swings herself along a hallway as we follow. I can tell she's been in the cast for a while, the leg muscles atrophied.

"What did you do to yourself?" I ask her.

"Shark attack."

"This isn't a good time to hear that," Tron complains.

"I hope it wasn't in the bay," Lucy adds.

"There are sharks in there for sure, don't let anyone tell you otherwise," Dixie says with all seriousness. "Supposedly even an alligator now and then, but I've not seen one of those. I tell everyone a shark got me just to see the look on their face. Truth is, I slipped while walking my boyfriend's dog. Busted my ankle in two places and tore my Achilles. He wasn't worth it, either. The boyfriend, not the dog."

She stops at the locker room, opening the door for us. It's little more than a bathroom tiled and painted institutional green. Inside are four metal lockers, a toilet stall and a shower. Sunlight seeps through the slats of the dusty Venetian blinds in the only window. On a shelf next to the sink are a blow dryer, a hairbrush, a large bottle of baby powder.

"Give me a holler if y'all need anything else. I'll be in the kitchen eating lunch," Dixie says as we set down our bags. "Maybe next time, I'll go down with you. I know where some of the old shipwrecks are."

"You don't really see sharks in the bay." Tron is back to that.

"All the time." Dixie nods her head. "The bull sharks are the worst, aggressive as hell and can swim up rivers."

"That's not really true." Tron laughs uneasily.

"It's true," Lucy answers as Dixie swings back down the hallway on her crutches.

"Shit." Tron digs inside her backpack. "I'm one of those who saw *Jaws* and never got over it."

"What's to get over? Shark attacks really happen," Lucy says. "I won't swim in the ocean."

"Yet you don't mind diving," Tron points out.

"Down there it's a level playing field because I can see what I'm doing."

"It's not a level playing field," I remind them. "We don't live there."

As they continue to discuss sharks and other things that can kill you while diving, Tron tosses me a pair of stretchy bike shorts. Not keen on stripping in front of others, I disappear into the stall. Sitting on the closed toilet lid, I take off everything except my sports bra.

The shorts fit like a second skin, and I stand up to shimmy into them. They have padding I could do without when I check myself in the mirror. I emerge from the stall to find Lucy and Tron dressed the same. But I sure as hell don't look the way they do.

"You're smokin' hot." Tron grins, sensing my insecurities. "Seriously." Giving me a thumbs-up.

"You'd flunk the polygraph," I reply as we pack up the clothes we had on earlier.

CHAPTER 28

O utside the sun is hot, the wind a cool whisper that barely
stirs the trees. Pink and white dogwood petals litter the
grass and pavement, the air fragrant with the lemony scent of
magnolias. It's a good day for diving but the problem will be
the visibility, never decent in the bay to begin with.

After yesterday's storm, a lot of silt will be stirred up. Hopefully, the winds will stay calm and we won't be fighting waves
and the currents. Our feet thump along the marina's long pier,
and I'm conscious of how I must look in bike shorts, a sports
bra and tactical boots, all black. Lucy and Tron walk in front
of me, and I'm reminded that I need to spend more time in the
gym.

I stare at the definition in their arms and backs. And the
way their calf muscles clench as they move, things flexing,
nothing jiggling, their every movement effortless. Nearby, people eating lunch at the Deadrise restaurant are watching from
the covered upper deck. Some are looking out at the emergency
lights, pointing and taking video with their phones.

The windowless black van from my Norfolk office is parked
with the flashers on in front of the marina. Nathan the death

investigator rolls down his window, assuring me that what I need is on board.

"I'll be waiting right here," he promises.

Our boat is the *Sea Hunter,* a thirty-footer with a wide dive platform, racks for scuba tanks and twin five-hundred-horsepower outboard engines. Two police divers are waiting in swim trunks and T-shirts. They introduce themselves as Liam and Henry while handing out dive gear the Secret Service agents dropped off a little while ago.

"I'll be leading you down," Liam informs us, about my age I estimate, bearded, with friendly eyes. "Henry will stay on the boat with the captain, ready to assist with the body bags and whatever else is needed."

"Also, keeping a lookout for other vessels coming through," says Henry, rail thin and tan, with a nice smile. "The biggest worry is military ships and subs. They don't publicize their schedules for when they're in and out of the naval station or doing maneuvers. We're not going to know most of what they're doing, for obvious reasons."

"We'll hope nothing major comes through," Liam adds. "But we can't guarantee it, and whatever it is? It has the right of way."

"They won't even slow down, don't care a flip about us, assuming they even see us," Henry echoes. "It's up to us to stay clear."

On that happy note, Lucy, Tron and I sit down on the aluminum bench seats, taking off our boots. We pull on three-millimeter-thick wetsuits, helping each other with the back zippers. The outboard engines begin chugging, and soon we're speeding away from the shore, skimming over the light chop, the bow rising and falling more rapidly the faster we go.

We clean our masks with baby shampoo, rinsing them in a plastic barrel of fresh water. My borrowed mask is heavier than I'd like because of the small camera mounted on it. I make sure everything fits properly and that the lenses aren't going to fog up. Seeing will be hard enough without that added problem.

"The plan is for the three of us to get the body to the surface and into the boat," Lucy says to us. "Then we'll let the Coast Guard and others deal with raising the wreckage. I think we're in agreement? We won't be able to chat underwater so I'm making sure we understand each other."

"Nobody touches the body but us," I confirm. "And it will be me who gets him out before anything inside the cockpit is disturbed."

A battleship cuts sharply into the blue horizon, slowly making its way to the Norfolk Naval Station. I'm reminded that where the helicopter went down is in the shipping channel, and I think about Henry's warning. The police can't secure the scene above or below water. Our law enforcement and forensic concerns are of no relevance to an attack submarine armed with torpedoes.

We're closing in on the police boats and Coast Guard cutter where debris from the helicopter drifts on the water. I can make out what looks like blue strips of cabin liner and a blue seat pillow. Lucy and Tron continue to talk, and I can feel their eyes on me as I carefully get up from the bench. The boat rocks up and down, leaving a frothy wake, an American flag whipping from a railing.

"Need some help?" It's Tron asking.

"No thanks."

I feel as if I'm standing on a seesaw, lifting a bright yellow aluminum tank out of a rack.

"You sure?" Lucy is on her feet.

"I've got it."

Making my way back to the bench seat, I strap the tank to the back of my buoyancy control vest as Lucy and Tron finish getting ready. I'm attaching the regulator hoses as the boat begins slowing down, the police diver named Liam making his way toward us from the cockpit, zipping up his wetsuit.

"The water's pretty murky," he announces over the noise of the engines, throwing on his tank as easily as a sweater. "Best thing is to follow the anchor line at all times. Plus, the current can be deceptively strong even when it's calm like it is right now. But that won't last as the wind picks up, and you don't want to be swimming against the current or pushed off course."

I sit down on the bench seat to put on my fins, strapping a sheathed knife around my left ankle in case I'm entangled in something. Working my arms into the vest attached to the tank, I adjust the straps to fit snugly. I stand up feeling the pull of fifty pounds on my back, and it's a challenge keeping my balance in fins on a moving boat.

"I'll lead us to where sonar shows the wreckage on the bottom about a hundred feet down," Liam continues his briefing.

Steadying myself with a rail, I check the dive computer on my regulator and the one strapped around my wrist. Both read that I've got a full tank.

"And hopefully it's reassuring to know that I grew up

diving for oysters in the bay," Liam is saying. "I know my way around. Sometime we should go when I can show you the cool stuff."

"Are there really sharks?" Tron won't let it go, reminding me a bit of Marino right now.

"Oh yeah. You might see one today."

"Something to look forward to," I mutter.

"For the most part they don't want to mess with us any more than we want to mess with them," he says.

"Oldest story in the book," I add.

"*For the most part* isn't good enough," Tron replies. "I don't want to have to shoot anything, but I will."

"Blood in the water, and we'll have even more sharks," is Liam's answer. "Lucy and Tron will buddy up. And Doctor Scarpetta, you and I are dive buddies."

We attach rolled-up salvage and collection bags, and flashlights to D-rings on our vests. I tuck folded plastic garbage bags inside one of my wetsuit's thigh pockets, and set up my dive computers while Tron and Lucy put on tactical nylon belts. They holster Heckler & Koch P11 underwater guns that fire flechettes, or metal darts, instead of bullets.

Henry drops the anchor, attaching a dive float to it while the captain cuts the idling engines. He places the folded bright yellow body bag out of the way on the wide dive platform, and we step down to it. The metal ladder is off to the side well away from the powerful outboard motors. Just beyond is the red dive float connected to the anchor line.

"Since nobody's been down yet," Liam says, "we don't know exactly how close we are to the helicopter. We may have to swim a little way once we're on the bottom. But based on what we're seeing on sonar, we'll be in the right ballpark."

He clips a lanyard to the handles of an underwater camera, looping the cord over his shoulder. Pulling his mask over his eyes, he places the regulator in his mouth, covering it with one hand. With the other he protects his hoses and dive computer, stabilizing the camera close against his side. Striding off the back of the boat, he splashes down, bobbing in the water, inflating his vest.

Tron and Lucy are next, and then it's my turn. Putting on my mask and making sure the seal is tight, I turn on the mounted camera. I take a big step off the platform, splashing down, the water cold against my face. Pressing the inflator button, I add air to my vest, peering through the water-dotted lenses of my mask. Using my snorkel to conserve the air in my tank, I swim to the dive float, joining the others.

"I'll go down the anchor line first," Liam tell us. "Doctor Scarpetta will be right behind me at all times. Once we locate the helicopter, how do you want to handle it?"

He's asking me this, and I explain that I can't know what I'll do until we get there. It's important that nothing is disturbed before I see it while filming everything we do. Regulators back in our mouths, we release air from our vests in loud hisses. Liam's head slips below the surface in a froth of bubbles. I'm right behind him, sunlight filtering through the water.

*   *   *

Following the yellow nylon anchor line feet first, I pause every few seconds to pinch my nose and blow, clearing my ears. I have my knees hiked up, careful not to kick Liam with my fins. I make my way down hand over fist to the sound of my rhythmic breathing and loud clinking bubbles. As we descend, suspended silt shines like gold flecks. The light dims, and I keep a check on my dive computers.

When we're forty feet down, I can see Liam below me but nothing below him, and I clear my ears again as the water pressure builds. A small school of striped bass shadow by, vanishing in the murk. A loggerhead turtle paddles close, giving me a bug-eyed smile. Seconds later I catch the vague shape of something much bigger zigzagging languidly the way sharks move.

Oh God.

I continue glancing up at Lucy and Tron, and at sixty feet they're no longer backlit by the sun. It's as if we're in an eclipse, and I search for the sharklike shadow again, seeing no sign of it. Eighty feet down it's as dark as dusk, the temperature hovering at fifty degrees Fahrenheit. I can feel the chill through my wetsuit as we reach the sandy bottom, turning on our flashlights, careful not to shine them in each other's eyes.

We illuminate the anchor half buried in sand, the chain tied to the nylon rope stretching up and disappearing in the gloom. Following Liam, we stay in sight of each other at all times, bubbles boiling up, giving the OK sign every so often. We fan out our fins gently to the sides, swimming froglike, stirring up the bottom as little as possible.

Our lights paint over rippled sand scattered with barnacle-covered rocks and old oyster shells polished white, a horseshoe crab lumbering along like an armored vehicle. I illuminate a green glass Fresca bottle, and the partially buried wooden keel of a boat that sank long ago. We glide over several truck tires, a triggerfish swimming by flat and leathery gray with lips pursed, showing its snaggly teeth before flashing off.

A rusty anchor is entangled with fishing line that moves in the current, and an oyster bed covered in silt looks like a pile of tarnished coins. Scuttling on top, a dark-colored crab stares at us with rampant claws like an outlaw brandishing guns. We swim single file over a patch of seagrass, my light finding a seahorse hovering upright with a curled tail, fluttering its fins like a hummingbird.

According to my dive computers we're 103 feet down, and 72 feet southwest of the anchor line when we discover the first broken pieces of the rotor blades. They snapped off from the mast, possibly as the helicopter hit the bottom and tumbled. Some forty feet away we find the tail boom that separated from the upside-down cabin, and the sight is jolting.

The silvery inflatable floats are still mounted to the skids, and had they been deployed we wouldn't be here. I shine my light through the windows, the cockpit completely filled with water. The pilot is upside down, harnessed in the right seat, his bent arms and legs floating up. The doorframe is bent and I motion to Liam that I need some help.

We steady ourselves by hooking our legs over the helicopter skid. Carefully, we pull the door open, scraping it along the bottom, sending up a cloud of silt and sand that completely obscures visibility. We hold ourselves in place for several minutes until we can see what we're doing again.

Liam directs his light on me as I unclip a bright orange salvage bag from my vest. Removing my regulator from my mouth, I place it inside the bag's open bottom, inflating it with a loud rush of thick bubbles. Taking a hit of air, I give the tethered bag to Lucy hovering nearby. I fill the second bag the same way, handing it over while Liam and my mask-mounted camera film everything we're doing.

We move slowly, cautiously, staying in a supine position above the marly bottom as we look inside the inverted cockpit, a small eel undulating by while giving me a beady eye. The right seat broke free of its mounts, slamming the pilot's head into the console. His forehead is caved in from the impact when the seat broke free, his eyes staring blindly through partially closed lids.

The head injury happened when the helicopter hit the water, and if he wasn't dead before, the trauma would have killed him. Brain tissue shows through the open fracture to the front of the skull, and I wish the officer named Dixie hadn't mentioned sharks. Worse, I'm pretty sure I may have seen one, and for the next few minutes, I cover the head with a plastic garbage bag as I would do at any scene.

But in this case, I don't want the body seeping blood and tissue and attracting predators. Shining my light around the cockpit, I notice a mobile phone mostly covered with sand drifting over the inverted headliner. A bottle of berry-flavored vitamin water is suspended nearby, some of the red liquid gone inside, the cap on. Images flash of Briley Flight Services, the refrigerators stocked with the same brand of drink.

I'm careful not to get my hoses snagged as I reach down for the phone, then the bottle. Tucking them inside the collection bag attached to my vest, I ponder the best way to free the pilot without causing a brown-out and further damage. At least he's not trussed up in a four-point harness that would be awkward to manipulate with my neoprene-gloved fingers.

Releasing the buckle of his shoulder harness, I free him and he floats away from the seat. I'm careful not to send him into oscillation, banging into everything and stirring up more clouds of silt. Turning him around, I grip him under the arms as he moves away from me, his shoulder knocking into the cyclic. Then one of his legs is caught on the back of the seat, his sneaker coming off and drifting.

I manage to ease him out of the open door, and Lucy straps a salvage bag's tethers around his chest. Tron attaches the second bag, and he begins to float up as they hold on to him. I follow the anchor line, Liam behind me. We ascend slowly to prevent nitrogen bubbles from forming in our blood, what's known as decompression sickness or the bends.

I continuously check my dive computer, and I have half a tank of air left. I remind myself to sip and avoid deep breaths. It's easy to go through a tank shockingly fast when stressed and exerting oneself. Every ten feet Lucy and Tron stop on the rope where we hang perpendicular like windsocks. Then we resume our ascent through blasting bubbles.

At fifty feet below the surface, the dimly lit water suddenly blacks out as if someone closed a metal lid over us. We stop moving, hanging on to the rope while pointing our lights straight up as if we might see what's happening. We can't make out anything but suspended silt, another turtle swimming by in a hurry as if trouble is coming.

We're thrown into complete darkness, something huge slowly passing over top of us. I can feel the vibration in the water as we wait for what seems an eternity, shining our lights around. I'm feeling the thrumming in my very marrow when the anchor line suddenly is ripped from our hands. I watch stunned as it's tugged away, vanishing in the blackness.

CHAPTER 29

Slowly, the murky light is restored, the vibration dissipating. The inflated salvage bags tug on the body of the dead pilot as Lucy and Tron keep a firm grip. Liam gives us the OK sign, pointing up, and we resume our ascent.

Staying close behind him, we stop and wait as he directs, our fins gently paddling. We hold in place underwater without an anchored line to make it easier. The winds are picking up, the current stiffer and moving us along. We can't fight it without exhausting ourselves, and we're down to less than a third of a tank. It would be easy to suck in the rest of our air in no time, and that would be very bad once we reach the surface. We wouldn't be able to inflate our buoyancy vests.

I'm thinking about that as I press a button on mine, adding more air from my tank, feeling myself rising, sunlight shining through the water. I squint in the brightness as I break the surface and float. White cumulus clouds are building in the blue sky, and I look around for our boat, no sign of it. I can make out the retreating submarine's conning tower jutting up like a squared fin, some of the fuselage showing above the water like a whale's back.

An untethered dive float rocks on the water some fifty feet from us, the attached flag gently waving, and we snorkel toward it. I'm guessing that when Henry and our boat captain realized they had to relocate immediately, they untied the anchor line, lashing it to a bright red dive buoy. We hang on to it, the yellow nylon rope loose. It was either severed or the anchor isn't holding anymore.

I keep my scan going, hoping nothing else comes this way, another submarine, for example. Those aboard wouldn't have a clue we're here, and we'd have no means of getting away. I doubt the encounter would be survivable. A sub, an aircraft carrier, and we'd be sucked right under the hull. I can imagine it in detail and that we'd drown most likely.

"You can't be within five hundred yards of a military vessel." Liam interrupts my grim preoccupations. "When it's far enough away, our boat will come back for us."

"Well, I don't see them anywhere," I reply as brackish water slaps under my chin, and I spit it out.

"They'd know to come straight back to where they left us," Lucy says with her usual calm.

"Except we've moved," Liam says. "More bad weather's rolling in tonight, and the winds are now blowing out of the south at ten or fifteen knots, I'm guessing. The current's only getting stronger and pushing us closer to the naval station."

"Which means we're even more in the path of military ships," Tron replies as I think of Marino.

This wouldn't have been the trip for him.

"Well, I never thought my day would be like this," Lucy says.

"Most of all, he never thought it." I stare at the dead pilot floating facedown, rocking with the surf.

The orange salvage bags are deflated on top of his body, his black-plastic-covered head hanging below the surface, his arms and legs dangling.

"I wonder if he's married, has kids," Liam says. "Or if his parents are still alive. What a bad day for them."

"I already looked up stuff about him," Lucy tells us. "Unmarried. Thirty-two. Had just started flying for Dana Diletti at the beginning of the year."

He told reporters it was his dream job. A new chopper with all the bells and whistles. Working for a celebrity, she explains as we scan for military ships, floating on top of the water. And we wait. Then wait some more as I worry about something suddenly barreling down on us. None of our vests or the dive float are equipped with flashing emergency beacons.

We begin making small talk to distract ourselves, chatting about when we started diving. And misadventures from the past. And stupid things we've done like running out of air. Or forgetting to turn it on before jumping into the ocean. And whether it's true that divers pee in their wetsuits but don't admit it.

"Never," Liam says.

"Nope." Lucy shakes her head.

"Making the point that no one admits it," I reply, and next we talk about food.

"I'm always starved after diving," Tron says.

"Ravenous," Liam replies as I try not to think about what

might be swimming under us. "A good tuna steak on the grill, cracking a few cold ones. Top it off with a neat single-malt Scotch and a Cuban cigar."

"I go for pasta. I'm putting in my order now." Lucy looks at me mask to mask as we bob up and down, spitting out water.

"Thank God." Tron points, and I turn around to see blue lights flashing in the distance and getting closer.

We wave our arms in the air, yelling when it's not possible for anyone to hear us. Closing in and slowing down, the Hampton police boat eases to a stop next to us, throwing Liam a rope that he ties to the dive buoy. Then he slides out the knife from the sheath strapped to his ankle. He cuts the yellow nylon line that may or may not still be attached to the anchor.

Henry has a bright yellow body bag unzipped and ready. The tightly woven mesh allows water to flow through, and we unbuckle the deflated salvage bags, handing them up to reaching hands. I help maneuver the spread-open body bag under the dead man. Zipping up three sides of the pouch, Tron and I hold on to it in the rocking surf as Lucy and Liam climb the ladder, shedding themselves of their gear.

They lean over the side of the boat, grabbing the bag by the handles, hoisting it on board, water draining through the mesh. The aluminum ladder bangs and sways, the chop getting stiffer. Hanging on to a rung, I take off my fins as Lucy reaches down for them. I feel the weight of the tank on my back as I climb up, taking off my mask with its attached camera, my neck stiff from the weight of it.

I pull off my gloves and sit down on the bench seat, shoving my tank into the holder. Unbuckling my vest, I work my way out of it and all the hoses. I bend down to pull off my dive socks, unstrapping the knife from my ankle. We struggle out of our wetsuits, dropping them in the barrel of water. When it's my turn to stand under the shower nozzle, I wash the salt and silt out of my hair.

"What do you need to do now?" Henry asks me this as I'm toweling off.

"There's no point in taking a liver temp or doing anything else," I reply. "We have a pretty good idea when he went into the water. The best thing is to let my Norfolk office handle it from here. You'll want to make sure that Doctor Peace has the video and photographs."

"What if he was already dead when the F-16s caught up with him?" Tron asks. "Is there any way to know that?"

"I won't be able to tell unless the toxicology gives me a clue," I answer. "But it seems you may have two separate events. He either passed out or died while on autopilot. Why? And fifteen or twenty minutes later his helicopter sputtered and crashed into the bay. Why?"

I explain that while Bret Jones was flying, he might have had a few swallows of a berry-flavored vitamin water. I hand the collection bag to Tron, pointing out that I noticed vitamin water inside the private terminal Dana Diletti and her crew flew out of this morning.

"I noticed the same thing," Lucy replies as our boat speeds back to the marina. "They always keep it in the little refrigerators, including the ones in the pilots' lounges."

"Bottles of orange- and berry-flavored vitamin water,"

Tron says to me. "I think we can assume that's where the pilot got the one you found inside the cockpit."

"We'll look at the video taken by the flight service's security cameras," Lucy adds.

"Good luck getting hold of that if Ryder Briley's involved." I trade my wet towel for a dry one, draping it around my shoulders. "Magically, the cameras will have been offline for some reason."

"They were on and working fine when someone turned them off early this morning. Or thought they had," Lucy replies with a trace of a smile. "As I've mentioned, Ryder Briley has been on our radar for a while. Suffice it to say that after Luna had her so-called fatal accident, I made sure it's impossible to turn off certain camera systems, including those at the flight service. You'll think you did. But you didn't."

*   *   *

Massive stone ramparts hulk on the bright horizon as our boat speeds closer to Fort Monroe. Dubbed the *Gibraltar of the Chesapeake*, the military installation was built after the War of 1812. It probably doesn't look all that different from a distance than it did hundreds of years ago.

News helicopters are following us, and I can make out the rescue and police vehicles parked by the marina, the docked boats shining in the sun. Our captain begins rolling back the engines, cutting our speed to avoid creating wake. Then we're gliding to the pier, and I spot the black windowless van from my Norfolk office. The death investigator named Nathan is climbing out of it.

He opens the tailgate and begins following the pier toward us, pulling on a pair of purple gloves, his feet loud on aluminum. Moments later he and Liam are carrying the bright yellow pouched body, loading it into the van. Texting Norfolk medical examiner Rena Peace, I give her the latest update. I mention the bottle of vitamin water that I'm having tested immediately, the toxicology in this case my top priority.

It's close to 3:30 P.M. when Lucy, Tron and I walk back to the Hampton police marine unit across the street as thunderstorms build to the south. The heat and humidity feel good as we trudge in our boots, our bags slung over our towel-draped shoulders. I can feel that my face is sunburned from floating on top of the water. Lucy's and Tron's noses are red.

The Dodge Charger is parked where we left it, the interior baking hot as I settle in the backseat, opening my jump-out bag. I pull a polo shirt over my damp sports bra, fastening my seat belt, draping the towel across my lap. The palms of my hands are pale and wrinkled from being underwater, my fingernails bluish, reminding me of what I see in drownings.

We're headed back to the NASA Langley campus, where the helicopter has been fueled and is waiting. It's a good thing we're getting the hell out of here, Lucy says as we pick up I-64 West by Hampton University. Thunderstorms will hit Tidewater within the hour, moving up to Northern Virginia and New England. Flooding is expected in coastal areas, and damaging winds could cause power outages.

She's wearing her computer-assisted glasses, the lenses tinted dark green in the sun. Both of us are catching up on weather reports, messages, emails as Tron speeds along the interstate, cutting in and out of lanes as usual. I see that trace evidence examiner Lee Fishburne has just now texted. He wants me to call as soon as I'm able. He's inside his lab with more test results, and I try him.

"Are you sitting down?" he asks.

"Actually, I am. And in a very loud car at the moment." I dig my notebook and pen out of my briefcase.

"Who would think that the deaths of an abused child and a Nobel Prize winner would be related somehow?" It's rare for Lee to show any excitement.

He goes on to confirm that the sparkling residue in Luna Briley's and Sal Giordano's cases is the same. They had a simulant of moon dust on them that glows cobalt blue under ultraviolet light. As he's saying this I'm texting Benton the information.

"I think it's safe to say that the simulant came from the same source," Lee is telling me. "It looks the same microscopically. The composition is identical. For sure it was made by the same manufacturer, the same machining used."

"And we've gotten no new information that might help us figure out where this fake moon dust could have come from?" I ask as we cross the Hampton River. "For example, if it's being shipped to someplace in Virginia?"

"No leads on that," he says as Benton texts me back.

With D1, he says.

My husband is meeting with Director Bella Steele and will be leaving Secret Service headquarters in a few minutes. He'll be home when I get there, and I can't wait to see him, to feel clean and civilized again. I text him that it would be helpful if he takes a container of marinara sauce out of the freezer. Also, the focaccia bread dough I put in there the other night.

"I wonder if Ryder Briley is involved in a business that uses fake moon dust," I'm saying to Lee while I type on my phone.

What about wine? Benton writes back to me.

Uncork a couple of reds, please, I type.

"Don't know," Lee is saying. "But there was a lot of microscopic debris on Sal Giordano's body besides the lunar simulant. Did he have a cat?"

Include Marino and Dorothy? I write to Benton while talking over the loud engine thrumming.

They should stay the night, and maybe Shannon would like to join us? She shouldn't be alone in the storm with all that's transpired. She's been skittish enough, and I know she's lonely.

"Sal used to have cats but hadn't for years," I'm saying over speakerphone while continuing to text. "Why do you ask?"

"Because he had cat dander on him. Also cat hair, but not normal cat hair that I've seen," Lee explains in his laconic voice as I think of the cheetah on the Yellow Brick Road.

Will invite all, Benton is writing back.

"And detritus such as bug pieces and parts, insulation, cobwebs and such," Lee explains as I hold up the phone for Tron and Lucy to hear. "What you'd expect if he was kept in a place that isn't cleaned very often."

"And all of this microscopic debris was all over the body, or only parts of it?" I look out at light reflecting on tidal creeks branching through salt marshes, reminding me of blood vessels.

"Yes," Lee says. "From all the swabs you took. He had this stuff all over him, head to toe."

"Suggesting he was unclothed while held somewhere," I reply.

"I guess that's one way to control someone."

"And humiliate." I feel a flare of anger that smolders in my core.

"Last but not least, something curious showed up in the fingernail clippings," Lee continues. "Nanograins of perovskite. And in case you don't know what that is...?"

"I don't."

"A calcium titanium oxide mineral used to make photovoltaic cells that convert sunlight into electricity. Solar cells, in other words," he replies. "But we're talking about a *synthetic* version of perovskite that's used in manufacturing. And not the naturally occurring mineral Sal Giordano had under his fingernails."

"Any theories about why someone would be accessing the real mineral? For what purpose?" I ask.

"Possibly for research. If you're making the synthetic version, for example, you'd probably want access to the real thing as a model. And it allows for additive engineering possibilities such as doping the synthetic with some of the real stuff. To cook up whatever your special sauce might be. I'm wondering if Sal Giordano was involved in projects involving solar-generated power? Perhaps something space-related such as the solar arrays used on satellites and telescopes like the Hubble and James Webb?"

"Not that I'm aware of," I reply.

"Possibly the grains of perovskite were transferred to him by someone else. Unless he had it under his fingernails before he was abducted and murdered. And if so, where did it come from?" Lee says as I'm thinking about the missing three hours.

CHAPTER 30

On Monday afternoon, Sal called me from Weyers Cave before turning off his phone as he ventured deeper into the Quiet Zone. This was around 1:30 P.M., and it should have taken approximately two hours to drive the rest of the way to Green Bank, West Virginia. But he didn't arrive at the restaurant until 7:00 P.M. What was he doing? Where did he go?

"Did you find perovskite on Luna Briley's pajamas or anywhere else?" I ask Lee over speakerphone.

"No."

Tron is driving the grumbling Dodge Charger through Phoebus, the shops and diners straight out of the 1950s.

"Are there companies in Virginia that make things out of solar cells?" I ask while speeding past a veterans' cemetery, the perfect rows of white headstones reminding me of teeth.

"Not many but some," the trace evidence examiner says.

"I'm wondering if perovskite might be mined anywhere around here. If so, that could explain finding traces of the real mineral." I can't stop thinking about Sal's mysterious trips to Weyers Cave.

He was a free spirit but not given to reckless impulsivity. He often told me that our summer romance was the most impetuous thing he ever did. He thought long and hard about most things, and if he stopped somewhere on his way to Green Bank, it was purposeful. If he periodically visited Weyers Cave, it was calculated.

"Based on what I've been reading, perovskite occurs naturally in the mountains where volcanic activity went on hundreds of millions of years ago," Lee is saying. "As the lava cools, it forms igneous or volcanic rocks, which is where perovskite is found."

"From fire and brimstone. That figures somehow." It's not easy taking notes as Tron drives like Formula One. "Where might we find volcanic rocks around here? Assuming the possibility that perovskite is mined locally?"

"The Appalachian Mountains for sure." Lee talks slowly and with a drawl that belies his facile intelligence. "Most perovskite is mined in Russia. Also Sweden and Mount Vesuvius, Italy. And Magnet Cove, Arkansas. I'm not aware of any actual mines in this part of the world. But there could be."

"I'll make sure the Secret Service has the latest update, and we'll keep this between us, Lee," I tell him. "Whoever left nanograins of perovskite and fake moon dust may not be aware of it."

Carrie.

"That tends to be what happens when it's something you can't see with the naked eye," he replies. "People don't think about what they're carrying around on their skin, their clothing, in their hair, leaving traces on everything they brush up against and touch."

"Carrie would think about it," Lucy says when I end the call as we pass through Hampton. "She understands about trace evidence and how it's transferred from one thing to the next."

"We can assume she knows a lot of the same things that we know." I look out at the Walmart Supercenter where my Norfolk office has an expense account.

"In some instances, more than we know." Lucy's tone hints of the deep-seated respect that she still has for her former mentor and lover.

It's like one world-class competitor admiring another at the same time they want to destroy each other. But what Carrie does isn't a sport, and it drives me mad when I detect the pilot light burning inside my niece. What they once had with each other isn't entirely gone.

"As long as she keeps herself under control, there's not much she can't master and figure out," Lucy is saying.

"It would be foolish to underestimate someone like her," Tron agrees.

"There isn't anyone like her," I reply with an edge. "And yes, it would be foolish."

The muscle car roars past the Virginia Air & Space Science Center, the soaring glass entrance reminding me of the cartoon *The Jetsons*. We have our windows partially opened and the air-conditioning off. I'm dryer than I was but the padding in my bike shorts is uncomfortably damp and squishy.

"Carrie might be decompensating," Lucy says. "It's happened before. And she crashes and burns."

"Usually not before she's done something hideous," I reply.

"Being cavalier about trace evidence that might be on your

person isn't like her." Lucy glances back at me as we're talking. "She's making mistakes."

"Possibly," I reply. "But I can understand not being aware of nanograins of dust clinging to her body and clothing. Especially if she's in and out of an environment where she's exposed regularly. People can get lax about PPE. They might wear a mask and gloves but not the rest of it. They think if they're passing through a room or not staying long, they don't need to bother. Or they'll reuse Tyvek that's become contaminated."

"Assuming Carrie's the one leaving the microscopic residues? I'm guessing she doesn't care." Tron glances at me in the rearview mirror as she drives like the proverbial bat out of hell.

Her face is unusually solemn. I can tell she's not entirely comfortable with the conversation.

"She wouldn't want to leave something unintentionally," Lucy repeats. "That's what I mean about her decompensating. When she does, she takes bigger risks and can be careless."

"I'm not sure she gives a damn about leaving evidence." Tron says the same thing Benton did as she blasts past a slow driver. "She figures we'll never catch her." A spike of hostility. "We don't even know where she is right now."

"Around here somewhere," Lucy says. "Or she was. Assuming she's involved in Sal Giordano's abduction and death."

"She'd be naïve to think she can duck the police forever," I reply. "Especially in rural areas around here where she'd stand out."

"She's spent a lot of time in Virginia," Tron says. "She knows her way around, and I suspect she can blend when it suits her."

"If she's the one leaving the trace evidence, then we also have some idea where she's been," Lucy adds. "Which is wherever Sal was held hostage. And maybe Carrie was around the Brileys, even inside their house. Maybe she had contact with Luna, explaining the sparkling residue on her pajamas."

"If she's the one leaving it, what's she doing with fake moon dust?" I ask.

"Don't know," Lucy says.

"What about perovskite and solar cells? What might she be doing with those?"

"Could be a lot of things. Electronics, including photovoltaic ones like lasers, LEDs, ceramic capacitors, aerospace technologies such as solar arrays," Lucy answers. "Also, and more pervasively, solar panels. As you've probably noticed when we're flying around, there are a lot of solar farms and solar-paneled rooftops."

"More all the time as companies and everyday people use them to generate electricity and profits," Tron adds. "I'm surprised a scientist like Sal Giordano didn't have solar panels on his property."

"Maybe that was something he was looking into," I suggest as more updates land, this time from forensic chemist Rex Bonetta.

I read the preliminary report he's sent, and Sal had high levels of haloperidol, lorazepam and Benadryl on board when he died. The powerful antipsychotic in combination with a benzodiazepine and antihistamine is known as a *B-52*. It's used as a chemical restraint when prisoners and psychiatric patients are out of control.

"That may be the explanation for the redness of his skin. Haloperidol, or Haldol as it's better known, has side effects." I'm looking them up on my phone as I'm talking, and what I suspect is confirmed. "One of them is photosensitivity," I add. "And Sal was fair-skinned to begin with."

"So, while he was dying in the sunny clearing, he was getting sunburned," Tron says.

"And he might have burned more quickly because he had Haldol in his system," I explain.

"A mixture of that, lorazepam and Benadryl is what was injected in his neck and elsewhere," Lucy surmises.

"It would be fast acting," I reply. "A B-Fifty-Two would cause ataxia and heavy sedation. Explaining why it's been used as a way of controlling violent and severely agitated people."

"And it's a favorite of the Russians," Lucy answers. "Used in prison camps and mental asylums to keep inmates in a stupor. Particularly certain political enemies of the Kremlin. A B-Fifty-Two cocktail is something Carrie would be aware of and probably utilizes when it suits her purposes."

As I'm listening, I imagine Sal driving his pickup truck away from the Red Caboose restaurant on Monday night. Minutes later, he stopped for someone. Perhaps it's as Benton says, and the person pretended to be in distress. I imagine Sal getting out of his truck. Or perhaps he opened his window, and suddenly was stabbed in the neck with a hypodermic needle.

He would have felt the onset of the drug cocktail quickly, and that could be when he swallowed the blue-and-white capsule. Maybe it was in a pocket, and he managed to take it without the assailant knowing. I envision the injection sites on his arm and buttocks. He was kept sedated possibly the entire time he was held captive. But that doesn't mean he wasn't aware of everything happening.

★ ★ ★

The low sun tinges the edges of building clouds, spreading pink across the horizon as we reach the NASA Langley hangar. Two Secret Service agents are waiting, and one of them takes the Dodge Charger from Tron. He guns the engine, squealing out of the parking lot.

"Back to a boring SUV." She stares wistfully after the blacked-out muscle car growling away.

"When we get to Washington National, I'll be dropping the two of you off." Lucy says this for my benefit. "Tron will drive you home. Benton's there with Marino and Mom, getting dinner ready. And Shannon is on her way. I'll meet you there later. First I've got to get the helicopter back to the training center and safely into the hangar."

They climb up into the cockpit, and it's the first time I've sat in the back cabin alone. I text Marino that I'm in the helicopter headed home. The weather's supposed to turn nasty again, and I don't want anyone on the roads if possible. I assume he and Dorothy are spending the night. He doesn't answer, and I hope they've settled their differences for now.

It's five P.M. when the Langley tower clears the Doomsday Bird to take off for Northern Virginia. The visibility is beginning to deteriorate, and Lucy has requested flight-following along the way. We'll be handed off from one air traffic control frequency to the next while Lucy routes us as a crow flies over

303

water and forests. She wants to beat the storm barreling in, the hail predicted to be as big as gumballs.

Without Marino to worry about, the intercom is left on in the back cabin where I'm harnessed in my silvery-gray flame-retardant seat. The partition blocks my view of the cockpit, and every so often Tron gives me details about weather and our present location. As case information is updated, I'm given the details, and Blaise Fruge didn't waste any time in the Luna Briley investigation.

A little while ago, she and other officers showed up with warrants at the Briley home. The couple was having drinks in the yard, enjoying the spring weather before it turns bad. I can imagine the looks on their faces as cops began searching their property for a second time. But now the stakes are different. They couldn't be higher.

"Ryder and Piper Briley have been arrested," Tron is saying. "They're being transported to the city jail as we speak."

"That's just the beginning of the charges brought against them," Lucy's voice promises in my headset.

When we cross the York River, the helicopter is full throttle with a fierce tailwind at an altitude of two thousand feet. Our groundspeed is 210 knots, or more than 240 miles per hour, Tron informs me. At Colonial Beach we follow the western shoreline of the Potomac River as ominous clouds continue to gather, the wind gusting harder. Quantico is off to our left surrounded by miles of backcountry woods.

A pale gash in dark trees is all I can see of the storied FBI Academy where Benton and I carried on our torrid love affair. We were sneaking around while Lucy was interning there, and she was none the wiser. I think of the two of us running the Yellow Brick Road obstacle course when she was in college. I remember getting rope burns and bruises together, cursing like sailors as we slipped in mud and climbed over walls.

Afterward Lucy and I would eat burgers in the academy's watering hole, the Board Room, hanging out with FBI agents, and I couldn't have been prouder. I believed that helping her land the internship was for her own good. She'd get physically fit and finally make a few friends. I thought it the right thing at that time in her development, but her mother had other ideas. To this day Dorothy reminds me what a terrible idea it was.

She was adamantly opposed to her only child pursuing a career in law enforcement, and I wasn't supposed to encourage it. My sister said she didn't want Lucy turning out like me. Morbid and fatalistic. Spending every waking minute focused on violence, death, cruelty and treachery. Always thinking about what might injure or kill something or someone.

Instead of dancing and making love under the moonlight, as Dorothy puts it.

In the end, none of us had control over what Lucy was drawn to or would become in life. But if she hadn't been at the FBI Academy when Carrie was, they wouldn't have met. They wouldn't have become lovers hell-bent on dismantling each other. Unless it was an inevitable karma they couldn't escape. Opposing forces colliding. A quantum entanglement, the two of them forever caught in a spin.

We near the Ronald Reagan Washington National Airport, the first drops of rain spitting as Lucy lands on the ramp we took off from yesterday. I retrieve my rain slicker from my jump-out bag, putting it on as she cuts the throttles to flight idle. Tron and I climb out, the blades thudding, the rotor wash whipping.

We hurry across asphalt speckled by raindrops, and I hear the pitch of the engines winding up as Lucy rolls open the throttles all the way. I wave as she lifts into a hover, making a pedal turn. For an instant we're eye to eye, and she nods. At the hold line she waits for the tower to clear her. I watch as she noses forward, taking off, sharply turning away from the airport, the helicopter's lights strobing.

"It's a bit chaotic inside." Tron presses an intercom button next to the door leading into the terminal. "As you're about to see, we've got agents searching Briley Flight Services. And I'm going to need you to tag team with me."

Employees are being questioned about any manner of things pertaining to Ryder and Piper Briley, she says. That includes Dana Diletti's ill-fated flight this morning. The expectation is that her pilot's incapacitation and fatal crash weren't accidental.

"The goal is to interview employees before they completely clam up," Tron explains as we wait for someone to open the door. "And to continue talking to them until they can't keep their lies straight." Peering through the glass, she knocks on it, ringing the bell again.

"Fear," I reply. "That's why they're loyal."

"I guess they'll get to pick what scares them most," she says. "Their disgraced employers who are chilling in the city jail right now? Or us?"

CHAPTER 31

We're buzzed inside by the same older woman who was sitting behind the desk yesterday when we were here. Her laptop is gone, her face resentful as Secret Service agents search the lobby and offices. I can feel her anger while investigators pack up computers and bottles of vitamin water.

"How are you doing?" Tron asks her as if this day is like any other.

"What do you expect?" She looks us up and down, taking in our windblown hair, our bike shorts and boots. "It's not fun being invaded." She stares at the investigators working.

"I'm sure not," Tron says pleasantly, a strap of her backpack slung over a shoulder. "Were you working early this morning when Dana Diletti flew out of here?"

"I've already talked to them." The woman continues staring at the investigators as if they're the enemy.

"And now you get to talk to us." Tron smiles patiently, treating me like her partner.

"It would appear I have no choice." She picks up a scrunchie and begins tying back her long dyed blond hair.

Every time I've seen her working the desk at Briley Flight

Services, she has on a skirt suit, this one navy blue with brass buttons, her figure matronly, her fingernails painted the same pink as bougainvillea.

"I've seen you in here before but we haven't been introduced," Tron is saying to her. "I'm with the Secret Service. Special Agent Sierra Patron, but everyone calls me Tron. This is Doctor Scarpetta who works with us. And what's your name?"

"I already gave them all my information," the woman replies icily.

"As you've mentioned, and it's much appreciated. What's your name?" she tries again, still smiling.

"Wilma Gaither."

"Wilma, where do you live?"

"Pentagon City and they already know all this." She stares at the investigators, a glint of hatred in her smoky made-up eyes.

"Were you here when Dana Diletti and her crew took off in their helicopter for Berkeley Plantation?" Tron asks.

"I work eight to five Monday through Friday," Wilma recites. "Sometimes I work additional hours if we're short-handed. Whatever my employers need, that's what I do."

"Then you were working the desk when Dana Diletti and three of her crew were here this morning with their pilot Bret Jones," Tron says.

"I wasn't watching them every minute." Wilma is getting flustered. "It was busy, and I had other aircraft to deal with. I do my best not to bother so-called celebrities. Especially ones who obviously want everyone to notice them."

"I would imagine you talked to Bret Jones," Tron continues.

"Of course." Wilma sits stiffly at her desk, her hands clasped in her lap. "But for the most part he was in the pilots' lounge, on his phone and checking the weather. Then when Dana Diletti arrived, they left."

"Did anything strike you as unusual about her pilot's demeanor early this morning?" I ask.

"He wasn't happy about getting called at the last minute." Wilma eyes me suspiciously. "Other than that, there was nothing noteworthy."

"Dana Diletti and her people were in and out of here a lot," Tron replies. "So what you're telling us is it was business as usual this morning?"

"That's right. Nothing seemed out of the ordinary except it wasn't the pilot she flies with most of the time."

"Do you have any idea why Bret Jones was picked for this particular flight?" Tron asks. "Did he mention anything?"

"I already told them." Glaring at the investigators again.

"And now we're asking." Tron will keep reminding her.

"He said that the usual pilot called him at four o'clock in the morning to say she wasn't feeling up to flying," Wilma tells us.

"What does that mean exactly?" I ask.

"She had a scratchy throat. It started during the night and she was hoping it would get better. But it didn't. That's what Bret Jones told me. And I don't know anything else."

"You're aware that there are cameras everywhere." Tron points out one directly over Wilma Gaither's desk as my attention wanders around the lobby.

I spot other cameras, and when I notice the bins of candy on the wall, I see flashes of Luna Briley on her bedroom floor. I see her on my table.

"The cameras aren't always working," Wilma answers with a hint of smugness. "Sometimes people turn them off."

"Who?" Tron asks, and she already knows the answer.

"Security has to do it."

"Were the cameras on when Bret Jones was here?" Tron knows the answer to that too.

Lucy has made sure the cameras can't be turned off even if it appears that they are. Wilma Gaither wouldn't know that.

"I have no way of telling unless I'm notified." She continues to evade.

"And were you notified about them this morning at any point?"

"Not that I recall."

"Which security officers were here when Bret Jones was?" Tron asks.

"I'm not sure."

"Did that person turn off the cameras?"

"I wouldn't necessarily know."

"Okay. That's fine. There are ways to find out what's true and what isn't," Tron then says with a shrug.

"I've told the truth." Wilma stares at me as she says this.

"Not to us, you haven't," Tron replies, watching her comrades walking around the flight service as they continue searching for evidence. "But here's a word of advice, Wilma. Now that your boss and his wife are facing criminal charges and possible prison time? Now that other people connected to them are being looked at very carefully? You might want to think twice about making false statements. Which security officers were here when Dana Diletti was?"

"It might have been Mira Tang. She's not here now but your colleagues were talking to her earlier." Wilma doesn't hesitate to throw someone under the bus when it's in her best interest. "Mira got here at seven o'clock this morning. An hour before her shift."

"Why was she early?"

"She didn't say. But she was here at the same time Dana Diletti and her people were. That's my point."

"Thank you for that," Tron replies. "Isn't it so much easier when people cooperate with each other? And it seems foolish to lose everything because someone else is in trouble. And you feel you have to protect them."

"Even though they might not do the same for you," I add as Wilma's cold face is touched by fear.

"You've been working for the Brileys a long time, haven't you?" Tron says in a gentler tone.

"Going on twenty years, but I wouldn't call us friends." Wilma lowers her voice to an upset whisper as the cameras secretly record her every word and gesture. "I never liked the way they treated their little girl when she was here with them. So impatient. The mother especially."

"Why would they bring Luna into this terminal?" Tron asks.

"When they were flying places on one of their private jets. I've been seeing them in here since Luna was born."

"And the last time you saw her?"

"December," Wilma says. "She wasn't in and out very often, as sickly as she was."

"Sickly in what way?" I ask. "What were you told was wrong with her?"

"It was generally known that she was...well, she wasn't right."

"Can you be more specific?" I go on.

"As I said, sickly. One was left to wonder what *wasn't* wrong with her. A sweet child, always smiling even when the mother would yell at her for no good reason." Wilma has a habit of looking askance at us as she talks. "Children are supposed to be curious. They're supposed to get into things even when you tell them no."

"And there's plenty to get into here." I indicate the bins of candy on the wall inside the sitting area. "I would think that was very tempting."

"Every single time." Wilma nods her head, the expression on her unfriendly face almost sad. "That child had a sweet tooth. And of course, candy wasn't allowed. Apparently, she was diabetic."

"How do you know that?" I inquire as I think about what Fabian told me.

Luna wasn't prescribed insulin, her diabetes yet another lie.

"That's what Mrs. Briley told me." Wilma Gaither talks in a conspiratorial tone now as if we're comrades. "She said don't ever let her get into the candy unless you want her in a coma or dead. And..."

Her voice trails off. She doesn't want to finish the sentence.

"And what?" I prod her.

"And when they were here right before Christmas, the little girl found a candy cane hanging on the Christmas tree we had near the fireplace."

She points to the spot in the sitting area, describing Piper Briley snatching the candy cane from Luna and throwing it in the trash. She grabbed the child by the upper arms, shaking her hard, telling her how bad she was.

"I was getting coffee." Wilma's almost whispering. "I don't think Mrs. Briley knew I saw the whole thing. The poor child was terrified, trembling like a leaf. And that wasn't the only time I saw things..."

Wilma's eyes fill with tears, and she impatiently snatches a tissue out of the box of them on her desk.

"Now look at what you've done. You've made me talk out of school!" she snaps at us. "Now I'll probably lose my job."

"You'd better hope you don't lose more than that," I reply.

Like your soul. If you still have one. But I don't say it.

"You could have fucking told someone that the parents were abusive." Tron turns to walk away.

"Maybe she'd still be alive." I look Wilma Gaither in the eye.

*   *   *

As we pass through the lobby, Tron checks with investigators sealing electronic devices in big paper bags. They quietly confer about evidence listed in the warrant. One of them gives her a key to an SUV waiting outside. Then the two of us leave as Blaise Fruge is parking her unmarked Ford Interceptor in the misting rain.

313

The lights in the parking lot have switched on, the wet pavement scummy with pollen. Fruge is in jeans and a windbreaker, trotting up to us, and she can't keep the smile off her face. She joins us beneath the overhang at the building's entrance, huddling out of the rain.

"What brings you here?" Tron asks her.

"Endless follow-up, talking to people who work for the Brileys. Most of them liars, what a shocker." Fruge is digging in a jacket pocket, pulling out a pack of cigarettes and a chrome lighter with an American flag on it.

"When did you start smoking?" I've never known her to do it before now.

"I used to and quit. Then I started and quit again." Sliding out a cigarette, she tucks it between her lips. "I'm not really smoking again, just sneaking one now and then."

Just like her mentor, Marino, I think. He chews gum to beat the band when I'm around because he knows I won't cheat. I refuse to break down and have a smoke when it would take nothing to be addicted again. But Fruge sneaks a cigarette with him when the urge strikes. That's the upshot of what I'm hearing.

"I know you're not supposed to celebrate the misfortunes of others." The Alexandria investigator turns her face away from the wind, blowing out smoke that goes everywhere. "But not much could feel better than locking up Ryder and Piper Briley's sorry asses. Let the games begin."

"We have interest in them for other reasons," Tron tells her.

"Well, you know where to find them. You can talk to the Brileys all you want, be my guest. They're what's known as a captive audience."

Fruge explains that when I ruled the death a homicide, she charged the parents with child abuse and first-degree murder.

"I was ready when you gave the word, and they didn't see it coming," she says to me, the rain gusting, water dripping from the overhang's eaves. "Me personally putting them in cuffs was a special pleasure, I must admit. I hope Luna's smiling wherever she is." Fruge flicks an ash.

"When will bail be set?" Tron asks.

"In the morning. But I'm making a big point of the obvious flight risk they pose considering the homes they own abroad and their private jets and all the rest. If I play my cards right, they'll be held without bail."

"Yours aren't the only charges they'll be facing," Tron promises. "Wait until we start piling on federal indictments."

"They could be locked up for a long time before trial," I reply.

"That's the idea." Fruge takes another deep drag. "I want to make sure they never see the light of day again."

The rain is falling harder, lightning veining the distant darkness. Fruge heads inside Briley Flight Services to see what other dirt she can find on the owners, as she puts it. Tron and I hurry through the downpour to the Secret Service black Tahoe SUV left here for her. I watch thunderclouds churning and lighting up dangerously, the storm front rolling in.

Driving away from the airport, we follow the George Washington Memorial Parkway along the Potomac River, and it's too foggy to see across it. I'm relieved when Lucy texts me that she's safe and sound at the training facility in Maryland. She'll be in her car headed home shortly.

"If Carrie Grethen's been in and out of Briley Flight Services, wouldn't it be on camera?" I ask Tron.

"Depending on whether she has the ability to turn the cameras on and off."

"I suspect that would be child's play to her," I answer.

"And I'll keep saying the same thing," Tron replies with surprising anger. "She doesn't care. In fact, if we find video of her walking in and out of Briley Flight Services, she's going to get a kick out of it. Wherever she is, she'll be laughing at us."

"Because she doesn't believe we can stop her." I squint in the bleary glare of oncoming traffic, the rain splashing against glass.

"I'm thinking she's flown the coop and doesn't give a damn what we find."

"I don't know what your plans are." I look over at her. "But you're welcome to join us for dinner. Lucy, Marino, Dorothy and Shannon, something relaxed and simple."

"That's really nice. But I think Lucy and I could use a break from each other." Tron is joking and she's not.

"You two getting along all right?"

"She can be pretty intense in certain situations."

The certain situation Tron alludes to is Carrie. She's not done. Maybe she never will be.

"I think you can understand why Lucy would be vigilant when that subject is raised," I reply with a reasonability I sure as hell don't feel.

"It's more than that, Doctor Scarpetta." Tron has yet to call me by my first name, and we've known each other more than four years. "What's between them is pathological."

I sit quietly in the passenger's seat, familiar with the terrain of Lucy's inner darkness. I know what lurks there, and I'm not about to discuss it with Tron. Or hardly anyone.

"Lucy gets fixated," she's saying. "No matter what she's doing I can tell that a part of her mind is on Carrie Grethen. It's been like that since last fall. Like something dormant that's wide-awake again, and it's not that I don't understand. But it's always there holding her like a tractor beam."

"I think that's to be expected when someone she once loved became her mortal enemy," I reply, feeling the heat of my rage.

"Once loved?" Tron stares straight ahead. "I'm beyond believing that Lucy can be objective about her. Or that she hates her as much as she claims."

Tron is driving less aggressively, perhaps because I'm sitting next to her in awful weather. Or maybe what we're discussing is causing her mood to shift. I wouldn't have guessed before now that her feelings for Lucy run deep. Deeper than work. Deeper than friends.

I don't know if Lucy feels the same way. Or if she's been with anyone since Janet and their son contracted COVID before there was a vaccine. By the time Lucy could get to their flat in London, it was too late.

CHAPTER 32

Puddles splash the undercarriage, trees thrashing in the wind, the Old Town Harbor shrouded in fog, the moored boats ghostly. It's 7:15 when we reach Benton's and my eighteenth-century modest estate surrounded by fencing that blends with the trees.

Tron stops in front of the closed wrought iron gate, and I tell her the code. Rolling down her window, she enters the numbers into the squawk box keypad. The gate begins to slide along its track as Lucy's AI-assisted cameras and spectrum analyzers relay our information. Video images are uploaded in real time as databases are searched.

Facial recognition software identifies whoever it is while the algorithm mines for other information such as someone's criminal history. Or if they have purchased firearms. Or made threats over the internet. Tron drives through, stopping to wait for the gate to close after us. She follows the winding driveway, lamplight shimmering on wet red bricks, the dark shapes of giant oak trees arching over us.

The guest cottage where Lucy lives is white brick with a slate roof, and has blackout shades in the windows. It's hard

318

to tell when she's inside. The presence or absence of her government take-home car doesn't mean she's home or away. She could be riding with someone else or out on her tactical bicycle. But I know she's not here now, and I remind Tron to keep a sharp eye out for Lucy's cat, Merlin.

"He shouldn't be out in this weather, but you know how he is," I explain. "A part of him will always be feral."

Rain slashes through the headlights as we near the main house, white brick with dusky blue shutters and doors. The roof is slate with two chimneys standing proud against the volatile sky. Parked in front is Benton's SUV, and next to it Marino's pickup truck, and my sister's white Audi convertible with a red leather interior, a Christmas gift to herself.

I step out into the rain, reaching for my bags as I'm thanking Tron. I dash inside the house while Marino holds open the door, shutting it behind me. In a sweatsuit, he's drinking a bottle of St. Pauli Girl, and I smell the aroma of marinara sauce warming in the kitchen while Mozart plays over the sound system. I drop my bags on top of the pumpkin pine flooring, taking off my rain slicker.

"Nice outfit." Marino looks me up and down in my damp polo shirt and bike shorts. He takes a swallow of beer. "The unlaced tactical boots really set it off. That and your hair."

I search his eyes for what was there earlier. But I see no trace of his old anger and hurt feelings. He and Dorothy must have worked out their differences for now, and maybe he won't project his frustrations onto me for a while. Then thought takes form, my sister making her way down the stairs, asking questions with every step.

"Where were you yesterday? Why all the secrets? It's like *name, rank, serial number* around here." Ice rattles as my sister carries her drink in one hand, a bottle of tequila in the other. "Pete repeats the same things over and over again. Being evasive, in other words..."

Dorothy is partial to onesies, and tonight she's the Jolly Green Giant because it's springtime, I suppose. A wide sash of green plastic leaves skimpily covers her bosomy figure, her long shapely legs in green tights with built-in green feet and curled-up toes.

"And of course, whatever you've been doing is related to all this UAP news that's everywhere. No point in being coy about that," Dorothy goes on. "Was Sal Giordano abducted by aliens? I must know the truth."

"I already told you we can't talk about what we've been doing because it involves military stuff," Marino says to her.

"What's the answer to my question? A simple yes or no will do." Another sip. "Did he get beamed up and tossed out? Like what happens to horses and cows when they're found mutilated and dropped from the sky, if the stories are to be trusted? Was he pushed out after the aliens were done with him? Meaning, they're brutes. Dear me, what a terrible thought. Who the fuck wants to be the *lesser children of a hateful God*?"

"Shit, Dorothy." Marino rolls his eyes at her. "Let's talk about something else."

"The two of you have been someplace you can't share, and obviously it's related." She directs this at me, sipping tequila, a healthy amount on the rocks.

As she continues to badger us for information, we're

interrupted by the sound of footsteps in the dining room. Then Benton and Shannon are joining us in the entryway.

"I trust you have everything you need?" I ask my secretary.

Staying in the guestroom on this floor, she's outfitted in a pink velour lounge suit and matching slippers. She's drinking what I detect is Irish whisky neat, no ice, probably the Jameson we keep on hand for her visits. But now and then she commits treason by drinking Scotch, she's admitted.

"You've had quite the day." Benton hands me a bottle of water, and a Manhattan with a cherry and a slice of orange peel. "I thought you might need some warming up," he says as thunder cracks nearby like a missile strike.

"Thank the Lord we're together." Shannon looks up at the ceiling. "It's like the universe is furious and lashing out. The planet is very agitated."

"I'll feel better when Lucy's home." Parched after diving, I drink the water first.

"She's going to be held up for a while," Benton informs us. "She just texted."

"It's always something." Dorothy rolls her heavily made-up eyes. "Nothing with her is ever as it seems. Well, it's not right she's not here. My only child's not going to join us for dinner when I've not seen her since last week?"

"Probably not," Benton says. "She just turned around and is driving straight back to the training facility. The cloud computer again."

"I hope that's not been hacked like so many things," Shannon says. "And speaking of mysteries, the hornet nest is where the exterminator left it." She directs this at Marino and me.

"I've made repeated calls asking when she'll return to remove it so more hornets don't move in. But nobody at her company knows who I'm talking about. The owner of Bug Off told me they have no women working for them and that they hadn't dispatched anyone to the medical examiner's office yet. For which he was most apologetic, by the way."

"I'm not sure who that exterminator was, but I don't have a good feeling about her," I reply, envisioning the woman in protective clothing that covered her face.

* * *

I explain that the vehicle bay cameras briefly turned off while the exterminator was near the ceiling's support trusses. While she was up there she could have tucked some type of surveillance device out of sight. After that, the cameras magically came back online, and the elevator went berserk, as did the parking lot security gate. Then at three o'clock in the morning the vehicle bay door retracted with nobody there.

I'm betting it was Carrie untethered on top of that ladder. She installed something that enabled her to take control of my building. I can't stand the thought that she was that close when Marino and I were arguing with the mortician from Shady Acres Funeral Home. She could have pulled out a gun and killed us right then. But she didn't. She'd rather watch, and I think about what Benton says.

The world's more interesting to her with us in it . . .

"Lucy needs to check my building as soon as possible," I add while wishing Carrie had fallen from forty feet up.

Maybe she would have suffered Sal's same fate, lying on

the ground with her head smashed in, slowly dying all alone. It would be what she deserves.

"Lucy doesn't know if she'll be back tonight." Benton is preoccupied with his phone, a red-checked apron over jeans and a tight T-shirt that look very good on him.

"I hope she's going to find some dinner and stay out of this weather." I take a sip of the Manhattan.

"I believe that's the plan," Benton replies. "Sounds like Tron's on her way to the training center, which is good."

"They should be together in this ugly weather and everything else going on," Shannon adds. "That makes me feel better."

"I understand the Brileys are in the city jail." Marino makes sure we know that Fruge leaked the breaking news to him. "That's at least something good, right?" He drains the bottle of beer.

"And a little while ago, our agents picked up one of Ryder Briley's security guards, Mira Tang." Benton offers another update. "She has quite the rap sheet. And owes him a lot of favors."

I remember Lucy saying that the ex-con would do anything for Ryder Briley. Including murder, it seems. Benton explains that video from the flight service's cameras shows the security guard inside the hangar where Dana Diletti's helicopter was kept. Mira Tang was wearing gloves, carrying a bottle of berry-flavored vitamin water and a red plastic gas can.

"The helicopter was waiting to be towed out to the tarmac," Benton is saying as I stand near the stairway, wrapped in my limp towel. "There was nobody else around. And you can tell she wasn't worried about the cameras. She's the one who turned them off at around seven o'clock this morning, assuming everything she did from then on would be unwitnessed and unrecorded."

She didn't know that earlier Lucy accessed the flight service's security system, making sure the cameras can't be disabled. Even if the software indicates they're turned off, they aren't. Mira Tang is on video opening one of the helicopter doors and placing the bottle of vitamin water between the front seats. Then she removed the fuel cap and emptied the contents of the gas can inside the tank.

"She was sabotaging it, pouring in water," Benton says. "We know that because there's video of her filling the gas can in a sink inside the hangar. She's getting ready to cause the deaths of five people if all goes according to plan, and figures no one will be the wiser. But we're seeing everything she did and so will a jury."

"Obviously, she was following orders," my sister deduces with another splash of tequila in her glass. "She didn't decide to do this on her own. Why would she?" Setting down the bottle again.

"Ryder Briley's orders." Marino begins massaging Dorothy's neck, and they're getting along fine now. "He and his wife ordered a hit on Dana Diletti because of all the shit she said about them on the TV news." He wraps his arms around Dorothy's waist, pulling her close.

"The Brileys are horrible human beings," she declares, her eyes half shut as Marino kisses her ear. "What they put that little girl through is unimaginable. But did they really believe it would never catch up with them? Why don't people think about consequences?'"

"Hardly anybody does. Including me, if I have enough of this." Shannon holds up her glass of whisky. "But there are a lot of people out there who believe they can get away with murder."

"Stupidity like that is what keeps some of us employed." Marino holds Dorothy tight, and usually he's not this amorous when there's an audience.

"But Dana Diletti should have anticipated what Ryder Briley might try to do to her," my sister reasons.

"Most people never assume someone will go that far," Benton answers. "And Dana Diletti is a raging narcissist herself. She thinks she's invincible and came extremely close this morning to finding out she's not."

"A miracle." Dorothy is starting to slur her words, getting *clumsy-tongued*, as she describes it.

"Had the engine flamed out sooner, had the pilot been incapacitated earlier in the flight?" Benton says. "The result would have been vastly different."

"It's a miracle," Dorothy repeats. "The engine could've quit over a crowded neighborhood right after takeoff. Or landed on a school..."

"God forbid." Shannon is shaking her head.

"Or a beach where people are sunbathing," Dorothy continues. "Or in the middle of Fort Monroe for that matter, destroying a national monument and lots of people living there..."

"I talked to Lucy before you got home," Benton says to me. "She explained that if you pour water into an aircraft fuel tank that's already full, it's unpredictable how long before it hits the fuel line, causing the engine to flame out and quit. But it could take a while, which fortunately is what happened in this case or there would be at least five people dead instead of one."

"It's just a miracle that things weren't ever so much worse." Dorothy takes a sloppy sip of her drink. "Dana-fucking-Diletti narrowly escaped. We've all been hearing about it ad-fucking-nauseam, her near-fucking-death experience. Never mind the pilot is fucking dead. Not near-dead. But dead-fucking-dead."

CHAPTER 33

Dorothy insists on following me upstairs as I carry my Manhattan. The pumpkin pine flooring gleams a deep orange in the glow of caged copper sconces mounted on paneling. Rain drums the slate roof, the wind moaning around the eaves.

She holds her tequila in one hand, the other on the railing. I know what she's going to do, and she starts in as we reach the top landing.

"Where were you yesterday and last night?" she asks in a hushed voice, bending close, ice rattling as she takes another sip. "No one can hear us, Kay. Now you can tell me the truth. I promise not to let the others know." She zips her lips.

"There's nothing to tell, Dorothy," I reply as we follow the hallway past antique maps of the Chesapeake Bay that make me think of diving earlier today.

"It's just the two of us, sis. It's always been just you and me. So tell me." Dorothy rubs my arm.

"I had to take care of a case at a military installation—"

"Shhhh!" she interrupts. "You were in Oz before that. Because your old beau Sal Giordano was dropped out of a UFO in that tacky theme park Lucy was so wild about."

I pretend I didn't hear her comment about Sal being my old beau. Dorothy is saying a lot of things she may not remember come morning. She's going to have a wicked hangover and isn't done yet. We pass the upstairs guestroom's open doorway, and I see my sister's and Marino's bags on top of the made bed.

"I'm glad you're staying over." I look at her drink.

"I know much of what's on the internet isn't to be trusted." She's slow and unsteady walking in her green slippers. "But it's being said that we shouldn't try to contact aliens if this is what happens. I'm dispirited. Feeling downright existential, and I didn't before."

"I don't think it wise for you to pay attention to what you're seeing on social media," I reply.

"Of course I'm going to fucking pay attention to it!" she protests. "I'm a fucking award-winning influencer!"

"That you are, Dorothy. That you are."

The main bedroom at the end of the hall has a view of the river and not a whole lot of privacy when my sister is staying here. I walk in and she's right behind me, ice rattling in her tequila, smelling like a tequila bar.

"Come on, pretty please?" she coaxes as I walk into the bathroom. "Sisters trading secrets just like the old days."

"We never traded secrets, Dorothy." I'm in front of the sink talking to her through the doorway. "In fact, I didn't really have many secrets. Not like you did."

"And now that's all you've got. Bloody secrets." She hovers in the doorway, staring past me at the mirror while fussing with her short platinum-blond hair. "I need to know where you and Pete were. It's only fair you tell me since the two of you were together all night."

"I was with Benton *all night*. Not Marino, and you know that to be the case. I believe the two of you were on the phone a good bit." I take the drink out of Dorothy's hand and set it down on the sink countertop. "Maybe you've had enough for now."

"Oh, don't you go narcin' on me, sis." She reaches past me, retrieving her drink, taking another swallow. "I don't need one of your lectures right now. I've had enough of them from my husband. He told me what a rotten time he had in Atlantic City. He thinks I'm selfish and doesn't believe I'm really being stalked."

"Hopefully you aren't being stalked. Has anything else happened?" I ask, and she shakes her head no.

"Obviously, he said those things when he was upset," she goes on. "We're fine now, the air cleared. But is it true? I simply won't have any peace until I know."

"Is *what* true?" I sit down on the toilet lid and take off my boots as Dorothy gets increasingly tipsy.

"Was Sal Giordano abducted and killed by aliens? Not so long ago it would be laughable to suggest such a thing. It would be *War of the Worlds* science fiction. But not anymore with constant sightings all over." She dramatically sweeps her arm like a game show host. "Including stories about aliens killing people. Is that what happened? I have to know."

"It's highly unlikely."

"*Highly unlikely?*" she exclaims in horror. "Meaning it's possible?"

"I certainly hope not," I reply. "But is that what I think happened to Sal? Hell no. He didn't have that kind of encounter."

"Oh." Dorothy's face is stricken as if I've given her awful news. "Well, in some respects that's a damn shame."

"I would think it's a good thing if we don't have to worry about extraterrestrials abducting and killing us." I take a swallow of my drink.

"I just want there to be something out there. Something besides us." She's getting teary. "You know these shows that Pete and I are addicted to? Well, they offer hope that there's more to life than the failed fucking mess I see every damn time I turn on the fucking news. I want goodness to win. I want something bigger and better than us to make sure we don't kill the entire planet."

"Me too," I reply.

"And I want to feel I matter."

"You matter very much, Dorothy. You always have."

"I want to matter to them." She points up at the ceiling.

"I'm sure you do. Now let me take my shower."

"I want to tell you I'm sorry about your friend Sal." She's getting more emotional, pulling a tissue out of her green sleeve. "I met him only a few times but understand why you liked him."

"I did like him. I liked him quite a lot."

"And I can see why there would be something between the two of you." She wags her finger at me, listing in the doorway as if on a rough sea.

"Why would you say that?" I'm not telling her. Never.

"You know, I can sense these things." She looks ridiculous in her Jolly Green Giant outfit, rattling the ice in her glass, her swaths of green eye shadow iridescent. "When you'd ride with Sal to one of your highfalutin meetings at the Pentagon, the

White House or wherever, I could tell that Pete was unhappy. He'd make all these snarks about what a piece of junk Sal's truck was compared to the amazing one I bought Pete. And that Sal didn't own a gun when of course my husband has an arsenal. And when Sal was on TV, Pete would change the channel."

"I didn't know that."

"I can read him like a book." She looks at me with a rare hint of empathy that conveys she knows about Sal.

It's not merely a premonition. No doubt Marino gave up my secret without overtly doing so, and that's typically how the proverbial cat is let out of the bag. He never meant to, but Dorothy can find the truth behind his darting eyes and bluster. My sister is aware of Sal's importance in my early life.

"The first time I saw you after you were back from Rome, I knew you'd been fucking somebody," she says as if there can be no denial. "You were relaxed and seemed almost joyful for you. Naturally, it didn't last, which was a good thing in hindsight. Long-distance relationships die if they stretch on forever, and yours would have, my dear." She sways closer, rubbing my shoulder. "You weren't going to move and change careers for him. And he wasn't going to change anything for you."

"Our lives wouldn't have been compatible," I reply.

"Must you talk as if your heart's a block of wood?"

"You know it isn't, Dorothy."

"I just wish you'd told me at the time."

"No offense, but you were the last person I was going to discuss my love life with." I take another hit of my Manhattan, desperate for a cigarette.

"As much experience as I've had with men?" She's getting

more emphatic. "I'm exactly who you should have asked, sweet pea. Well, I'm sorry you were sad and I wasn't there to help," she adds unexpectedly, tears spilling.

Then I'm overwhelmed by emotions I've kept walled off for days, even longer. Some of the sorrow I feel is ancient and no longer visible on the surface.

"Come here." Dorothy gives me an awkward hug, patting my back as I hear Lucy's cat Merlin muttering and meowing. "Oh!" my sister exclaims. "I guess when I said *come here,* he thought I meant him!"

She laughs hysterically as Merlin saunters into the bathroom, looking up at me with owl eyes, his ears flat like a helmet, his tail twitching. Dorothy starts crying again, clinging to me, her sash of plastic leaves tickling my skin. Lucy's cat jumps up on the back of the toilet where he often perches.

"You'll feel better after you eat." My only sibling stumbles over the words, nodding her head knowingly. "And you need to put something on your sunburned schnozzle." She pokes my nose that's bright pink from my floating on the water while waiting to be rescued.

"I'll see you downstairs." I shut the bathroom door, turning on the shower.

*   *   *

After I've cleaned up, I find that Merlin has vanished as he so often does. I change into pajamas, putting on a robe and slippers, headed downstairs. Carrying my empty drink glass, I walk into the kitchen, my favorite room in the house.

Old bricks show through the creamy plaster walls, a rack

hung with polished copper cookware suspended from an exposed beam overhead. The deep fireplace works, and during cold weather Benton and I use it often. There's nothing cozier than sitting at the table before the window, having breakfast while looking out at snow, a fire burning.

"What are we talking about?" I ask as he takes my empty glass, big gleaming pots of sauce and boiling water steaming on the stove.

"We were just imagining what a nice night Ryder and Piper Briley must be having in the detention center." Marino has switched from beer to bourbon. "I'm thinking about them mingling with the general population. Inmates don't take kindly to child abusers. Especially spoiled rich ones."

Dorothy is slumped in a chair at the kitchen table, half comatose now, and he's rubbing her neck again.

"They'll be killed in there before it's over," she says, or I think she does.

It's hard to understand her now, like listening to a new language she's invented. I tap Advil out of the bottle, making her take three. I stir the marinara sauce, adding olive oil to boiling water that's ready for the pasta.

"The phone calls to our office won't help Ryder Briley one bit," Shannon is saying. "The recordings of the nasty things he said clearly show he was trying to threaten us and interfere with the autopsy. And I'm assuming it was him or his wife who's been making the crank calls, not saying anything, trying to spook everyone."

"Are we still getting them?" I ask as Benton makes me another Manhattan.

"Well, Fabian did mention he had one today that he was certain was the same as the others." Shannon sips her whisky. "As I was heading out this afternoon he stopped by and told me. He said his direct line rang in the investigation's office, and when he answered it, nobody was there. The caller ID was *out of area* again. And he mentioned he could hear a radio or something in the background, maybe a talk show host, but he couldn't make out what was being said."

"Then it's not Ryder or Piper Briley doing it," Marino decides as I'm reaching the same conclusion. "They were being arrested right about then."

"Let's eat while we still have power," I reply as the lights flicker again.

"I'll round up some candles just in case," Benton says as Merlin saunters into the kitchen, jumping into my sister's lap.

She doesn't react, her arms dangling at her sides, her head slumped, softly snoring now.

"I believe that's all she wrote for tonight." Marino excuses himself to help her upstairs.

When he returns, I serve plates of spaghetti marinara with grated Parmigiano Reggiano. Shannon helps Marino set the table in the dining room while I make spicy Caesar salads and bake loaves of my special garlic bread. I open a Chianti that gets better as it breathes, and it makes me think of Sal. If he were here he'd be helping with dinner like he always did.

Benton swirls the ruby-red wine in a glass, holding it up to his nose, tasting it. Candles flicker in the dining room as he fills our glasses, and we seat ourselves, draping big red-checked napkins in our laps.

"First we raise our glasses to Sal." I hold up mine. "Not present but never forgotten."

As I say this the lights go out for a second, the candle flames wavering as if there's a draft. The storm has gotten fierce, the wind buffeting and whistling. Rain pounds the roof, lashing the trees on our property. The lights continue dimming as we eat, and everyone decides to turn in early. During a power outage, tucked in bed is a good place to be.

"I for one am beat." I push back my chair.

"I need to make sure my better half is okay." Marino drops his napkin on the table. "She's going to feel like total shit tomorrow."

"Whenever able, make sure she drinks a lot of water." I start clearing the table.

As we carry dishes into the kitchen, I remind our guests that each room has battery-powered candles and flashlights. I assure them that the backup generator should kick on.

"And at least we'd have some of the basics for a few hours," I explain, hugging Marino and Shannon good night.

Benton and I carry cups of tea upstairs, setting the alarm, his pistol on the bedside table. We talk quietly for a while with the lights out, pressed close to each other. I'm not aware of anything else until I feel him touching me awake at three A.M.

"Hi." His breath against my ear as I feel him bending close.

"What is it?" I reach for the lamp on my side of the bed.

Benton is in cargo pants and a black polo shirt with the Secret Service crest embroidered on the shoulder. His gun is in a pancake holster on his hip, and I smell his musky cologne.

"I've got to go." He kisses me, his face silky from shaving.

"What's happened?"

"She's been spotted, and I need to get to headquarters." He's talking about Carrie.

"Where?" I sit straight up, arranging pillows behind me.

"She was caught on a security camera in a private terminal at the airport in Warsaw, Poland," he says. "Facial recognition software identified her. The name on her passport is Zofia Puda."

Benton explains that Carrie's alias Zofia Puda was renting a house in Dooms, a tiny town out in the middle of nothing some fifteen miles from Weyers Cave. He says agents are headed there to search the place.

"But she's not here," I say to him.

"She's not in Virginia. She's not in the United States. Not anymore."

"Then for sure she was."

"Yes. Two nights ago, Zofia Puda a.k.a. Carrie Grethen took off in a private jet from the Shenandoah Valley Airport. As you know, that's in Weyers Cave. Clearly, she'd been spending time in that area. But she's gone now, Kay. She's nowhere near here."

"We're sure?" I can't stop asking it.

"Yes." Benton is checking his phone. "Most likely when she realized the Brileys were about to be arrested, she split. I suspect it will come out soon enough that she was doing business with them, that they were working with the Russians. More of the same, stealing our technologies while interfering with our elections."

"I wonder if Carrie was at their house on Monday," I reply. "Maybe she'd been there before when discussing business with

Ryder Briley. And maybe she saw Luna not long before she was shot."

"Carrie would have been nice to her. She considers herself good with children." Benton says this as if talking about someone normal. "She would have detected that Luna was mistreated, identifying with her because of her own abusive mother. Maybe Carrie hugged her and transferred the fluorescing trace evidence to her pajama top."

"If the candy-covered peanuts she ate came from the Briley Flight Services terminal, then maybe Carrie is the source. If so, she should have been picked up by the security cameras," I remind him.

"We already know that the cameras were off the Monday afternoon before Luna Briley was shot," Benton informs me.

"Carrie probably did that every time she was passing through. She's a pilot or used to be. Who's to say she's not been flying in and out under an alias? Maybe she went to see the Brileys at their house, and brought Luna a bag of candy from the bins in the terminal. Not a nice gift to give someone supposedly diabetic."

"Carrie must have known she wasn't," Benton says, kissing me goodbye.

CHAPTER 34

I sink back into a deep hole of sleep, and when I come to I'm not sure where I am, the storm still raging, rain beating the roof like sticks. I feel for Benton, his side of the bed empty and cold. Then I remember him waking me up with the news about Carrie. Cool air whispers across my skin as the wind whistles and roars.

The deluge lashes and drums, thunder cracking while my eyes adjust to the dark. I listen to the familiar electrical hum of the antique ceiling fan that came from a bank once robbed by Bonnie and Clyde. That's the story told by the owner of the Louisiana junk store. I check my phone, and Benton texted hours ago that he was safely in Washington, D.C.

All okay, he wrote then, confirming that Carrie Grethen isn't a factor.

He's telling me not to worry. She's in Poland or she was. Where she can't be right now is here, and I wander into the bathroom, washing my face and brushing my teeth. As I ponder what to wear today, I'm torn by indecision. The Brileys are behind bars and Carrie's being hunted down in Eastern Europe.

I should feel a sense of relief and resolution, but I don't. There are too many unanswered questions.

I'm stealthy as I follow the hallway in the glow of the patinaed copper sconces Benton and I came across in New England. All is quiet inside the guestroom where Marino and Dorothy are staying.

I don't hear any signs of Shannon stirring as I head downstairs. I'm making a cup of coffee in the kitchen when my smart ring alerts me that Lucy has sent a message.

Can you feed Merlin? she's texted. *Sorry. Didn't know I'd get stuck here all night.*

Not seeing him so far, I answer.

Hopefully in my place.

Her cat wears a collar embedded with a sensor that opens the small electronic flaps she installed in doors at our house and the guest cottage. If Merlin can't come and go at whim and on demand he wails like a banshee. He tears things up.

I don't want Mom going into the cottage, Lucy continues to explain. *I'm running a special operation with the software and she needs to stay out.*

Will head over there now to feed Merlin, I write back. *Where are you?*

Lucy answers that she's with Benton, and I imagine them in a situation room surrounded by data walls. They're tracking Carrie Grethen. Maybe she'll be caught, and what a gift that would be, taking her out even better. Turning off the alarm, I put on a slicker, opening the kitchen door to the amplified sound of the heavy rain splashing.

The sky is solid gray, the rising sun a vague whitish smear on the soggy horizon, big cold drops of water pattering the top of my hood. Beyond the kitchen door the courtyard is flooded.

The heavy branches of the magnolia rock in the wind, the big white blossoms manhandled by the storm.

The wet brick walkway glowers in the glow of carriage lamps as I carry leftovers from last night, the plastic containers cold from the refrigerator. I walk quickly, surveying deflowered tree peonies and dogwoods, pastel petals scattered everywhere like little bits of trash. Centuries-old evergreens and hardwood trees thrash and bend, leaves and pine needles scattered.

I think about what Shannon said, and she's right about the universe seeming agitated. It's as if the weather is alarmed, warning me to be careful.

It's not over, amore. I hear Sal's voice in my head.

Getting out my keys, I climb the front steps of the quaint white brick guest cottage, a cat flap in the lower part of the door I unlock. I flip on the lights inside, taking off my slicker so it doesn't drip everywhere, hanging it on the coat rack. The wide board pumpkin pine flooring, the exposed brick walls are the same as the house, and I call out to Lucy's cat.

"Merlin? Hello? Time for breakfast!"

Beyond the front door is the small kitchen, and I place the containers of food inside the refrigerator while calling out to Lucy's capricious and elusive pet rescued from a parking lot. It's unusual that he's not slinking in to greet me. Lucy jokes about him being a watch cat, and to some extent he is. When he's here and the front door opens, he flies in to see who it is.

"Merlin?" I drop my keys on the kitchen counter. "Please don't tell me you're outside somewhere!"

"He's in here with me," a familiar voice answers from the sitting room, and my heart slams against my chest.

No. Please God, no.

"Sitting right here next to me purring," the voice adds, and I didn't bring my gun.

"We're looking each other in the eye, friends now. Aren't we, Merlin...?"

Frantically opening drawers, I find the Sig Sauer pistol Lucy usually keeps in here. Holding it in both hands, the barrel pointed up, I quietly leave the kitchen. The next room is the living area where tables are arranged with laptops, arrays of video screens and spectrum analyzers with blinking lights.

*   *   *

"Hello, Kay, it's been a while," the voice says, and it's not Janet talking through Lucy's computer.

I walk to the desk, and Merlin is sitting on top of it staring at the curved computer monitor.

"What do you want?" I ask Carrie Grethen.

"I see you're armed and dangerous, but it's not like you can shoot me." Her scarred face smiles at me remotely, her hair dyed the same color as Lucy's and cut similarly.

She's seated on a green leather couch inside a room with fine art on the walls. In the background are antiques, arrangements of fresh flowers, a window overlooking the skyline of an old city.

"Let me adjust this a bit." Carrie moves her computer monitor, making sure I don't miss the wicker gift basket, the bottle of red wine uncorked on the glass coffee table.

The focaccia bread I baked has been torn into pieces she's dipping into a saucer of the olive oil I gave Sal for his birthday. For an instant, I can see Carrie's left hand, mangled by the drone that flew into her years earlier. The propellers sliced open her face, and severed the tips from two of her fingers. She's wearing Sal's inexpensive beaded bracelets, the ones he always wore, my rage so intense I almost can't bear it.

"The Tignanello has hints of violets and strawberries. It's quite nice and travels well." She takes another sip, savoring it like a sommelier.

Holding the glass of Tuscany red in her mangled fingers, she makes sure I never forget the damage I inflicted when she showed up on my property. This was before I moved back to Virginia and my sister inadvertently led the wolf to the door in Cambridge, Massachusetts. All I did then was finish what Carrie started. She makes her own choices. They always turn out catastrophically for someone.

"Not a bad year." She sets down the wineglass with a sharp clink as I set down the Sig Sauer on top of the desk.

"What do you want, Carrie?"

"I have a few things to share with you, Kay."

I pet Merlin's head, and he's purring. But it's not his normal purring. It's the sound he makes when threatened, a mixture of a purr and a growl with the hint of a yowl. As if he's gargling unsettledness and about to bare his claws.

"It's okay, it's okay," I tell him, and he twitches his tail, staring at Carrie's face on the monitor. "What did you do with Janet?" I ask.

"Oh, she's here somewhere." Carrie's gaze is like looking into chaos. "Janet, oh Janet? Where are you?" Carrie laughs. "Oh, there we go, come here, baby." She switches to baby talk, smiling lovingly on a curved monitor big enough for gamers.

342

She holds out her damaged hand, and I again notice the bracelets. Around her neck is Sal's fossilized shark's tooth on a gold chain, my fury smoldering.

"Come, Choo Choo." She pats the sofa, and the big spotted cat jumps up next to her.

The male cheetah I saw in the Oz theme park. Or I'm assuming it's the same one, purring so loudly I can hear it, and no wonder Merlin is growling and ready to pounce.

"You remember Choo Choo from Somewhere Over the Rainbow, don't you, Kay? That was him you heard moving around while you were borrowing the ladies' room in the Witch's Castle. Well, both of us were right above your head at one point," Carrie says, rubbing his ears. "Until I zipped away into the fog."

"Where did you steal him from?" I envision the location of every camera Lucy installed in here, enabling Janet the AI avatar to engage in a meaningful way.

"Not steal but liberate. He did surprisingly well on the plane. Put him in a dog carrier, which he didn't love," Carrie is saying. "I admit it's helpful flying private."

Standing by the desk petting Merlin, I can't look into Carrie's eyes on the monitor without being pulled in. And I won't go where she is. I won't let it happen and never have. I keep my attention on the cheetah sitting next to her like a porcelain statue.

"Lucy's slipping up, hate to tell you," Carrie goes on. "Otherwise we wouldn't be having this tête-á-tête, Kay. So much for her failproof firewalls. Well, here I am. In fact, I'm in a lot of places, in case you've not figured that out yet. Your office, for example."

I envision the exterminator on top of the ladder.

"And, oh dear, the problems your poor niece and her love-sick partner Tron are having with the cloud computer. *'Lucy in the sky with malware...,'*" Carrie sings.

Lucy's not here right now because of the problem. Meaning, I showed up to feed her cat. Carrie goes on to boast about how clever she is compared to the rest of us. The problem is we let our emotions get in the way of the mission.

"And then one loses focus...," she explains as I'm thinking how to send a message without Carrie seeing what I'm doing.

She's in front of a video display somewhere, possibly some expensive house or apartment in Warsaw. She's sending out electronic signals, and the longer I can keep her talking to me, the more likely it is that law enforcement will locate her.

"What do you want?" I sit down at Lucy's desk, rolling the chair close.

There won't be cameras on the floor beneath me, and using one hand I carefully slide my phone out of my slicker pocket. I type in the password, barely looking at what I'm doing while Carrie tells me how sorry she is about Sal Giordano.

"It doesn't feel good when you lose someone important, someone who goes way back," she's saying with saccharine sympathy as if we're close and share much in common.

"No, it doesn't," I reply with forced civility while typing, my phone out of sight in my lap.

"Feels even worse when someone takes them away. And you've done it more than once, Kay..."

She's hacked in, I text Lucy.

We know, she answers right away, and I realize this is what she wanted.

She's set up an electronic trap that's giving the Secret Service Carrie's location even as she talking to me over the internet. It would seem Carrie hasn't a clue what I'm doing. She's none the wiser that Lucy has hacked into Carrie hacking into Janet.

Keep talking, Lucy then texts me.

"And when bad things are done, someone has to pay," Carrie is saying.

"I feel you blame me for many things," I reply. "Now's your chance to explain your side of things."

"From the beginning you involved yourself in matters that were none of your business. In fact, that seems to be your trademark, Kay. And look at the trouble it's caused you and everyone."

Her crazy eyes are steady on me, and I look between them, a trick I learned long ago in court. It appears I'm staring someone in the eye but I'm not.

"What do you want?" I again ask.

"It's obvious you could use some help..."

Suddenly her face vanishes from the monitor as a video begins to play. Within seconds I recognize Luna Briley's pink bedroom. She's on top of the bed, eating from a small paper bag of candy-coated peanuts when her mother walks in.

"What do you think you're doing, you little shit?" Piper Briley screams, and she sounds inebriated.

Snatching away the bag of candy, she shakes Luna by the shoulders. Piper is shrieking and throttling her. Then Ryder Briley appears in the doorway, shirtless and in boxer shorts, his face livid.

"*Let go! I told you not to leave marks on her, you fucking bitch!*" he snaps at his wife.

"*I told you she won't listen!*" She turns around, glaring hatefully at him as I feel myself getting angrier.

"*And it's your fault. You're the fucking mother. Now do a better job or I'll find someone who will!*"

"*You'll find someone who will?*" she screams at him. "*I think you already did, you sorry motherfucker...!*"

Piper storms off, and is back seconds later, their child sitting up in bed, sobbing and cowering.

"*What are you doing...?*" Ryder bellows as Piper storms back into the bedroom, pointing the pistol at their daughter. "*WHAT ARE YOU DOING...?*"

"*Making sure I don't leave any marks...!*"

BANG!

The video abruptly stops. Then Carrie is back on the monitor, her scarred face twisted by a mix of hatred and ecstasy.

"All those antique dolls on shelves in there?" she says, the cheetah rubbing against her. "They have hidden cameras looking out of their pretty little glass eyes. Piper and Ryder liked to keep a close watch on their prisoner daughter. They liked to witness the power they had over her. They got off on hearing her cry herself to sleep. After the bad thing happened, they deleted the video, of course. And I undeleted it, naturally. I'd been watching what was going on for a while, you see. It's important to know who you're working with, don't you agree?"

"You gave Luna candy while you were at the house," I reply.

"As I had before, would sneak her a little bag of it when her daddy and I discussed the various big ventures we're involved in. I happen to like candy-coated peanuts myself, and I'd share them with her. There's video of that too, if Lucy's ever smart enough to find it."

Carrie goes on to explain that Piper Briley was furious when she walked into the bedroom after lunch and found Luna eating candy. But that's not what tipped the scale.

"It was finding out that her loving husband is fucking his jailbait helper Mira Tang. Well, he won't be anymore, and you can thank me for that," Carrie says with a contemptuous smile that's crooked because of the damage I caused.

"I don't intend to thank you for anything," I tell her.

"You're secretly just as pleased as I am. Let's be honest, the Brileys are bottom-feeding scum."

"You have no idea how I feel about anything. You just think you do."

"Speaking of bottom feeders, reminds me of that poor pilot on the bottom of the bay. I can't recall his name." Carrie sighs. "Nobody special but there was no need to kill him. I wouldn't have done that. But Ryder insisted on tit for tat with that over-blown TV journalist."

Carrie tells me I'll find the same B-52 cocktail in the vitamin water that Mira Tang spiked. The vials of haloperidol, lorazepam, the liquid Benadryl are in a gym bag at her house under her bed.

"I assisted Ryder Briley with one last favor before he and his trashy wife rot in prison. And believe me, that's the worst thing for them." Carrie feeds the cheetah from a plate of ground steak tartare. "Terrible to imagine how they'll be treated for the rest of their days, depending on how long they last. All because of me. Payback."

"For what?"

"They didn't do as instructed. And I know about being a helpless child when you're trapped in a nightmarish home, completely controlled by fuckers." She feeds Choo Choo another raw steak meatball.

"You didn't deserve to be mistreated as a child, Carrie. But how tragic that you've turned into the same monster," I reply as pounding sounds in the background...

Then wood splinters...Voices shout *POLICJA!* as the monitor blinks out. I look down at the phone in my lap, reading Lucy's last text.

We got her, it says.

CHAPTER 35

By early afternoon the volatile weather has moved on, the sun slipping in and out of clouds as Marino and I drive through the Shenandoah Valley. Lucy, Tron, Benton and other key federal agents have landed in Warsaw. Before that they were monitoring my remote chat with Carrie Grethen.

"Pretty damn smart." Marino has his Ray-Bans on, chilling in shorts and a T-shirt. "Carrie Grethen must be so pissed she can't see straight."

"It was brilliant." I'm in a baggy tracksuit and sneakers after stopping by my office.

I took a last look at Luna Briley's body, the marks on her upper arms and neck vivid after more time in the cooler. They verify what I saw in the video Carrie Grethen played for me early this morning. Moments before Luna was shot to death, her mother grabbed her violently in a fit of rage directed at her cheating husband.

The Brileys and Mira Tang are being held without bail, and Marino and I are taking the rest of the day off, sort of. This isn't a pleasure trip to the mountains in the western part of Virginia. It's something I have to do. I won't have peace until I

349

know why Sal had been making trips to Weyers Cave, carrying thousands of dollars in cash, since last June.

"Whatever Lucy cooked up with Janet, the two of them caught Carrie Grethen, end of story," Marino is saying. "They set up something in cyberland, and the psycho fell for it hook, line and sinker. But I'm surprised Lucy did it."

"What do you mean?" I look out at the range of Appalachian Mountains rolling in the distance, thinking about what Lee Fishburne said about volcanic rock.

"She basically turned Janet into a honeypot." Marino slides open the ashtray, digging out a pack of Juicy Fruit gum. "She used Janet to seduce Carrie into letting down her guard. Hell, the two of them have probably been talking for a while depending on when the hacking started."

"The two of who have been talking?"

"Carrie and Janet. Point being, Carrie hacks into Lucy's computer, and Janet herself helps lay the trap, is right there waiting. I mean, it's beautiful when you think about it. Lucy and Janet are crime-busting partners again." Marino continues talking about the AI-programmed avatar as if she's a living person.

Carrie is in the custody of the police in Warsaw, assuming she's not been relocated already. What happens next and where she'll end up, I won't be told. I suspect she'll be taken to someplace where American officials can interrogate her. International deals will be made that I may never be told about.

Marino exits I-81, and a few minutes later we're driving through the rural hamlet of Weyers Cave, population a couple of thousand, famous for its Grand Caverns where soldiers camped during the Civil War. Hundreds of them from the North and South alike sought shelter inside the cave at some point, their signatures carved into the stone walls. I remember Lucy's amazement when I took her through rooms that looked like a cathedral, and a zoo with features resembling animals.

Marino cruises past the post office and a Methodist church. He picks up Route 256, the Little Rebel convenience store off to the left. We pull up to the gas pumps, and after driving several hours it's a good idea to refuel anyway and make a pitstop. But that's not why we're stopping.

Sal was here multiple times, filling up his old truck, getting a coffee and using the facilities. The white frame building is old with a faded green-striped awning over the porch, and signs for specials taped in the windows. One of the two pumps in front is for diesel fuel.

"That might explain the reason Sal picked this place," I suggest. "His truck is diesel."

"Maybe. But there are plenty of places to get diesel fuel." Marino turns off the engine. "That's not the only reason he was coming here."

"While you pump, I'll go inside and pay," I reply as we open our doors. "I'll see who's working the cash register."

A bell jingles cheerily as I walk inside an old market that reminds me of the one my father had when I was growing up in Miami. The wooden countertop is scarred, and on top is a steel cash register that belongs in an antique store. There are racks of candy and gum, and small freezers with ice cream, a ceiling fan whirring.

An older woman appears from an aisle, drying her hands on a paper towel. Her face is wrinkled like tidal sand and framed by short gray hair with bangs. I detect a shadow of suspicion in her dark eyes.

"Can I help you with something, ma'am?" She returns to the chair behind the counter.

"I wanted to pay for fuel," I reply. "Fifty dollars' worth."

"You can pay at the pump with your credit card." She points out the window. "But I'm just as happy to take cash."

I give her two twenties and a ten as she studies me carefully while glancing at Marino filling his truck. I look around at snack foods, breads, canned goods, cleansers, toiletries, most anything one might need. But nothing I'm seeing gives me a clue about why Sal might have come here beyond making a mundane pitstop.

"You here to visit some of the caves?" The woman opens the cash drawer, tucking in the money. "This is a good time of year to do it. Pretty soon it gets really crowded. Especially during national cave week. We've got some good ones around here."

"You certainly do. I used to take my niece to a few of them."

"That why you're here today? The caves?"

"No, it isn't." I'm not going to lie.

"Where are you coming from?" She's grilling me now.

"Alexandria." I glance out the window at Marino hooking the nozzle back on the pump.

"Looks like he went over by fifty-two cents, ma'am," the

woman informs me. "And I can tell you've got something on your mind. You're not the only one who's come in here lately, full of questions about that rocket scientist abducted by a UFO and killed by aliens."

"Who's been asking?" I find a five-dollar bill in my wallet, telling her to keep the change.

"The feds," she says.

"The scientist you're talking about is Sal Giordano, and he was a friend of mine," I tell her as Marino texts me.

Should I come in?

I look through the window at him and subtly shake my head. No. Don't come in.

"That's godawful," the woman says. "But I'll tell you the same thing I told the Secret Service agents. I didn't know him. He'd come in every now and then to fill up his truck and use the men's room. Sometimes he'd buy other stuff. I don't think what happened to him had anything to do with him stopping here."

"Did he ever say anything about anyone following him? Anything like that?" I ask.

"No, ma'am. He was always in a good mood except this last time. Monday afternoon. He was feeling blue. I could tell."

"Do you remember the first time he came in?"

"I've been working here most of my life and never saw him before last summer," she says. "He came in on a Saturday in early June. I remember because he was friendly and had an Italian accent, which we don't hear much around these parts. After that he was in and out."

She gives me a long, penetrating look, her expression turning sad.

"You were close to him, weren't you?" she says kindly.

"I was, had known him much of my life," I reply. "I'm trying to figure out what happened to him. And I know he'd want me to do that."

"I'm sure he would."

"Did he ever mention what he was doing out here?" I ask.

"No, he didn't say a thing. I had no idea who he was until I saw the news about him being killed. I didn't know he was important."

"So he'd pull in and get fuel, and then continue on his way," I reply. "And that was it?"

"Well, now sometimes when he'd stop in and leave, he didn't head back to the interstate. He went that way. Toward the airport." She points, referring to the regional airport Carrie Grethen flew out of for Warsaw.

*　*　*

Returning to the truck, I tuck packs of Clove and Fruit Stripe gum in the ashtray while telling Marino what I learned. Instead of returning to I-81, we continue west just like Sal did on occasion, following the two-lane road past silos and green fields.

Weyers Cave is famous for its flower farms, and we pass acres of chrysanthemums and a barn with a gift shop. By now it's midafternoon, the sky clear, the air hot and steamy. A Gulfstream jet is taking off from the Shenandoah Valley Airport, catering mostly to private flights, a number of expensive cars in the parking lot.

"Sal may have driven this way, but I don't see why he'd stop here," I comment.

"Me either." Marino glances out at the modern brick terminal, the airfield going by our windows. "I got no clue why he'd come this way. It's not like he was here to pick flowers or fly somewhere. What do you want to do, Doc?"

"Let's keep going for the next ten miles or so. Last time Sal was here it took him three extra hours to get to Green Bank. That's not a lot of time, and there's only so far off the beaten track he could have gotten."

As I'm saying this I detect the silvery silhouette of some type of industrial plant way off in the distance. Rock quarries are carved into the hillsides, and large pools of runoff water are an unhealthy teal green. Getting closer, I can see that the industrial plant is crisscrossed with chalky white unpaved roads, rows of parked transfer trucks glinting in the sun.

"What the hell is that up ahead?" Marino asks. "Must be new. Of course, it's been a while since I was out this way."

"I think my last time was when I took Lucy to Grand Caverns while she was still in high school. Whatever this plant is, it wasn't here then."

I can make out metal silos, warehouses and other buildings. As we get closer, I begin to recognize towers, vertical kilns, transfer chutes and belt conveyers. Then we're driving past vast expanses of solar farms. Field after field of the glassy blue panels are tilted up in perfect rows with grass growing between them where sheep are grazing.

"They must generate a lot of their power here," I decide.

Up ahead is the sprawling plant's entrance, and there's no

security gate. But I notice signs warning about trespassing and industrial hazards. Multiple big dome cameras are on top of tall poles, and the name of the company doesn't spark at first. Then it hits me like a high-voltage jolt.

"True North Industries," I say to Marino. "*True North*, as in the initials *TN*."

"The code in the capsule Sal swallowed. Holy shit."

"Maybe."

"Here goes." Marino picks up his Colt 1911 from the console between us, sliding it out of the holster. "Just in case we run into anybody unfriendly."

Placing the hefty pistol in his lap, he drives through the cement plant's entrance, white dust billowing up. We realize in short order that the streets have no names, only numbers, and I recall what Sal wrote in the note he microphotographed.

"TN. Five-L. Seven-R. Nine-L," I recite to Marino while sending Benton a text.

I let him know where we are and why.

"There's street three," Marino says as a dump truck coated in dust rumbles past us. "There's four. Next is five, and I'm taking a left."

We make the turn and continue to street 7. Taking a right, we keep going to street 9. We turn left, and looming in front of us is a huge metal structure built into the side of the mountain. A small sign over the front door says *Bando Solutions*, and I text the name to Benton. Beyond this building are others, the parking lots filled with transfer trucks and earthmoving equipment.

"A Japanese aerospace company based in Tokyo, with

offices all over the world, including one in San Francisco." I'm looking it up on my phone. "There's no listing of Bando Solutions having a location here at this cement plant or in Virginia or West Virginia. Nothing near this area."

"Sounds like they don't want people knowing they have a presence around here." Marino shifts the truck into park, both of us staring out the windshield at the enormous windowless structure. "Shit. You could probably fit a couple of football fields in there."

"And whatever's going on was of interest to Sal. Very keen interest," I reply. "Or he wouldn't have led us here. There's something he wants us to know."

Around us are several dozen SUVs and pickup trucks, and by all indications there are employees working inside Bando Solutions. We're uninvited and have been picked up by the security cameras. Right now, there are two choices as I see it. We can turn around and leave. Or we can walk inside and ask a few honest questions.

"Come on." I open my door. "The worst they can do is tell us to get lost. I don't think anybody's going to shoot us in here."

"I'd say that's a safe bet." Marino checks the Colt, making sure a round is chambered, putting the safety on. "But I'm bringing my friend all the same."

He slides the pistol into the pancake holster, clipping it to his waist. We climb out of the Raptor, its gleaming black paint coated in the tenacious dust. He points the remote, locking the truck as we walk toward the entrance. The door opens before we reach it, and a young man steps outside unzipping his dusty white coveralls, taking off his safety goggles, his hair cover.

"Afternoon." He digs out a pack of cigarettes, lighting up as we head toward him.

"How's it going?" Marino asks.

"Can I help you with something?" He eyes us curiously with a glint of anxiety. "Are you looking for someone?"

CHAPTER 36

In his thirties, I'm guessing, the man has a heavy Japanese accent and a crew cut, the backs of his hands tattooed.

"We're here about Sal Giordano." I come right out and say it.

"Is there someone in particular you're meeting?" The man smokes the cigarette, leaning against a pillar supporting the entrance's overhang.

"How about we start with you," Marino suggests, and the man shrugs, a shadow of uneasiness touching his face.

"It's awful what happened to him." He squints at us through cigarette smoke.

"How well did you know him?" Marino asks.

"I'd see him when he'd stop by. It wasn't all that often. Who am I talking to?"

Digging out his wallet, Marino flashes his bright gold badge, and I do the same, playing the role of his partner like I did long years ago. We introduce ourselves, and the man's first name is Daku. He almost seems relieved to see us while at the same time visibly nervous.

"We're investigating Sal Giordano's death," Marino explains before I get the chance, reverting back to lead detective mode as if he never left it.

"Like I said, it's horrible," Daku replies. "But I don't know anything about it except what's been in the news."

"But you know something, don't you," Marino states rather than asks. "I mean, you know why he'd been coming here since last summer. Let's hear your version instead of somebody else's. Or you can wait until the feds are crawling all over the place."

"I know that Doctor Giordano was fired up about what he was doing." Daku begins to talk as if he needs to get it out. "It was his life's passion, and I felt kind of bad for him, truth is. I didn't want to discourage him, though."

"About what?" I ask.

"He was well aware how many patents out there never see the light of day," Daku replies. "I'm assuming that's what you're curious about. What he was doing here right before he died."

"It was one of the last places he stopped before being abducted and killed," Marino says.

"When I heard about it I was shocked." Daku takes another hit on the cigarette.

"What patent are we talking about?" I ask him.

"Let me guess," Marino says. "Something to do with fake moon dust."

"We don't use the word *fake* around here." Daku taps an ash. "Obviously, you know about Doctor Giordano's research and what a cool idea it is even if it never comes to anything."

"What patent are you talking about?" I again ask.

"Well, he has more than one filed. But the point is to make concrete from a simulant of lunar regolith," Daku explains.

"Huh?" Marino scowls.

"He'd stop in and buy some of the stuff to experiment with in his cellar," Daku goes on. "Small amounts, and then he'd drop by to discuss his progress, bringing samples. And he'd call from time to time. We were working on his idea together, sort of on the side, you know."

"What you're saying is he was paying you under the table to assist in his research," Marino replies. "Sounds like a sweet deal. Do your employers know about that?"

"It would be most appreciated if the details of our transactions remain private." Tension touches his face again.

"I can't make any promises, and we're not who you need to worry about." Marino turns up the investigative heat, talking the talk. "This is just the start, and the more truthful you are, the easier it will be for you later."

"Making concrete to build structures on the moon?" I ask. "Is that why Sal Giordano was experimenting with moon dust simulants?"

"We manufacture them here. Also, Martian and other simulants, shipping tons of them to Japan and elsewhere," Daku says.

The entire building we're in front of makes nothing but regolith simulants. There's other research going on with solar cells because of the perovskite mined. He explains that's the reason Bando Solutions decided to locate here, staring off at the quarries gouged into the mountainside.

"That and the deal they made with Briley Enterprises, which owns True North Industries," he adds.

"Well, isn't that something," Marino says nonchalantly, both of us masking our shock. "You know what's happened to the Brileys, right?"

"I saw it on the news. I didn't know them." The way Daku says it, I believe him.

"I'm assuming you're making simulants of perovskite as well?" I ask.

"Yes. Doping it with the real thing."

"Was Sal Giordano involved with perovskite research?" I imagine he'd be intensely curious.

"He was quite familiar."

"When he was here this past Monday afternoon, did he do anything involving perovskite?" I think of the nanograins Sal had under his fingernails.

"He was always interested in whatever's going on," Daku says. "And on Monday, I showed him some of the newest solar cell panels we're making to generate our own power. He was thinking about installing panels on his property in Alexandria."

But that's not why Sal was visiting Bando Solutions, Daku goes on to say. His focus was the lunar dust simulant, and his patent has nothing to do with building habitats on the moon or Mars. NASA and other space agencies are already working on those sorts of things.

"His dream was to build the first telescope on the moon," Daku explains.

"Out of fucking cement?" Marino blurts out.

"Absolutely." He lights another cigarette, and I can see Marino looking at it lustfully.

"You mind?"

"Sure." Daku taps a cigarette out of the pack, offering it to him, flicking the Bic lighter, and I can't believe it.

Marino is cheating right in front of me. He doesn't look at me or give it a thought, and we're back to the old days just like that. He's the big tough detective blowing smoke, swearing, flaunting himself like a peacock.

"What you'd do is fabricate a humongous dish by filling a crater with cement made from lunar dust." Daku is telling us the gist of Sal's patents. "Find a way to heat it up enough that the material turns to glass, and you'd have one hell of a stationary radio telescope up there. It would be the most powerful one ever because there's no atmosphere on the moon to distort everything."

"I guess that's pretty cool," Marino says, enjoying his bummed cigarette while I stay upwind. "But I'm not understanding how something like that could work."

"Without question, what he designed would have. It's a shame he's not here to see that happen." Daku seems deeply disappointed. "He promised me that if it did, he'd bring me into the project."

"Obviously, you're a scientist," I say to him.

"A geologist."

"How long have you been working out here?"

"Two years."

"Do you remember the first time you met Sal Giordano?" I ask.

"Last June. He got word of what we were making here, and paid us a visit. It was quite the big moment for a Nobel laureate to show up, as you might imagine. We sat down and talked about the project he had in mind. He didn't want anyone knowing what he was doing."

"Why not?" Marino asks.

"Mostly he was worried about the government taking his idea for its own use," Daku explains with a flash of resentment. "He said he'd pay cash for the bags of simulant necessary for the research. And he'd compensate us for our time."

"*Us* or just you?"

"Well..."

"Hey, Daku?" Marino blows a perfect smoke ring. "Ask if we give a shit about that."

"It was just me. And it was important that there'd be no electronic or paper trail."

"Isn't that something?" Marino looks at me. "He just happens to walk out on a smoke break when we pull up."

"We have security monitors everywhere," Daku says. "I saw you pull up and knew you didn't work here. Nobody drives anything black around here. It was only a matter of time before someone showed up asking questions."

"Better to cut it off at the pass, right?" Marino says.

"Yes. Doctor Giordano was a brilliant scientist and a good person. He shouldn't have his ideas stolen from him by the government or anyone else."

"And his actual research was done here," I make sure. "That's what the purchased simulant was for?"

"Nothing left this facility except the small amounts he'd

take home to experiment with," Daku says, and I envision the residue that sparkled cobalt blue under UV light.

There were traces of it inside Sal's pickup truck. That makes sense if on occasion he visited the facility and hauled some of the simulated moon dust home. As fastidious as he was, I have no doubt he wore face masks while working with it. But it wouldn't have been possible to get rid of it. You might not see the residue with the unaided eye, but it would still fluoresce.

"It would be helpful to take a look around inside, and then we'll get out of your way," Marino says as if it's our right. "Maybe you can show us what you're talking about. And where Sal Giordano would hang out when he'd visit."

* * *

Zipping up his coveralls, the geologist puts on his hair cover, his goggles. He punches in a code to unlock the door he stepped out of earlier. We're shown inside a vast work area divided into different stations, everybody covered from head to toe by white Tyvek.

In an anteroom are shelves of PPE, and Daku hands us coveralls to wear over our clothing. We put on booties, face masks and goggles. The noise of grinders and other machinery is loud, and we're given earplugs should we want them. Putting on hard hats, we follow Daku across the dust-covered floor, and I can't imagine working in such an environment without a respirator or at least a surgical mask.

Against a far wall are pallets of lunar regolith simulants in fifty-pound bags for shipping, the writing in Japanese. Daku walks us into another room with a ball mill that finely grinds the necessary minerals. Workers are driving forklifts and utility terrain vehicles (UTVs), nobody paying us much mind as we're given a tour.

Our geologist guide goes into detail about the process of extracting ore and reducing it and other minerals into a fine dust. The individual grains are too small to see without magnification. He complains about how tenacious the dust is.

"Sticking to everything like Velcro," he says.

The next connected building produces solar cells and panels. From there we pass through a vehicle bay where trucks are loaded with pallets of lunar, Martian and perovskite simulants. We pass through a series of doors leading to a small windowless office with two desks, a copying machine, a coffeemaker, a water cooler.

"This is where I would talk with Doctor Giordano," Daku says.

But I'm distracted by the radio tuned in to a talk show, the host ranting about political conspiracies. I feel a chill touch the back of my neck.

"... *The reason is to keep you in the dark. To control your every thought and feeling....!*" the host declares.

I'm reminded of what I heard in the background when I got the hang-ups in the morgue and on my cell phone. The air is dusty in here, and I notice cobwebs and dead bugs. Pink fiberglass insulation protrudes from a damaged wall.

And detritus such as bug pieces and parts, insulation, cobwebs and such, Lee Fishburne said.

I think of the trace evidence I collected from Sal's body. Lee also mentioned cat dander, and I ask Daku if anyone might bring a pet to work.

"No animals except what's in the caves. Bats, an occasional rat snake. Spiders, salamanders, millipedes." He indicates the far side of the room.

Through an open doorway I can see the interior of a gloomy cavern, the rough stone walls unevenly lighted. I remember what Lee told me about volcanic activity forming igneous rocks that are necessary for the fabrication of moon dust and also perovskite.

"...*They want us to be their slaves, brainwashing us into believing it's for our own good...*" The talk show host continues spewing his venom.

"Sorry about that." Daku finds the radio, turning down the volume. "One of the security guys listens to it nonstop. Me, I can't stomach any more politics."

"Tell me about it," Marino says as we look around at wall-mounted video displays.

The livestreaming images are captured by the network of cameras throughout the True North plant, its quarries and mines, and also the operations going on at Bando Solutions. I'm not surprised to realize that Marino and I would have been spotted the moment we approached the plant's entrance.

We're being observed now, I suspect as I continue looking around. But it's not Carrie Grethen or the Brileys spying on us. It can't be Mira Tang either.

"What is this room we're in?" Marino asks.

"Sort of mission control," Daku says. "Where we make sure everything is as it should be."

On monitors are live images of the grinders, the crushers, the kilns, the silos. I notice that a faux leather sofa opens into a bed, a corner of a wrinkled sheet hanging out from under a cushion. There's a small refrigerator, a kitchen table, a sink with a dish rack, everything needed to camp out.

"So, I'm going to show you the most recent result from when Doctor Giordano was here last month," Daku says. "This is very close if not exactly the right formula depending on how it would do in the extreme conditions of outer space. During solar flares and meteor strikes, for example. And gravity's not the same on the moon, of course."

He sits down at a desk that has a knapsack on top along with a SpaceX coffee mug and the photograph of a pretty young woman. Unlocking a drawer, he pulls out a blue cloth briefcase that has a black shoulder strap, and I'm startled as I recall what Gus Gutenberg said about a briefcase fitting that description.

"Did Sal Giordano bring this when he was here on Monday?" I ask.

"Yes." Daku opens the briefcase, pulling out a cardboard box.

"When he gave the briefcase to you on Monday, it had your payment in it, I assume," Marino says.

"And his latest sample."

He proudly hands the box to me, and I remove the lid. Inside on a nest of cotton is a small pale gray block of what looks like everyday concrete. I feel its weight and smooth, polished texture, imagining how excited Sal must have been about a dream he didn't divulge to NASA, the NSA, the CIA, the president of the United States or scarcely anyone, including me.

He was determined to invent a lunar telescope that would help us better understand how the universe was formed, and who we are. His invention would be built on the moon, leaving his legacy, and I'm pained he didn't share this with me. I'm also not surprised in the least. Sal didn't go into much detail about his work in general, and I understand why now better than ever.

He never mentioned his patents, and I was unaware that he'd filed any. But in the end, he wanted me to know about his dream and make sure it wasn't forgotten. Or more likely stolen, the lunar telescope built by the Russians first. Now that Carrie's been caught, hopefully that won't happen as easily, if at all.

Whoever rules the moon, rules Earth, Sal used to say. *It's called King of the Hill, amore . . .*

I envision the code in the microphotograph he must have taken recently:

TN-5L-7R-9L

Its childlike simplicity touches me. I'm reminded of a scavenger or treasure hunt, an innocent game. I hand Marino the concrete block made from simulated moon dust. He looks at it, returning it to the box with a shrug.

"I still don't get how you turn something like that into a telescope any more than I could shoot somebody with a cinderblock," he decides.

"Not an optical telescope. But a radio telescope," Daku reiterates as if that settles the confusion.

"Then I guess you could turn a sidewalk or empty swimming pool into a telescope," Marino says a touch snidely.

"Ummm . . . I don't think so, but not sure." Daku ponders this for a few seconds.

"Is there a way to get out of here without walking back through the entire fucking place with all this damn PPE on?" Marino the tough guy asks him.

"The next connecting building is the crop-dusting hangar. The door's probably rolled up because the fumes are strong in there, especially now that it's warmer. You can go out that way if you'd rather."

"That would be better." Marino is sweating in his coveralls, and I'm desperate for fresh air.

My eyes are watering and itching from the dust. Daku walks us through a storage area, past a bathroom that Marino decides to use. He takes off his PPE, and I do the same.

"To leave you go through the door right there." Daku shows me. "Walk through the hangar, and you'll be outside a couple streets away from where you're parked. You'll have to walk a little way. But not too bad."

"Who does your crop dusting?" I ask him.

"This really amazing scientist from Poland who's also a pilot. Zofia Puda," he says, and there's no question that Carrie was here.

"What type of aircraft does she fly?" I ask as if it's no great matter.

"The Cessna that's in the hangar. But she's in the process of switching over to the chopper in there."

"Where is she now?" I ask to hear what he says.

"She doesn't work every day," he replies. "I've not seen her in a few days."

"Thank you very much," I tell him. "You've been very helpful."

He disappears through the office, returning to the first building where we met him, I presume. I text Benton the latest update as I hear the toilet flush inside the bathroom. Water runs in the sink, paper towels yanked out of the dispenser. Marino emerges, his eyes everywhere as I tell him about Zofia Puda a.k.a. Carrie. She held Sal hostage here all night long, pumping him full of drugs to keep him sedated.

"Probably nobody here has a clue who Zofia Puda really is," Marino says. "I wonder if the Brileys even know her real name."

"I'm sure not. This way." I head to the door that Daku pointed out to me.

CHAPTER 37

The instant Marino and I walk inside the hangar we're hit by the sharply pungent odor of white vinegar. Dozens of big white plastic drums of it are on pallets against a wall.

...A pungent odor... Sort of vinegary, I remember Lucy describing what she smelled around Sal's body at the scene.

I notice the single-engine Cessna plane Daku mentioned, and I suspect Carrie used it often to get around. Perhaps she'd fly it to Ronald Reagan Washington National Airport when she had meetings with the Brileys or other business in that area. Marino and I walk past a windowless white cargo van with a folded ladder on top. It looks like the van I saw on Sal's driveway and also inside my vehicle bay.

The van fits the description of the one Dorothy believed was following her. There are no license plates, front or back. Nearby is a ground power unit (GPU) cart that's plugged into a weirdly configured single-engine Eurocopter Carrie was just starting to use for crop dusting. The four doors have been taken off and are stored in a rack.

The helicopter's skin has a chameleon paint job that changes colors as we move closer. The point may be aesthetic, but the pigments reflecting light differently would interfere with radar. Bolted to the undercarriage is a metal spray system rig, and there are others on the floor near a workbench.

Stainless steel booms, some ten feet long, are equipped with multiple spray nozzles, and attached to either side of the helicopter's chassis. I envision Sal's contused upper leg. I remember the periodicity of the pattern, the four abrasions exactly the same distance apart. I dig a tape measure out of my briefcase, and the space between the nozzles is the same as the abrasions.

I look through the openings where the doors should be, and on the cyclic is the spray rig's trigger. I wonder if Carrie accidentally hit it while struggling to push Sal's body out of the left seat. Perhaps in the process she doused the scene with the vinegar solution. Or maybe when he struck the boom on his way down, that somehow released an acidic-stinking shower. Either scenario might explain why the odor was strong when Lucy and Tron first arrived at the Oz theme park.

Harnesses are fastened on top of the seats in front and back. That's the proper way to crew an aircraft, and I remember the fastened seat belts inside Sal's crashed Chevy pickup. It would be habit for Carrie to leave them like that, and I suppose that could be the reason. Or more likely, she didn't want the seat belt alarm chiming while she drove Sal to an awaiting vehicle before sending his empty truck off the mountain.

I wander closer to the fifty-five-gallon drums of vinegar that would be diluted with water and pumped into the white plastic tank attached to the helicopter's belly. As Marino and I continue searching and taking pictures, I'm glancing around for cameras, wondering when someone's going to interfere with our snooping. Digging out gloves from my briefcase, I hand a pair to Marino and we pull them on.

We walk over to the workbench, where he roots through a pile of magnetic signs, one of them for BUG OFF, another for FIRST FAMILY FLORISTS. There are shop cloths, tubs of grease remover, and a mechanic's trolley case with drawers of aviation tools. I notice a box of transparent plastic food service mitts typically used in restaurants and delis, and they strike me as strange in this context.

I pull out one of the mitts, and it's like a sandwich baggie, only mitten shaped. They make sense when preparing food but also would be a convenient way to safely handle certain materials and substances such as vinegar that can be caustic on the skin. Designed for one-time use, the mitts are inexpensive, two thousand to a box. Another benefit depending on who we're talking about is the wearer won't leave fingerprints, possibly not DNA either.

I think of the odd impressions lifted from the glass of Sal's pickup truck. I envision Carrie's left hand, the two missing fingertips, the scars on her finger pads and a thumb. Gloves wouldn't fit her the way they once did, I'm explaining to Marino as I take more pictures with my phone. He's looking through a stack of Virginia license tags that he guesses are stolen.

I look on as he riffles through a pile of aviation and agriculture magazines. They're mixed in with other mail on top of the workbench. Picking up a manila envelope, he reads the address label.

"Zofia Puda," he says, showing me the printed label:

Zofia Puda, Sabo Solutions, Aviation Unit Chief...

"Sabo Solutions hired her as their crop-dusting pilot, having no idea who they were tangling with," I explain.

"Meanwhile, she's stealing all their tech secrets, who knows what the hell else. And she targeted Sal Giordano," Marino says. "Maybe she was out here when he showed up to do his fake moon dust research at some point."

"That could be what happened. We may never know," I reply. "But I seriously doubt he ever met the alleged Zofia Puda here or even caught a glimpse of her face. Otherwise, he would have realized that's who was following him in Rome several weeks ago."

"Assuming it was Carrie he saw."

"I think we know."

"You're probably right," Marino says. "She grabs him as he was driving up to the lodge. Then she kept him here all night trying to get intel out of him and whatever else she wanted. Finally, she choppered him to the theme park and pushed him overboard."

I remember when Carrie learned to fly helicopters long ago, using one to escape from the Kirby Forensic Psychiatric Center on Hart Island in New York City. She has to do everything that Lucy does, only in a way that causes the most harm. As we're talking, I continue glancing at my phone, hoping the police are headed in this direction.

A lot of evidence to collect here, I text to Benton.

Help is on the way, he answers.

"She's been working at Bando Solutions, likely doing aerial spraying with a vinegar solution to clean the miles of solar farms," Marino is saying.

"The same thing I use to clean the old glass windows in our house," I reply. "As long as it's not too concentrated, vinegar and water won't harm livestock like the sheep we noticed earlier. And it also helps mitigate weeds..."

I'm interrupted by footsteps, someone coughing behind us.

"Finding anything interesting?" An aggressive voice sounds as Marino and I spin around.

*   *   *

Norm Duffy strides toward us from the hangar's big square opening. The security officer I fired last fall is in jeans and a loose-fitting denim shirt with the True North logo on it. He has an evil smile on his bearded face, his fists clenched at his sides, coughing quietly as if he has asthma.

"Take it easy, man...," Marino starts to say.

"You're trespassing, assholes!" Reaching around to the back of his pants, Norm pulls out a pistol.

Then Marino has out his gun, pointing, and nothing happens. He frantically switches off the safety, firing and missing as Duffy ducks for cover. The cartridge case is sticking up from the ejector port, the pistol jammed. Marino tries to clear what's called a stovepipe while we run toward the door, zigzagging behind the helicopter, then the van as gunfire explodes.

Bullets ping as we dash back inside the building with Norm in pursuit, another shot ripping through the door as Marino slams it. We shut the office door, locking it, blocking it with a chair. Yawning open next to us is the entrance to the cavern, and I grab Marino's arm, pulling him toward it. As claustrophobic as he may be, for once he doesn't argue.

We hurry inside, the air instantly cooler, the sound of water dripping in the uneven shadows. Caged overhead lights push back the darkness as we duck into a recess as Marino clears his pistol jam. We listen, barely breathing, and I know Marino's plan. He'll wait until Norm Duffy steps inside the cavern, and then Marino's going to blow him away. I hear footsteps at the cavern's entrance, Norm Duffy coughing quietly and clearing his throat.

"Nighty night!" he yells, coughing again.

The light of his flashlight probes past us, then vanishes as the door bangs shut. For an instant I'm too shocked to move. That can't just have happened.

"Jesus," I whisper. "I hope we didn't just get locked inside here."

Marino has his pistol ready, making his way back to the door, trying the knob.

"Fuck." He keeps trying to force it. "FUCK!"

He kicks the metal door hard, and suddenly it flies open to the sound of gunfire as Marino falls inside with a loud heavy thud. Then silence. I listen for him, hearing nothing, and I'm seized by dread. He would be calling out to me if he were okay, and I wait. Nothing except the sound of footsteps returning to the entrance of the cavern. Then they're headed toward me.

Please no ... Please no ...

I make my way deeper inside, my heart hammering, sick with worry about Marino. The tunnel I follow is wide enough for a car, water drip-dripping from a ceiling of stalactites that look like icicles of all sizes. Reaching up, I break off one, and it crumbles in my hand, ruined after the thousands of years it took to form.

God forgive me for my sins, I think as I try another one, unable to break it.

I try yet again, this stalactite snapping off about eighteen inches from the tip. It seems sturdy enough. The lights inside the cavern suddenly go out, throwing me into blackness as complete as outer space. I feel my way along a wall, not daring to turn on my phone's flashlight or make a sound.

I have no idea where I'm going, and should I get lost in here I might not be found anytime soon. Or far worse, Norm Duffy finds me first. The cold, rough stone is uncomfortable against my back, and I'm inching along when I see the first beam of light probing. I hear footsteps heavy on stone, loose pebbles clicking and clinking.

"I know you're in here somewhere, Kay!" Norm calls out, followed by a wheezy cough. "Where's the big bad chief now? Cowering somewhere, aren't you?"

I can hear the triumph in his mocking voice as he closes in on me, breathing heavily, coughing some more. I think of the dangerous dust he's been exposed to chronically if he's out here often while making the security rounds for Briley Enterprises.

"As usual, Kay, you stick your nose where it doesn't belong. And guess what happens?" Norm takes another step. "Nobody better than *yours truly* to take care of bitches like you, and I've been waiting for this moment a long fucking time. Come out, come out wherever you are, Kay!"

He can't be more than ten feet away, and I'm aware of the broken bits of stalactite I'm still clutching. I toss a piece of it beyond the beam of probing light, and Norm chuckles again, wheezing.

"You know, Kay, it all goes back to what motivates someone." Another step, another cough. "And I have plenty of motivation when it comes to fucking you."

I toss another piece a little farther this time. Then the last chunk, and he chuckles again. I can smell his sweat as he pauses by the recess where I'm flat against the wall like the moth trapped inside the SLAB.

"This is getting tedious, Kay!" he calls out, the red dot of his pistol's laser sight bouncing around the cavern walls.

Then I see the vague bulk of him in the glow of the phone he holds in one hand, his pistol in the other, and he's inches from me. Gripping the intact stalactite like a dagger, I lunge, throwing my weight behind the stabbing motion from low to high. I feel the sharply pointed tip pierce fabric and flesh as he screams, the pistol clattering to the rock floor.

I drive the stony shaft up under his ribs, into his chest cavity as he shrieks and shrieks, grabbing at me, but it's too late. I back away, and he falls heavily, my hands trembling and slick with blood. Turning on my phone's flashlight, I shine it on him, his eyes wide open and fixing on me. The thick end of the stalactite protrudes from his torso, blood soaking his shirt.

He moves his lips as if begging for help, and I won't give it. Finding his gun, I pick it up, a Glock 9-millimeter that I'm taking no chance he might retrieve. I don't see how he could survive what I just did to him. But I'm not trusting anything right now, maybe never again. Following my light, I find the way back to the door Norm Duffy left open wide.

Texting *MAYDAY* to Benton, I tell him to send an ambulance as I hurry back inside the building, terrified.

"Marino?" I yell.

Please be okay.

"Marino?" I call out, passing the bathroom.

Please God.

"Yo! In here!" he shouts to my enormous relief, my knees going weak.

He's inside the office, bare-chested and sitting in a chair, his face dazed. The floor under him is spattered and pooled with blood, his pistol some distance away halfway under the sofa.

"Jesus! Don't move." I wash my bloody hands in the sink.

"I'm not moving," he says. "I don't even know how I got in the chair."

I take away the shirt he's holding over a gaping bullet graze at the back of his head. "An ambulance should be on the way shortly. Do you remember falling and hitting the ground? Were you unconscious?"

"When?" he weirdly asks.

"You're going to be all right, Marino," I assure him even as we hear the wailing of sirens.

"Is there a fire somewhere?" His eyes are glassy.

On the security monitors I see a caravan of police cars and ambulances charging through the cement plant. Benton has gotten my texts and taken care of it from Poland.

"How'd you get here, Doc? We're not flying the helicopter home, are we?" Marino asks, and he's not thinking straight. "Tell Lucy we're driving, okay? Where is she anyway?"

"Take it easy," I reply.

He winces as I gently palpate his scalp, making sure the bullet didn't penetrate, and it didn't. But another fraction of an inch and it would have smashed through his skull. My bigger concern is that he fell and hit his head. We need to get him to the hospital as soon as possible.

"Tell me what you remember." I tie his bloody shirt around his wounded scalp, making a bandage of sorts.

"About what?"

"About Norm Duffy shooting you."

"What's he doing here?" Marino looks baffled. "I don't remember getting shot. Are we sure I was?"

"A graze, but you might have been knocked out," I reply.

He begins to ramble about maybe coming to on the floor, trying to stop the bleeding, not knowing where he is or what happened.

"Then you walked in, Doc, and I couldn't believe it. Where'd you go?" he goes on drowsily. "I thought, oh no! She's been beamed up the same way Sal Giordano was. And I've been left behind..."

TEN DAYS LATER

Sal used to say that in a perfect world no one would say goodbye on a Sunday. The subject came up our first weekend together that summer in Rome. It wasn't practical for me to spend the night with him when I had an early lecture at the university every Monday morning.

But I did it anyway, making my getaway in the dark, throwing caution to the wind. I stayed up late, got up early, gave my lectures, and throughout it all I never left him on a Sunday. Today will be the first time, and at least the weather is good, church bells tolling in Old Town, a lot of people visiting graves and strolling the winding lanes in Ivy Hill Cemetery.

A small group of us have gathered, the dogwoods profusions of pink and white. Butterflies alight on tombstones, birds chirping from branches as if there's nothing sad going on. It's just Benton, Dorothy, Marino, Lucy, Tron and me. Cemetery workers are stationed nearby, ready to cover the grave with the Italian pottery urn inside it.

We're having our own private remembrance, and are filming it for Sal's sister, Sabina. She couldn't come. It was too sad, she told me over the phone. But she'll see us next time we're in

Rome, very soon she hopes. The plot I chose is appropriately close to where the father of the U.S. space program Wernher von Braun is buried. I know Sal would like that.

I can't say for sure what he would choose as an epitaph on his simple marble headstone, and it was left to me to pick what made sense. *Continua a guardare in alto,* I can hear him saying. *Keep looking up.* Pointing to the stars.

"I know he wouldn't want a big fuss made. But if anybody deserved one it was him." I'm standing by the open grave, everybody gathered around it. "Most of all he would want to be among his friends."

Nearby on a stone bench is the small shovel I bought at Walmart the other day. Each of us takes turn sprinkling soil, and it clinks against porcelain at first. Then the dirt is quiet as more is layered. When I add the last shovelful, I can't hear the dirt at all or see the colorful ceramic urn I found for Sal online.

"When I'd get bogged down in all the messes of this world, he would point up," I tell everyone. "He'd say never forget what we come from…"

Dorothy is teary-eyed in a low-cut black dress and sweeping black hat. She's hanging on to Marino's arm as if she's lost her closest friend, and leave it to my sister to make everything a drama. The angry red scar on the back of Marino's head is something he's quite proud of now. He'll be telling that war story the rest of his days.

He still doesn't remember being shot. More important, he doesn't remember that he forgot to take off his pistol's safety. Knowing him, he would have fired a first round and that would have been the end of Norm Duffy, sparing us the trauma and the trouble of what happened next. Marino simply thinks that we got ambushed and I ran for cover, hiding inside the cave where I stabbed Duffy to death.

I won't let Marino know or think that maybe what happened inside that hangar wasn't his finest moment. As it stands, he's feeling quite pumped up about himself. I can't remember the last time I saw him in a suit, this one black with a black shirt and tie. His Ray-Bans are fixed on me as I continue remembering Sal.

"He always reminded me of what's important, most of all what we're capable of...," I'm saying to my family.

Lucy plays a recording of Mendelssohn's Symphony No. 4, a favorite of Sal's. We used to listen to it on his rooftop in Rome when we'd look up at the night sky and he'd tell me that the moon is the gateway to all that's beyond.

"Which is why we can only hope that his telescope is built up there one day, and appropriately named for him." I'm saying this to Benton later when we're walking through the cemetery, returning to our cars.

"I hope that's what happens," he says. "And some huge tech company doesn't steal his idea. Which is the more likely scenario."

"The Russians are my worry."

"They'll try to beat us building anything up there." Benton pulls out his phone, looking at it.

"Really? You have to do that this very second?" I put my arm around him. "You can't keep in it your pocket for longer than ten minutes?"

"That sounds dirty." He kisses me.

"We're in a cemetery, Benton." I resist the urge to laugh uncontrollably. Then I feel like crying again.

"I used to make out with my dates in cemeteries," he says.

"You never did with me, and I'm feeling a little jealous."

We climb inside his car as everyone else returns to theirs. We're headed to the house, where I've planned a simple meal that Sal would approve of and no doubt help me prepare. Ravioli filled with ricotta and covered in a spicy gravy that's heavy on the fresh basil. I'm making a rustic Italian bread, and an antipasto with the cheeses and olives he loved.

We'll drink toasts and celebrate his life while feeling at least some peace knowing that Carrie is behind bars. The cheetah she stole and transported to Poland has been rescued and placed in an appropriate habitat. Eventually, it will be returned to the wildlife institute in Virginia where Carrie stole it from.

Apparently, the cat followed Carrie like a shadow, suggesting that she was inside the theme park at the same time we were working the scene. She was in the Witch's Castle while Marino and I were there, explaining the noises we heard. When we checked out the rooftop, the cat may have been hiding and watching. Carrie was gone, having clipped herself to the zipline, streaking away in the fog.

She may have been close by when the cheetah stopped us on the Yellow Brick Road. At any time, Carrie could have taken out all of us. But she didn't. Benton believes that we're the only family she's got, and I can't stomach hearing it. She gets a rush from being close to us, watching, calculating, feeding off our emotions, vicariously feeling what we feel. And it's all I can do to listen to comments like that.

"...The Sal Giordano Lunar Telescope. I like the sound of that," my husband is saying as we pass a monument with white roses climbing over it. "I think we should get the word out to some of our colleagues, such as the director of NASA."

"When his massive disk is built up there from moon dust, we'll be able to see as far back as far back goes. All the way back to the Big Bang, and we'll watch it happening." I reach for Benton's hand. "We'll finally see for ourselves how we were made."